WREQUIEM
AT THE RED ROCKS

A NOVEL OF BRUTALIST SATIRE
& FUTILE GESTURES

JASON MAKANSI

Author of *The Moment Before*

ALSO BY JASON MAKANSI

The Moment Before: A Novel

*Painting by Numbers: How to Sharpen your BS Detector
and Smoke Out the "Experts"*

*Carbon IRA & YouTility: How to Address Climate Change
& Reward Carbon Reduction Before It's Too Late*

*Lights Out: The Electricity Crisis, the Global Economy,
and What it Means to You*

An Investor's Guide to the Electricity Economy

Numerous Published Short Stories

WREQUIEM
AT THE RED ROCKS

A NOVEL OF BRUTALIST SATIRE
& FUTILE GESTURES

JASON MAKANSI

Author of *The Moment Before*

Layla Dog Press | Tucson, AZ

Typeset in Adorn Condensed Sans and Baskrville
Cover art: Shutterstock Digital Illustration: Beautiful Sedona by AloneArt
Cover design: Kristina Blank Makansi

Library of Congress Control Number: 2026909108
Paperback: 979-8-9912722-3-0
Ebook: 979-8-9912722-4-7

THIS WORK IS HUMAN AUTHORED
& HUMAN DESIGNED.

To all those out there who can still find strength,
action, and purpose while the nation and
the world crumbles around us.

THE MAJOR PLAYERS

Bradley Maniopolis :: *Lead facilitator battling CMD, emergent ethnic, gender-fluidity, and career identity crises.*

Colloquium facilitator for Neo-anthropocentric Models of Retrospective Freedoms, on the verge of retirement, but suffering from compulsive masturbation disorder (CMD), ethnic and gender identity crises, someone who has spent a career trying to be recognized for something beyond a "subject matter expert" in his industry.

Gail Bartholomew :: *Packs heat whether she has a gun or not, willing to sacrifice it all for her squad.*

One of three main colloquium panelists, ex-military, just retired Director of the Cold War Missile Museum, has an axe to grind about how the Air Force is ignoring her and her fellow Missileers (who staffed the land-based US nuclear deterrent facilities), deathly ill from years of exposure to "the most dangerous materials known to man, "packs heat" whether she has a gun or not.

Azul Ebunoluwa :: *In transition from a rich Nigerian heir to an American Afro-beat superstar.*

Second main panelist, representing the History of Musical Instruments Gallery (HOMI-G), thirty-something affluent émigré from Nigeria, percussion player extraordinaire, negotiating the space between the wealthy museum benefactors and his artistic ambitions.

Ashera Winters :: *Finding her place in a world that devalues what she values the most.*

Third main panelist, Director of the Tomahawk Hill Preservation Society, ardent defender of the earth and its non-human inhabitants, coming to grips with her lack of earning power, turns to her pet Gecko for comfort.

Raj Magellan :: *A Brahmin Indian American turning the chip on his shoulder into a persona and a bank account no one can challenge.*

(née Rajamahedron Majundar) Ranked in the "under 40, over a billion" club, Principal funder of the Center for the Study of the Philosophy of Freedom, and founder of the men-only "Primates Festival", Raj seeks to be President someday but first wants to rival Aspen and Davos with his own annual Freedom Conference by restructuring the global economy around quantitative models of freedom as the primary currency of life.

Dr. Keshawn ("Kerry") Washington :: *Can't avoid being kicked around like the football that once made him a collegiate star.*

Ex-football star and Raj's hand-picked African-American Director of the Freedom Center, in the eye of the scandal erupting over the replication years ago of his penis as a sex toy, and a primary target of the post-feminist culture warriors of the #VeeToo movement.

Dr. Victor Haviland :: *A brainiac stuffed into the maturity of a South Park character.*

Bradley's best friend from college, math nerd, leading authority worldwide in Associational Statistics, whom, through constant texting during the conference, badgers Bradley about how many girls he's slept with, then launches an unrequested, clandestine intervention to help Bradley deal with his CMD.

Rachel Schiff :: *Lifelong Jewish New Yorker who converts adolescent trauma into feminist celebrity.*

(a.k.a. Naomi Wasila) Friend of Bradley and Victor's from college (and Victor's former girlfriend and lifelong confidant), self-professed expert in smashing the patriarchy and sexual relations, marshals her #VeeToo faithful to the conference venue, in protest of the Primates Festival and faulty penis replicas, all the while staging Bradley's intervention.

Nascha Sunsee :: *An ambitious, grounded woman pushing against the tide of hierarchy and privilege inside and outside the Yavapai Nation.*

Overworked, underpaid manager of the Conference venue, Song of the Sun resort, in Sedona, Arizona, owned and operated by the Yavapai nation, sister property to the nearby Coins of the Canyon Casino, trying to monetize the stupid white-people comments she puts up with every day, satisfy her boss' ("Big Chief") ever-escalating quotas for resort guests losing money at the casino, and keep order as the colloquium decorum deteriorates and the multiple protests escalate.

Avi Kauffman :: *Down but not out, he's got one more fight left in him, and he's not going quietly.*

Professor, former hippie and social rabble-rouser, force-retired by his Sociology Department management, head of the newly formed "Collective for Liberation from Unfreedoms and Extant Inequities (CLUED-IN), or "Unfreedom Center."

Conrad Bolton :: *No one pushes a billionaire like him around. Until someone does.*

HOMI-G benefactor, heir to the Bolt-Mart fortune running gas/retail stations and dollar-store equivalents around the world, gets wind of what's going down at the Colloquium and rushes to Sedona to protect his family's good name.

Catherine Isabell Keener :: *It's her party and she'll make someone cry if she has to.*

One of the Carefree Ladies of Cave Creek (a group of affluent married women who "take a break" annually from their hubbies) who is a guest at the resort while the Colloquium is being held. She befriends Bradley and escorts him into unknown territory.

Stephanie Plemmons :: *It's always the patriarchy. Always.*

One of the esteemed Colloquium speakers, livid that an "old white guy" is running the event, can't stop needling Bradley about his lack of "fitness for duty."

Rolex Williams :: *Representing Carver University, a storied HBCU, he is exhausted from doing the White man's work.*
Longing for the day when he doesn't have to explain why Black Americans deserve Reparations or why Blacks are allowed to use the n-word, and myriad other nuances of cultural conversation. Loves nature, but feels strongly that his people should get their full civil rights before geckos.

There is nothing as satisfying as creating your own mythology
or as dangerous as believing it.

—Unknown

CHAPTER 1

THE COLLOQUIUM

The straight white male of *your* generation is an endangered species.

That's what the woman told Bradley at the evening reception. True, he had interrupted the conversation she was having with another woman, but he'd done so courteously. As conference facilitator, he wanted to introduce himself to as many participants as possible during the kickoff evening reception.

He asked for the woman's name after stating his. She was not unattractive, maybe early 40s, dressed in a maroon skirt, matching heels, and a form fitting buttoned-up jacket below an icy look that preceded the chill from her handshake.

"Dr. Stephanie Plemmons."

He left the right angle of his arm hanging between them, daring her not to shake.

"Hygienic protocol," she protested, glancing down at his hand with an upturned side of the lip.

"Ah, okay, I get it. No worries."

He nodded hello to the other woman who said her name more pleasantly.

Bradley maintained his professional demeanor, near neutral, on the north side of enthused.

"I'm trying to get acquainted with as many of our speakers and guests as possible by asking, 'What does freedom mean to you?'"

That's what he'd been asked in his interview for this gig, a clever icebreaker, he hoped.

Dr. Plemmons didn't hesitate. "Freedom is when white men no longer dominate the global power structure."

She barely smiled. Her assertion was followed by an animated discussion between the two women about patriarchy, misogyny, and how men, simply by their presence, pose a danger to women. As Bradley politely excused himself and headed toward what he hoped would be less hostile territory, he heard Plemmons laugh and say something about endangered species and how she'd been assured they were not going to appoint an old white guy as facilitator.

"He looks ethnic to me. Maybe Italian or something?" the other woman said as he moved out of earshot.

Thankfully, most of the other participants behaved more appropriately for a reception, so he wasn't too bothered. Maybe Dr. Plemmons had a bad flight, trouble in her romantic life, or was already just plain pissed off.

More worrisome was the text message he received from Dr. Keshawn "Kerry" Washington who'd hired him and who was the director of the Center for the Study of the Philosophy of Freedom. Turned out Dr. Washington would not be attending the first day of the conference, "Neo-Anthropocentric Models of Retrospective Freedoms," which meant that Bradley was on his own as facilitator. The major benefactor for the Center, Roger Magellan, was supposed to make a token appearance in the morning by video. Maybe he'd explain the absence. And why wasn't he showing up to his own conference?

After shaking more than a dozen hands and engaging in requisite small talk, Bradley headed for the ballroom exit. On the way, he noticed the wallpaper featured a repetitive print of the prickly pear cactus, certainly one of the weirder plants Bradley had grown accustomed to in Tucson. It seemed to have

4

a face, to be smiling at him. No. Not just smiling. Snickering. Like it knew something he didn't.

An attendee walked quickly after him, holding a glass of white wine sloshing dangerously. He caught up with Bradley in the hallway. Facing each other, Bradley realized the guy had been trying to catch his eye for a while.

"Dr. Maniopolos, I just wanted to quickly introduce myself. Dr. Mikhail Tseitinsky, from Stanford?" He had a spray of white hair poking up from the sides of his head and spoke with the last vestiges of a Cold War accent.

"It's Mr. Maniopolos, haven't yet earned that PhD. I remember your name from the attendee list."

Maybe Tseitinsky had checked out some of his work through an internet search, wanted to chat about it.

"I only learned about this conference two weeks ago, from a colleague. I was glad I could still register."

Bradley nodded. "Glad you could make it."

"As am I. My biology background and research in genetics and neuroscience has led me to some provocative conclusions about free will. As you can imagine, I have a special interest in the Thursday session."

"Weighty areas for research. I'm also quite interested in the free will session, a topic I've never thought much about."

"Then perhaps you might consider my book, Predetermination: How the Lack of Free Will Makes the World a Better Place.

"I feel like I've heard of it."

"It was on the *New York Times* bestseller list for months—not boasting, mind you, just explaining where you might have seen the title. I wrote it for a lay audience."

"I'll check it out!"

"That's quite kind of you, Dr. Maniopolos. I won't take up more of your time. I'm sure you have many responsibilities as the conference facilitator, so I just wanted to introduce myself."

"Glad you did. See you in the morning."

Bradly headed back to his room thinking that Tseitinsky seemed like a pretty humble guy given his status as a NYT best-selling author and Stanford prof.

Putting his hotel room door between him and the outside world, he decompressed for a few minutes, unpacked his bag, then plopped himself and his thoughts—marinating in three cocktails, a few morsels of finger food, and the mild portent of being out of his element—down on his bed and proceeded to do what he often did when he first laid down on a hotel bed. He stripped down to his underwear and masturbated.

Once his climactic moans subsided, he entered that brief, liminal state at the Venn diagram intersection of satiation, exhaustion, and guilt.

He never understood the guilt part.

Bradley Yannis Mohammed Maniopolos had self-identified as white his entire life. Whenever anyone asked about his ethnicity, and most people did soon after meeting him, he'd say, half Greek, half Lebanese, and all American. He was an assimilationist, he'd tell people, when the subject of ethnicity came up or when he and his daughters argued about pronouns. Ever since, at age seven, when he was conned by his older sister into thinking that rubbing olive oil on his skin would make him less brown, he knew he was supposed to be white. All the neighborhoods his family lived in were white. The schools were white. His friends were white. Everyone he interacted with in any material way was Caucasian. He ticked white on his census and medical forms. He'd even married a Heinz 57 chick from Texas.

Turns out, his sister wasn't so wrong about the olive oil either.

He was white, damnit! And straight too. Problem was, he was still the darkest guy in any group of peers, neighbors, or friends. Six decades later, he wasn't so sure. That uncertainty infiltrated his mind the way seaweed and fish reminded you that you are an intruder in their ocean.

That wasn't his immediate problem, though. A few years earlier, at the tender age of 66, he'd sworn off sex. He'd carefully explained to Valerie, his spouse of 35 years, that he had no more bullets left in him and had resigned himself to a second life of celibacy. This fresh approach would be enriched by all the mental space he would then have to devote to more productive pursuits once all that anxiety over sexual performance had drained away from him permanently. Along with the anxiety around all the other performative acts which seem to dominate his life.

He felt so strongly about this late-course correction, he made it part of his private retirement plan. He even confided it to his lifelong friend, Victor Haviland, who was taking monthly testosterone injections to keep up with the demands of his third wife, 15 years younger. Another friend, from high school, who Bradley asked if he was able to still maintain his erection until his partner was satisfied, looked at Bradley, puzzled, with a furrowed brow, and said, "What?"

Celibacy was short-lived, though. Valerie was having none of the "no more bullets" theory. Get a 'scrip for Viagra, she urged. Of course, she didn't *demand* that Bradley do this, although she was happy to point out that Bradley, over the decades, had no problem swallowing gummies, Valium, anxiety relievers, and even occasionally, amphetamines—and before that, dropping acid, doing quaaludes, and even snorting coke from time to time.

"That was all recreational," he pleaded.

"And sex isn't?"

Then he confessed that he was afraid of asking his doctor.

"Millions of men have asked their doctors for boner pills," she retorted.

"Yeah, well, billions of women have had babies, but we had to take Lamaze, EMS, Heimlich, Mozart-listening sessions, sonograms, yoga, and who remembers what else to have ours."

"I have no idea what that has to do with your refusal to talk to your doctor. Besides, what role did you play in giving birth to our kids that was so onerous?"

"Aw, come on, I accompanied you for all that. I was even there in the hospital room at delivery."

Valerie still held a grudge because a photo of Bradley holding their first daughter in the hospital room just after birth graced their kids' photo albums, but no one thought to take a photo of her and the baby. And, as Bradley has reminded her, that's because the nurse put the baby in his arms and took the photo. Bradley had nothing to do with it.

"So, are you saying you no longer find me desirable? Or is it that you need your ego assuaged to get you in the mood?" She gave him a come-hither look. "Come on, Bradley baby, want me to blow your blue-veiner?"

"Jeez. I can still *get* it up. I just can't *keep* it up as long as I used to."

He couldn't keep it up long enough to satisfy Valerie.

He added. "Blue veiner. Did you have a secret life writing copy for Blockbuster porn videos?"

"I learned from the ones you brought home and stashed in the closet."

"You knew about those?"

"If I could find them, the kids could find them. I had to hide them better than you did."

"So that's why I lost track of 'em."

"They're still in the garage crawlspace."

"The lost video fees I paid on those ..."

"I'm sure half those adult videos were never returned."

"Can't you go ask for the 'scrip on my behalf? I mean, let's face it, it's really for you. You're the one who wants to keep having sex."

"Bradley, you're acting like an infant. You already told me you're still able to get it up, and I assume you're still masturbating as per usual. So, if you don't find me appealing as a sex partner, just tell me."

"Hey, it's my body. I don't want that pharma shit in it."

"You stop doing gummies, and I'll believe you."

Valerie put an end to the months-long arguments by threatening the polyamory they had experimented with years ago.

He knew this was a thing, the horniness of the post-menopausal, post-career, post-child-rearing woman, another reason Bradley was certain God didn't exist. What intelligent designer would make men top out at nineteen and women at ninety? Well, maybe not quite ninety.

The last thing he needed in his life was another person demanding equal attention in the love and sex department. He was trying to shed responsibility and performance demands, not add to them.

So, he caved. In time, the Viagra righted his intimacy with Valerie but had a side effect. Compulsive masturbation disorder, CMD. He'd looked it up. It was worse than when he was in his 20s, when he'd sometimes masturbate two or three times a day, even on days he'd had sex with a girlfriend or one-night stand. Hell, sometimes not even an hour after.

Now that Valerie was getting off regularly again, what did she care about his problems? "Go join a Facebook club for Viagra users," she'd joked. Except he wasn't really sure the Viagra correlated with his masturbatory excess. Like most medical questions, you couldn't depend on the internet for a straight answer. He was just thankful that this time around, Instagram offered an endless supply of scantily clad women to figuratively rub up against instead of having to buy his porn from newsstands and convenience stores and take it to the counter where the overweight, under-resourced, pizza-faced cashier invariably would look at you, offended, like 'We only sell smut here because of the First Amendment.' Or, if it was a guy, snickering like Beavis. Or was it Butthead?

If kids today only knew how tough it was back then. 'Aw, *dude*, we had to buy our pornography in a store.' He remembered this commercial with a guy web-searching while his wife was paying the bills. Then the computer screen says, in a HAL-like voice, "You have reached the end of the internet. Please turn back."

Today, there was no end to internet porn.

He rearranged his pillow and gazed out the hotel room window wondering if the canyon the resort was nestled into was one of those Sedona energy vortices he'd read about. Maybe the whole place was on some sacred land or something. Although there was nothing particularly Native American-ish about the place even though the resort was supposedly owned by some tribe. There was a long, curved desk built into the wall, and a table piece underneath on wheels that rolled out, a work surface for a keyboard, he guessed. Very modern. Three framed photos were mounted above the desk, one was a close-up of some wildflowers, the second an even closer-up of tree bark, and the third a cactus in the foreground with the side of a mountain behind it. Nice, but nothing screamed Indian or magical vortex.

Just before he swiped Cuddles4UFOxoxo off the screen, a text alert from Victor appeared at the top of his screen, cutting Cuddles's head off at her eyebrows.

How many girls have you slept with?

WTF? That's from left field. Bradley thought. Victor was up late. It was eleven p.m. in Miami. He texted back.

The brilliant, tenured professor asks ... what?

You read it right.

You can't be serious.

I am.

Then you've reached a level of immaturity best handled by your therapist.

I'm dead serious.

I don't have time for this. He paused. As the sun set, the eastern side of the cliffs out his window were glowing like embers at the bottom of a fire pit. *Anyway, I can't even begin to answer that until we get some definitions in place.*

Like what?

Like, do you mean how many beds I've slept in also occupied by a woman, how many times I've had sex, how many times I've had intercourse, I mean, what's your definition of 'slept with' or 'sex'?

You know what I mean.

No, I don't. Is making out 'having sex'? Or does genitalia have to be involved?

Uh, genitalia, then.

Okay, buddy, what's prompting this awkward line of inquiry?

IDK. Just curious. Maybe this whole 'MeToo' thing I keep seeing on the news.

I'll think about it. Gotta run.

Lying still, in a bit of shock, Bradley shed his briefs, then got up, went to the john, took a leak, glimpsed himself in the mirror, then stared longer than he should, something he'd been doing since puberty. He placed his hands on the counter and leaned in.

He looked down at this pecker, wondered if he could give it another go. Like, right now.

Maybe the pud-pulling had less to do with Viagra and more a consequence of being almost completely retired. He had more free space in his mind. Like a computer CPU when you cleaned out the idle apps and useless files.

Why wasn't Valerie taking something to ease their whole sex thing? Her orgasms had been taking forever ever since they first slept together. Hell, if it didn't take her half a day to climax, his hard-ons wouldn't seem so brief. They have pills for everything these days, why couldn't she take one to speed things up?

He soaped and washed his hands of any remnants of semen, grabbed a hand towel from the rack with a fastener screw that was coming out of the wall on one side, then tossed it on the counter. Is there a hotel in the world where towel rack attachments aren't coming out of the wall?

How many women *had* he slept with?

No one ever actually answers the question, not truthfully, except perhaps Tino Lamborghini, who probably lost count at fifty before he was even out of college. Tino used to say, back in the day, if you talk to ten women a day, you'll convince one to sleep with you. Sure, if you looked like Tino, were built like Tino, and were as flirtatiously persistent as Tino. Hell, half the *guys* at college would probably have fucked Tino if there was no shame in it.

Now, it was looking like Tino could be the Harvey Weinstein of his class cohort.

Bradley was no Tino, but he started counting anyway. Number one was easy. Everyone remembers number one. Well, maybe not Wilt Chamberlain. But then again, that would depend on Victor's definition. Number two was surprisingly hazy. Number three? Shit, number three might have been Victor's girlfriend back in college, Rachel Schiff. In fact, he'd found out about CMD in a book Rachel had authored about women and their vaginas.

Victor, Bradley, and a number of other guys on campus were subjects of experiments concocted by Rachel for "Immersive Novel Construction," an experimental creative writing course offered at the women's college across the street. These guys, Bradley and Victor included, appeared as characters in Rachel's debut novel draft, illicitly obtained and read by a later boyfriend, who got royally pissed off and accidentally-on-purpose left it on a table at the college pub the next evening for the rest of the student body to get a look at.

Call it an early version of doxxing.

The exposure of Rachel's draft was a bona fide campus scandal, topped only by the two a.m. Sunday false fire alarm at the largest campus dorm which emptied out the rooms onto the quad and revealed just who really was sleeping with whom.

The two men Rachel spilled out with that night were neither Bradley, Victor, nor the guy who leaked "The Penis Papers," as Rachel's draft had come to be known. Rachel didn't have boyfriends or lovers or hook-ups or whatever you call them today, friends with benefits. She had temporary sexual gratification accomplices, which she then leaped on and over to cross that wide, raging river she called the patriarchy—a term very much in vogue now but which, as Bradley understood it, got its initial burst of academic momentum in the 1970s at women's colleges in the Northeast. Women's colleges like the one Rachel attended across the street.

As much as Rachel feigned outrage at the unauthorized release of her work, she reveled in the attention it brought, and later, the contract from a major publisher a few dozen blocks south on Broadway for three works of fiction, none of which were bestsellers, but which were instrumental in her entry to Hollywood as a scriptwriter and consultant for some of the industry's budding female pornography producers. The industry needed help appealing to women.

Thinking of Rachel was not helping his count. He was feeling the four-hour drive from Tucson and needed to do something, or he'd fall asleep. If he did, he'd be awake before midnight. He went down to the lobby. The line at the front desk was long. He walked around it and headed toward the bar.

It was never too late for a nightcap. And what was up with Victor's question, anyway?

CHAPTER 2

NASCHA SUNSEE

Nascha Sunsee Array, manager for the Song of the Sun Resort, rushed back from checking on the Freedom Center reception room to find the registration line nearly out the door. There were no backup employees. Several of the hotel's staff had been called to the casino property down the interstate for what was forecasted to be a banner week. It wasn't like COVID protocols had disappeared entirely, which added time and aggravation to just about every task on the property. If they'd just allot the resources and a little money for marketing and promotion, Song of the Sun could really take off.

Overworked as she was, she was grateful for her position. Yet she couldn't help but think of better ways to make a living, ways that didn't involve pandering to tribal leaders, or those who pretended to have enough Yavapai blood to qualify to work in tribal administration. Plus, she didn't think the quota system she had to operate under was ethical. That wasn't her call, though.

Years ago, she'd attended a weekend workshop promoted by a famous talking head news anchor who never showed up but instead addressed the attendees, crammed into a Country Living Inn & Suites meeting room outside Flagstaff, remotely. The conference, targeted at women, was titled "Know your Value." Fees for staff with management potential, like Nascha, were paid by Song of the Sun. There she got the idea for her book.

"How do you pronounce Yavapai," the guest in front of her asked politely. Just the kind of question that would hold up the line even more.

"Just think of it as 'have a pie,'" Nascha replied, sweetly.

"Oh, that's cute, but really—"

"It's pretty close, actually, to how it is pronounced." She arched her eyebrows and twitched her head towards the line.

"And is the have a pie reservation close by?"

"Just up the highway."

"Are 'have a pies' Apache or Navajo? Someone told me both occupied this area."

"Neither. We're Navapache. And we still occupy this area."

"Is that a thing, Navapache?"

"It should be."

Who the hell knows. Just possibly, the Heinz 57 concept could apply to nonwhite people from Europe living on this continent, too. Maybe brown people could call it the Sriracha Scoville Scale 1500. Doesn't exactly roll off the tip of the tongue, but who cares?

This exchange wouldn't even make it into her collection, *The Tonto Chronicles,* which she hoped to publish one day and be rewarded for her "value." In the preface, Nascha had written, "The 'Lone' Ranger had a constant companion. His name was Tonto." Perhaps that short quote alone summed up the typical American's perspective on the "Wild West."

Nascha waved up the next person. Audible sighs of frustration were becoming uncomfortable. Yet this one guest didn't budge.

"Is there someone to help with the luggage?"

You can't roll a roller bag?

Nascha smiled. "He should return from assisting another guest any minute, if you wouldn't mind waiting over there." She pointed to a comfortable fiery-red lounge chair, backed up against a midnight-blue wall decorated with turquoise and silver trim.

One bellman for a 300-room property. Who doubled as the handyman, and sometimes the concierge. What was the Chief thinking?

Nascha motioned again to the next person in line, who was not impolite enough to move forward until the present guest fully exited.

The man paused and came to attention.

"I respectfully acknowledge that I am on land of the Native Americans of this area, and am committed to building sustainable relationships with the, uh, sovereign and indigenous ..."

Nascha looked at him, puzzled.

"Uh, okay ... your name, please?"

"I thought I was supposed to say something like that," the man said. "I even tried to memorize a land acknowledgement before I got here." He seemed crushed.

"May I see a driver's license?"

While she was registering him, Nascha remembered when a representative of the Center for the Study of Freedom and Philosophy called to discuss a "land and people preamble" that participants could announce at the beginning of their colloquium. At the time, she'd thought it courteous of the person to want to craft it and clear it with her, but she had no authority to do so. Truthfully, she didn't even agree with the practice. Just another way for those who now control the land to make themselves feel less guilty about the people they took it from.

She'd referred the lady on the phone to the Tribal Council at Camp Verde, realizing that the odds of her getting a timely response was worse than the odds of the Yavapai and the Hopi ever settling their dispute over who owns the valley below the three mesas.

The only "acknowledgement" Nascha could abide by was the one embodied by a famous tale in Southwest Native American circles, told in as many variations as there are tribes: A native chief was once asked by NASA to contribute something for a radio signal of a collection of messages NASA planned to send out into space for any life forms who might have the sophisticated technology to receive and translate it. The Chief refused. NASA asked again. The Chief refused. Finally, a deal was struck. He would craft a message in his native language but would not divulge it to NASA. After being pestered about the message the rest of his life, he whispered it on his deathbed: "Don't believe a word these people say."

The previous registrant was still waiting for help with the luggage. Nascha ducked quickly into the office behind her, got on the radio, and pleaded with Rodrigo to hurry. He was probably sneaking a smoke. She returned to the desk. The line now snaked out to the parking lot. She'd have to start handing out free drink tickets.

With each guest she registered, "Nascha's Have a Pie," that bakery she'd always wanted to open, seemed like a better and better idea. The pie shop idea predated the Know Your Value conference, but she figured she could sell *The Tonto Chronicles* in the shop. Bottom line was, there had to be a better way to earn a living than managing a severely under-resourced resort or sitting in a dilapidated booth selling jewelry to white people along the highways to Flagstaff and the Grand Canyon.

She was certain *The Tonto Chronicles* could be a bestseller. Who wouldn't laugh at stories about ridiculous things white people say, like when a guest said to her, "a buffalo nickel for your thoughts" and then burst out laughing. They didn't even have buffalo around here.

At the very least, she wished the Big Chief would take seriously her idea of converting the golf course into a full-blown arena for vortex-focused pharma and psychedelics-fueled parties organized by and for the wealthy white women in Phoenix and LA. Nascha had already proved it could be a serious revenue producer. She'd prove it again later this week when the Carefree Ladies of Cave Creek showed up.

Nascha didn't have the kind of power that allowed her to make big decisions about the resort. It didn't have to matter that the Song of the Sun wasn't located in one of the mythical seven energy vortices of Sedona. Who said there could only be seven? There was no reason why her resort couldn't be an eighth. With a little marketing, they could create their own mythology.

Mythology, she thought, was the one thing they were really good at. Identify some sacred spot where mother earth crawled out of the other side of the black hole, put up EMF sensors, and set the dials to some fictitious zone of synchronicity. Or some such BS. Their patrons wouldn't know the difference. Or care. But the elders instead decided it was a good idea to build a golf course in a charming canyon with a dry riverbed.

She needed to focus on the present, though. How was she going to make her quota for the month?

CHAPTER 3

COLLOQUIUM: DAY ONE

The next morning, Bradley entered the empty hotel elevator car from the top floor where his room was. By the time it got to level two, it was packed with colloquium participants.

"Oh, hello, Ashera," he called out across several people's heads and necks after the door opened and one of his principal panelists squeezed into the remaining space. She hunched her shoulders and pulled her bag closer to her body. She tried unsuccessfully to respond to Bradley with a half-smile and quarter turn of the head.

Ashera, whom he'd met at the reception, could be N+1 or whatever Victor's number turned out to be. She had the kind of thick, wild hair that made you ignore the color and just admire how much you'd like to bury your face in it. Her ethnic blend must be a cocktail no genetic mixologist could duplicate. It was clear from her bio he'd read earlier how she identified—them, they, Mexican, Moroccan, Tohono O' Odom, and vegan. *To-Tonto what?* He guessed she was tattooed to the hilt, including the knobby flower shooting out of an aloe plant wrapped around a vein in her neck.

Bradley had wanted to fill out his pronouns as "It" which elicited a smiley face from Dr. Washington, when he responded to an email about pronouns. The emoji was by no means permission to violate present-day norms for making sure others understood the source of your victimhood.

Victor could get away with using "It," since he was adopted and was indeed a victim of anything or anyone that didn't involve the highest order statistical analysis methods on the planet. Despite being raised in a strict Anglican household in New Hampshire by whiter-than-white, and Britisher than British parents.

After sharing a proper good morning after they exited the elevator, Ashera and Bradley walked side by side in silence past the registration area, then through an outdoor canopied walkway that felt like a curtain of heat. Making conversation with Ashera during the reception had been difficult. Like talking to your cat. Even when you didn't have one.

The Conference Center was freezing, even though it was sweltering outside. Immediately, he was jolted by the views from the floor-to-ceiling windows of gorgeous jagged red rocks and cliffs on either side of the golf course, views that forced contemplation. Introspection. Retrospection. All of the above. Although the fiery color palette of the rising sun had receded, the western canyon wall seemed to radiate back the warmth it had absorbed, like a baked pie coming out of the oven.

During his interview, Dr. Washington explained how he viewed his role as facilitator. Bradley summed it up as, "So you want me to act as a discussion catalyst without dissociating and becoming part of the product content." Something like that, Keshawn replied back, looking a bit puzzled.

He was also instructed to make sure that the Freedom Center comes across as a champion of diversity, equity, and inclusion, DEI—or, as Bradley thought when he first saw the acronym, God in Latin, or close enough to God based on the one year of the dead language he was forced to take five decades ago at prep school. To the extent possible, he was supposed to make sure no one felt left out of the discussion, and to make a special effort to engage, or call on, those who might take offense at not being engaged or otherwise called on.

"You know what I mean, right?" Keshawn said, without a wink or a nod.

"Well, not exactly. I'm to achieve 'equity' by paying special attention to some and less attention to others?"

"It does sound nonsensical when you put it that way. Just make sure no one dominates over, interrupts, or demeans other participants."

"You mean white men?"

"Okay, I mean white men!"

"Ah, then, I will ensure no mansplaining takes place!" He pulled that word from straight from Valerie's lips.

"That's it, that's right," Dr. Washington said, smiling happily like the man in front of him had finally hit upon the right answer.

As Victor had been bitching about the last few years, DEI had become God-like in the halls of higher learning. Bradley had wanted to push it with Washington, an African-American, and ask if he should prevent all men from mansplaining, or just white men. Were black men off the hook? What about indigenous men? Indian Subcontinent types? Asians? Mexicans? What were the rules?

Victor said it had become more important to not offend any single individual in your class than it was to instill some collective level of understanding of the material, whether it was in the highest level graduate courses Victor taught or Intro to Statistics. Victor, and other professors he knew, complained incessantly that standardized college entrance exams had gone the way of the Neanderthal, because they weren't fair to, in Victor's words, Neanderthals. Grade inflation had reduced the assignment of marks to the first two letters of the alphabet. Almost any comment a professor made about the work, written or oral, could be challenged as "having come from a place of non-objectivity regarding the person's ethnicity, race, gender, socio-economic status, sexual orientation, generational poverty, genetic structure, and general physical and mental impairments not the fault of the individual."

Although Bradley engaged with academia tangentially in his own career as an industry and technology analyst (he dealt with "complex engineered energy systems," he liked to say), and as a parent seeking the best schools and universities for his kids, he hadn't understood the depth and breadth of the changes. He wasn't "down in the weeds" of the DEI movement, as Victor said, so he couldn't possibly understand how bad it had gotten.

The academy had come a long way from when Bradley's college freshman chemistry professor propelled his 5-foot-4 yarmulke-topped frame into the 300-person lecture hall, saying, "Okay, look at the person to the left of you." All fearfully, if with bewilderment, obeyed. "Now look to the right of you." Some 270 heads, many with unkempt, robust manes swishing through the air, turned as if on orders taken from a boot camp drill instructor. "Good job. One of those two people won't be here next semester, and the other won't be here next year!" He hadn't seen that professor express such glee for the rest of the year.

The job of a freshman chemistry professor back then was to weed out one-third of the students who thought they had a chance at getting into med school and force another third into other majors. On top of that, women had only recently even been allowed to attend the Ivy League university he and Victor went to.

Two of the women in his engineering program could have qualified for the list Victor was asking about.

He saw a text come in from Valerie.

Do you know where the olive oil is?

CHAPTER 4

PACKING HEAT

Ashera, Bradley, and one of Bradley's other panelists, Azul Ebunoluwa, who had not been at the reception, were all seated at the dais. Bradley poured water into the short glasses set near each seat, taking care not to let the ice in the pitcher cause a spill.

When he finished and turned to look over the gathered attendees, he was astounded to see the number of women in the audience. At most of the conferences Bradley attended, women were usually less than five percent of the crowd, often a lot less, like zero. Here, he guessed, they made up between half and two-thirds.

Gail Bartholomew, Director of the Cold War Missile Museum, the third panelist, had also missed the reception and was still a no-show. Bradley was getting nervous. Hell of a start if there was no Gail, no Dr. Washington. He looked at his cheat sheet with his opening remarks. Well, Bartholomew didn't have to be here for his intro or the remote video feed with Roger Magellan.

He checked his watch again. Surely Gail was just delayed. Bradley, along with the other panelists and speakers, were being well-compensated by the Freedom Center. Washington had said, "The Center wants to ensure there is no poaching of expertise from people or groups lacking power just because the Center has political and cultural clout." Bradley wasn't sure what the director meant. What kind of clout did a brand new Freedom Center wield?

Bradley and Dr. Washington had ordered the program so practical material would go first, then empirical research, and finally, the conceptual and speculative topics. He'd asked Gail to lead off, if only because he knew her from his volunteer work at the museum.

"I figured that was you when I saw the program," Gail said warmly, when Bradley had introduced himself on the phone, "Maniopolos isn't exactly under M from the Daughters of the American Revolution."

Bradley laughed. "But it is from a country proud to be the birthplace of democracy."

"And how's that going for them?" Gail snickered. "So, tell me, how long does my presentation need to be? I don't have to prepare a PowerPoint or anything, do I?"

"That's up to you. We'll have AV equipment set up, but the only requirement, per se, is to address the topic suggested by the Freedom Center for your institution, which I've captured as, 'Achieving Peace and Freedom Through Military Strength.' Working title."

"Yeah, I remember from your last email that freedom could be thought of as protecting the 'collective peace of mind of a nation' in this context, through mutually assured destruction."

"Kind of a contradiction in terms, no?"

Gail had paused a moment. "Perhaps."

"Or a *Catch-22*."

"Never read it."

"So, MAD did not lead to peace of mind?" Bradley pictured Slim Pickens riding "Little Boy" in *Dr. Strangelove*.

"Fear is what keeps citizens in their place, not peace," she countered.

"Well, Ms. Bartholomew...."

"It's Captain Bartholomew," she said sternly. Then in a more relaxed way. "Or Gail. I'm just funnin' you."

"Gail, you are free to frame your presentation within the context of the question in any way you wish. You're the expert here."

"Don't worry. I follow orders. Most of the time." She chuckled through a labored breath, like she was suffering from asthma. "This isn't my normal kind of assignment, though. I mean, I haven't led tours at the museum for years, I can barely do that kind of walking anymore. I sure don't seek this kind of extracurricular work. This just seemed, well, the right thing at the right time."

"We appreciate your willingness to join us. And you'll be receiving the first half of your remuneration in two weeks or thereabouts."

"Now there's a big word. Gotta admit, it's pretty sweet money. And paid in advance!"

"Can't disagree with that," Bradley added with a laugh.

"By the way," Gail added, "I am now the former Director of the CWMM. There was a recent re-org by the Air Force. I accepted an early retirement."

"Even better. Now you aren't bound by their restrictions. We'll get the real story!"

She snorted. "You might at that."

By 8:10 a.m., the audience was getting restless. Bradley had to do something. Valerie had once described comfort-building exercises used to open large meetings at the company she worked for.

"Before I make formal introductions, why don't we all take a few minutes to breathe deeply, stretch, introduce yourself to the people next to you, and tell each of those folks something interesting about yourself that wouldn't show up on your CV. Just make sure it's G-rated."

He overheard someone grumble in the first row. "What is this, church?" Everyone else seemed eager to comply.

That took them to 8:20 a.m. Still no Gail. He'd just go ahead with the Magellan introduction. He didn't want to make a multi-billionaire wait.

He already had Magellan queued up on his laptop. He went to the podium.

"While we're waiting for any stragglers getting their coffee and pastries, let me be the first to welcome all of you to the inaugural International Conference on Neo-Anthropocentric Models of Retrospective Freedoms, sponsored by the Center for the Study of the Philosophy of Freedom, or the Freedom Center, affiliated with Sonoran Community College in Tucson, Arizona. My name is Bradley Maniopolos, and I am honored to be your facilitator for the next few days."

Dr. Plemmons, that enemy of the patriarchy he'd met at the reception, immediately rose from the audience. "I was assured this conference would not have an old white guy for a facilitator."

Trouble already, Bradley thought. He could turn over his two ethnic cards but that just wasn't him.

"Well, you don't really know how old I am," Bradley said, with a chuckle.

Before Dr. Plemmons could retort, Bartholomew burst through the thick cypress-wood double doors at the back of the meeting room. All eyes turned in her direction, as the first ones who noticed gasped and nudged the person next to them. One attendee in a middle aisle seat bolted towards the other double doors. A third took cover under the flimsy narrow conference table in front of each attendee, spilling a pitcher of water in the process.

Gail marched towards the dais wearing a mauve-colored holster strapped to her hip, handgun snapped into it. Most of the audience was too stunned to react, even as her stride and manner seemed to suggest that she'd have no problem using the weapon. Bradley glanced quickly at Ashera and Azul. It was unclear whose mouth had the larger diameter opening. Azul's certainly had the whiter teeth. Gail was out of breath by the time she reached the dais.

Bradley recalled that Gail walked like a Brontosaurus—or was it Apatasaurus now? She'd always dressed like a drill sergeant and strode about with unwavering purpose, even when she didn't have one. Her ruddy complexion, reddish-orange hair, spherical frame with short, stumpy limbs, and a pumpkin of a head could be startling when combined with her bull-in-a-China-shop manners. As she approached the dais, he tried to exude nonchalance, even as, for a split second, his legs vibrated under the table. Since it appeared she wasn't going to fire the weapon anytime soon, the agitation in the room subsided. Barely.

He'd seen all sorts of weird shit at conferences. That time a speaker told him he'd never done public speaking before, then took the stage, promptly fainted, bashed his head, bled like a mother, and was taken away in an EMS vehicle. Then there was Bump Brummit, a guy who sold machines three-stories high and thirty feet in diameter. He decked a guy in a meeting room because the man dared to move his briefcase a few feet without asking Bump's permission.

Maybe the worst was when one of his speakers at a conference Bradley had organized told an off-color joke, offending a woman attendee, who reported it to the engineering society which sponsored the conference. Next thing Bradley knew, the president of the society called him on the carpet and demanded that he and his speaker apologize.

No one had ever shown up overtly packing heat, though, and some pretty tough dudes worked in his industry.

After Gail took her seat at the dais, Bradley said, "Now that we have a quorum, and a good gal with a gun ..."

He hoped for a few laughs, got none.

"Let me quickly introduce Roger Magellan, a tireless advocate for the Freedom Center who will make a few remarks on the big screen." He hit a few buttons on his computer and wondered whether Magellan would mention some of Bradley's publications, his books, his interviews on CNBC, features in *Newsweek*, quotes in the *The Wall Street Journal* and *The New York Times*. He'd applied for this gig and sent in his creds as a lark, thinking it was something different to do as he eased into retirement, and was still mystified as to why they'd selected him.

"Roger, we're ready."

Bradley was surprised the video feed wasn't live in real time, but instead an IG-like reel of someone emerging from a thick forest into a clearing, wearing a presidential dark suit and red-blue-white tie who didn't look like a guy named Roger Magellan. He looked as Indian subcontinent as anyone could, darker than Bradley. His hair was straight, slicked back over his head in a pompadour with some shiny goo that reminded Bradley of Brylcreem. He was tall, lean, and clean, with an angular face, a cherubic smile, a confident demeanor, and an air of superiority.

Bradley was yanked out of the moment. In his decades of professional experience, the men he'd worked with who came from the subcontinent never did squat. They were self-important know-it-alls who wouldn't shut up during meetings, but who never completed the work they were assigned. They always tried to get out of paying their invoices by claiming you didn't perform to the letter of the agreement. They always had lofty degrees from great universities, certificates for this or that, and dozens of plaques on their office "I love me" walls, but it was always all talk and no action. They loved presenting papers, leading committees, and seeing their name in print, but hardly ever did actual work. Bradley had ended up holding the bag more than once.

Well, he figured, Magellan sure wasn't going to mention any of Bradley's work.

"A hearty welcome to beautiful, one of a kind Sedona, Arizona!"

Ugh. His ebullience was off-putting, especially since the man hadn't bothered to show up for his own conference.

"My name is Roger Magellan of the Magellan Foundation. Before I say anything more, let me apologize on behalf of Dr. Keshawn Washington, the Freedom Center Director, who is not attending due to a personal emergency. He will make every effort to arrive just as soon as he is able."

Not a real explanation, Bradley noted.

Magellan went on to thank the speakers and panelists and the institutions they represented, and then reviewed some of the highlights of the agenda. He made special note of a presentation by a Professor Wertmuller. The concept behind her work deserved a patent, Magellan said, but certainly the mathematical model she was creating, with generous Freedom Center support, would provide the basis for multiple patents and intellectual property down the road.

Right. Keshawn had mentioned that Magellan was "high" on Wertmuller. "Quantizing Freedom" was the title of her talk. Bradley had no idea what that meant, but he was looking forward to finding out. Magellan also mentioned the Thursday session on free will and teased the audience with his possible virtual attendance to join the discussion.

Magellan continued, "All of you may think this is silly reverie on my part, but I have no doubt *whatsoever* that this conference will one day be considered the Davos or Aspen of its field!"

That comment turned some audience member expressions quizzical. Bradley thought he heard a snort from somewhere near the front.

"Now I will leave you in the capable hands of our facilitator, *Mr.* Maniopolos ..."

He stressed the mister! Like he was lesser. Couldn't the guy at least mention one of his books, his years of policy work in DC, his exposure of Enron? Something rather than emphasizing the "mister?"

"Thank you, Roger. We'll see you on Thursday!" Bradley shut down the video feed and looked out at the audience. "The Aspen of Freedom! The Davos of Liberty!" Bradley offered a half-hearted fist pump. "Well, I trust we can live up to those aspirations!" Then he turned toward Gail.

"For our first presentation, I have the pleasure of introducing not just the former Director of the Cold War Missile Museum, but a woman who was my superior officer, of sorts, when I was a volunteer docent at the museum, a lady who did far more for all of us during the Cold War than build a bomb shelter in the backyard or hide under a desk during a school drill."

"Now these poor kids have to suffer through active-shooter drills," a woman yelled from the floor.

Bradley ignored the outburst and read Gail's bio.

"Thank you for your service," someone yelled, scanning the audience in a way that implied that everyone else in the room should be grateful as well.

"Or is it 'thank you for your servitude?'" retorted a woman near the front, carrying a "Smash the Patriarchy" and "Black Lives Matter" bag, who turned around and looked venomously at the man who'd just yelled.

Gail had no words on her slides, just photos from the museum, some of her squad mates from back in the day, and close-ups of some of the equipment. She invited everyone to come down for a visit. They were only 30 minutes south of Tucson, she said, and bragged that the best, cheapest tacos and burritos in the land could be had at Tacho's Food Truck in the parking lot of the Green Valley Mall.

"Tacho employs very cheap labor and doesn't pay rent," she added, wryly. "He makes this secret salsa from a family recipe, so you know it's the good stuff."

From the photos, the museum appeared to be nothing more than an office building and a couple of connected trailers with a few instruments and antennae jutting up from the ground in the back. She called that "topside." A few small tanks, and a display of a rocket engine. Then a shot looking down into the silo from the bubble dome protecting it. She pointed at a huge earthen formation to the southwest.

"Other than the abandoned mine over thataway, not much between here and the border but mule trails."

"Mule trails?" an audience member asked.

Pointing with her hand-held laser, she responded, "Up here, between the site and the mine, is the pathway used for years by Mexican smugglers." She looked back at the questioner and added in a tone that Bradley couldn't tell was serious or not, "They leave their trash like coyote skat."

"Not exactly tight security," an audience member observed.

"If you only knew," Gail said.

Audience members shifted uncomfortably in their seats.

The last slide was a photo of herself in uniform in 1979.

"I didn't always look like the person you see in front of you today, fat, sick, health problems out the wazoo. But that's a separate story."

Indeed, Bradley thought. She looked even worse than the last time Bradley had been at the site.

When her power point was complete, Gail went off on a bit of a ramble.

"So, you folks, and the rest of the world for that matter," she said, as she carefully surveyed the audience, "probably wonder what we did down there. I mean, as I mentioned, these sites were manned 24/7/365. We did the things we were supposed to do, but that's kind of boring to talk about. Then we did the things we weren't supposed to do and we're not supposed to talk about. And then the site did things to us the Air Force definitely doesn't want us to talk about.

"We performed mindless repetitive tasks, proceeded through checklists, maintained the equipment, manned the control room—and no, it does not have the red button you see in all the movies—wrote the indicator and gage readings on clipboards during our rounds, regularly handled some particularly noxious gases and flammable, explosive compounds, and communicated with our superiors at the Bagman Air Force base up the road. We kind of did what the site crews do at other industrial facilities." She smiled at Bradley. "You and I talked about that. "We baby the equipment," she continued, "follow safety protocols and, to be honest, prayed that nothing really bad would happen. Elaborate instruction manuals guided every action we performed at the site. Almost down to how to take a shit."

Several in the audience gasped. A few chuckled.

"Hey, we're all adults," Gail said, with a shrug.

Bradley said, "Sorry to interrupt, Gail, but could you tell the audience about the guidance system computer?"

"Ah, yes, the guidance system for a warhead that would take out half of Moscow had a central processing unit with less brainpower than the ringtone on your phone."

Bradley had his own theory about those missile sites.

Gail went on. "You folks probably haven't thought about the Cold War in years. Too obsessed with global warming, 9/11, the War on Terror, MAGA, illegal immigration, school shootings, etc. What is a "cold war" anyway? We were fighting wars all over the world, not just Vietnam. The CIA ran them undercover. There was nothing cold about all the bullets flying and bombs dropping. But I digress.

"Then," she paused, for effect, "then there is what the site did to us missileers. I mean, there's a lot of publicly available info on how all of us were affected—site accidents, deteriorating equipment, long-term health effects—but there is a big difference between information that is made available to the public, you know, through Freedom of Information Act requests, and general public knowledge. I'll tell you one—this missile program was described as early as 1973 as 'an accident waiting to happen' by the Pentagon's own analysts. Accidents did happen. Occasionally, something went boom at one of the sites. Not ours, thank God."

Bradley got Gail's attention and gave her the one-minute sign.

"Okay, okay, I'll shut my trap. To conclude, did we achieve 'peace through strength' and did the missile program protect American liberty? I don't know, how do you define freedom anyway? That's what you're here to talk about. No Russian missiles ever struck U.S. soil. No American nukes landed on Russian soil. Did we 'win' the Cold War? Maybe, but who lost and at what cost?" She paused. "Questions?

Ashera raised her hand. "What if we saved all that money we spent building missiles like yours and instead negotiated with the Russians to achieve peace, a cold peace, if you will? Wouldn't that have done more to protect 'freedom' of Americans and Russians?"

Gail responded, "I stay away from high-patheticals ... and I'm not mispronouncing the word. No offense, it just doesn't do anyone any good to speculate."

Bradley interjected, "I like that! Hypathetical." Then he wondered if Ashera felt shot down. That would be against Dr. Washington's rules of engagement for the meeting.

"Oh, and if you're wondering why I have this pistol strapped to my waist, yes, I did mean to scare the shit out of all of you," Gail added. "I'm dramatizing the fact that site commanders like me carried a pistol in case any of the crew was, shall we say, reluctant to follow orders when we got the call to blow half of Russia."

Whew! Bradley thought, at least she has a reason.

An audience member yelled out, "You mean, you'd have to shoot one of your own?"

"That was the idea," Gail said.

Murmurs flowed through the audience like the peaks and valleys of multiple sine waves.

"Would you?" asked the lady with the BLM insignia on her handbag?

"Would I what?"

"Shoot a member of your own crew?"

That's another 'hypathetical.'"

Audience member: "So, in your estimation, did the Cold War enhance American freedom or not?"

"I suppose, if you define freedom as the spread of capitalism around the world and countering communism, then, absolutely, the Cold War was unarguably successful."

"But at the expense of the rest of the world, right?" The audience member asked. "Or at least those nations which were not our allies?"

"Depends on if you think global freedom is a zero-sum game. One nation gains freedom while another loses it. Or, as I like to say, there but for the grace of me goes you."

"That's kind of brutal," Bradley said, smiling, "but I think we'll have to leave it there. Before we break, does anyone have a final question or thought or two?"

Gail labored from the podium back to her place on the dais. The chair creaked ominously as she sat. "I prefer to sit," she said. One audience member raised a hand and asked, "Did you ever get to meet any of your Missileer counterparts in Russia?"

Gail shook her head. "Nah, Perestroika and glasnost didn't go that far."

Another audience member called out. "Could you comment on the false narrative of the so-called "missile gap" perpetrated by the Pentagon and the media in the late 1950s?"

Gail laughed. "No need. You just did."

"Can you say 'yellowcake?'" someone yelled.

Bradley held up a hand. "Okay, let's not get too far afield. On that note, it really is time for a break."

The audience exited out to the lobby area for refreshments and coffee. Bradley and Gail chatted on the dais. He pointed at the weapon.

"I mean, surely this is a case of an unnecessary action hero. Did you really need this?"

"I checked with the hotel. They have no publicly displayed prohibition against open-carry. It's an open-carry state."

"Right, but you couldn't just show a photo of yourself back then with the pistol?"

"It's part of my delivery." She winked.

An audience member strode up to the dais. "Thank you for standing up for our Second Amendment rights," he said, extending his hand to Gail. And then he was off on a rant, talking about how his freedoms were being threatened by the libs as Bradley left them to it and walked away.

After sucking down a cup of coffee, remarkably decent for a conference hotel, and chatting up a few of the attendees, Bradley had ten minutes left to duck back into his room. Several of the attendees had caught him during the break to share their feelings about the weapon, ranging from mild displeasure to extreme discomfort.

He texted Victor:

Holy shit! One of my panelists showed up armed.

It took a few minutes for a response.

That's nothing new. A weapon, or a pair, beats a hope and a prayer!

What?

It's a saying around Florida, the DeSanctimonious State.

You've been to conferences with armed academics?

No one comes armed to talk about associational statistics. Other colleagues have mentioned it, though.

That's it? No one cares?

Not enough.

Doesn't it change how people talk about their work?

I guess.

What do you do about it?

IDK. Turn it into a teachable moment?

LOL. Not!

Seriously. A break in the texting.

So, what's your count?

Bradley sighed.

I know it's not your strong suit, but ... be mature.

I want an initial estimate by the end of the day.

Go baby your stats students.

Then he realized that he had not communicated with Valerie since yesterday morning. They had parted on a tense note. He wasn't sure why. Something felt amiss. They'd even had sex the weekend before, and he had made sure that she reached her orgasm, even though he hadn't. So, it couldn't be that.

Well, he spent most of his married life trying to figure out why she was feeling whatever she was feeling and what he could do about it. Then again, she hadn't bothered to communicate with him either. Another one of those, who's on first, something unresolvable on second, I don't know on third, but let's talk about it ad infinitum always waiting at home plate.

Bradley stopped at the front desk on the way back to the conference room. He motioned to the lady whose name tag read Nascha.

"Excuse me. What is the Song of the Sun's policy on open-carry?"

"We don't allow booze to be brought in from the outside, not even brown-bagging, except in the privacy of guest rooms."

"I meant firearms."

"Oh, uh, as per state law, we allow it except where and when alcohol is served."

"Don't most hotels prohibit open-carry on premises?"

"The national chains perhaps. We are a one-off, affiliated with the Coins of the Canyon Casino down the interstate a ways. For obvious reasons, weapons are *not* allowed on casino premises in the possession of any guests. We have jurisdiction, as it's on Tribal land. I mean, it's really *all* our land, but you know...."

"Oh? What Native American nation are you affiliated with?"

"Yavapai."

"Yav a pai," Bradley repeated, slowly.

"Yavapai," Nascha repeated, eager for her next entry in *The Tonto Chronicles*.

"Ah, okay, thanks."

Nascha watched the guy nod and walk away without saying anything overtly stupid or racist. Bummer.

"Yava dabba do," Bradley muttered, with a quirk of his lips.

Victor had said to make it a teachable moment, Bradley thought, entering the meeting room, before he noticed an attendee with a pistol and holster strapped to his waist, the same guy who thanked Gail for defending the Second Amendment. Goddamn, what was this, a saloon in the Wild West serving shots of highbrow cogitation on freedom?

When the group had reconvened, Bradley began by suggesting they delay the next formal presentation until after lunch and take the opportunity of the unforeseen incident with Gail to have an ad hoc discussion about freedom in the context of gun possession, open and concealed carry, and the Second Amendment. That was when he noticed yet another attendee with a holstered gun. Well, at least there were only three good guys and gals with guns. The unarmed were still in the majority, if defenseless. Unless there were guns hidden in purses and pockets.

Ashera swiftly grabbed one of the microphones from the panelist table. Bradley could see her hands tremble around the handle.

"I'm not going to, uh, pretend nothing out of the ordinary happened this morning. While I have, um, great respect for Ms. Bartholomew and her fellow Missileers, I won't abide by this notion that the freedom one person is entitled to in carrying a gun should take precedence over the fear forced onto the rest of the audience and our lack of freedom to feel safe at a colloquium to which we were all invited."

"That's an unfreedom!" an audience member yelled.

Another audience member in the first row said, "Look at the precedent you established. Now there are two others carrying firearms. Jeez, a small army is materializing."

"Three," said one of two African Americans in the audience, who stood up, pointed to the firearm at his waist, and sat down. "It's an integrated army!"

Bradley did a spit take, but no one else laughed.

Gail, who was sitting next to Ashera, said, "All of us have the right to carry a weapon."

"Also the obligation to consider others who choose *not* to carry weapons. Your freedom to parade around with a gun on your hip effectively nullifies my freedom to feel safe in this space."

Gail considered Ashera's comment. "Fair enough," as she unclipped the holster, leaned over the table, and placed the weapon between herself and Ashera. "Take it with you to the podium during your talk. How's that for equity?"

Gail smiled as if she'd just won the lottery.

I'm sitting here at an academic conference, Bradley thought, and four attendees are packing heat.

He spoke up, "Well, look, there's the legal case, and then there's the ethical case. And the normative case. Surely, it's a 'norm,' meaning *normally* people do not brandish firearms while engaging and debating at an academic conference."

Gail looked over at him. "That norm was just challenged."

"That's what the last eight years have been about," an audience member said. "One party destroying norms, the other is trying to play by the norms."

"Okay, think about this," Gail said. "A bicyclist comes to a four-way stop intersection, slows down, then crosses, when a guy in a honking Camaro blows through the stop sign. The cyclist screams at the car and flips him off. Both broke the law because neither obeyed the stop sign. Who would have been at fault if the bicyclist got mowed down?"

"It's the degree of illegality," the same audience member replied. "What the motorist did was more illegal than what the bicyclist did. Bicyclists are not required to make a full stop at a stop sign."

Gail laughed. "Tell that to the attendees at his funeral. The 'norm' for motorists is that most do not come to a full stop at any stop sign, even though it's the law."

Bradley spoke up. "So everything is a gray area subject to interpretation."

"Let's face it," Dr. Plemmons spoke up from the second row, "the whole system of laws is constructed by those with power, flaunted by those with power, and used against those with less or no power."

Gail nodded, thoughtfully. "You get it, girl! So, who is really free in a society? Only those who make the rules. I spent all those years underground, wrestling with hazardous chemical tanks, faulty equipment, unreliable leak detectors. Missileers were exposed to some of the nastiest stuff humans have ever invented, not to mention radiation. We're all dying off early. We have every form of cancer you can think of, plus diabetes, skin ailments, you name it. We did all of that in the name of protecting American liberty. We didn't make the rules. But we did follow them."

Then she added, with a devilish grin, "Mostly."

CHAPTER 5

GAIL BARTHOLOMEW, CWMM

Three months earlier, Gail Bartholomew was at her desk after quitting time, about to button up the museum for the day, when she got around to reading the mail. The envelope with the return address, Center for the Study of the Philosophy of Freedom, resident at Sonoran Community College, Tucson, Arizona, was probably a request to schedule a customized group tour. Turned out it was an invitation to speak at a colloquium. Hm, she thought. She opened the rest of the mail, stuffing the invite into her pocket.

She went to the parking lot, got into and started her car, parked in the "Reserved for Director" space, turned on the air conditioner, and retrieved a manila envelope from the glove compartment. She exited the car and returned to the building, gravel crunching under her feet. She bypassed the admin building and walked directly into the topside area toward the farthest manhole grating, just inside the perimeter fencing, under which were junction boxes for electrical connections and space for one technician. She lifted the grating, descended the three steps of the wall-attached ladder, inserted her key into the lock on a hinged door opposite the junction boxes, pulled the knob, and retrieved the two packages that had been left on the other side of the door.

Then she placed the envelope where the packages had been, with the note she had written earlier on a plain piece of paper, in English and in Spanish: "IT ALL ENDS TODAY!" Funny, that could have been the plain English version of the command she would have received to launch the warhead back in the day.

She climbed out of the manhole, laboring to breathe in the stifling desert air. She pulled the invite from her pocket. Just a few days ago, she had received notice from the Air Force that her position as director would be terminated within the month.

She read another few lines. A Bradley Maniopolos would be the facilitator of the colloquium. Maniopolos? She only had to turn that name over once in her mind. Had to be the same character who worked as a volunteer docent for a year or so. How many people in southern Arizona could have that name? How many people in America?

Who would be inviting *her* to an academic colloquium? She said colloquium out loud, like it was a bad medical condition. She read a few more lines, noting that directors from the Tomahawk Hill Preservation Society and the History of Musical Instruments Gallery had also been invited. Who would even think to utter the names of these three institutions in the same breath?

She glanced behind her towards the sun making its way west over the old copper mine nearby as she scrunched through more gravel. She pushed the button for the rickety elevator which descended underground to the control room. Technically, she was breaking rules riding it alone. They really should replace it, but its authenticity was prized higher than its reliability.

From there, she walked through the 10-inch thick blast door down the long corridor to the 12-story silo where the missile still resided, sans nuclear warhead.

She had difficulty climbing the short six-step ladder up the wall adjacent to the pedestal supporting the old inertial measurement unit, the collimator in tech speak. The ladder was tucked away behind the pedestal. It led to a storage cubby hole, a platform large enough to serve as a bunk bed. Nobody remembered why this cubby hole was included in the design of the facility. Gail suspected it was to keep a spare collimator. They were large devices used to provide the missile's guidance system a true-north reference point. If the primary one malfunctioned, it had to be replaced quickly. Before Gail's tenure at the complex, it had been replaced with more sophisticated technology, leaving the cubby hole empty.

When Gail was a missile combat crew commander, the cubby hole was prized as an isolated place to "chill out" or sneak in a nap. A small air conditioner, mounted on the ceiling, was needed to keep the machine cool. One wag on her staff called the cubby the Dollymater after a deflated sex doll was found back there.

She placed the thick package wrapped in brown paper and twine as far back as she could reach, then felt and counted the others. She knew every inch of this facility like the back of her hand; this cubby hole held particularly fond memories. Now, she could barely fit back there, much less with another person. She gave the packages one final look. She had no idea what the contents were worth. She performed her tasks and took her cut, then deposited that into a savings account at the credit union.

She went back to the car and climbed, with difficulty, into refrigerated paradise. She could no longer spend more than a few minutes in the heat without turning red and struggling to breathe.

On the 10-minute drive home, she stopped off at Tacho's Food Truck at the Green Valley mall, parked behind it. Tacho's partner came around from the front. She handed Gail her dinner and her cut in a bag. Gail in turn handed her the package from the Collimator cubby hole.

Gail had managed to carve out a comfortable lifestyle working at the same place she began her career, one of the eighteen nuclear warhead missile launch sites in southern

Arizona. Her site had been converted into a museum after it was decommissioned. Most of the other sites in Arizona were returned to fallow land, except for one purchased by an aging 1960s rock 'n' roller.

His platinum-attaining album, "Surf's Up, So's the Missile," contained the hit single "No More Roads to Moscow," which went national in sales, charting even in the UK back in the late 1960s. His band, Nu Clear, was considered by many in the military to be a welcome antidote to the prevailing peace, love, and protest music of the 1960s, although the band, outside of the "Moscow" hit, only enjoyed air play regionally in the Southwest.

She passed a begging family, poorly dressed, soiled, obviously Latino, sitting at a traffic light. She worried about the illegals overrunning the border, the damn tear-jerkers who insisted on providing water to the ones trying to cross the desert. It was too bad that the bill the legislature passed to make it a crime to allow illegals access to water and provisions was not signed into law by the governor. What a chickenshit he turned out to be.

She stopped at the Bolt-Mart on the corner just beyond the interstate, filled up with C12, and bought a pack of Marlboro Lights. She was supposed to have quit smoking, but that idea had gone nowhere. At least she'd switched to lights.

Bolt-Mart had initiated a novel advertising campaign a few years ago in rural areas, labeling their least efficient gasoline C12, the mid-range C6, and the most expensive, but most fuel-efficient C2. C stood for carbon.

The company had made a strategic decision to sacrifice numbers for loyalty, catering to the climate-denial segment of the customer base. Wherever you found jokes about dark Brandon on the dark web, you now found advertisements for Bolt-Mart's high-carbon fuel. It was mostly a gag, the three choices were the same as at every other fueling station, and met federal and state fuel specifications, but Gail and other like-minded customers felt like they were "owning the libs" every time they filled up.

Heading home, she turned into her neighborhood, noting the flapping flags on gleaming silver flagpoles in nearly every yard. The houses were mostly occupied by active and retired Air Force hailing from all parts of the country. Years ago, they'd successfully lobbied the developer to change the names of the streets from a Sonoran desert theme to the Cold War. La Cholla Circle became Cul de Sac de Cuba. Kingfisher Lane became Kennedy Lane. All the cactus and cutesy critter names were thrown out in favor of Castro, Khrushchev, Kremlin, Pravda, Titan, as well as ICBM, Minuteman, NASAMS, Trident, Patriot, Lee Harvey, Oswald, Ruby and others.

She pulled up to her place at the intersection of Titan and Moscow and gathered the mail from the box at the end of the driveway. After parking the car in the garage, she went inside, opened the fridge and popped a Bud Light. She wasn't supposed to drink, but at least it was a light beer. She sat on a stool at her kitchen counter, pulled the invitation from her pocket. Neo-Anthropocentric Models of Retrospective Freedoms. What the fuck did that even mean?

Suddenly it dawned on her she'd be the *former* Director of the CWMM when the conference took place. It presented an opportunity to deal with something which had been quietly nagging at her for years. She held up the bottle and watched the Bud label vibrate before her eyes. It all shook loose an adolescent memory, when she went with a classmate to a Friends Meeting House and learned that Quakers sit in silence during worship service unless they are "moved" to speak.

"You mean, there's no pastor?" Gail had asked her friend.

"No."

"There's no leader?"

"Not a formal one. We call it quaking," her friend continued, "when your body begins to shake because your soul has something to say."

With so little time left, maybe her soul finally had something to say.

Several books were published on the missile site's technical and engineering features, and even an expose of the catastrophic mishaps which occurred at several of the sites. They couldn't cover those up completely. Nothing on the human beings assigned to turn the keys and honor the orders from strategic command. Little on the ailments and health effects of living and breathing in a confined area containing some of the most dangerous materials known to man. Nothing on the psychological impairment from the thought of having to hold a pistol to a squad member's head if he or she was reluctant to obey the orders. Nothing on carrying out the orders to annihilate an entire city of millions.

She gulped the last of her beer. What did a bunch of academic eggheads know about freedom anyway? She looked at the paper. Who even came up with subjects like "Neo-Anthropocentric Models of Retrospective Freedoms"? The invitation made it sound like Sedona, "with its seven energy vortexes," was the spiritual capital of the planet. They want to talk about underground energy? They'd have to travel to a death star to find more underground energy than she was responsible for all those years.

She often just wondered how far from the end she really was. She could no longer deal with the paperwork and haggling with the Air Force, insurance companies, care providers, pharmacies, all made more difficult by the Pentagon's need to cover it all up. She was a poor advocate for her own situation, but she could at least make sure her compatriots had some resources to fight back with after she was gone. Her body quaked in anticipation.

CHAPTER 6

BRADLEY GETS THE GIG

D r. Kerry Washington was especially impressed, after the interview, with Maniopolos' fifteen minutes of fame elevating the electricity industry to national prominence at a time when the industry was imploding from its own greed and avarice.

A Wall Street analyst had exposed the tip of the Enron iceberg in May 2001. Around the same time, Maniopolos revealed, in a book he'd written as an independent consultant (to much acclaim in the business and popular press) that the failed energy company's business model was being pushed by Wall Street onto its competitors. If regulators didn't rein in the industry, Maniopolos asserted, the entire country—and not just California—would soon be suffering from severe blackouts.

Despite the glowing book reviews in outlets like *The Wall Street Journal* and speaking gigs from Harvard to UCLA, his celebrity for exposing Enron soon receded. Then he found some acclaim elevating public awareness of an industry which preferred to work in the shadows delivering a product—electricity—which everyone took for granted, critically depended on, yet complained incessantly about due to pollution, carbon, ash landfills, rising prices, etc. Kerry had memorized a quote from one of Maniopolos' numerous articles and speeches, repeated in *The Wall Street Journal*, "Public perception of our industry is solely based on our byproducts, not our product."

He may have lacked a PhD, but had gone back to school in his 50s, earning a master's in Sociology. He had better publication credits than most of the PhDs he knew. He had no connection to any universities or colleges, didn't seem to have any axes to grind against the institutions involved in the colloquium or the Freedom Center. His resume was studded with conference facilitating appointments, even if they were mostly in the areas of technology, venture capital, and energy. The sociology professor he studied under back in the Midwest, and listed as a reference, spoke highly of him.

Mr. Maniopolos was an "old white guy," but Kerry wasn't going to hold that against him. The Freedom Center was a firm believer in the meritocracy, even if they had to pay lip service to passing cultural fads.

Best of all, Maniopolos appeared to be politically and culturally agnostic, at least based on the forensics of his public record, no evidence of support for either political party, or work for partisan institutions. Social media activity was zilch. He had a stellar professional record but was not a public figure with the ego that usually goes with it.

Washington convinced Magellan that Maniopolos was their guy. Magellan did his own due diligence and concurred. In Magellan's words, he was the kind of guy who could be a catalyst for discussions, without becoming the object of them. In the same call, he mumbled something about Maniopolos' unpublished work, still available on the web, which indicated his alignment with the Freedom Center's mission.

But Magellan's due diligence went deeper. In a bit of serendipity, he had discovered a photo of Maniopolos with his arm around Dr. Victor Haviland and a few other classmates from their 25th college reunion, then dug deeper using his contacts in cyber-forensics and learned they were still close friends. Magellan had identified Haviland as someone who could create the complex probabilistic models around freedom concepts using advanced associational statistics. He'd already hand-picked his expert with deterministic models, Dr. Fredricka Wertmuller, who, together with her father, had been applying such models to the concept of freedom for decades. The Holy Grail would be when the results of these two models converged.

If all went well, Maniopolos would serve as an intermediary between Magellan and Haviland. He'd get them both to a Primates Festival and make certain it happens.

When the director mentioned to Bradley the title of the colloquium, Neo-Anthropocentric Models of Retrospective Freedoms, Bradley recalled reading something about a group with freedom in its name being a front for white nationalists. The main donor backing the group, Roger Magellan, was the same uber-wealthy founder of the Primates Festival, which began as a modest, ultra-secret gathering of men held in a remote location on private land, cultivating all the traditional male traits that modern society, in their view, was attempting to squelch. The festival had ballooned into an extravaganza celebrating and embracing these traits in a way that an over-achieving journalist doing the expose captured in a meme entitled "Tuff Mudders Meet Tech Bros." Another news piece put it differently: "Insufferable Incels Root for their Roots."

The only rules, according to the AI summary from Bradley's Google search, are "What happens in Primates Festival stays in Primates Festival" and "No one leaves dead." The summary explained that men could be men at the festival—fight, wrestle, play rough sports—but you couldn't kill anyone. That they had to call out no killing as a rule seemed over the top, but Bradley assumed it was all part of the machismo branding.

Two of the traits especially prized by the group, accounts noted, were initiative and perseverance. Men who were able to figure out how to pierce the secrecy of event logistics and membership and get themselves into the festival were not turned away as interlopers, but welcomed as ranking members and given a club hand-carved from a tree branch and a blow-up doll to drag around by the hair.

This was not the case for two women who once managed to penetrate the grounds. They were summarily shown the exits, but not before a small subset of members demanded to vote on allowing an exception to the "no one leaves dead" rule.

When Bradley was asked in the interview how he would define freedom, he had said, "It is something undervalued by those who have it, overrated by those who don't, and wielded as an implement of hypocrisy by those who claim to represent those who want it." He remembered how Washington smiled as he munched through his bagel.

"So, are you implying that freedom isn't nearly as vital as we make it out to be?" One woman board member had asked.

"Freedom doesn't appear on Maslow's hierarchy of needs, does it?" Jesus, where had Bradley pulled that one from?

The woman responded. "Couldn't you argue that freedom, manifested as free will, is part of the critical support structure for self-actualization?"

Dr. Washington interjected. "I'm so glad you brought free will into the discussion. We haven't set much of the agenda yet, but we are planning a session on that topic, freedom and free will."

Washington had asked if any of the board members had any questions for Bradley.

"I do have one," chirped a Board member, "I note that your conference experience is all in the *commercial* sector, not in academia. Are you as comfortable with inductive arguments as you may likely be with deductive ones?"

Bradley retorted, "I have facilitated workshops and symposia at Harvard, MIT, Carnegie-Mellon, Vanderbilt, Washington University in St. Louis, the University of Michigan—"

"But the topics were of a business and technological nature, rather than cultural, or, uh, philosophical."

"True, but even discussions of the evolution and implementation of technology can devolve into questions of best practices vis a vis users and communities, environmental impacts, and corporate responsibility, among other topics that relate to the question of freedom. And I've studied extensively about freedom in the context of economic and political systems as part of my graduate work in sociology—"

"Yes, but the concepts presented at this colloquium may be deeper and more complex than what a masters' recipient may be exposed to."

God, Bradley thought, these people and their goddamn PhDs. He wanted to choke the bitch down.

"If I may," Bradley asserted, "even inductive arguments rely on distinctions that tend to narrow down broad assertions in order to ensure rational integrity."

Kerry had looked up from his dwindling plate of food and beamed.

Bradley continued. "I believe that's taken directly from 'The Philosophy of Freedom and the History of Ethics,' published in *Philosophies* in 2020?"

He could not believe the lady board member did not know he was referencing Dr. Washington's own research.

Kerry broke in, still beaming. "One of Mr. Maniopolos' strengths is an ability to apply his analytical capabilities in real time to facilitate discussions without, you know, putting his thumb on the scale."

"You can't see that I'm blushing, Mediterranean skin and all."

"No blushing required." Washington said on a laugh. "So, do you have any questions for us?"

Bradley asked what was the dust-up in the media about the Center being a front for white nationalism. Washington replied that an overzealous reporter was conflating Magellan's support of the Freedom Center with his Primates Festival.

"If the community college thought for a cold minute that we were in any fashion promoting white nationalism, we'd be thrown off campus," one board member added.

Bradley told the group he found the whole thing ironic.

"The fact that the Primates Festival celebrates self-reliance and resourcefulness from those who manage to burrow their way in, I mean, doesn't that represent what this country has always been about? The rugged individual challenging the system, carving off his or her piece of the pie? Breaking a few rules and norms, if necessary?"

No one challenged his assertion.

Before the interview, Bradley looked up the definition of Neo-Anthropocentric, knew that neo means new, that anthropocentric means the current era in the earth's history when human domination was irreversibly changing the conditions of the planet for all other living things. He knew what models were, generically, but in this context? Retrospective freedoms? What were those? He asked for clarification from the room.

One board member offered, "Think of it as a reaction to 'post-humanism,' that humans must remain at the center of moral and ethical discussions, because, well, for no other reason than humans are having the discussions."

Right, Bradley thought. How circular is that? Which must mean that Freedom Center types were fearful that humans would *not* remain at the center of a moral discussion?

Other snippets of the conversation rattled around in his head.

"We're exploring whether nonhuman life forms have rights, implying that they have the 'freedom' to demand those rights. Even if *they* cannot articulate them, are we obligated to articulate them on their behalf?"

"Not to be provocative, but isn't that the pro-life argument with fetuses?" Bradley had said, cautiously, wanting to show his chops.

"Which also could be construed as applying to animals and plants," a board member added.

Boy, does that open a can of worms, Bradley thought. And if worms have rights, surely they—or their advocates—would be opposed to being treated as bait.

"Retrospective Freedom also offers a roadmap for previously prevalent human groups, such as native peoples, to position and reclaim their rights to land, artifacts, customs, and rituals," another board member added.

That'll be the day, Bradley thought.

A board member with a doctorate in computer science and artificial intelligence had spoken up, in a voice reminiscent of Carl Sagan:

"When we gaze into the future, when robots are fully functional and integrated into human society, we must begin now to understand how to ascribe to them the same derivatives of freedom and liberty as we might ascribe to nonhuman living things."

But are robots going to be *alive*? Bradley had wanted to ask. And then he wanted to ask himself why on earth he'd majored in engineering when he could've studied a discipline in which right answers didn't need to be actually correct, only clever.

Much as all of this made Bradley's head hurt, he was going to happily accept the gig if offered—a little out of his comfort zone, but he could gloat about this one to Valerie till the cows roamed off the campus commons. She was the one with the double major in political science and philosophy, master's in education, and doctorate in international relations, and would happily argue between morning coffee and evening cocktail hour whether AI robots would ever truly be intelligent or not.

He could stick it to Victor, too. Best friend or not, he had the same affliction as all these other academics, tossing around phrases like *primary sources*, implying that in Bradley's work, he relied on less rigorous *secondary* sources. Or making distinctions between pure science, applied science, and, God forbid, practical engineering. Hell, it was applied science and engineering that paid the freight for people like Victor to sit around poking their theories into their navels, seeing if they'd come out their assholes, and to get validated when they regurgitated them to their peers.

What disturbed Bradley more than anything else from the interview was the mental image of Dr. Washington on his knees giving him a blowjob, an image which had appeared like those triangular tiles with pearls of wisdom in the Magic 8 Ball toy he remembered from childhood. Why was a homo-Afro-erotic fantasy just now deciding to make itself known? He'd had brief glimmers of homosexual thoughts in the past—he presumed everyone did—but usually with white men who had power over him.

Maybe it was the cream cheese smeared across his full lips.

After the interview, Dr. Washington lingered over a third bagel. A voice mail had come in, from a colleague at a former institution. The colleague sounded distressed—but also, ominously, seemed to be choking back a laugh. He hit the call back button. His friend answered immediately. Anyone who had still been in the room with Kerry would have seen the color drain from his face, if he wasn't black as the night sky with no celestial light.

"Oh shit." Then his screen lit up with an incoming call from Raj Magellan. The windowless conference room suddenly felt like a prison cell and the warden was coming to call.

CHAPTER 7

RAJ MAGELLAN

Rajamahedron Majundar (a.k.a. Roger "Raj" Magellan) paced around the expansive glass-walled Florida room he used as an office. The enclosed porch alone had more square footage than the average American home. If he opened the door to the back side of the property, located outside of Indianapolis, he could hear the burbling of the White River flow down the sloping manicured yard beyond the adjacent woods and the paved multi-use nature trail. He liked nothing better than watching from afar as users of the trail paused to gawk at his estate.

While he contemplated what to do about Kerry Washington, he straightened the framed undergraduate diploma hanging on his Zoom wall. Electrical engineering from The Ross-Holliman Institute of Technology, Next to that was the diploma for his MBA from Notre Dame. And he'd also framed his first patent, for a medical device implant to cure sleep apnea. The technology never worked as intended, but he'd made his first $50 million before all the lawsuits against Med-Technobie1, the company he'd sold the license to, were filed.

There was also a framed copy of that company's original business filing with the state of Indiana. That company was how he'd gotten his start despite his engineering degree being from a "substandard" school, as his investment consultant from San Jose had told him in no uncertain terms. The conversation had stuck with him like the earworm of a song you can't stand.

"Look, I can't sell an investment principal someone with a degree from Rose Hummus," the man had said in thick Brooklynese, "you're competing with the Ivies, Cal Tech, Stanford, MIT ..."

Magellan had scoffed. "You're selling a company and a technology, not a—"

"No! How many times do I gotta repeat this? I sell people. Money invests in people, not inanimate devices or ideas. It buys credentials, status, the trend. Just like stocks. Investors don't understand what the technology is. Or care. They invest based on the one in ten rule."

The rule was then impatiently explained to him as if he was an idiot. One out of ten of the venture investments returns big enough to cover the losses of the other nine.

"It's like gambling, just more zeros after the digits of the dollar amounts being risked. And the zeros are attached to other people's dollars."

The other rule: "You buy the team that's already done it."

Raj had retorted. "So, find me a partner with a degree from a university who's already 'done' it."

The consultant did just that, after demanding a higher percentage than standard of the money he raised, and Raj was off to the races. By the end of the first decade of the new millennium, he was a billionaire with a Brahmin ancestry and a chip on his shoulder about the circles of elite power he had to circumvent to be successful. Why should he have ever needed to partner with a Jew and a German to get what he deserved on his own merits?

Still, he'd used them like they'd used him. And after Raj won the grudge match lawsuit over who really owned the IP for a social media company they'd founded together, they'd parted ways as bitter enemies. Raj didn't care. He no longer needed them. He found the other key to success. Remain in the background. Let the white guys do the face work.

After seeing too many 30 under 30 and 40 under 40 listings of rising stars in urban and regional business magazines, Raj, with the help of his well-heeled partners, convinced the national entrepreneur's bible, NorthStar Weekly, to start one called the Under Over ranking - Under Forty, Over a Billion. He made that list at age 38.

His current crisis, though, wasn't about money or ownership or IP or even white guys. He wasn't about to let a personal market choice Dr. Washington had made years ago at one of Raj's Primates Festivals derail his first freedom conference in Sedona. This colloquium, which he envisioned as the annual equivalent of Davos or Aspen, would be the linchpin in his grand strategy to elevate the field of Freedom Studies the same way economics had spawned the much loftier and far more profitable field of financial engineering.

He opened the porch door. The wind rustling through the branches and leaves and the faint burbling of the river calmed him. He often called upon the ambient sounds of nature to help make a big decision. Evidence of private insolent and scurrilous behavior at his festival helped him achieve his business objectives. A public scandal was an affront to his Brahmin ideals. He could fire Washington. And maybe he should. But firing a Black professional wasn't a good look these days.

What would Musk or Bezos do? Ah, he couldn't use either of them as a mental model. They had multibillion-dollar companies to run. When reacting to public crises, they had to be conscious of equity and debt holders, customers, regulators, and government officials, despite whatever tough talk came out of their mouths and X accounts. Still, unlike other billionaires, Raj didn't have shareholders to answer to. He was beholden to no one. He had a net worth of $1.8 billion, validated by Forbes, and was not even technically middle-aged. He could ditch Kerry Washington and no one would blame him.

Building his center and turning freedom studies into the most coveted field in academics was a quintessential American aspiration. It was *forward-looking*. His way of giving back. Liberty was the backbone of America. He was proof-positive. Elevating such an intellectual endeavor would be a testament to his Brahmin ancestry. They were the masters of all knowledge worth knowing and interpreted it for the lesser among them. In earlier epochs, they encoded creation myths and sacred texts. He'd do the same for the study of freedom in this era!

As he had learned between the lines of his MBA program, those European Jews at the University of Chicago, devotees to the Austrian school of economic thinking, created valuation models for options, futures, and derivatives, and elevated finance from the simple arithmetic of accounting to the complex calculus and differential equations used in modern financial engineering. The rise of financial engineering, in fact, reversed the socialist path the country was on post-World War II, and ensured that American Jews would take over from their German brethren and remain in charge of money. Everyone at his business school knew this and praised them privately, even if the feat was never acknowledged publicly. In the 1990s, the entire global economy was hitched to this engine of specialized, quant-intensive knowledge.

Raj's ambition was to mimic the Chicago School's success for his fellow Brahmins. It would involve more than just making freedom studies as valuable as a STEM field, but that was central to the cause.

Magellan suddenly had a thought. Could Maniopolos replace Washington? His public credentials were more than sufficient. He was the first to expose, beyond Wall Street specialists, the mark-to-market valuation models energy companies like Enron were abusing to inflate their profits. Which meant he understood financial engineering. His master's research focused on how the use of ever more complex, opaque, and proprietary models had progressively, since the 1970s, collapsed the U.S. and global economies several times, though not fatally, culminating in the 2007-2008 global economic crisis, which was close to fatal. What was a math model, Maniopolos had concluded, but information used by financial elites to control transactions? Models aren't used to represent the markets, as most people assume. Models are the engines which drive markets, Maniopolos said. And he was right.

Hell, if Maniopolos had a PhD, he'd hire him. When he discovered his friendship with Dr. Haviland, his mind was made up.

This would be his gift to the America that had given him so much. Afterwards, he could charge into the public eye and run for president, though the last election cycle showed that America wasn't quite ready for a President who only looked like 2 percent of the American population. It wasn't even ready for one who looked like 50.5 percent of the population. Presidents were going to be white men for a while longer, Obama notwithstanding. He had plenty of time, and plenty of money.

First, he had to take care of this minor bump in the road with Washington's penis.

CHAPTER 8

ASHERA PRESENTS

The morning of her panel and presentation at the colloquium, Ashera woke early, boiled water in the small electric pot she traveled with (to avoid the taint of coffee from an in-room device) and prepared a cup of mint watermelon black tea. She left herself enough time for a full Yoga workout led by one of her favorite YouTube instructors, followed by 20 minutes of meditation, burning her travel-sized three-wick candle.

She attended to her breathing, remembering her therapist's guidance to focus on the friendly faces in the audience. She'd only made a few public presentations, in small, intimate venues where family or close friends could send positive vibes a short distance.

Afterward, she munched from a bag of mixed dried fruit while watching calming, happy YouTube videos of people with their non-traditional pets—pigs, goats, tortoises, and even mountain lions—and checked in on Gordon. Then she went directly to the colloquium meeting room for the opening session, her confidence burnished because the facilitator had noticed her in the elevator.

Mr. Maniopolos introduced her then chuckled over a short anecdote about walking Tomahawk Hill. It wasn't funny.

"Can you hear me okay?" Ashera asked, when she got to the podium and tapped the mic nervously. The audience nodded politely.

"First and foremost, Tomahawk Hill. I am mortified the name has not been changed to something less offensive, let me put that out there—Tomahawk Hill is a space protected originally by an antiquities permit granted by the state of Arizona, later by designation as a National Historic Landmark, and finally placed on the National Register of Historic Places. In the 1970s, the desert laboratory was elevated by the Department of the Interior to a National Environmental Study Area. However, most people in our area know 'The Hill' as a very steep and challenging hike, four miles round trip."

She clicked through a few photos of hikers struggling to get up the steepest incline of the path, some walking backwards very slowly. She breathed deeply, and exhaled, taking comfort by placing her hand in a pocket and gently clutching the foam gecko she kept in her pocket for good luck.

"At the academic level, the Hill acts as a research preserve for wildlife in the area, including coyotes, lizards, Gila monsters, javelinas, and the plant life and flora, notably our irreplaceable saguaros. Deeper still, archeologists are scraping through the rocks and dirt to uncover one of the earliest communities to live in southern Arizona. I'll refrain from the jargon that may not be familiar, like 'extensive complex of stone trincheras features that reflect a pre-ceramic village'...."

She paused, smiling.

"... and just say that evidence suggests a pre-Hohokam peoples' village. The Hohokam are a general designation for Native Americans from which I am proud to say includes part of my ancestry, the Tohono O'odom nation." She advanced the slides.

"Other than humans, here is the greatest threat to the Hill, and most of the Sonoran Desert, for that matter. Bufflegrass, an invasive species spreading like the kudzu vine did in the southeast United States.

An audience member raised his hand and asked, "How long does a species have to be in a location before its designation is changed from invasive to indigenous?"

She took a short breath through her nose, with a long exhale from the mouth. "That's a difficult answer, which maybe we could save for the discussion?"

Another audience member jumped in, "Just like people. White Europeans are an invasive species in North America."

Another audience member spoke stridently: "Humans are an invasive species, period! The climate is paying the price!"

"How did we get from crab grass to climate change?" Bradley asked into his mic.

Audience member: "Speaking of invasive species, Zionists are an invasive species in Palestine."

Audience member: "Palestine is the home of the indigenous Jews from the Bible. Therefore, they can't be invasive."

Audience member: Bangladesh and Pakistan used to be India. That wasn't even a hundred years ago!"

A different audience member: "Arizona used to be part of Mexico!"

What all this had to do with anything, Bradley couldn't tell. "Let's stay on topic, please?" he pleaded.

Ashera continued. "In the context of the question posed by the Freedom Center, one way we might think of the Hill is, who has rights to this area and why? Rights are intimately intertwined with freedom."

Gail leaned in towards the microphone: "Those who conquer it."

Ashera ignored her. "Legally, the University does, especially with its full takeover of the Preservation Society, which you may have read about in the news. Do the Tohono O'odhom have rights to this land? Could it be proven that the early peoples from this community were in fact related? That would pose a situation similar to the Jews and Palestine, historic ties dating to antiquity. Do the students who walk the hill, and frankly, abuse it by sneaking in at night, partying, leaving their trash, have rights to use the land in this way?"

Gail grabbed the mic closest to her. "Like the illegals in my neck of the woods!"

Ashera turned to look directly at Gail. "Certain acts may be illegal, but *people* are not." Then she glared harder, her legs shaking. "You want to see who has no excuse for disrespecting the land?" Her next slide showed a photo of a pile of beer cans and fast-food wrappers a few hundred feet off the trail with a group of college age kids hiding their faces behind their caps and giving thumbs up."

She went on. "This doesn't happen every week but it happens often enough. University students who think it's funny to trespass on protected space. We've photographed poachers seeking relics and ancient artifacts, although legally I am bound not to reveal those people. No amount of 'off limits,' or 'please remain on trail,' 'no trespassing,' or signs warning of poisonous snakes deter them. And these people are most definitely not refugees.

"The hill is a protected space," Ashera continued, making air quotes around 'protected,' "yet we lack any enforcement authority."

"That's why someone has to be in charge," Gail said. "Conquerors make the rules."

Dr. Plemmons raised her hand but spoke before Ashera or Bradley was able to call on her. "So, freedom for one group requires policing to enforce the limitations of that freedom against those for whom that freedom is prohibited?"

Ashera considered the question carefully.

"Having jurisdiction without the means to enforce it implies no guarantee of the rights of those within that jurisdiction, yes."

She cleared her throat and gulped from her water bottle, letting the fluid relax her throat.

"Then there's the wildlife," she continued. "What rights might they have in a protected land surrounded by a metropolitan area of one million residents? While we say Tomahawk Hill Preservation Society 'speaks for the Hill', legal protections can be removed with a few strokes of the pen in Washington, Phoenix, or at the University. How do we protect the Hill acknowledging that, in the context of economic growth in the region, it is a hugely valuable piece of real estate? Developers salivate over the potential for multi-million-dollar homes with spectacular city views."

Gail interrupted again from the table: "The tribal folks help the illegals smuggle marijuana, cocaine, and fentanyl over the border. They could use some legitimate means of making money."

Ashera responded, "In fact, representatives of the O'odom have broached that very subject. But do you really think the tribe would be granted development rights if houses were to be built on such a prime piece of real estate?"

An audience member said loudly, "They'd just build another casino."

Ashera gritted her teeth and clicked to her next slide, a photo of the Geico insurance company gecko, then followed it with a short video animation of a real gecko darting across the walkway. She felt in her pocket for her portable "Gordon" and gave him a squeeze.

"My own research, preliminary, suggests that this gecko has to move at twice its normal speed when it crosses the walking trail pavement in the heat of the afternoons, which can be up to 150% hotter than the dirt around it. Moving faster takes more energy, upsetting the lizard's physiological balance. In southern Arizona, pet owners often put protective mitts on their dogs' paws when they walk them."

Here, she inserted a pause of gravitas to underscore her point. "I invite you to contemplate the plight of the gecko navigating this multi-use, protected space, paved just to suit human recreational needs with little thought to how that pavement affects wildlife. Remember, to those more powerful than us, we are all geckos."

Ashera returned to her seat.

Bradley thought of how at the beginning of his career four decades ago, the lowly snail darter, in effect a minnow, had held up the construction of nuclear power plants. Geckos and snail darters and poor humans, all at the mercy of those at the top of the economic food chain.

"Okay!" Bradley proclaimed, faux brightly, "that was illuminating, I, for one, hadn't thought of the hill in that way. We have a few minutes. Questions?"

An older man seated at the back of the room, one of the three armed attendees, spoke up.

"Help me out here. I'm trying to draw a through-line from the experience of a missileer sacrificing her health holed up in a bomb silo in defense of this country for fifteen years to the rights of a gecko to run freely with no obstructions or dangers imposed by humans? Does our system of jurisprudence accommodate such an expansive definition of rights and freedoms?"

Dr. Plemmons rose and turned toward the man in back. "We can't even pass a constitutional amendment that legally guarantees equal rights for all *people*. Can you believe it? In the first half of the 21st century, the group who makes up 50.5% of the population, a majority for those not familiar with percentages ..."

Boy, that was snarky, Bradley thought.

"... is not guaranteed equal rights under the law! Are geckos more important than women?" Plemmons turned back to the front and sat down as if she'd settled the matter.

"Does the Freedom Center support passage of the Equal Rights Amendment?" Another asked.

Gail pulled a mic toward her. "The Missileer community has been trying to get reparations from the Air Force for our health impacts for two decades now. If veterans or women can't get our rights recognized, it'd say it'll be hard for geckos."

Jesus, everybody wants reparations, Bradly thought.

A dreadlocked young Black man raised his hand. "I don't think that is the correct use of the word, reparations."

Gail frowned. "It most certainly is. Look it up."

The young man retorted, "Well, there is the strict definition of the word, and then the generally accepted connotations."

Gail shook her head. "Blacks don't get exclusive use of a word."

The man pursed his lips. "I don't know, Jews pretty much have exclusive use of the word Holocaust. With a capital H. Why can't Black Americans have Reparations? With a capital R?"

Bradley suspected Gail used the word to be deliberately provocative, just like she'd walked in with a gun on her hip. It never ended well when 'Jews' was uttered cavalierly in a public forum. Sure enough, next thing he knew, the guy who accused Zionists of being invasive rushed to the floor mic.

"Because there are more Jewish civil rights groups than there are Jews—B'nai Brith, the Anti-Defamation League, American Israeli Public Affairs Committee, the Jewish Congress, the National Council of Jewish Women, Emeritus Jews of the Heritage Foundation, Israeli American Civic Action, Rural Jewish Council, the Ashkenazi Jewish Foundation, the Sephardic Jewish Association, the Anasazi-Ashkenazi Israeli Trilateral Council—"

Yeah, Bradley thought, and all of them will be up my ass and the Freedom Center's if they catch wind of what this guy just said. Under the table, Bradley quickly looked up Ashkenazi in his dictionary app. Funny, but he'd never noticed before that the word included "Nazi." The next entry listed in his search said something about Nazis being associated with *Northern* Germans. Man, everyone splits hairs.

"Let Ashera respond to the original question," Bradley said, looking up from his phone.

"The rights of geckos, or animals in general, don't have to be mutually exclusive to the liberties of Americans, or humans in general. Yet we should always have the same amount of respect for the weakest among us."

That prompted a belly laugh from Gail. "Okay, that's never going to fly. That's against the natural order of things."

"Respect for the weakest was a central tenet of Jesus and his disciples, Gail," Ashera responded, "not that I'm a Christian, or even religious."

Bradley sighed, turning to gaze at the cliffs through the tall windows. They had transitioned from rust red when he woke up to a fiery orange now that it was mid-afternoon, glowing in fact, like the briquettes in his Weber. Could he sense the energy vortex from the golf course? He shifted in his seat. He was feeling an energy vortex in his crotch. Both were better than the tremors emanating from this room. Time for a break.

As he stood up, he noticed Ashera check a text on her phone, then utter audibly, "Oh, for God's sakes," in a tone of abject disgust, as he passed her to the podium. He wanted to pause and look over her shoulder, but it would be too obvious. Still, he couldn't help but be curious.

CHAPTER 9

ASHERA GETS AN INVITE

It was when she leaned over to grab her backpack that Ashera Winters noticed the envelope wedged between the seat and the floor. The return address read Center for the Study of the Philosophy of Freedom, Sonoran Community College, Tucson, Arizona. She clutched her purse, and shoved the envelope into it, half sticking out of the top, as she entered the building, late for her somatic therapy appointment. She'd pay for the lost minutes anyway. Thankfully, the pain from the $700 tattoo she got three weeks ago had finally subsided.

She pulled her brand-new hybrid SUV into a space labeled "clients," unplugged from her dashboard screen, cutting off the Afro-diaspora band she was listening to and the mapping app she depended on.

The Honda CRV replaced the 2004 van, a gift from her grandmother, at 260,000 miles on the odometer. School loan payments were going to start up again, now that the federal pandemic emergency relief programs were ending. Clearly, after ten years in the real world, her degree in Intersectionality Studies from Mount St. Helens College was going to keep her in debt until retirement.

Friends warned that turning thirty does something to the way you think about your place in the American economic system. She'd resisted for as long as she could. She rationalized away the impact of the CRV on her carbon footprint—it was a hybrid, after all. While she had enjoyed riding her bike to and from Tomahawk Hill, her new boss at the university suggested that a director-level employee not arrive to work like she came straight from hot yoga. She supposed it was also time to trade in her pink backpack with fluorescent green trim for a proper work satchel.

As a kid, she often had nightmares about climate change. She channeled that fear into activism during and after college. In time, she recognized that one person collecting recyclables, which may or may not actually be recycled, or even a billion people doing the same, wasn't going to stem the relentless quest for global economic prosperity based on over-consumption. Two and a half billion people on this planet wanted the same lifestyle Ashera enjoyed. Who was she to deny that? Who was anyone to deny that? Those who had everything wanted more. Those who had nothing wanted something. She just wanted to make a positive difference. A higher salary would be nice, too.

Maybe the moment she consciously realized diligently washing her recyclables and foregoing plastic straws was little more than an exercise in futility was when she saw an Instagram ad for a new company that would deliver gourmet pretzels anywhere in the country. Pretzels? How much carbon would be associated with each delivered pretzel? Carbon from one pretzel delivery could liquidate five years of one person biking to work.

She yanked at the phone cord still plugged into the dashboard port, put on her yellow-orange sun hat, slung her backpack (saguaro-green with strawberry red trim) over her shoulder, picked up her health insurance card (which she thought was lost, but later discovered on the passenger seat underneath some clothes she needed to launder at her parents' house), grabbed her notebook and favorite pen, and her water bottle plastered with decals: Smash the Patriarchy, Trees Are Life, A Carbon Coin for Your Thoughts?, and Sufficiency NOT Efficiency!

Well, she still believed in sufficiency, even if she was giving up on sacrifice in a world of excess.

The new car and the therapist visits were courtesy of serendipity and COVID-era unintended consequences. The modest nonprofit she worked for, the Tomahawk Hill Preservation Society (THPS), loosely affiliated with the University through the archeology department, had lost some big donors during the pandemic. At the same time, the department was shrinking, not faring well against its competitor departments at peer universities. To keep the Hill solvent, the U agreed to take it fully under its wing, a move that the U intended, so it claimed in the press release, to help them compete with Arizona's other big universities for Native American students. Taking custody of the protection of sacred land would be a meaningful gesture to the local indigenous population. It also meant a surge in pay and benefits for THPS employees, as, by law, pay and benefits had to be brought up to par with all others employed at the U in comparable positions.

It also meant that the Hill was now owned by an institution answering to the Board of Regents in Phoenix, all political appointees. Whether there would continue to be an "arm's-length" relationship between the U and THPS was a question Ashera and her colleagues debated incessantly in their Slack channel. The most recent revelation that the U's CFO had made a $350 million error in the institution's financial statement made the future of the Hill that much more uncertain. It worried her. Like everything else in the world worried her.

But in the meantime, she could benefit from the better benefits package she had, thanks to the U. As she took a seat in the waiting room, she surveyed the bookshelves and knew she was going to like this therapist when she saw that two of the books on her shelves were ones that Ashera lived by: *How to Relax* by Thich Nhat Hanh and *The Body Knows What the Mind Doesn't* by one of her favorite professors at Mount St. Helen's.

The titles that really blew Ashera away were the fiction and nonfiction of Naomi Wasila (aka Rachel Schiff). *Dismantling the New Patriarchy: Penis by Penis*, was a richly illustrated memoir, presaging the graphic novel genre, recounting the author's experiences with men at college. Considered far ahead of its time, it was a cult classic around the dorms at Mount St. Helen's, what her father called one of the anarchist schools. The trilogy set the stage for the classic *Vanquishing the Penis: A Battle Plan*, under the Wasila name. It had been published in 1991, the year Ashera was born.

Vanquishing the Penis was considered a work of academic rigor for many years, until a small group of counter-academic women, primarily at southern and Christian universities, began to pick it apart. When a band of conservative moms from Florida took offense at the volume residing on the shelf of a media talking head's Zoom background, they launched a national movement against the book, getting it banned from many libraries and college programs. Then the #MyVagina-Too movement (later shortened to #VeeToo to cut back on the knee-jerk provocation) took up the cause, hired the best progressive lawyers, and fought back.

The amount of feminist-oriented research and analysis reputed to be "defective, spurious, unsubstantiated, juvenile, and irreproducible" just kept growing, with whole programs losing funding. Then the research quality arguments got lost in ugly, pitched accusations of antisemitism and anti-Christian sentiments. That many academics abandoned Wasila, labeling her a pseudoscientist, only made admirers like Ashera stick with her more fervently. She was #VeeToo all the way.

The therapist opened the door to her office and offered Ashera a welcoming smile. "I love the gecko!" Ashera held out her arm to show off her latest tattoo. "Thank you. It's my own design."

"You hardly have room for any more, at least on your arms."

"Right?!"

"How's Gordon?"

She patted a pocket on her backpack where she stashed her comfort squeeze toy. "He's always great."

They spent most of the session talking about the car, turning 30, and the new management at her job. The therapist encouraged her to think about her feet, hands, and buttocks, the body's touch points with the automobile, and to reflect on any trauma Ashera may have experienced. She was the one who'd convinced Ashera to acquire a synthetic, portable gecko she could rely on as a touch point, when live Gordon wasn't available.

The doctor excused herself to visit the restroom. Ashera took the time to open the envelope from the community college.

"Oh wow, this is weird," she said, as the therapist returned, "I've been invited to make a presentation at a colloquium on freedom." She grabbed at the back of her neck, pulled at her hair, with one hand. Then she fingered the edges of the paper, furrowed her eyebrows then raised them, and then pulled at it like she was enlarging the invitation.

She read further. "It's in Sedona."

"Ah, I hold semi-annual healing workshops there. Gorgeous area."

"I've heard."

"Are you feeling any specific sensations in your body about this opportunity?"

"Mostly butterflies in my stomach, weakness in my knees, lightness in my head."

"The classic presentiments of someone not necessarily comfortable speaking in public?"

Imposter syndrome, too, Ashera thought. She bit her lip. Sipped from her water bottle.

Suddenly, her attitude did an about face. "To be honest, though, maybe this signifies an arrival of sorts. Bought a new car, paid $700 to a tattoo artist, and now got my first invitation to a peer-level conference. And yeah, it's been a banner year, and its only May!" She chuckled. "I mean, I'm only out of college eight years. Haha."

She took a cleansing breath and pushed away the purple and pink woven strands that made a kaleidoscope of her hair, hanging like wrapping paper ribbons around her face.

"Let's focus on the conference."

"Actually, I think it's going to make me cry!" She choked back tears and sniffles, as she straightened her shoulders and stiffened her back.

"That's worth dissecting. Let yourself go. How so?"

"It's a validation. Someone thinks I have something important to say about my work at the Hill."

"Where in your body are you feeling something extraordinary?"

"My esophagus. It contracted, like something coming up the GI tract didn't have enough propulsion to get out." Ashera's face went pale. The periodicity of her nervous twitch, shaking her leg, seemed to double. "It's okay, I'm fine."

"Remember to titrate through those arousal sensations."

Yes, Ashera thought, she remembered the session on titration. All the modalities seem to refer to the same actions, humming, breathing, swaying. She loved the sound of those words. Titration, pendulation, enteroception.

"Your sensations in the esophagus, it's your feeling of genuine self-worth struggling to break free. What is the title of the conference, if I may ask?"

"Uh," she peered more carefully at the invite. "Neo-Anthropocentric Models of Retrospective Freedoms?"

"Hmm," the therapist mused.

"Yeah, right?"

"Well, conference aside, it could be restorative just to immerse yourself in Sedona's energy vortexes. I hold my workshops at Cathedral Rock."

"I'll certainly keep that in mind."

"The indigenous tribe in the area, the Yavapai, recognize Cathedral Rock as one of the vortexes. They call it the birthplace of humankind."

Did she just say, *have a pie*? Ashera wondered.

If she accepted, she'd have to find someone to take care of Gordon. Or bring him with her. She could get him a little travel cage. Maybe that's just what Gordon Gecko needed. To get out in the world.

CHAPTER 10

BRADLEY TAKES A BREAK, AZUL PRESENTS

Bradley didn't stop for a refreshment or sweet during the break after Ashera's presentation. He dashed to his room, lay down on the bed, whipped out his phone, tapped Instagram, and scrolled through his "saved" InstaBabes. He warmed up with the ten-second clips of women juggling their breasts in tiny swimsuits, mooning their admirers through the narrowest strip of thong, or stretching a new bikini with their hands and their body out of the photo, then jumping into view with barely anything covering the good parts. Was there no end to the creative ways they could suck you in?

Then he picked one, switched over to Google, searched for "Breastbalcony83xtraxx porn." Dozens of images of Breastbalconyyy popped right up. He stroked, scrolled, stroked, tapped, stroked, swiped left, and stroked until he settled on an image of her on her hands and knees tonguing a massive erect penis attached to an African American body with no face, getting drilled from behind by a buff white guy. He ejaculated right when the Black guy came, then congratulated himself on achieving self-stimulatory synchronicity with the virtual world. Surely there was a vortex for that.

What else in the world gave him such pleasure 24/7 with complete control, physically and mentally, independent of anyone or anything messing it up? It supported entrepreneurial, sex-positive women and was the highest form of self-care. He was doing good in the world. Plus, there really was no better way to get a nap.

When he woke, the remorse took over, as usual. He berated himself for all the time he had wasted over the years pleasuring himself.

When his thumbs worked again, he texted Victor.

Hey, man, did you start masturbating more frequently after the T injections?

I'm not a serial masturbator, like you. Remember, I am of the repressed Anglican sect, according to, uh, you!

Don't give me that. Every guy masturbates. Does testosterone make you masturbate more, is what I'm asking?

I don't do it.

You got to be kidding.

Nope. Got caught once by my parents. Seeing my mother's face staring at my hand wrapped around my dick turned me off for life.

This is getting chronic. For me, I mean.

Wow. I remember when we shared a dorm room, you thought you were getting away with it with your bed behind the bookcase and the desk.

Arranged for that purpose.

Nice try.

I tried to be quiet.

Ha. I don't recall an "only masturbates privately" line on the forms we filled out about the qualities of our preferred roommate.

This is serious. Guess I'll have to talk to Valerie about it.

She doesn't know?

Well, she knows I whack off. She's not stupid. But this frequency. My foreskin is chafing.

TMI, TMI!!!

Bradley paused to check on the knock on the door, then told housekeeping he'd be out of the room in a few minutes.

On the other subject, what's your count?

C'mon, Vic. Gimme time.

How much time do you need??

Memory fades, you know. But I promise.

How's the colloquium?

Additional weapons introduced. No shots fired. We have our team-building exercise tomorrow. Hopefully weapons remain behind.

I contacted Rachel, BTW.

How is she?

She says hi.

Say hi back. I have to go.

He gathered up his things and rushed out. The elevator seemed to take forever. He shuffled his feet and pushed the down button a dozen times. As he was pushing his sleeves up, he noticed that the carpet had a pattern to it, just like the long hallway he walked through to the meeting room. Tips of arrowheads touching each other. Was it a sacred Native thing?

He returned to the head table in the meeting room, arranged his favorite pen, notebook, and conference program, leaned over to say a few words to Azul, then went to the podium.

"Now I have the pleasure of introducing ..."

Bradley realized he hadn't learned how to pronounce his name.

"Uh, A-zoo-boo-eeke ... well. Sorry about that."

Geez, he didn't want to be using the word zoo or boo introducing someone from Nigeria. Too late. He turned to Azul, who waved his hand like it was nothing.

Speaking through his embarrassment, Bradley said, "Welcome! I'll let you pronounce your full name, Azul. Azul represents a truly unique museum space and will share his thoughts about music and freedom in your soul."

Bradley felt his phone vibrate as he sat down and sneaked a peek under the table. "Oh shit," he uttered, when his screen lit up. He hadn't closed out of Google. He hunched his shoulders and closed in his arms. The image of Fleshbalcony rimming that dick. He panicked for a moment and forgot where the X was to delete. Then he found it.

Whew. That could have been bad. Thank God Dr. Plemmons wasn't nearby. He checked to make sure his settings were on private, no tracking, and no history.

Then he noticed the text from Victor.

Maybe you should discuss your "problem" with Rachel.

Christ, was Victor nuts? Rachel 'destroy the patriarchy' Schiff? She was too busy being a national hero to women across the country victimized by their partners' lack of attention to their vaginas, G-spots, and inner labia. Or whatever.

Don't you fucking dare mention this.

"Thank you, esteemed Mr. Maniopolos, and colleagues. As Mr. Bradley has mentioned, I am Azubuike Ebunoluwa, Azul for short. Manager for Special Programs at the History of Musical Instruments Gallery, HOMI-G for short."

Azul's voice was low and resonant, like he was singing "Amazing Grace," the way Obama sang it that one time after that school massacre.

HOMI-G! Bradley stifled a laugh. Sounds like the title of a Kendrick Lamar album.

"I can't hear! Stand closer to the mic," someone in the audience yelled, impatiently.

"If you will not mind ..." Azul took the remote mic from its holder and jog-hopped down three stairs from the dais to the floor.

"I will be more comfortable if I am able to move around." He paused to survey the audience, then looked up at the ceiling.

"Let me start by saying I come from a country that is in many ways the antithesis of freedom."

One of the shithole countries, Bradley thought.

"Now I live in a country that believes itself to be a beacon of freedom, a shining light on the hill. In fact, I can be considered one of the most free people from Nigeria, because my family is very wealthy."

Bradley nearly snorted. Money buys freedom no matter what country you live in.

"Truth," someone called from the audience.

"Amen," another said.

"And therein lies the problem," a third added.

"It is not the truth that sets us free, but freedom which makes the truth," Azul continued. "Did you know? We are sixth happiest country in Africa! One thing to know about Nigeria you may not have known before. Also, Nigeria is the Saudi Arabia of Africa. Petroleum reserves. Black gold. Texas tea."

That got a ripple of laughs.

Azul walked slowly from one end of the room to the other, looking down at the carpet, then up toward the chandelier. He stopped to consider the view of the red rocks from the windows, then pointed to them, his free arm extended, palm up. "This extraordinary landscape! Look at it. I can't imagine a more beautiful place. I praise God for this!"

Mention of God raised a few eyebrows while some in the audience nodded in agreement.

He paced to the center of the middle aisle. "How is it that a rich child from Nigeria ends up at HOMI-G? So. Music is my love. It's what makes me the happiest man from the sixth happiest country in Africa. I feel 'free' when I am immersed in music. Listening. Playing. Contemplating. Discovering."

He paused between each gerund.

He switched the mic to the other hand, and rubbed his chin. "As a young man with recently completed doctorate in music history from ASU, with a concentration in percussion, and tens of thousands of dollars in student loans, I learned of HOMI-G, which had only recently opened, and thought, "This should be the perfect place for Azul Ebunoluwa to work!"

He gazed upward again, as if seeking inspiration from a higher power.

"For many years I spent applying to HOMI-G, volunteering in their programs, suffering rejection after rejection, often with no explanation. Finally, three years ago, I was given an employment!"

He looked again at the ceiling. "God had smiled on me."

That was at the height of the Black Lives Matter movement, Bradley thought. HOMI-G had been a whiter shade of pale the one time he'd visited. They must've decided a little diversity would be a strategic move for fundraising.

"The important question I am invited to address by your Freedom Center is 'How does music set the soul free?' Perhaps nothing connects people around the world like music. But it is not the only thing which is connecting people. Global trade in petroleum connects people. The exchange of currency connects people. Communications technologies. Modes of transportation. We are connected. 'We are the World' was the chorus at Bob Geldof's Live Aid concert for Africa in 1985."

Azul pointed to his throat.

"The human voice emanates from a windpipe, and the mechanism to create this sound is similar to every wind instrument on the planet. Soon, AI will create music for you. Perhaps you are thinking that Pandora and Apple selecting playlists for you is cool. You have not seen anything yet!"

Bradley wondered if he could sync his list of Instababes with the songs on his Apple playlist. Now that would be cool.

You could hear the bustling in the adjacent hotel service area, the audience was so mesmerized.

"If music is nothing more than tones, pitches, in certain arrangements, in combinations, in certain registers, sound waves deconstructed to amplitude, frequency, and cycles, how is this freeing our souls? HOMI-G is a place to admire artifacts and relics which may soon have no place in our daily lives. Because the playing of instruments is no longer needed. AI can make perfect music for us from a tone bank and represent the acoustical characteristics of any famous music venue in the world!"

He went on to argue that HOMI-G had nothing to do with freeing the soul. That instruments as museum pieces are all fine and good to study and learn from, but they aren't freeing. Stored behind glass or on a pedestal out of the reach of humans to blow or strike or pluck them, instruments represent only the *potential* for music, not music itself. They're static. Immobile. Dead. The very opposite of what music is. Of what freedom is.

Bradley wondered how HOMI-G would take that declaration.

"In conclusion," Azul said, "I posit that music, per se, is not what sets the soul free. Rather, it is the *alchemy* that occurs when people take up those instruments and play and people gather together to listen. The magical certain something that everyone feels in these moments, like the aromas of petrichor and creosote that scent the air after a desert rain. When you are realizing that performers are no longer performing, that what everyone is hearing, *sharing*, is simply pouring out of them. You realize you are not alone. These short, rare, precious moments. This feeling of connecting. No conversation necessary. No money, no oil, no wealth. No possessions. You simply exist among others, connected. It is this emergent property that frees the soul."

"Imagine no possessions," wormed through Bradley's ears.

Azul caressed the mic with both hands, then walked back to the podium. Geez, what's he doing with that thing? Bradley wondered.

Ashera grabbed a mic from the dais.

"That was beautiful," she gushed. She gazed at him like she'd found her soulmate.

Azul paused before he replaced his mic on the podium stand. "For the only thing your soul truly wants is to not be alone. This is true freedom!"

Bradley had to ponder that one. He was pretty sure his soul found its alone time pretty damn freeing. It did just a few minutes ago.

The audience remained rapt. It was the hour in a conference day when the air hangs heavy, the eyelids droop, blood sugar is low, and attendees are not even absorbing 10 percent of what was said. Yet they'd hung on Azul's every word.

Bradley could almost imagine Barack Obama suddenly appearing beside him and the two of them leading the audience in "Amazing Grace." It almost brought tears to his eyes.

Then his phone vibrated again.

CHAPTER 11

AZUL IS HONORED

Late for a staff meeting two months earlier, Azul wondered about the envelope he'd just received in the mail with the return address, "Center for the Study of the Philosophy of Freedom, Sonoran Community College." The envelope appeared to be personally addressed, though, not a printed label. At the bottom left, in fancy script, was "From the office of the Executive Director, Dr. Keshawn Washington."

He read the name of the center aloud. Then he inserted his letter opener shaped like an Ida sword, one of his prized desk accessories, and pulled out the paper.

An invitation to speak at a conference! His heart raced. The cadence of his breathing stuttered. He had never been invited to address others off-site. He'd wait until he returned to read the body of the letter, then savor it over a cup of tea.

He walked past the American Popular Music display, thanks to a gift to HOMI-G from the late drummer for Nu Clear, Rasta Masta Collins, and stopped, as he frequently did, to admire Collins' drum kit, as elaborate as Neal Pert's, the drummer for Rush. Collins generously endowed the percussion program at his university in Phoenix, making it one of the top in the country.

This would be the first time the regular Tuesday staff meeting would be discussing a proposal of Azul's. Usually, he was content to simply do his part in programs designed by others, but the VP he reported to had dinged him, albeit courteously, in his last "career chat," for "not taking more initiative to propose and drive projects which would enhance the HOMI-G experience for its patrons." In truth, he had no ambition to rise through the ranks. He had trouble, in fact, with the whole American notion of "getting ahead" in one's chosen career.

He mulled over the working title of his proposal as he stopped by the rest room, then took a drink at the water fountain. "Percussion: Where Music Began, Where Life Ends." In his wildest expression of the concept he planned to present, he would invite percussion players to create a soundtrack in real time for horrific events like the bombing of Dresden, the detonation of the A-bomb over Nagasaki; the collapse of a condo building in Miami; the boiler explosion and sinking of a ship carrying slaves on the Mississippi. He thought of including images from *Amistad*, but figured most of HOMI-G's clientele couldn't tell the difference between Amistad and Amadeus, and if they did, they didn't care.

He thought music was long overdue for the equivalent of a "German Abstract Expressionism" period. When he was invited to a seminar in percussion at the University of Missouri - St. Louis, a school with little national reputation but with a wonderful music program, he visited the city's art museum and became obsessed with Gerhard Richter's November, December, January series. The triptych grabbed him by the throat. Ever since, he had dreamed of a percussion ensemble that could evoke similar raw emotion. An ensemble he could be a part of. Maybe lead. Maybe make a difference in the world.

He could imagine it. See it. Taste it. Hear it. *So exciting.*

He came to his senses just before he entered the meeting room. What was he thinking? Of the hundreds of school groups, old ladies' auxiliary clubs, and the other typical patrons he saw each day on-site, what fraction of them would appreciate such a performance, especially if they had to buy a separate ticket?

He stopped to catch his breath at the picture window with the view of the Superstition Mountains. His pulse raced with what was feeling like a mild anxiety attack. His hands felt clammy. The blood was draining from his head, even as he felt the fluid around his skull swelling.

Deep down, he knew perfectly well why he'd submitted such an outlandish proposal. He'd satisfy the boss's request for "more initiative" without having to carry it out because it would never be approved. He'd done it so many times that he understood his predilection to sabotage his own success.

Thank God he had not sent a slide deck around ahead of the meeting. When his name came up on the agenda, he sketched out some ideas for performances from musical groups which "lean into" percussion, whether they were jazz, rock, folk, or contemporary art house. He truncated the title to "Rhythm: Where Music Begins."

No one looked unhappy when the meeting ended twenty minutes early.

No one except his boss, who wore the *womp womp* smile, as one of his musician friends called it, the cartoon sound effect when someone failed or something didn't happen quite as expected.

His VP took him aside as they exited the room. They stood by the railing overlooking the crowd of enthusiastic patrons in the entrance lobby below. They were almost all white. His boss, also whiter than white, had that look of struggling to find the right words.

"I'm looking forward to hearing more, uh, robust concepts."

"Awesome!" Azul exclaimed, as he mentally tried to shrink in height. It was always difficult talking to a person in authority in a deferential way when you towered over them.

"On another matter," the VP continued, "look for an invite from the Center for the Study of the Philosophy of Freedom in the mail."

"You can bet I will!" Azul replied, visualizing the invitation waiting for him on his desk.

"Honestly," the VP said with a smile as wide as it was shallow, "Dr. Washington, the Freedom Center Director, who I know personally from our University days, had sent me a courtesy heads-up about the invite. Star football player in our day, I might add. But—"

Azul swallowed his spit. It tasted awful. He could sense bad news.

"I apologize, Azul, but I really think the assignment is best handled by someone at my level. I'd like to see you take the time you would have devoted to this endeavor to craft and execute on a HOMI-G special event, as spelled out in our last career chat." His eyebrows lifted with the last few words.

Azul tried his best to appear earnest. He nodded with a knowing frown that expressed how he would go forward and do his best to satisfy the request. Guess he'd read the invitation over a lukewarm cup of Lipton.

"Anyway, I have a timeshare in Sedona so the Gallery will save on expenses, too."

In Sedona? Azul had heard so much about Sedona. The vortexes! Just looking at the photos of the area, he'd dreamed of staging a performance there, like Pink Floyd at Pompeii.

They stopped in the hallway at the point where they would proceed in opposite directions to their offices, and his boss continued. "It'll be fun to 'riff' on the intersection of music and philosophy. I'll be sure to get your input when it's time to prepare my remarks and slides and even credit you at the conference."

What did this short, puffy, white guy know about riffing? Although he had an MBA, the man couldn't even play the washboard.

The director's countenance turned a bit more serious. "On the other matter. Azul, I was expecting your proposal to the group this morning to take, well, a bit more risk, not "out of the box" thinking necessarily, but at least pushing the envelope?"

"Yes, I understand."

"Attaboy!" Before Azul could respond, the director patted his arm, gave him a short nod, and said, "Okay, then, I think we understand each other."

Upon return to his office, Azul read the invitation in full. "Neo-Anthropocentric Models of Retrospective Freedoms," he sounded the words out loud. What? He read it again. And again. It sounded like an archeological expedition. Oh well, he shouldn't get too upset. He was honored to have been selected but, on the bright side, he was relieved of extra work. But he couldn't get out of his head how the boss had appropriated his opportunity. He always tried to refrain from thinking too hard about the family behind HOMI-G, but thoughts of appropriation and expatriation and exploitation were hard to banish.

Coworkers whispered about the criminal enterprise, the expatriation of valuable artifacts from so-called third-world countries. He knew as well as anyone that no place of employment was free of ethical contradictions. They liked to rant off-site about HOMI-G's principal benefactor, Conrad Bolton, heir to the global Bolt-Mart Fuel & Convenience store chain fortune, branded for "shedding up to 120 seconds from your fueling stop." Its "schtick" was tallying up the total seconds they had saved customers and displaying it on the sign at each station. "12 billion seconds shaved off customers' pitstops nationally since 1966." Which in time gave way to the generic "trillions and trillions of valuable minutes shaved off pitstops worldwide," after they had quit counting at the turn of the millennium.

After 9/11, Conrad took his share of the fortune, accepted a passive role at Bolt-Mart as a member of the Board, and started Allegiance, the global equivalent of a chain of dollar stores.

In a marketing strategy now taught in the "Black Belt Master Class" at top business schools, Bolton branded each store in its respective country under the name of the older version of the nation's currency. France had "the Franc Store," Greece "the Drachma Store, China "the Yen Store." It was a little trickier in the countries which had been under colonial rule, like Nigeria, where it became "The Kobo Store." Patrons still transacted with the official currency, they had no choice, but the walls and shopping bags and other store paraphernalia were decorated with images of the old currency. One older HOMI-G display design manager couldn't help but bring up "the Dong Store" in Vietnam every chance he got when he was yakking with Azul. Then the man would invariably crack himself up like he was some comic genius.

The sentimentality for old currencies appealed to customers, as did the feeling of thumbing your nose at the global financiers pushing dollar and Euro-based transactions. The torrid growth of Conrad Bolton's stores coincided with growing nationalist sentiment around the world. Consumers responded well to the nostalgia, a potent token from a time when life was thought to be simpler and Western capitalism wasn't running roughshod over the rest of the planet, oblivious to the fact that it made a fervent capitalist like Bolton wealthier.

The rest of the Bolton clan remained sequestered in southern Mississippi (rumor had it that they *owned* Mississippi south of Jackson), establishing and stocking elaborate cultural centers in Jackson and Oxford, a few reputed to be involved with white Christian supremacist groups.

Azul sympathized with them in many ways. The wealthy are always targets. He had become a more serious Christian in America, after attending an evangelical church service, just when the loneliness of living in a foreign country was about to send him back home for good. There, he learned that his wealth would grow with his faith and positive attitude, after the family money was cut off when he quickly switched his major at ASU from business to music. He had been expected to return home and take his place within the family—and the family business. Where his family grew up in Lagos, Christians were a minority but controlled much of the economy, politics, and culture. He had been groomed from birth to do the same.

Conrad himself was known around HOMI-G to be an avid lover of music, a guy who could play enough keyboard to get through some of the more simplistic 1960s-era rock 'n' roll (Chicago's *Color My World* was his signature go-to whenever someone beckoned him to play), and began collecting musical instruments from all of the countries where Allegiance stores were located. Including Nigeria.

He had bragged in an interview article in *The Atlantic* that HOMI-G had more visitors in five years than the Bolton Fine Arts Complex in Jackson had in 20. HOMI-G staff liked to joke, when Bolton was on site, that they could hear him approaching, humming *Color My World*.

Azul shuffled a few items on his desk and leaned over to drop the invitation in his trash bin when his computer dinged. His email platform was configured to alert if a note came in from his boss. He looked up and saw a window pop up, subject line "Sedona."

He clicked and the email opened. "Just off the phone with Dr. Washington. You'll be going to Sedona, after all. Let's chat earliest opportunity."

In that later meeting, his boss explained that Dr. Keshawn Washington was thrilled that senior management thought so highly of the colloquium that the VP would claim seniority and want to present, but one of the conference objectives was to diversify voices and perspectives.

"In other words," the boss told Azul, "they want a Black guy."

CHAPTER 12

VICTOR'S DONE IT AGAIN

At lunch, Bradley hobnobbed with the attendees over tortillas, black beans, salsa, and roasted agave hearts, a Yavapai delicacy. He had a stimulating conversation with a Dr. Francis Malpense about his research "at the intersection of behavior, ethics, and the law." But he was preoccupied with Victor's question and didn't linger long.

After he found a quiet nook equipped with several lounge chairs and a set of bookshelves, he sat down, picked up and flipped through a novel, Requiem by Lauren Schechter, then returned it to the shelf. He picked up another book and set it down without even opening it. Then he picked up his phone and typed:

So, about your juvenile line of inquiry ... intercourse and fellatio?

Victor texted back immediately.

Fellatio? Who uses that word?

Blowjob isn't very accurate.

What about finger jobs?

Getting to third base doesn't count.

There are far fewer triples in baseball than home runs.

True. Even I know that.

Victor had never been as into baseball as Bradley.

What if the girl had an orgasm? That's not third base?

Well, okay. Can you really remember who had orgasms?

Actually, I can!

Bradley always prided himself on controlling his climax so his partner would come first. Maybe this was part of the problem with Valerie

Wow.

I'm sure you could, too, the number being thusly satisfied counting on one hand.

That's mean.

Sorry. You can't define the bases from the guy's point of view.

Why not?

How about cunnilingus?

Why not make Victor squirm a little. Such a prude.

What the...? Sure, I guess.

Aren't you glad I didn't say, eating at the Y?

You just did. That's Tino speak.

Or muff-diving.

Cut it out.

Long pause. Bradley typed. *Okay, are we done?*

Another long pause. Bradley suspected something wasn't right.

Jiah left me.

WTF? Oh shit, Bradley thought. Victor couldn't even hold onto an Asian wife?

Been back on dating apps. Feeling super insecure. Kind of on the verge of a breakdown.

Bradley had wet-nursed Victor through his earlier divorces and dating follies. He'd even flown to Miami to serve as his wing man for a long weekend. He remembered when Victor emailed Bradley that a Match prospect had sent him a photo of herself topless. Victor insisted on sending it to Bradley, but Bradley told him he'd have the Coral Gables police at his house, and he didn't care what kind of gated community he lived in. Victor's excuse was that she was so proud of her "reconstructed breasts," she'd want the whole world to see them.

What does your pending separation have to do
Bradley hit *send* too soon.
with the number of women I've slept with?
Have you any idea how jealous I've been of you all these years?
What?
You always got the girls.
What planet are you on? That was four decades ago. Ancient history. Tino Lamborghini, he got the girls. Look what happened to him.
What happened to Tino?
#VeeToo accusations out of the woodwork. He's on the hook for about four decades of date rape, sex with minors, and serial non-communication with women after he'd bedded them down.
That only happens to really rich people who have assets to go after.
Those are the only cases we hear about.
Well, I have a chance to catch up to you, at least. Testosterone shots are not cheap, you know.
You're not exactly poor, either ... Anyway, you're too old for this. We're both too old for this.
I think my count is six.
Six what? Shots!?
Six women.
Ha, you better double those testosterone shots, add a heavy dose of courage, and find the charm you lack. Back to esoteric discussions on freedom ...

Now, it made perfect sense, Victor contacting Rachel.

Bradley finally remembered number three. What a doozy. He was visiting his brother at college, during spring break. Two older girls picked him up at a club in a renovated church after he had been wandering around the bars blitzed on orange goofies. Next day, all he remembered was that she'd been on her period. She'd said it didn't matter to her, and so Bradley pretended it didn't matter to him, even though it scared the shit out of him. As soon as he'd ejaculated, he pulled his bloody penis out and looked at it, wondering what he was supposed to do now. Camilla—he even remembered her name!—climbed out of bed and got him a wet paper towel. He remembered nothing more of the episode other than, period or not, fear or not, coming inside a woman still felt great. And she was older. Even if by just a few years, that had meant a lot back then.

Shit, though. Thinking about how Jiah was gone and Victor was in a bad way was sad. Pathetic, actually. All Victor ever wanted after college was a stable marriage, a family, and a musty office at an institution of higher learning doing and teaching the world-busting statistical math few others could touch.

Well, he got one out of three. Better than lots of their friends. They were both in a way better place than Tino.

CHAPTER 13

GUN, GUNS, AND MORE DEBATE

In the afternoon's first session, academics covered voting rights, systems of justice, and education as key elements of freedom. One presenter, as part of the session on freedom and systems of democracy, focused on polling research that showed that over the last fifty years Americans had grown to favor abolishing the electoral college. Of course Americans want to abolish it, Bradley thought. It was a stupid system. But that didn't mean it would actually happen, so why dwell on the improbable? Or even the impossible?

The presenter who followed, a stately white woman with a gray streak in obviously dyed black hair, reviewed what she claimed were the latest statistics revealing that the disparity in how the U.S. justice system treated Black Americans compared to all other ethnic groups was growing smaller. So, therefore, America was on the right path.

Dr. Rolex Williams, a Professor at Carver University, immediately and vehemently contradicted those numbers with his own research revealing an insignificant positive impact on that disparity in the wake of the Black Lives Matter protests, but stating that, if you combine the data from state level police reports and prosecutions with the data from federal courts, you find that that the overall level of injustice simply oscillates. In some states, it got better, in some states it got worse. But the combined trend line trajectory was definitely headed toward worse. The hope of continued progress after the Civil Rights Era, Williams contended, was evaporating before their eyes.

Bradley couldn't even follow the presentation on Freedom, Democracy, and Education. He knew two things: 1) It was too damn cold in the room, and 2) every attempt to make public education equitable fails. End of story. It was demoralizing and, despite an astonishing factoid or two, he could barely keep his eyes open.

Where was Gail? He kind of wished someone would fire a gun.

Then he had an epiphany. Victor, for once, was right. Make Gail's gun into a teachable moment!

At the break, Bradley asked Dr. Malpense if he, as part of his upcoming talk, would offer a few remarks on how his research applied to this morning's incident. He readily agreed.

After he introduced Malpense, he leaned over to Gail and whispered, "You know what *mal pense* means in French?" She shook her head, and he said, "bad thought." She did a spit take.

Bradley sat back in his chair as his head spun from words and phrases like aggregate utility, deontology, teleological, maximum vs average utility, universalization, act-centered perspective. Try saying that last one ten times before semantic satiation sets in. Act-centered perspective, accented perspiration, action perspicaciousness, supercalifragilistic ... when Malpense uttered the "repugnant conclusion." Bradley heaved a sigh and let his mind wander.

Was Kim Wildebaer number four or five? They'd been standing around a pinball machine in a downtown bar back home, summer of junior year, frosted mugs of beer sitting on the glass top dripping with condensate, ignoring the "DO NOT set mugs on glass" sign. Kim smiled at him, asked if he remembered her. He stared, and stared, and then it hit him. Janice Wildebaer's younger sister! He hadn't seen her since elementary school.

"I remember when your family moved to Lancaster Heights, and you and your sister joined the swim team," she remarked. "Your family was so exotic looking!"

If he had a nickel for how many times he'd heard that one since.

"Well, you were the best butterfly swimmer I've ever seen."

"Being double-jointed helps." She joined her hands behind her back and brought her arms over her head. "Still got it."

"Ugh, don't do that," Bradley said, shielding his eyes.

"Yeah, it's freaky."

"How's your sister?"

"Married."

"She's not even out of college."

"She didn't go to college."

They moved to a table and reminisced about elementary school. "Remember when Keith Mallard peed in the socket in the boy's bathroom?" he asked with a laugh.

"Are all boys that stupid? A friend told me that happened at her school too!" They both laughed at that and kept talking, pounding a few more beers. He told her about college life in New York City. She told him how boring it was to go to college in your hometown. He gave her a ride home since she lived only a few miles from where he was staying at his parents'. She mentioned something about always wanting to go to Silver Dollar City, a theme park near Gatlinburg, and Bradley offered to take her over the weekend.

Once they got there, they'd watched some of the historical re-enactments—Indians and bad guys robbing trains—and when they got to the waterpark area, they shed their outerwear and spent the rest of the day in swimsuits.

They got more playful and intimate with each slide into a pool of water or ride on which they sat side by side, later found a secluded spot, where Kim went down on him, while he rubbed and pinched furiously at her nipples, until some kid peered from around the corner and yelled, "Hey!" which startled a parent who then also saw them, and started screaming, "Stop that! This is a Christian entertainment place!"

They untangled themselves, zipped up, buttoned up, and ran, laughing their heads off.

"Thus the question is often not what is wrong with the act, but what kind of person would do it, or what kind of person would oppose new behavioral norms which, on their face, are non-threatening to those in opposition?" Dr. Malpense asked the audience.

Bradley tried to focus on what Malpense had just said because he didn't think anything at all was wrong with the act. Of course, he was still thinking of Kim giving him a blowjob. Still, for all the indecipherable jargon at the beginning, Malpense's conclusion seemed to make sense. It's not always about a *right*, or a *law*. It's about just being the kind of person that does the decent thing. Or not.

"Whoa! Whoa! Just wait a sec," Gail blurted out, after pulling her chair up to the dais table and leaning halfway across it to look directly into the eyes of Dr. Malpense at the podium. Bradley thought her weight would push the entire table—pens, notebooks, mics, pitchers of water, cups and all—off the raised dais and onto the floor.

"This is a thinly veiled attack on the person—or persons—who legally carried a firearm into the room!"

"Gail," Bradley said, "I think the professor is talking in the generic sense—"

"Well, I am centering a theoretical reference and context," Malpense continued, "but in the functional sense, it is appropriate to speculate about the type of speaker who would bring a firearm to an academic conference. No one else did, after all. Until you did."

"How did I know I would be the only one? It's not like I make a living attending conferences with PhDs—pin head dopes, as my compatriots used to say! I told you the pistol had a purpose."

Ashera spoke up. "Gail, I think what the professor means is that a person may have the *legal* right to bear a firearm at a gathering like this, but perhaps also an *ethical* obligation not to ... or maybe ask ahead of time if it was to be used as a prop."

"That would spoil the surprise!"

"And likewise," someone chimed in from the audience, "a conference facilitator has the obligation, though perhaps not the right, to require pronouns of a group of academics so that no one person feels uncomfortable, especially since such a requirement is considered normative for this type of group."

Wait, what? Bradley blinked. Now they're attacking me? Because I didn't require pronouns?

Gail regarded the audience. "What if some shooter barges in here? I'm the good gal with the gun. You're all dead meat."

"Gail," Ashera said, patiently, "can you honestly say that you did not think once about whether strapping on a firearm and walking into an academic colloquium was appropriate? You made a choice."

"Well, maybe I didn't think hard about whether it was appropriate, but I did think about the fact that maybe I wanted to show some respect for the Second Amendment in a group that would likely be hostile to it, and impress upon you why a missile site commander carried a gun to enforce the order to end life as we knew it. Do you know what that does to your psyche? I mean, look at me. People are uncomfortable just being around me."

Suddenly, she looked less like a retired Air Force captain and more like someone who was ready to unload to her therapist.

"I think we all understand how difficult it is to be the odd person out, for whatever reason, in any group." Ashera's voice was kind, placating.

Bradley instinctively grabbed a mic. "Exactly! I remember when I entered prep school in seventh grade, I was the darkest kid in the school. The upperclassmen used to beat me up on the bus, just because. Then in ninth grade, the school admitted its first Black kid. They couldn't call him a nigger to his face, so they called me a nigger. But that wasn't nearly as bad as when they called me Sirhan Sirhan—"

He stopped talking and sucked in a breath. He sensed Rolex Williams staring at him. He didn't want to face Azul either. What the hell was he doing, personalizing the discussion? It simply wasn't in his DNA to make the professional confessional. How was he triggered into that? He couldn't recall ever mentioning any of this before, not even to Victor. He turned towards the huge windows overlooking the canyon. Was there some mystical truth vapor emanating from the vortex?

"Excuse me, that was way, way off-topic and out of line. I'm so sorry. Dr. Malpense, uh, do you have any closing remarks? We have a minute before the session is scheduled to end, and we can all get ready for the culinary treat we have planned at the Vortex Cortex, which I understand is one of Sedona's finest restaurants."

The audience filed out. Ashera and Gail stepped down from the dais separately, and walked awkwardly towards the door. Soon they were side by side.

"If that wasn't the most convoluted bullshit I've ever heard," Gail groused. "Who pays them to think up those words?"

"Unfortunately, I did, and took on loans for the privilege. Reminds me of most of my college courses."

"Well, I hope you didn't go too deep into debt to learn how to say 'universalization.'"

Ashera let that one lie. After a few seconds, she said, "Thanks for leaving your firearm in your room. I really appreciated that. I think we all did."

"Thanks for having my back in there."

"Being a vegan, I know what it's like to be the lone whoever wherever. Every party, every restaurant, every picnic. I always have to bring my own food, makes it even more awkward."

"I thought you vegans existed just to make the rest of us feel guilty." Gail smiled.

"You're not the only one." They approached the elevator. "I think I'll take the stairs," Ashera said, quickly, "gotta get my steps in." She paused while Gail pushed the button.

"Hey, you want to go with me to the firing range tonight? Ditch that group dinner? I don't want to listen to those blowhards anymore today. You probably don't want to relive your college vocab quizzes."

All Ashera wanted right now was to meditate, soak in a hot bath, burn some incense, drink a glass of wine, say hi to Gordon, chill to some ambient tunes, scroll through heartfelt animal stories on Instagram, and see if her therapist might agree to a short Zoom session. Like, right now.

Then again, she'd never fired a gun.

"Can I let you know? I may spend the evening contemplating the meaning of life through the 'repugnant conclusion theory.'"

"Sure, just come knock on #217 or call the room before 7."

"Cool," Ashera trotted up the stairs.

Bradley drew the strip key card through the slot, pushed the door open into a far more reasonable 78-degree room, threw his stuff on one bed and splayed himself across the other. He needed a cat nap like nobody's business. Fastest way—sometimes, the only way—to fall asleep was to spank the monkey. First, he needed to text with Victor.

Do you remember the girl everyone called green teeth at college?

It took a minute for Victor to reply.

No. Wait. Did you sleep with her??

No, you idiot. Just asking ...

Was that the girl Tino called Smegma.

God, don't remind me.

What is smegma anyway?

Don't ask. Or look it up. Everything is knowable now.

Her face was a war zone of acne.

I called her Meg one time. To her face. I thought that was her name. No one used her real name behind her back.

God, we were mean.

Weren't kids mean to you?

I don't recall anyone. Maybe I was called a nerd or whatever you get called for not being into sports.

The privilege of being a straight-up white guy.

Damn, Bradley thought, now he was parroting the words he saw and heard in the media.

You're white, too.

Mostly.

Were kids mean to you?

Forget it. Hey, I'm up to eight.

And what year does that take you to?

I'm not through junior year.

You suck.

Actually, eight depending on the definition we're using.

We haven't resolved that?

I thought anything that involves genitalia.

What is the definition of sex anyway?

Ask Bill Clinton.

Clinton knows the definition of sex. He doesn't know the definition of 'is'.

What about BJs that don't result in ejaculation?

Those definitely qualify.

Damn, Bradley thought, under that definition he would have to include Rachel. Is that why Victor asked?

Okay, I gotta nap before dinner. C ya.

Now he was paranoid that Victor knew. Maybe he knew all along. Although he still couldn't remember for sure. Bradley had gotten to know her first. They'd had a pretty intense friendship for a month or two, but never went beyond heavy making out. He even introduced her to Victor.

He remembered how drunk he was, how he had taken half a quaalude earlier that one evening, that he'd run into Rachel on the quad, how she had, in fact, invited herself into his dorm room, pretty much forced her way in, even after he had asked, "What about Victor?" and she waved her arm as if it was a superfluous question.

She pushed Bradley down onto his bed, garbled something about "unfinished business," unbuckled his belt, unzipped his Levi's, and wrapped her hand around his cock. He wasn't one to use the word greedy too loosely, but that's how she took it into her mouth, like it was hers for the taking. He was well on his way to a climax, apparently she wasn't interested in any reciprocating, at least not yet, then he thought a little bit too hard about his best friend. He felt a little nauseous, whether that was the drugs or Victor, and went flaccid in short order. I'm too high, Bradley said, breathless. I'm too drunk, she responded, though she acted frustrated and disappointed. Maybe they both were right, but it wasn't the last time she mentioned "unfinished business" to Bradley.

CHAPTER 14

NASCHA AND THE CHIEF

Nascha looked forward to when the resort would enter the 21st century and start using back-office management software. In the meantime, she'd finally finished her paperwork for the day, and should've been heading home except that she had been working so much overtime recently, she felt like she was living on the premises.

Everyone was overworked. The resort was surely violating state labor laws, but since it was under reservation jurisdiction, it was a moot point. Her employer was the Yavapai Nation, the location was technically within Sedona city limits, and the property straddled both Yavapai and Coconino counties.

Everything was fucked up like that in Indian land.

At the moment, it was quiet in the lobby, so she picked up the book she was reading, *The Only Good Indians*, and found her place. She could eye the guests, coming and going, just beyond the registration desk. She wished she could turn off the goddamn generic "Native American music" piped in all over the facility. Even white people gotta be tired of listening to a flute sounding like it was emanating from a distant cave, accompanying wisps of smoke.

The Chief's choice, though.

The telephone interrupted her thoughts. Nascha had a pretty good idea who it would be. Few people called the landline at this hour.

"Good evening, Nascha Sunsee, how's everything going?"

The Chief. She could hear the clinks and jingles from the casino's gaming floor where he spent most of his time.

"Fine. Everything's fine."

"That's good, good to hear.

"How are things going down there?" Nascha ventured to ask.

"Picking up, but still too slow. We need more warm bodies and deep pockets with big holes."

How about a credible, sustained marketing program, Nascha thought. Casinos around Phoenix advertise during Diamondbacks games.

"How's the resort traffic?" he asked.

"Still slow. Can't believe it hasn't picked up since COVID."

"Eh, you know," Chief said, "America sneezes, the reservations catch the flu and die."

Literally, Nascha thought. She knew what was coming next.

"Speaking of such matters, it's getting to be the middle of the month and ..."

"And I'm behind on my quota."

"You're one thought ahead of me."

"I get it. It's slow up here too, though."

"Well, I don't have to repeat the business model."

Nascha knew he would anyway.

"The resort is a feeder into the real revenue generating operation: gambling. We expect the percentage of guests coming down to the Casino to grow. It's not stretching the truth to say that the wellbeing of the entire Yavapai Nation depends on this casino revenue, and casino revenue depends on you."

She tapped her fingers on the office table. "Spare me the guilt trip. I get it. I'll see what I can do."

The tribe didn't have much of a choice about what land would be ceded to them back in the day, but whoever thought guests coming to experience Sedona would want to take precious time to get to that casino location was smoking way too much peyote. Coins of the Canyon was 45 minutes south on SR79 and Interstate 17, then 15 extra minutes along a potholed reservation road once you got past the filling stations and fast-food joints at the interchange catering to the Montezuma's Castle historical site. The last mile was a hard-packed dirt road, with plenty of washboard surfaces to rumble vehicles, vibrate eyeballs, and jiggle passengers' internal organs.

"If you think the quota is unreasonable, we can discuss that."

"Could we discuss a bigger bonus for making the quota?"

"No, nothing like that. Not now while we're still recovering from COVID."

"Although if it wasn't based only on white Euros, it wouldn't be so difficult."

"Well, we're not out to fuck those who haven't fucked us."

"Everyone has fucked us."

"Well, let's focus on the original fuckers."

"Then we should only fuck the Mexicans."

"Funny."

"It's true."

"We have an incentive for this weekend," the Chief continued. "The Nu Clear cover band, Kremlin, will be playing a four-night gig beginning Thursday evening." He paused for a reaction. She gave him silence. "They're pretty popular, no?" he asked, uncertainty in his voice.

"Chief, cover bands that cover groups with a national or global following are popular. Rolling Stones, Led Zeppelin, REM, Metallica, Nirvana, U2, acts like that. Nu Clear had a regional following for about five years way before I was born, one or two big hits in the Vietnam vinyl era. They've been living off the royalties ever since. Which makes Kremlin a draw for just about no one. They usually play small venues attached to roadhouse bars where motorcyclists overnight on their way to Sturgis or Vegas."

"Well, it is what it is. I don't select the entertainment."

"No, but you approve it," Nascha said. The entertainment manager was his elder sister, overly susceptible to gratuitous overtures from salespeople.

"Well, let's work with what we have, not wish for what we don't."

One of the Chief's favorite sayings, from some parable combining the worst of Yavapai mythology, Christian Bible verses, and the wit and wisdom of Donald Rumsfeld.

Nascha had only two real options to satisfy the quota. A large percentage from the group currently at the hotel would just meet her quota, but the Freedom Center crowd didn't seem like gambling types. Academics weren't big spenders, in her experience, with their limited travel budgets. Let's face it, that's why they were staying here and not at a fancier resort actually in Sedona. The only exception would be if the conference was accompanied by an expo, and the booth sales teams paid to wine and dine attendees. But the resort rarely played host to those types of meetings. If only Chief would look at the marketing plan she'd put together before COVID. She figured it was moldering in some drawer in his office.

The biannual gathering of the Carefree Ladies of Cave Creek, or CLCC, now there's real potential. They spared no expense when they were in town. Problem was, the Chief only awarded three fifths of a credit for a white woman, compared to a white man. "They don't drop as much coin," he insisted.

The trick would be dragging them away from their vortexes, magic rocks, hot tubs, psychotropic drugs, and kaleidoscopic YouTube videos on the big screen while basking in the glow of the red rocks. She recalled the time a friend working the Red Rocks Arena told her about them all being in a trance, watching

Yanni's "Live at the Acropolis" on a huge screen. That told you everything you needed to know about their cultural tastes. Folks in a red-rock arena watching music performed in a limestone arena half a planet away.

How much more money they could make if they claimed that the valley the golf course ruined was Sedona's eighth primary energy vortex. Groups like the Cave Creek Ladies would flock to the Song of the Sun. Hell, they could even be on Sedona's Pink Jeep tour!

It didn't take an MBA to recognize that the best way to make money in America was to make it by selling nothing.

CHAPTER 15

PISTOLS AND CRYSTALS

Ashera's therapist did not have time for an impromptu Zoom session. Like a kid seeking permission from her elders, she asked in a text message about firing a gun at a range. In her response, after initially recognizing the act as somewhat out of character, the therapist encouraged Ashera to go for it. There are many ways to relieve the tension the body feels, she said. You should document how your body responds and we can discuss the experience at your next session. Ashera loved that idea. Then she thought better of the whole thing. She was 100 percent opposed to personal weapons. Even if you lived in the back country among wild animals. Because you shouldn't be doing that in the first place.

She called room 217 and waited for Gail to pick up.

Bradley was disappointed when Nascha informed him that only 20 of the registrants had signed up for the group dinner. Small groups often made the conversations more intimate and productive, though, so there was that. Just after he had his second shower for the day, and dressed, he saw a text box light up on his phone lying on the bed. Victor. Damn, he was already a few minutes late.

Aren't you with some Freedom group?

Yes, why?
The Center for the Study of the Philosophy of Freedom?
Yes, gotta hurry. Late for dinner.
And the Director is a guy named Dr. Keshawn Washington?
Look, not now ...
Oh, boy, are you going to love this one ...
Shit. Gotta go. Van is gonna leave without me.
I think you're gonna want to know about this ...

Bradley sat next to Azul in the van. "So you're a drummer?"

"A percussionist," Azul corrected, "but yes."

"My parents got me a drum set for Christmas as a young teenager."

Azul smiled. "I have come to learn every American boy, it seems, had either a guitar or a drum set.

After a pause, Azul continued. "I understand you have visited the HOMI-G. May I ask what were your impressions?"

Bradley blinked, then recovered. God, every time he heard HOMI-G, he thought of thick gold chains, medallions, and matching orthodontics dangling off some hip-hop overlord's neck, surrounded by big-breasted soul singers grinding their implanted booties.

"Oh, first class, really unique place. I love museums."

"I see. HOMI-G did not come across to you as perfidious?"

Guy has a big English vocabulary for someone from Nigeria, Bradley thought. Probably went to some fancy boys school in London.

"Uh, not really."

Azul let it drop. "We have special performances. At the HOMI-G, I mean to say."

"Scottsdale is kind of a haul from Tucson for a concert."

"Well, should you ever have the opportunity to hear the Superstitious Afro-Centric Mountaintop Brothers Orchestra, SAMBO for short, I guarantee it will be worth the drive."

"Cool." It sounded like the kind of music Bradley and his friends used to call "jungle boogie." A phrase his kids recoiled from the one time he'd used it. But wasn't it verboten to use the word Sambo too?

"This is the band I play in."

"Even cooler!" Jesus, he sounded lame, even to himself.

As they approached the restaurant, Azul turned from looking out the window. "Your classmates in high school. Did they really call you Sir Han?"

Bradley again felt embarrassed about his outburst. "It was junior high school, but yes. I'd still like to beat the shit out of David Sarnoff, the guy who started it." He was startled at how vehement he sounded.

"Who is this Sir Han? And why would your classmate do this?"

"Oh, we had an argument about the Middle East. Sirhan was the guy who assassinated Robert Kennedy. Sarnoff knew what he was talking about. I knew next to nothing, other than the Israelis were responsible for the mess, which is what my mom and dad told me. It's all old news."

Suddenly, Bradley realized how Azul was saying the name.

"It's Sirhan, one word, he was Middle Eastern. I don't remember which country."

"And why did they call you the n-word?"

"Well, that wasn't Sarnoff. A couple of rednecks in the upper classes." He pointed to his arm. "I get pretty dark over the summers." Should he tell him about the olive oil? Probably not.

"What is this, redneck?"

Should he even try to describe a redneck? Maybe being called a redneck was as offensive as being called the n-word.

There's no official convention for it, though. There was no r-word like n-word, kike, wop, spic, dago, kraut, slant eye, and all the rest he'd grown up hearing spouted by classmates, and used himself even though he knew what it was like to be on the receiving end.

"It's not important. Anyway, I shouldn't have blurted out something so personal. Forget you ever heard it."

As the van came to a halt in the restaurant parking lot, Azul, in the outer seat, got up first to stand in the aisle. "Did your classmates call you the n-word frequently?" he persisted.

Bradley thought about it, and shrugged. "Eh, maybe a few times."

"Isn't it fascinating, the insults and offenses, which stick with us even decades later?"

"It's not healthy to dwell on them," Bradley said, while they waited for the line to move down the van aisle. "Did you have any nicknames while you were growing up?"

"Not until I arrived in America."

"Oh."

"Booty scratcher."

"What?"

"This is a nickname used by Black Americans for Nigerian Americans."

"Kind of like a redneck? What some poor, uneducated white Americans are called."

"I supposed that would be correct."

"Geez, where does it all end?" Bradley said, giving Azul a collegial clap on the back. Azul didn't react. He was staring intently at a message on his phone as any hint of joy in his countenance drained away.

"Well, this seems quite unfair," Azul muttered, eyes glued to the screen.

"It sounds private, so I won't ask," Bradley responded.

While they stood around the restaurant's private dining room having pre-dinner cocktails, Dr. Penelope Zabel, Professor of Ethnic Studies, UNLV, she/her on her badge, pulled Bradley aside.

"Did you happen to catch the six o'clock news?"

"No, why."

"Apparently, your Dr. Washington is in some hot water. I mean, the allegations seem preposterous, but as we know, the coverup can be worse than the crime."

"What crime? What coverup?"

"It's not exactly polite cocktail hour conversation. I'm sure the news segment will be repeated."

Damn, Bradley thought. *Was this what Victor was trying to text me about?*

He soon discovered that the big news may not have been appropriate for cocktail hour conversation, but it quickly took over dinner conversation. Attendees could hardly talk about anything else. He'd never heard anything like it, even in this era of minute-to-minute outrage on social media, doxxing, ghosting, whatevering. As if gun-toting speakers, pronoun conventions, and repugnant conclusions turning into personal slights weren't enough, now there was this mess. He tried to remember why he'd thought taking this gig would be a good idea.

As desserts were being served and conversation ratcheted up to a cacophonous crescendo, a rainstorm pounded the roof like bags of hammers dropped from an airplane. Furious winds kicked up, pushing rivulets of gravity-defying water up the windowpanes. Branches and tree debris washed into the streets. It only lasted ten minutes, but by the time they were ready to get back into the van, raging streams flowed in the gutters by the sidewalk and everyone was still talking about the Keshawn Washington Dildo Debacle.

"This town is too cute for its own good," Gail said, "too many Californi-cating plates."

"It's pretty idyllic, though." Ashera replied, looking out the window.

"Crystal Gratitude Exposures," Gail read from a retail sign. "These towns around the mines turned into centers of woo-woo. Like Bisbee."

"Jerome, too, where we're supposed to go later in the week."

"I rode my motorcycle through Jerome once. My ass wouldn't fit on it now."

"That's not true, I see grossly overweight men on motorcycles all the time, often with grossly overweight women wrapping their arms around their bulging waists."

Damn. Had she offended Gail?

"My Indian motorcycle was pretty bad ass—"

"Isn't that pejorative?" Ashera reproached.

Gail sighed. "That's the brand name, Indian. It's like a Harley."

"Oh, sorry." Ashera countered, "I try to ride my bike as much as possible, cut down my carbon footprint. But it's a pedal bike. I refuse to use an e-bike until the electricity it uses comes from renewable sources and we take climate change seriously."

"Eh, the weather's just going to do its thing."

Gail was not a person Ashera wanted to pick a fight with over climate change. Still, unable to stop herself from speaking up, she persisted. After all, she'd memorized appropriate responses from the Sierra Club education pamphlets, so she turned to Gail.

"Weather and climate are two different things."

"I don't know. I don't trust those brainiacs who come up with those complicated prediction models. The Pentagon spends millions on those things. They start with the answer they want and have those beltway bandits build the models that prove them correct. Surprise, surprise, the answer is always more funding for new weapons programs, never money for taking care of ailing vets."

"I get that, but almost all of the climate models now come to the same conclusion. We ... are ... fucked."

"Hey, weathermen want funding too. They just suck it from a different government tit."

"I can't argue with that, although weathermen and climatologists are not the same. And when 95 percent of the world's scientists agree—"

"Ninety-five percent of Germans seemed to be okay with throwing Jews in gas chambers."

Ashera gasped at that one. "That's not even close to the same thing, Gail, and you know it."

"Most everyone in the southern states thought slavery was just fine. Until it wasn't."

"Again, not the same thing. One is *science*. The other is *sentiment*." That one, without Sierra Club coaching. She was proud of it.

"You know how much money the Air Force has allocated to study the diseases we Missileers are suffering from? Lymphoma, Parkinson's, thyroid cancer ... "

"No idea."

"I don't either, because it doesn't matter, the answer is always the same."

"It's not their fault?"

"Bingo. They're not liable. Launch Control Centers are safe working environments," she said in a mocking voice. "The evidence does not support the notion that each site is a cancer cluster. Blah, blah. We don't need an epidemiological model to forecast how many of us are dying. We just count the bodies."

"That's terrible. But isn't that typical of all industries when it comes to toxic materials?"

"The other two women pioneer Missileers in southern Arizona, good friends too, are both dead. I'm probably next."

Ashera didn't know what to say. But she wanted to ask, how to put it delicately.

"Gail, did you ever feel like you were, like, a token woman, for the Air Force?

"We weren't tokens. We were replacements. Word got around how unsafe the work environment was. Men wouldn't enter the program. So, they encouraged naïve, idealist women who could be *convinced* they were brave patriots, pioneers carving the path for women in the military, all that bullshit. You know, combined with the feminist ideals of the time ... " Gail muttered under her breath. "No wonder no one trusts the government."

Ashera went quiet again.

Gail's voice was hard-edged when she spoke again. "That's the price of your freedom to choose your pronouns."

Ashera's voice, in response, went down a notch. "Gail, you know that's not fair. There's no connection between the suffering of the Missileers and the desire to identify where on the gender spectrum someone wishes to be recognized."

"Look, I don't begrudge you or anyone else the right to live however they want. But it doesn't have to be in our faces all the time."

"Well, let's not re-litigate the afternoon."

"Sure, no reason to. Anyway, whatever is happening with the climate, there are better things to worry about."

"Like what?"

"World War III. It's already begun, in Ukraine. We're just waiting for the signal to go in."

"You mean NATO?"

"I mean us, the U.S. of A. Question is which side we go in on." She paused. "And don't get me started on the Middle East. We don't call any of this a war, because Congress hasn't declared one. The War on Terror gave the President the authority to fight wars anywhere and everywhere. And the President all the peaceniks love, Let's Go Brandon, and his lackeys in Congress, won't invoke or revoke the War Powers Authorization. Fucking cowards have just handed over power to the president to do whatever he wants. And bodies like mine—and everyone who signs up to do their duty in uniform—are just cannon fodder. We've just become numb to it all. But mark my words, the war has already started."

She looked over at Ashera, "You know what I mean?"

Ashera nodded. Finally, something they could agree on.

When they were done shooting, Gail looked at Ashera's target sheet and clapped her on the back. "Not bad!"

Ashera spent the last few minutes of the ride back to the resort staring quietly out the windows at the glistening ground. They hadn't heard the rain through their ear protection.

Thinking Ashera was disturbed by Gail's opinions, Gail took pains to assure the younger woman that her thoughts were "nothing personal against her." She was grateful Ashera made the effort to spend time with her.

Ashera was consumed by a graver threat to her world view than Gail's opinions. Firing that gun had made her feel something she'd never felt before—a gut-level sense of *power*. It had emerged from a place so deep inside her, beyond her physiology, her heredity, from a latent area of her genetic code, an inner body experience so primal, so disturbing, she decided then and there that she would never allow herself to feel that way again.

She vaguely recalled a movie her parents loved that won an award, with a scene where a real estate agent convinces his lover that firing a gun is the best way to relieve stress. It became an iconic statement from her father, whenever he'd had enough of her, her siblings, her mother, or the whole bunch of them.

"I think I'll go fire a gun," he'd quip.

God, that made so much more sense now.

She was going to email her therapist (she was only supposed to text if an emergency, and even then, not after 8 p.m.) as soon as she was back in the room. Could she possibly do an emergency session first thing in the morning?

Gail parked at the resort. As she got out, she reached into the back seat and handed Ashera her target sheets.

"Don't forget these. You can guard my six anytime!"

CHAPTER 16:

DEFECTIVE DILDOS AND EAGER LADIES

Bradley caught the late news edition on television back in his room. Sure enough, there was a brief segment on the protest at Sonoran Community College in front of the building that housed the Freedom Center. The whole thing seemed preposterous. He needed a drink.

He went to the bar for a nightcap, just one. He had the place to himself, but had to interrupt the bartender, name-tagged Andre, to order a Grand Canyon bourbon on ice with a splash of water. The man was earnestly mixing and filling pitchers with some frozen concoction as if catering to a full house.

He gazed out at the first tee box in the darkness beyond the lights around the swimming pool and hot tub. Residual moisture made everything shimmer, though the rain had ceased.

Bradley thought about the Keshawn Washington Dildo Debacle and shook his head. What was the world coming to? The idea of a mold of Dr. Washington's erect cock replicated and sold as a dildo was mortifying. The idea that the whole thing was exposed because some lesbian allegedly victimized by said dildo claimed the product was defective and that its use did not, in fact, guarantee multiple orgasms. The fact that she was suing for damages was ... well, ridiculous. Then again, he thought, a clever lawyer could prove almost anything in an American court of law.

Bottom line: Dr. Washington may not be showing his face in Sedona anytime soon. Bradley was on his own.

Why did he take this stupid gig in the first place? Good question. He did this stuff in his sleep with other subjects in other contexts. Hell, he'd facilitated hundreds of conferences and meetings, technology, energy, sociology, even public hearings on zoning and permitting. Why was he here? Just to prove something to Victor? To Valerie? To himself?

A burst of activity in the hallway from the lobby startled him, the sound of roller bags being dragged in, vivacious conversation.

"Ladies! We've been expecting you!"

Andre hurried from his side of the bar to where they were filing into the registration area. He gave the first few of them faux hugs and air kisses. "Nascha has all of your room keys laid out over here," he said, pointing with a flourish to the table.

They must have all pre-registered. Real keys, too! What hotel still used those?

"Your complimentary pitchers of bacanora-laced frozen pina coladas are waiting in my fridge. Texting me in advance gave me plenty of time to get ready for you!"

Suddenly, Andre was strutting around and talking like he was emceeing a drag show. Not that Bradley had been to a drag show. Well, once, maybe. If that's what that was.

Within minutes, the bar was swarming with a dozen or more women who looked to be in their 50s and 60s, all dragging expensive-looking bags perfectly sized for their owners to ask for a pair of strong masculine arms to lift them into the cargo compartment of an airplane. And they were all adorned in summer outfits suitable for the Caribbean. All manner of precious metal and gemstones dangled from necks, wrists, ears, and ankles, and in one case, a nose.

"Don't look so lonely," one of them remarked as she passed Bradley, "you're among friends now."

"I like making new friends!" he said cheerily, draining the last of his bourbon. He turned to Andre and immediately ordered another.

Turns out he'd had his first brush with the Carefree Ladies of Cave Creek, from a town on the outskirts of Phoenix, arriving in Sedona for the 10th anniversary of their annual weekend getaway. No spouses, no plus-ones. The vacays began, he learned, as a response to their spouses' "boys" weekends set aside for golf, hunting, gambling, boating, four-wheeling, and motorcycling. Bradley thought he overheard something about psychotropics.

"What brings *you* to Sedona?" One of the women asked Bradley.

"Oh, you know, a scintillating colloquium on the philosophy of freedom."

"Sounds dreadful," her companion observed.

"This is where we put *our* theories of freedom into practice," the other said, laughing.

"Hey handsome, when you're ready to take refuge from *that* alien land, we have an open border over here!" Another yelled, from two or three women away.

Bradley thought about texting Victor that his count was about to go up. Surely there was an N+1 or even 2 in this crowd. He was beyond tipsy but not quite weaving after his third bourbon. The splash of water he requested was more like the tears of someone struggling to cry with joy. When was the last time he was the only guy in a bar with a dozen women intent on partying all weekend? Never. But he had a colloquium to attend to, so he reluctantly departed.

Why shouldn't I add one to my lifetime count, he reasoned, on his way to the elevator and up to his room. He was still spooked by that image of Dr. Washington's cream-cheese encrusted lips wrapped around his dick from the interview—how did that even happen?—and needed reassurance that he was still 200 percent heterosexual. He wasn't looking for some primal celebration of machismo, just an escape to the women of the 1980s. Was that so much to ask? Turn the clock back a few decades, not a century or two. To when sexual freedom was the mantra of the era.

The hardest thing he did every single day, he thought as his back crashed against the elevator's back wall, was not cheat. He remembered when Valerie used to read him passages from one of the many books on male vs female biology, genetics, psychology, anthropology, and whatever other "ologies" she was into at the moment, and there it was: Men are hard-wired to copulate with as many women as possible, to spread their seed far and wide. And, for every man who cheated, there was a woman complicit in the act.

Why was the onus always on the guy? Valerie had laughed at that.

Once, much later, during a heated argument, he had said that every day he didn't cheat is a win. She looked at him like she was contemplating two options: stick the knife she was holding in his gut or leave the room and not talk to him for the rest of the day. She chose the latter. But what was wrong with what he said? She was the one who read him that stuff! At that moment, it was indelibly impressed upon him that what was understood, even accepted, in the collective world of academics had absolutely no bearing on what two people as individuals would ever tolerate.

He slid his plastic key through the door lock slot, lay down on the bed, opened his Instagram app, then promptly fell asleep before he could even get his dick out of his trousers.

CHAPTER 17

DAY TWO - BONDING ON THE TRAIL

Bradley waited outside the registration area on the canopied sidewalk to meet the tour guide from Seduced by Sedona LLC, providing *"GREAT GUIDES AND GREAT GEAR!"* for hiking, rafting, rappelling, mountain biking, and other area activities, including Pink Jeep Tours of the energy vortex sites. He wanted to check in with the guide before everyone headed out for the colloquium's low-stress bonding event, hiking in Red Rocks State Monument, a primary vortex area.

Across the highway snaking around the resort's southern perimeter, the sun was making its way over the towering cliff of burgundy and red strata, a formation that seemed to stand guard proudly, though ominously too, over everything in the canyon below, including the resort.

Large bulbous clouds appeared above the cliffs, moving ever so slowly. The juxtaposition of the cliff—dense, statuesque, permanent—against the cloud—vaporous, agile, in motion—captivated Bradley. After a wide gap of blue, another pillowy set of clouds followed. The cliff face darkened. It didn't take much change in light for those rocks to reveal how many different shades of vermillion they were capable of. Very chameleon.

A van pulled into the lot and up to the curb with haste. Out sprang a sculpted young man in camo shorts, sporting a man bun, belt with a thick Western buckle holding back a tucked-in knit shirt with *Seduced by Sedona* embroidered in orange, yellow, and red over his left breast. Its sleeves fit snugly at the shoulders. The guy carried a vented straw hat, had a skin tone that patrons of tanning salons would give their right tit or left nut for. The name tag across his breast said Finnestraw "Finn" Hernandez.

"Mr. Ma-nipples!" he said, with a smile as long as the name he just tried to pronounce, a gait worthy of a gazelle.

"Finn?" Bradley said, with a partially outstretched hand no match for the one approaching his like a lunging aquatic animal.

"Please, call me Bradley." Few could say his last name without stumbling over it.

"Bradley! Awesome to finally meet you!"

"Likewise," he replied, hoping his tone of voice was at least moving in the direction of the exuberance implied by Finn's.

They talked logistics, how many of the attendees had signed up for the outing, the need for plenty of water and sunscreen, the signing of waivers absolving Seduced by Sedona of any legal responsibility for accidents.

"It's a pretty diverse group, a wide range of ages too," Bradley reminded him.

Finn beamed. "As long as they can walk with no supports, other than a walking stick, we're good!"

"Cool! I'll run upstairs and get my water bottle. The others should be gathered here in a few minutes."

Nascha noticed Finn as soon as he bounded through the big cypress wood doors. Her toes curled. Her fingers went numb. Her heart fluttered. Her privates pulsed. OMG, she thought. He was probably 20 years younger, but she didn't care.

"Hi there!" Finn beamed sunnily. "I'm with Seduced by Sedona, picking up the group from the Freedom Center? Uh, do you mind if I just take a seat here until they assemble? It's sizzling outside."

Did she mind? She'd like a 6-by-6 painting of him on her ceiling, preferably wearing nothing but maroon leather chaps while riding a horse and shooting an arrow into a buffalo.

"Not at all."

Despite the hit of Blueberry Head Band he'd bonged at the shop just before he left, Finn tried to focus his mind on the task at hand. Be at the trailhead by 8:30 a.m., back at the resort by 11:30 at the absolute latest. He'd grab lunch at Red Roxy, take it easy during the afternoon, then spend the evening hanging out at the Airport Grill, a good place to meet out-of-towners.

He was gonna love the time-and-a-half pay he was promised since the company was so short-handed. He pulled the cheat sheet out of his pocket and reviewed the stuff he was supposed to say.

"I believe your group is assembled," Nascha told Finn, then admired his leap from the chair, bouncing past the counter like a gymnast starting his floor routine.

Finn found the group mingling near the van. It was a beautiful morning, and he'd landed the easiest job in the world, walking in Sedona with a bunch of strangers eager to enjoy the scenery. He could not wait to complete his inaugural tour for the company.

When they piled out of the van at the trailhead, Bradley could feel a breeze pick up. There was considerably more cloud cover than yesterday. Or even earlier this morning. Perfect conditions for a hike.

As they gathered at the trailhead, Finn gave a boilerplate spiel about the hike. He waved toward the restrooms and cautioned everyone to fill their water bottles, as there would not be another opportunity until they returned to this spot.

"It's a 3.2-mile trail classified as easy to moderate, but even for experienced hikers not used to these conditions, it'll definitely feel like you're getting your steps in!"

His manager had informed him that they'd struck a deal with Prickly Pear Beverage Co to distribute their latest concoction, Sensa!, so he told the group, "We'll have fifteen minutes to relax and take selfies at a meditative overlook where I will have an offering of a light mocktail, replete with botanicals and adaptogens designed to refresh your psyche without unduly pressuring your bladder. But all along the trail, please be mindful, present, and aware of your inner spirit and try to detect when the Earth's electromagnetic force synchronizes biodynamically with your nervous system."

That garnered more than a few raised brows and several rolled eyes.

"This trail is for pussies," an Asian woman said, loud enough for everyone to hear. Bradley couldn't see her name tag. "Look, it's like walking around a track!" She looked like she'd outfitted herself for a 24-hour survival test by cashing in five-years' worth of REI gift cards.

As they circumvented the visitor center, Bradley overheard the talk among some of his attendees, phrases like "normative ethical theory," "meta-theoretical questions," and "freedom of choice based on a Gladwellian distinction between an immediate, intuitive first-order system and a second-order system of higher analysis." What planet were these people from?

"Malcolm Gladwell kind of looks Orwellian," Bradley said, as he sidled up to the pair. One reminded him of a physics TA in college who often showed up to labs with half his breakfast rappelling down his considerable beard.

"He's the master at spinning the Sapir-Whorf hypothesis for the common man," the bearded one chortled.

That was enough of that. Bradley fell back to bring up the rear as the trail led them along the creek. The crushed stone below their feet was firebrick red as they passed under a huge tree with thick, gnarly branches spasmodically extending from the trunk. Beyond the branches, fast-moving clouds fractured the sunlight, creating a kaleidoscope of soothing reflections and shadings on the ground and in the trees. Sloping upward to the west were the cliffs, not as starkly red and brown as the ones by the hotel. Suddenly, everything was shaded, like a great being had plucked the sun from the sky. The temperature dropped, and he wished he brought a light jacket or sweatshirt.

His mind drifted from the ethereal sense of his surroundings to Victor's question. He couldn't recall the order after five. Who was number six, anyway? He probably didn't want to remember.

The temperature had dropped considerably by the time they began to climb the path up the side of the cliff. Steps chiseled into stone were bald from wear, the gentle incline scattered with scrub brush, ocotillo, creosote, and prickly pear. Prickly pear everywhere, in fact. Then more smooth step faces. Not much evidence of the rain from the night before. Why was it that every prickly pear reminded him of that iconic "hooded man" photo from the Abu Ghraib prison in Iraq?

He was well behind the group now, but as long as he kept them in sight, it would be fine.

Number seven was a cheerier thought, the girl he went out with most of junior and senior years. He still had fond memories of her. Who was number eight? *He was number eight*. During that trip to Daytona. Well, no one was going to hear about that one. He'd passed out after a night of drinking and smoking crushed aspirin or something, and awakened to the guy whose luxury condo they were staying in between his knees blowing him. He'd never worked through that one psychologically.

Thank God that unfortunate encounter was quickly followed by number nine, two days later. Nice girl. Went to college in Boston. Red Sox fan. He was in New York. Yankees fan. It was not destiny. All he remembered of the sex was how urgent it was to cancel out that homo experience. He'd been raped by a gay guy who had power and money over him. Well, not raped raped. There wasn't any penetration, but it was definitely sex. And definitely nonconsensual. He'd always blamed himself for it, though. What happens when you are not in control of yourself or your surroundings.

His right big toe hit a rock stuck in the ground. He stumbled, didn't fall, wincing at the sharp but fleeting pain. Suddenly, the wind gusted, blowing dust across the trail. He shielded his eyes. Tree branches swayed, and leaves and Palo Verde needles shook more insistently. Now he was downright cold. Valerie always pestered him about layering up, and he resented it when she was right. It felt like another storm was coming, except that it rarely rained here in July, and never in the morning. That's what he'd read.

They kept walking along the path, occasionally stopping for a photo of the valley spreading out below them. Above them, the clouds were now dense, gray, and angry. The sun was no longer being cute, poking out from behind a cloud, making tiny leaves and bark and plant stems glisten, exposing dancing dust particles on the ground and spider webs in trees. Could storms form this quickly around here? Everything weather-related these days seem to happen more frequently, more rapidly, and more furiously than in anyone's recorded experience. Even the paddle-shaped limbs of the prickly pears were swaying in the wind.

Two members of the group were now hurrying toward him.

"I don't know about you," said the Asian woman with the name tag, Dr. Xin Zhou, who thought the trail was for pussies. "I'm turning around. It's shorter going back than it is going forward." She appeared to be in her 50s, in good shape. She was already walk-running, her fanny pack with the price tag still hanging off it spanking the top of her butt. The woman with her didn't look like she could run from the bedroom to the kitchen.

"Is that wise?" Bradley yelled to their receding backs, "I think Finn should tell us the best course of action. Maybe it's just a brief sun shower?"

He stopped to take inventory of the group ahead. The two had fled the other way, but the group seemed smaller than just two missing. There'd been a trail intersection at one point climbing the cliff. Did a few of them make a wrong turn? Had Finn not yet realized the group had dwindled? How much effort did it take to keep track of 23 adults on a hike?

Without further warning, the clouds opened up, releasing a fury of pent-up moisture. Twenty minutes earlier, it was warm, partly sunny. Now, the temperature had dropped at least ten degrees, the sun had disappeared, and the rain sounded like bat day at Yankee stadium when all the Bronx ghetto youth fourteen and under banged their free 15-inch Louisville Slugger replicas on the hard plastic empty seats in front of them.

Bradley rushed ahead, passing everyone rapidly retreating the other way. He saw the first bolt of lightning, just as he caught up with Finn and Ashera.

"It's only five more minutes to the overlook!" Finn screamed at the now-distant hikers running tail for shelter.

"Are you out of your mind?" Bradley yelled at the two, "It's fucking lightning out!"

"I know," Ashera yelled back, sticking out her tongue, arms spread wide. "I've never been out on a mesa during a storm! I'm going up to the overlook."

The woman must have a death wish, Bradley thought. But at least she was smart enough to bring a rain jacket. She had experience on hills and slopes anyway.

Finn reminded her about the waiver she signed.

It was still pouring by the time they all—all except Ashera—made it back to the trailhead, including the two who'd taken the wrong turn. Dr. Zhou had a bloody leg from a fall while she was running down the rain-slicked steps. The "normative ethics" guy looked like he'd smeared war paint all over his face and extremities, mumbling about having fallen onto slippery rock and sliding a few feet.

Red rocks don't look so magical when turned into paste smattered over skin. There wasn't a dry stitch of clothing among them. Shoes squelched and squished, except for the one guy who wore hiking boots. No happy campers. Several pissed off ones. The rain kept coming down, but Ashera did not show. Everyone else was cold and grumpy. Teeth were chattering. Tempers were flaring.

"Look, we can't wait any longer, I've got to get ready for another tour this afternoon," Finn lied.

Bradley agreed. They would have to leave Ashera behind. All of them were adults. She made her choice.

In the van, the talk centered on the rainstorm, but apparently not an awful experience for everyone. Bradley overheard the professor from last night, Dr. Zabel, comment to her seat mate that she felt like twirling and undulating like a Siren. There was just something about a hard rain against the parched earth, she exclaimed. And the botanically-saturated air! The creosote. It's magical!

Dr. Zhou took a photo of herself and one of her leg wound before she had bandaged it with the contents of a first aid kit she was carrying, then posted both to her social media accounts. Bradley guessed she wasn't divulging to her followers that she'd retreated even before the rains began. But at least it didn't appear she was calling her lawyer. She wasn't complaining about a trail for pussies, either.

"These storms seem to come faster and more furiously these days," he commented to the person next to him.

"It's Sedona," she said, matter-of-factly.

The normative ethics guy was lecturing Finn on the various weather apps he could have used to more precisely gauge when the rain would begin. "Even AccuWeather has Minute Cast, which breaks down the weather pattern by the minute. You should download WeatherBug now. It tells you when and how close lightning strikes are to your present location."

One by one they marched past Nascha at the desk, dripping onto the lobby floor, leaving a pale pink liquid sheen over the tile. Nascha couldn't remember the last time she'd seen so many drenched guests. What a mess! Thank God she'd have time before the afternoon registration rush to get it cleaned up. Finn was the last one in. To his credit, he did try to wipe himself with a hand towel he had in the van.

He was about to sit in one of the lobby chairs, when Nascha cried, "No!" and quickly brought out a folding metal chair from her office.

"Use this."

He sat, his head in his arms, dejected. Bradley came in, stood over him.

"How hard could it be to keep track of two dozen adults and the weather on a three-mile hike?"

Finn peeked out through his fingers. "I'm so sorry, sir."

"Your management is going to hear about this!" Bradley groaned, then left to get out of his wet clothes.

"Boy, did I fuck up!" Finn muttered into his hands.

"It can't be that bad," Nascha said, wanting to mother him in the worst way. Well, she really did not want to mother him. Comfort him, sure. With him on top. Or her on top. Didn't really matter.

Poor guy was almost in tears. "They never gave me any real training. I had no idea what I was supposed to do. When does it ever rain in July in Sedona ... in the morning?"

Uh, like, pretty often if you've lived here a few decades, Nascha mused.

He kept his head in his hands. Then real sobbing ensued.

"I don't even know first aid. I had to memorize all this stuff about the vortex. They taught me what words of zest and uplift to use. I had to carry all this food and drink in my backpack for them, but they didn't even give me a first aid kit, not even Band Aids!"

Nascha could sympathize. It had been so difficult to find workers lately. Everyone was scrimping on training, getting people online as fast as humanly possible. At more than a few of the establishments around town, it looked like the proprietors had waited at the exits of Arizona's prisons to find workers. Hell, she'd had to hire people whose repair work looked like they were mimicking YouTube DIY videos for the first time.

"Honey, you look like you could use a strong cup of hot coffee."

She led him to the restaurant bar area, poured him a cup from the tank the resort kept full for guests, asked him if he preferred cream or no, put the lid on, and walked it over to him. I'll take your cream in my coffee, she dreamed.

"But don't sit there!"

CHAPTER 18

#VEETOO BARGES IN

Nascha could breathe a little easier now. The rain had passed. She'd gotten the mess from the hiking group cleaned up. Most of the registered guests were staying for several days so the morning checkouts and the late afternoon check-ins would be more easily managed.

She picked up *The Only Good Indians* again and found her place. She'd known from the opening line of the novel, "Indian man killed in dispute outside bar," that she was going to enjoy it. Ever since she'd read *The Last Final Girl*, Nascha had made her way through Stephen Graham Jones's earlier works. There was just something about how that guy was able to mix Native mythology and stories with Hollywood-type slasher tales. He spoke truth about life on reservations.

No sooner had she completed the first page when one of the housekeepers rushed into the registration area with a look of concern. She pointed in the direction of the highway, mumbled something in Spanish. Nascha couldn't wait until English speakers were available again. She was definitely on board with those who thought English should be the official and only language used in public-facing situations in America.

Finally, they quit trying to communicate. The housekeeper pulled Nascha forward. They walked out front. She pointed to the entrance of Song of the Sun, up the short but steep hill, to the roadway that followed the contours around the layered cliffs of red rock and the monolithic formation Nascha liked to call "Big Brother," not because of its Orwellian reference, but because it loomed over the resort like an older brother ready to take out anyone doing bad things to his siblings.

Near the large pink stone wall of a sign with "Welcome to" above an abstract sculpted half sun, with "Song of the Sun" below it, Nascha saw a crowd of a dozen or so carrying signs and walking in lines back and forth. What the hell?

"Okay, thank you Esmerelda, you may return to work."

Nascha walked with purpose across the parking lot. It was eleven in the morning and already the temperature was in the mid-90s. You wouldn't have thought a deluge had just occurred.

As she approached the group, she could make out a few of the signs.

IF THE DILDO DON'T FIT, YOU CAN'T ACQUIT

KERRY'S WANG AIN'T NO THANG

WASHINGTON'S COCK DON'T CROW

OUR BODIES OURSELVES

THE GENUS WITH THE PENIS WON'T GET BETWEEN US

Each sign had a prominent #VeeToo in the lower right-hand corner.

One woman held a digital camcorder recording the whole event. Nascha made sure to avoid her.

"Excuse me," Nascha yelled over the vehicle traffic, then louder, "Excuse me, I'm the manager here. What seems to be the problem?"

One lady broke from the line and approached Nascha. The one with the camera followed her.

"Shut that thing off!" Nascha demanded. "Otherwise, this is going to get ugly fast. I represent the Yavapai Nation here."

Nascha thought about her weapons back at the office, but decided she really wouldn't need them.

"This is a Native American owned business?"

"Sure is. We have our own laws on our sovereign land."

"Well, we have no intention of violating the rights of indigenous peoples. Solidarity with you, always! Especially Native women!" The woman raised a fist.

Right, Nascha thought. The only "solid" thing about that declaration was how elastic it was.

"This is a public sidewalk, though." The lady's voice lilted upwards. We're not breaking any laws by assembling here."

"Technically, the Song of the Sun is responsible for the maintenance of this sidewalk, so we have jurisdiction over its condition." It was true that the resort paid for repairs and upgrades to the sidewalk, and resort employees kept it clean. The part about jurisdiction she wasn't quite sure of.

"We have a permit from the city of Sedona to assemble."

"I'm not arguing. But what is all this about?"

"We demand that Dr. Keshawn Washington hear our message."

"Who?" That name was vaguely familiar to Nascha. Oh right, the signatory to the contract for the rooms and the Freedom Center's group rate, the conference facilities, and the special events. But he wasn't registered at the hotel. What did he have to do with dildos and cocks?

"I think you have bad intel. There is no Dr. Washington registered here."

"Isn't the conference ... " The woman had to look at a piece of paper she retrieved from her pocket. " ... Neo-Anthropocentric Models of Retrospective Freedoms," being held here, sponsored by the Center for the Study of the Philosophy of Freedom?

Nascha knew the resort was hosting a freedom conference, that the Freedom Center was paying the freight, and that the name sounded like something from a diorama of Indian life in a musty museum on the East Coast. Which made her wonder what was the latest on that initiative in Washington, D.C., to have that racist, outdated crap ripped out of those places.

"There is indeed, but Dr. Washington is not registered here. You folks need to take your beef elsewhere, preferably for your own sake, somewhere cooler and more comfortable."

The rest of the group had gathered around their leader.

"You mean he's not here?" someone muttered.

"Damn, we drove all the way from Phoenix."

A few of them looked like they were also picked up from the Phoenix homeless shelters, Nascha thought. The others looked like students. All of them lily-white. Such babes in the woods. She watched a car pull into the parking lot, slow and hesitantly, the driver peering over the steering wheel.

"Does this mean we're not getting paid?" another asked.

"Yes, yes, you'll be paid for the hours you worked," the apparent leader said.

"It wasn't our fault your organization got bad information. We want the full three hours and drive time originally promised."

A young man got out of the car, opened his trunk and pulled out a sign.

"Is this a straggler from your tribe?" Nascha asked the leader.

"Hold on. What does the sign say?"

Nascha walked toward the car. The guy was now holding his sign up proudly.

"Women will not displace us," Nascha read, loudly so the lady protesters could hear. "Okay, YOU sure as shit aren't getting any airtime on my property. Scoot! Now!"

"What about them? If they can be here, I can be here."

"They're leaving. You're right behind them or I'm calling tribal police!" She walked towards him with a vicious look on her face, cocked her arm like she was going to slap him silly.

Just as quickly as he appeared with his sign, he threw it in the back seat, got his ass into the driver's seat, and took off.

"He's with the Velvet Sovereign Pact," the leader-apparent said. "Wholly incompetent white supremacists trying to stage counter-demonstrations to ours. The rest of his group must have gotten lost."

Good God, Velvet Sovereign Pact? What the hell was that? Nascha wondered. Way too many white people with way too much time on their hands. As far as she was concerned, all white people were white supremacists.

"Well, I've got a resort to run," Nascha said. But please, get yourselves some water and get out of this heat. In fact, I'll have someone bring you some."

"As long as it's not in plastic bottles. We don't do plastic."

"Well, fuck it then." She lost her patience.

Oh, and if that is your van over there," she pointed to the area near the tennis court, "it is illegally parked on private property. I won't have it towed, as long as you make a timely departure."

The last thing she heard from the group as she walked away was, "Look, the actual protest doesn't matter. We just need the footage."

CHAPTER 19

#VEETOO & DILDOS

As soon as she returned to Phoenix, Ivy, the leader of the protest group, called the cell phone of her local #VeeToo contact.

"There was no Dr. Keshawn Washington at the Song of the Sun Resort in Sedona."

"Oh? What happened? We have a pretty good ground operation in Arizona, especially around the campuses … "

"I figured you'd tell me."

"There was, though, a conference there sponsored by the Freedom Center?"

"That's what the hotel manager said. She chased us away."

"But not before you got the footage?"

"We got some video. Not the best. I sent a copy to headquarters as instructed."

"Good, good."

"So, why were we scheduled for three hours in the blazing sun, after we got drenched during a downpour, when all we really need is the video?"

"We don't want to look like we're just showing up to create memes. I mean, #VeeToo still believes we have to put in the work. It's a movement after all. Plus, it gives us an opportunity to get a few dollars into the pockets of students, the unhoused, the under-employed, unemployed, under-resourced, under-funded, and under-the-overpassers who can use the money."

"So, we're a wealth redistribution organization too?"

"Kinda. I mean, let's face it, our donors and patrons are affluent white women, a few wealthy gay men. They don't want to stand out in the sun and protest themselves, so that's why we pay you to do it."

"So when is this group going to become public anyway?" Ivy asked. "I'm always nervous about applying for permits using these aliases and phony licenses. We're lucky no one does the same kind of investigative reporting on us as we're doing on our targets."

"Yeah, lame local journalism is our friend, for sure. We need to exploit this golden period while the media continues to give angry women a free pass and our enemies haven't sufficiently organized."

True, Ivy conceded. It took the Federalist Society 40 years to pack the Supreme Court, Wasila wrote, in her last essay in *Mother Jones*. It took women and Blacks hundreds of years to get the vote—or even to be allowed to own property. And a century or two of European Jews saying, on Rosh Hashana, "Next year in Jerusalem," before they were handed the keys to Palestine and created the myth of paradise from the desert. Societal change takes time and perseverance.

"Speaking of enemies, some lame-o from the Velvet Sovereign Pact showed up. God, was he pathetic. He retreated almost as fast as he arrived."

"That won't last forever. History teaches us that power blocs may stumble, but they're always out there scheming and undermining."

Ivy remembered how excited she was the first time she read Naomi Wasila's manifesto on smashing the patriarchy. And while supporting lawsuits like the one against Dr. Washington weren't specifically in the plan, neither was getting a law passed in New York State that would later force an ex-President of the

United States to pay millions in damages for sexual assault that occurred 20 years earlier. When it came down to "he said/she said," women, finally, were winning big. At least every once in a while.

The truncated bonding hike gave Bradley an extra hour to decompress and regroup. He returned to his room, shed his hiking clothes, spread them out on the balcony railing outside, took a hot shower, got under the covers, and gazed out the window.

He got up and took a piss, looked at his old sucky, wrinkled self in the mirror. He was getting old and showing it, especially the flappy gobble of flesh on his neck bisecting his chin, like the folds of a tent about to be spread out and impaled by its support poles. His gut never went away, no matter how he ate or exercised over five decades. It wasn't big, but it was annoying. He sat back up in bed, arranged the six pillows, and tried to think through the rest of the day. He could no longer ignore the string of texts from Victor.

Freedom must mean strange things to your Freedom Center guy.

Saw a clip on the news last night about your Freedom Center guy.

Rotsa ruck with that one!

Jesus, a replica of a star athlete's pecker ...

Just gets weirder and weirder out there in the real world ...

This was as good an excuse as any not to get out of bed just yet. Finally, he had to respond.

How would you know, Mr. I-can't-be-fired tenured professor? The last time you were a member of the real world, Clinton had just become president.

It must make life pretty easy, waking up every day knowing you can't be fired.

He'd always resented Victor for that. Jealousy or resentment. Same difference, right?

Give me some credit. I achieved tenure faster than anyone ever in my peer group.

Your peer group consists of 50 people worldwide.

The power of small numbers! Hey, Rachel said look into the Primates Festival.

Why?

One of the big events at their confabs is a huge circle jerk.

Haven't heard that phrase in a while.

Yeah, when a bunch of guys stand in a circle and masturbate ...

Fuck you, Victor, I told you to keep your mouth shut about that.

I didn't tell her. I swear.

Well, how did it come up then?

She was telling me how she met that billionaire tech bro, Roger Magellan.

Probably slept with him.

No doubt.

Or wants to.

No doubt

Or will.

For sure.

Glad you can take all this so casually.

There's some connection between him and your Washington Freedom Dildo Guy, but she wouldn't say what.

She's in the middle of all of these women's issue things, even if it's just at the periphery.

That statement violates Euclidian geometry, Bradley.

True. I'm still dazed by a washed-out hike this morning.

What happened?

Never mind.

Ok.

Really, somewhere between the eye and the tail of those gender-

issue tornadoes, Rachel's mucking around.

Ah, I see your point. Good graphic.

You know, maybe Jiah would still be with you if you didn't invite Rachel to spend the weekend with the two of you that time.

That has nothing to do with it. Jiah swore she wasn't bothered by her.

God, you're an idiot when it comes to women.

Not necessarily denying that ...

You two have had some strange chemistry reacting between you for decades. Anyone could sense it, you know, like tremors from an impending earthquake.

Is it that obvious?

Yes.

She's a friend.

True. But Rachel is a past girlfriend, and one of the most intense women anyone could hope to meet.

So ... on to bigger and better things ... where's your count at?

Will you quit fucking obsessing about my count?

A pause.

It's up to 10.

Is your memory that bad?

No, but the circumstances are a bit fuzzy. It was the '70s. And the '80s.

Well, good luck today. Don't take any wooden dildos. They give splinters.

Bradley dragged himself off the bed for the second time that day. The space at the back of his eyeballs ached. Instead of dwelling on the failed hike, he ruminated fondly on the lady at the bar who had graciously invited him to join their group. That was before she mentioned the gummies. She reminded him of one of his InstaBabes. Surely not.

He looked down at his crotch. Was it the woman at the bar or the InstaBabe image? Maybe he should take this glimmer of a hard-on to its ultimate conclusion. He reached for the olive oil and went at it, undressing the woman, whatever fragments he remembered about her. Then he got bummed out and quit. His sucky old self looked back at him from the mirror. At least he still had the smooth Mediterranean skin. Because no one could take away the fact that he was *exotic looking*. *Swarthy*, Valerie's old boss had called him admiringly. He hated that word. Too close to Smarmy.

Did being friends with people like Victor reinforce his need to identify as white? All of his good friends over the years were straight-up white people. He'd never even had a friend who was Black, or Hispanic, or Greek or Middle Eastern for that matter. Always white. Or Jewish. He was always the darkest one.

He slathered his arms, face, and neck with olive oil and regarded himself again in the mirror. It really did make his skin seem whiter. As long as he turned into the light a certain way.

CHAPTER 20

NASCHA TEMPTS BRADLEY

Before she dispatched him, Nascha managed to ferret out of Finn the name of a professor at Northern Arizona University who had published books. The bonus was a new entry for her *Tonto Chronicles*. When she mentioned the working title of her book, Finn asked, "Who's Tonto?" Not quite as much fun as if an old white guy or gal had said it, yet still.

He said he'd be happy to introduce Nascha and the professor by email. He made it clear that he didn't know what good it would do. He was just a rising senior. He didn't earn that great a grade in her class. She might not even remember him. A she, Nascha noted.

"Oh, I'm certain she'll remember you," she said, her lusty expression dripping like glistening agave syrup ready to be lapped up and licked off his waxed chest.

She stared at her third cup of coffee, as if trying to recall the movements necessary to lift her arm and grasp the cup. She read a note from Andre. He was able to take care of her little favor for the Cave Creek Ladies. On behalf of women of all kinds, she resented the Chief's three-fifth's rule for white women. Note to self: Show the Chief the actual receipts for their expenditures. Maybe that'd change his mind.

After she'd sorted and organized papers aimlessly strewn on her desk, and reviewed her standard afternoon checklist, she saw the guy running the Freedom Center meeting step out of the elevator.

"Mr. Maniopolos, how is the conference going, apart from the aborted hike, I mean?"

"Yeah, about that."

"Unpredictability has its own charm, though. Right?"

"Yesterday's sessions went pretty well, if you discount the firearms and the pronouns."

"Well, aren't weapons usually involved when freedom is at stake?" She replied with a smile.

"I suppose."

He sounded dejected.

"Is there anything the resort can do to make things more than all right?"

"Oh, I didn't mean to imply there was anything wrong with the services."

"I'm grateful to hear that."

"It's just that discussions about freedom are a bit more, uh, serpentine than I expected."

"I'll take your word for it."

"Nothing we can do about the weather," he added.

"It's not completely out of the ordinary. Though we usually get less than an inch of rain in July."

"I think we got two inches in fifteen minutes."

"Deluges carry special blessings."

Bradley looked at her, puzzled. "How so?"

"In Yavapai lore, a woman survived the third catastrophe, a flood, by taking refuge in a log which eventually ended up in a canyon north of Sedona. She is the supreme mother-goddess of the Yavapai people."

"Kind of like Noah's ark?"

"Maybe, if you're white and Christian," Nascha thought. But another entry into *The Tonto Chronicles!*

"What were the first two catastrophes?"

"They weren't important, apparently."

"I guess we all have our mythologies."

"Some more than others."

"Maybe the fourth catastrophe is upon us," Bradley said. "Curious, what is the Native American attitude towards climate change? I mean, do they accept the idea?"

Nascha groaned inside. What did it take for these damn people to understand that we're not one monolithic race with hive-mind opinions?

"I can't speak for the hundreds of Native American tribes and their members. Personally, I see it as a Second Peoples problem."

"Second Peoples?"

"Yeah."

"Well, I should get back to it."

"I wish you earnest discussions about freedom," she said, earnestly.

"Thank you. Thank God there are no right answers, only clever arguments!"

Nascha suddenly had a thought.

"Mr. Maniopolos ... "

Bradley paused, stepped back to the desk.

"I know your group had a walking tour of Jerome and Tuzigoot planned for tomorrow evening. There's more rain in the forecast. I wondered if you might consider changing your plans. Our sister property, the Coins of the Canyon casino down the highway a piece, has some great deals for Thursday nights, and some special entertainment. A Nu Clear cover band will be performing.

"A what? Nu ... Clear? I'm sorry, but I've not heard of them."

"They were quite popular in this area years ago."

"Wait. Do you mean, Nu Clear, as in Nuclear?" Or New Clear, as in some newly found clarity?

"I believe the former. The band's name is Kremlin."

"I'll see if they come up in Apple Music. But really, the decision isn't mine. I can poll the attendees, though, and see if they'd like a change in venue."

"As an inducement, management will give each person in your group $10 in chips as a token of appreciation." She had no idea if the Big Chief would approve, but sales were sales, and she had a quota to meet.

"Good enough. I'll let you know."

He paused. "Speaking of music, this background music is so soothing. Is this Galway?"

"Who?"

"James Galway, Irish guy, I think."

"No, it's Carlos Nakai. From, uh, here." This guy is a treasure trove for my Chronicles, Nascha thought.

Bradley nodded, headed to the conference center and then quickly returned to the front desk. "Ms. Sunsee, are there any other groups at the hotel going to the casino Thursday evening?"

"Let me check the list." She reached underneath for a clipboard. "Uh, yes, the Carefree Ladies of Cave Creek. They are here for their semi-annual ladies weekend. They'll be at the resort through Sunday."

"Ah," he said, walking away but then back-stepping, "Hey, may I ask you a question?"

"Fire away," Nascha said, "I mean, sure."

"Is there a Native American tribe that *doesn't* operate a casino?"

She could sense a new entry.

"I hear the Sioux do not. Or to their way of thinking, the Lakota, the Dakota, and the Nakota."

"Sounds like different brands of Coca-Cola."

"Good one!"

"Why are they the only ones?"

"They're getting their reparations by charging admission to the Monument to Crazy Horse on the other side of Mount Rushmore, even though it's not even close to finished."

There's that word again, reparations, Bradley thought. "No kidding?"

"No kidding."

"Okay, hey listen, I've really got to get myself into that conference room."

"My apologies for holding you up."

"Oh, not at all."

Yeah, Nascha thought, the Sioux considered the Black Hills so sacred that they decided to carve up one of the highest mountains in that area to make a memorial. At least when miners blast out a mountain, they extract something humans could all use, like copper or iron. Her mother taught her, if you're going to do something, do it for the right reason. Revenge for carving out Mount Rushmore was the worst reason to destroy another mountain. But that was a "Lakota, Dakota, Nakota, Coca-Cola" problem. And another entry for *The Tonto Chronicles*. Whatever. If the Freedom group decided to go to the casino, along with the Cave Creek Ladies, she'd clear at least eighty percent of her quota before mid-month.

She was beginning to feel downright jaunty. How long could this mood last? The problem with all good moods. She picked up *The Only Good Indians*, found her place, and started reading, then thought, hell. She put the book down, looked up the professor Finn had mentioned, and typed an email to her. She put in the subject line, "Humor book proposal: Stupid things white people say to Native Americans," mentioned in the text that she was Yavapai, hit send, then got back reading.

To her shock, a response arrived within 30 minutes. Yes, the professor would be delighted to share her insights on publishing options with Nascha. The timing couldn't be better. Publishers were interested in marginalized voices. In the aftermath of COVID ravaging Native American reservations, they would be particularly receptive to a female Yavapai narrative. She went on to say that LGBTIQA+ voices were "having a moment" in the publishing world and wondered, not so subtly, if Nascha could check any of those boxes.

Which boxes? What did all those letters stand for? What was the plus sign for? How come the professor assumed the Yavapai were "marginalized? I mean, we are, Nascha thought, but it's not her place to assume that.

CHAPTER 21

FREEDOM TO THINK

Back in the conference room, Bradley noted that Ashera had managed to return to the resort in one piece. He recognized the need to address the Dr. Washington issue, but agonized over what to say, then decided that the best course of action was to attack it head on, ask the audience to suspend judgment and gossip until the facts come out. Before Bradley could open his mouth to make those remarks, Ashera had picked up one of the dais table mics.

"Please, may I say something?"

"Of course, Ashera."

"There was an important inequity from the end of yesterday's program."

Geez, another one? Bradley wondered, how many can you have in a day?

"Getting *called* the n-word a few times as a white boy in school has no equivalency to being *viewed* as an n-word every time a white person gazes at you."

Bradley braced himself. "I'm not sure I follow, Ashera. Am I even, uh, white?"

Azul bent over and looked at her quizzically, too. He hadn't looked very happy this morning.

Jesus, does every slight have to be picked apart like an adolescent zit, Bradley wondered? He was only trying to be honest, even if it wasn't a premeditated comment. Maybe subconsciously lean into his own vulnerabilities to better relate to the participants and the subject matter.

Ashera continued. "Using a derogatory label on anyone is bad enough. While I do have sympathy with your feelings about being called Sirhan, this is, in the end, a minor point."

Since when was using the n-word a minor point? It gets career sportscasters fired on the spot, Bradley thought. For shit's sake, Azul must have mentioned to Ashera something he had said privately to him on the bus. That's not right. Maybe he should get even and say something about Azul's band being named Sambo. I mean, come on.

"You were seeking sympathy for the use of those words about you as a young boy. But there are still millions of people in this country who no longer utter the n-word, yet *think* the n-word every time they look at a Black person. They see 'inferior.' Language is only the surface manifestation of racism. An implicit, silent racist response is, however, baked into American society."

Dr. Plemmons—white woman and front-row occupant extraordinaire—blurted out, "I believe you are co-opting Azul's experience, Ms. Winters, and race-splaining to him and, for that matter, to other Black members of our colloquium."

All eyes diverted to Rolex Williams, one of two Blacks in the audience.

"Ain't my story," he retorted. "My mama was the first Black woman in the executive suite at Coca-Cola."

"You must be very proud of her!" Ashera responded with an achingly earnest, blindingly white smile.

"Ah, I'm just razzing yo ass. She was responsible for the C-Suite's coffee service first thing ever' mornin'."

Several in the audience gasped.

Azul responded, "Please, I am not Black-American. I am Nigerian-American. And a devout Christian."

Bradley suppressed a groan. What did being Christian have to do with anything, and how many times do we need to split this hair?

Ashera raised her hand like a student in class. "May I please finish?" Long pause as she appeared to gather her courage. "Having a few dents in the armor of your personal freedom as a youth, Mr. Maniopolos, is nothing compared to being 'unfree' in your very existence!"

"Which reminds me," an audience member yelled, "why wasn't the Unfreedom Center invited to this colloquium?"

The Unfreedom Center? What the hell is that? Bradley wondered if there was actually a competing group championing unfreedoms and why such a thing should exist.

"Avi Kauffman's methods have been thoroughly discredited many, many times," Dr. Zabel responded from a floor mic. "Let him sponsor his own colloquium."

"Speaking of language," a woman stood up and spoke loudly, 'can we talk about how the use of jargon and acronyms and multi-polysyllabic words joined together for no apparent reason than to code-talk among peers is also prejudicial? I mean, why can't we academic types speak in plain English? It's completely off-putting and intimidating to non—"

"Sorry, friend, but I've just got to," Gail said as she snatched the mic from Ashera. "Girl," she pointed at the woman in the audience, "now you're talking my language. I guarantee you the military is worse than every university combined in that department. They just do it to keep those lame Senators and Congress people and members of the lame-stream media confused."

"I resent being called 'girl,'" the audience member retorted. "I have a full doctorate, was tenured at one of the youngest ages of anyone in my department, and hold the Caitlyn Jenner Chair in Reconstructed Transgender Psychology at Bryce Canyon University."

"It's a term of endearment," Gail said, brushing her off. Then she added with a smile, "*Gurl!*"

"Yes, and rappers are using the n-word too," Azul pointed out.

"Yes, but as a disclaim on the word non-Black people are not allowed to use and as a way to promote solidarity," Rolex Williams retorted. Then he frowned as if pondering what he'd just said. "Even if the reasoning is a bit convoluted."

What would Rolex think of Azul's band name? Bradley wondered.

Dr. Plemmons turned in her seat to glare at him. "Could you phrase that in a way that omits the double-and-a-half negative?"

Dr. Williams gave her a crooked smile. "Y'all grammar-splaining to me?"

Bradley didn't think Arabs called each other sand niggers in a show of solidarity. He remembered a history teacher in seventh grade, who insisted that the n-word was also a term of endearment. Southern white slaveowners often held such great affection and respect for their slaves, he'd said, calling them "niggers" was like saying "buddies," and calling a Black man "boy" was like calling him "son," like a regular member of the family. That teacher probably had a sheet and a pointy white hat in his closet.

Gail handed the mic back to Ashera. "I'm sorry, just had to get that out."

"What is equivalent to Azul's example," Dr. Plemmons spoke up again, "is how men see a woman by herself—on the street, at a bar, or in the park, anywhere—and immediately think, she's fair game. But if she's with a man, any man, even a work colleague, the reptilian brain kicks in and thinks the woman is taken. She's a piece of property to be owned and controlled by a man. Unfreedom is associated with just *existing* in the eyes of the dominant caste."

"Shit," Bradley blurted out, "that's so true!" Then he placed his hand over his mouth, and mumbled, "Sorry."

But, Jesus, it was true! How many times had he been at a hotel bar on a business trip when a woman by herself sat down. Most likely traveling for business just like he was. But before you knew it, a guy was buying her a drink, or three guys were swarming her barstool. But if she was with a guy ... It was a Eureka moment! A thought so deeply embedded in his alligator brain coaxed out into the open for full examination. He needed to quiz Victor about this.

He watched as a short man near the back of the room stood and walked to the mic stand set up in the middle aisle.

"Well, how is any of that different than when each of you ladies, and each of you men too, looks at someone like me and thinks, he can't be a 'full' man."

"Yeah, you'll never get elected president," Gail yelled.

Audience member: "Hey, that's totally inappropriate!"

"Word!" Rolex Williams said.

"Truth," Gail countered, "Look at me. I ain't getting elected president anytime soon either, not even of my neighborhood association."

True that, Bradley thought. Chris Christy proved that in spades. Shit, was it okay to say "spades" anymore?

The short man continued. "Do you know that the average height of an American male is 5 feet 9 inches and the average height of a corporate CEO is 5 feet 10½ inches? If that doesn't prove bias in hiring and promoting, I don't know what does."

That's not such a big margin, Bradley thought. But maybe that's why one of the only things in life he ever regretted was not being 6 feet tall. And losing his hair in his 40s. And that little bit of gut that refused to go away. And having dark skin.

Azul got hold of a mic. He seemed agitated. "So you are then saying to us that a short white male is treated in an equivalent way in the eyes of others as a black individual is by white people?"

Gail jumped in. "Oh good God, now short white men will demand reparations from tall white C-suite types ... "

"That's blasphemous," Rolex yelled from the audience. "Well, maybe not blasphemous, but you know what I—"

"All of us girls who represented the UN wing in high school should demand reparations from the cute white girls who always made cheerleader," Dr. Zhou chimed in.

Ashera agreed. "Short white guys suffer the same indignities as women? Come on."

We should build a pyramid of victimization, Bradley thought, a Mazeltov's hierarchy of triggers. Or maybe someone in this crowd had already done that. He waved his arms and crossed them in front of his head and chest, then made a time-out sign with his hands.

"Namaste!" He cried. "Isn't all this a perfect segue into our first presentation this afternoon, "Freedom to Think: A Human Right?" And without waiting for anyone to protest, he introduced Dr. Thomas Helvig, PhD, Professor of Practice at UC Santa Barbara's Newer School for Research, Director of the Center for Post-Racialized Power Structures, and head of Constitutional Scholarship at The Claremont Institute.

What in the world was post-racialized? And Santa Barbara? He'd been there on more than one occasion and to his knowledge, only one race lived there. Extremely affluent white people.

Still, he sat back and tried to pay attention. Deep into the presentation, Bradley was struggling to decide whether Dr. Helvig was advocating *for* the right to think or *against* it. How do you even articulate a right to think? Don't you just, uh, think? Nobody knows what you are thinking if you don't say anything about what you are thinking, but everyone is thinking all the time. Aren't they?

Helvig droned on. Bradley could see audience members nodding off. "Psychological mediation ... right to mental integrity ... paradigmatic violations of the rights to freedom of thought ... paternalistic thought modulation..."

What the fuck? Paternalistic thought modulation?

He texted Victor under the table.

Just heard about 'paternalistic thought modulation'

You mean when our dads tried to brainwash us?

Funny

During the Q&A session, an audience member asked, "Professor Helvig, may I request a clarification? What are you referring to when you mention marketing and false advertising? I read a book in high school called *Subliminal Seduction*, about how advertisers embed things like naked women and cocktails into ads to appeal to the viewer's subconscious. I mean, is any of this new?"

Ashera glanced at Helvig standing at the podium and grabbed a mic. "One could argue that the entire U.S. economy, indeed its very power structure, is based on false advertising and has been since the nation's inception. I mean the Constitution guarantees liberty for all, but calls slaves three-fifths of a person for voting purposes. Yet that part of the Constitution is ignored, while the Second Amendment is gospel."

"Careful," Gail said, smiling this time.

An audience member spoke up. "Right, no authority has yet infringed on the corporation's right to push sales through misleading advertising, and promoting claims which can easily be proven to be false, or dubious at best. Precious few companies are ever held accountable."

"It's buyer beware," Gail said, flippantly.

"Caveat Emptor," Helvig nodded appreciatively.

Another audience member raised a hand and stood. "Let's say a certain someone has been indicted for spreading lies about the loss of an election. If that person *truly believes* that he's won the election, then he can't be found guilty of lying when he claims in public that he won. Is that an example of a subjective mental feature being objectively defined for legal purposes?"

A collective groan. "Oh no, let's not bring Trump into this!" someone yelled.

Please, God, let's not, Bradley silently implored.

"Well, let's step back," Professor Helvig said. "What we mean by autonomy of thought and thought modulation is, for example, when a social media platform algorithm sees that you are clicking on, say puppies, scantily clad women with enormous breasts, or scantily clad men with throbbing you know what's in their shorts—"

Dr. Plemmons: "If you can say breasts, you can say penis!"

Another audience member: "One's a norm, and the other isn't."

Bradley tried to be funny. "These days a Norm is just a guy on *Cheers*." It didn't work.

"—and the algorithm keeps sending you more of that to keep you engaged," Helvig continued, raising his voice above the crosstalk. "That could be considered a violation of one's autonomy of thought by strategically modulating your thought processes. Not saying it *should* be considered this, but it could be."

"Hey, if you don't like what's on the screen, you have the *freedom* to turn it off," Gail blurted out. She didn't need the mic to make herself heard.

"Personally, I am kind of grateful when Pandora tunes its recommendations to my musical tastes," Azul added.

"Me too," Ashera agreed, "I love the algorithm's suggestions. YouTube's as well."

Bradley spoke up then. "I mean, the algorithms are only feeding us more of what we want, right? Is that wrong?"

Bradley was thinking about the cosplay models that just keep coming into his Instagram feed. Man, why would *that* be a bad thing? It all started months ago when he was looking for some sexy outfits to buy for Valerie and make up for a particularly nasty argument they had gotten into and, if he was honest, he instigated just to be mean. Within seconds, his feed became a firehose of InstaBabes in every conceivable outfit, posed in titillating five-to fifteen-second reels in front of their phones. He had never gone down a rabbit hole so rapidly. Or rabidly.

Audience member: "Well, yes, but that doesn't mean it's good for us. When food companies sell us more of what we want, which generally isn't nutritious and good for us, it's usually the least expensive stuff they can get away with selling and that they can sell the most of, because, let's face it, that's what capitalism is. Buy low. Sell high. Make money on the margin."

Audience member: "Is this not an indictment of the entire American way of life?"

What's next, Bradley wondered, double secret probation?

Following Helvig's presentation, Bradley remained at the dais during the break. He wanted to text Victor and ask him if he'd ever thought that a woman sitting alone was fair game. In his reptilian brain. Victor probably didn't know what a reptilian brain was. Before he could formulate the thought in a way Victor would understand, he got a text from him.

I'm thinking about getting my penis enlarged.

Bradley looked around to see if anyone was close by.

What??

Just read an article. Thousands of men do it.

Are you fucking stupid?

No, desperate. Getting no responses on Match.

Tenured statistics prof at UMiami doesn't cut it anymore?

Nope. Nor does being 67 years old.

How's a longer dick gonna help? Did you stop to think that maybe you shouldn't be chasing 40-year-old tail at your age?

I've upped the age filter a bit.

Ah, you've gone from robbing the cradle to raiding the rest home.

Jiah read once, in Brazil you have the right to be beautiful.

So ... ?

So ... I have a right to be ... impressively endowed.

You have the right to anything in this country, as long as you got the money.

How big is your pecker?

For shit's sakes, Victor.

It costs twenty-five grand.

Holy shit.

That's less than what I paid for Jiah's wedding ring.

Are you serious?

A pause.

What's been the response to your director guy's uh, pubic relations problem?

Ha ha. So far no one has left. We really don't know the details.

How's the count going?

I've remembered number 11.

Doesn't seem like you are getting to 30 anytime soon.

Hey, I'm a little preoccupied right now. Putting down my first academic mutiny ...

We don't have those problems at our Symposia on Bayesian Quadratic Regression Methods with Univariate and Multivariate Posterior Distribution Functions.

That's a mouthful.

We lead with our jargon, not our penises.

It'll be both after you get your Dexter extended.

What's a Dexter?

Do some research.

Number 11. Bradley couldn't remember her name. A true one-night stand. He was out with a friend celebrating his birthday. He'd downed a Valium before they hit the bars, the last one they were at for the night, packed in like the No. 1 train during rush hour. The only details he could pull from his memory was the sex was pretty good, the mattress on the floor they fucked on was uncomfortable as hell, she had only moved to the city a few weeks earlier, but fortunately there were only a few hours before daybreak.

She'd told Bradley that he was her reward for reaching her goal of losing 50 pounds. When he offered to call her and asked for her phone number, she told him no need, kissed him sweetly at the apartment door, and gently pushed him out. The beauty of Manhattan. Dawn could blend into day along with the insignificance of whatever just happened. Even when you're the one being used.

CHAPTER 22

AVI KAUFFMAN AND THE UNFREEDOM CENTER

Avi Kauffman was ready for severe resistance tactics against the university president's office, the Board of Regents office in Phoenix, and, for good measure, the office of the Center for the Study of the Philosophy of Freedom's office across town. The university's financial fiasco had been in the news for months. Now the hammer was coming down. Fifteen percent budget cuts. A hiring freeze. Layoffs. All because the CFO's accounting models had made a $350 million error.

How could an accounting model make that large a mistake? He knew how. It didn't. It was just a manufactured excuse for the president to make all the major changes he'd wanted to for years but had been prevented from carrying out by saner people.

He knew this. The papers weren't reporting it, though. The papers rarely reported the truth.

He suspected the president from the moment he'd spent $10 million gilding the "executive" box at the football stadium. He knew the guy was corrupt. Were they going to cut the football program's budget 15 percent? No way.

Meanwhile, his boss, the director of the sociology department, was talking about slashing costs. Again. Seemed like that's all he talked about. They'd been incrementally whittling away at the department for over three decades while programs like Entrepreneurship at the business school doubled their budgets and students every five years. What was entrepreneurship but the capitalist's way of saying, fend for yourself?

Even Avi's job might be at stake. Every year during his career conversation, Jerome Hogarth, the director, chastised Avi because he and his grad students didn't publish enough. Hogarth wasn't impressed when Avi insisted he researched real-world social dynamics while working with community groups "at the grassroots," rather than conducting research projects whose conclusions depended upon spurious data and dubious statistical correlations.

"That's just not the way it's done these days," Hogarth repeated. "The '60s are over, as are the '70s, '80s, and '90s."

Hogarth was really urging him to retire. Sooner rather than later.

"The '60s were the last time anything positive happened," Avi countered. "You can't study social change in the classroom. You have to be in the field."

"Dean Whitmore doesn't want you out on street corners and overpasses holding signs and hollering through a bullhorn," Hogarth said. "He wants you working to establish a new center through which we can apply for more grants from places like the Center for American Progress and the Pew Research Center."

Avi knew exactly what that meant—begging and pleading for money from groups that were supposedly progressive, but eventually gravitated to the middle just like the others. Whatever happened to groups standing up for real progressive ideas? They all caved, that's what happened. Occupy Wall Street and Black Lives Matter and every other so-called leftist group eventually gave in to the Man. It was infuriating. He needed to be on the front lines, for god's sake. He would've gotten more involved in the whole #MeToo thing on behalf of his female colleagues, but at least one of them threatened to file a grievance against him after that conference in Maui. Everyone was so touchy about touching. Nothing like the free love days of sit-ins and sleepovers and Woodstock.

Maybe it really was time to retire.

Still, Hogarth and Whitmore had let him slide until 2018 when Sonoran Community College announced it was establishing the Center for the Study of the Philosophy of Freedom with the help of a massive grant from the Magellan Foundation. Hearing that Magellan was funding a competitive center motivated him to get off his ass. It was the last straw for Hogarth and Whitmore, too. They weren't about to let a billionaire and the local school for apprentices, cooks, and welders get out ahead of them.

"I mean, come on," Hogarth had said. "We're supposed to intellectualize on the philosophy of freedom. They're supposed to turn out skilled labor for the local economy."

Dean Whitmore was emphatic. "It's no longer a choice, Avi. Either you work with Hogarth to get some kind of center established, or we'll find ambitious junior faculty who will. We need funding partnerships with outside organizations now! With your seniority, it's your job to bring the money."

Avi had been cultivating an idea, CLUED-IN, The Collective for Liberation from Unfreedoms and Extant Inequities. He wanted to use the word "collective" since he was, at heart, a socialist. "Liberation" would appeal to women and other minorities subject to domestic colonialist power structures. Unfreedom, he told Hogarth and Whitmore, was a concept gaining traction in social movements as an antidote to the corrupt intentions of those who merely *espoused* American freedom as something our enemies want to take away as an excuse to tighten the noose of late-stage capitalism.

And "extant"? He searched and searched but could not find an academic center with that word in its name. It was accurate, too. The inequities faced by those not centered in the white power structure had been lingering for decades, centuries even.

It wasn't his fault that CLUED-IN's launch occurred just before COVID. They'd managed to raise $50,000 in the first two years but the Dean set a goal of half a million by the end of fiscal 2021.

So it was inevitable, Avi thought in hindsight, when Hogarth and Whitmore pulled him aside and into his office after he'd dismissed the last class he still taught, "Contemporary Sociological Theory as Actionable Protest," a four-credit course consisting of two credits of independent research into a current social movement, and two credits of "lab work," code for embedding graduate students into Kauffman's pet policy, extra-legal, and NGO organizations.

"Avi, I hate to be the one to tell you, but we're going to replace you as the head of CLUED- IN."

"But I just got started! It's my baby!"

"It's not going according to plan."

"Well, COVID has had a lot to do with that."

"COVID has nothing to do with it. We've decided you need to step aside and allow our upcoming faculty some opportunities. You're 78 years old, Avi."

"Some people around here are 80."

"Yes, our academic celebrities with buildings named after them. You can still be a professor. Unless you want to retire. How does Professor Emeritus sound?"

"It sounds like I'm being marginalized for ageism, that's what it'll sound like to my lawyer. Who's taking over the Center?"

Hogarth looked at the floor.

"Don't tell me you've picked Benowitz."

"We've picked Benowitz."

"What the hell?"

"She's got everything. Her mother is African-American, her father is Hispanic, and she's married to a Jew. She's an alum who grew up here, went on to Princeton for undergrad, Yale for her

PhD, and did a postdoc at Oxford. She could have gone anywhere but she came back home because she loves the Sonoran Desert. Her scholarship is vast and her research credentials impeccable. She's impressive as hell and she's already agreed."

Avi smirked. "What about that plagiarism situation?"

"That was assessed and dismissed years ago," Hogarth said.

Yeah, Avi thought, *after* the definition of plagiarism was relaxed in a way that absolved her.

"Anyway," Whitmore went on, "we're more interested in her overall scholarship than if more than a few words were taken from another source. And she's got a high profile in the field and a stellar social media following."

"You mean she checks the boxes so she can fundraise off her so-called qualifications. How many times has she been arrested? Huh? Tell me that."

"She's never been arrested, thank God."

Avi grumbled. "So, you're cutting me out."

"Avi, you're a '60s radical who had to change your name after that incident during the Columbia sit-in."

"I was never charged."

"No, but organizing an orgy with undergrads while locked in Hamilton Hall did stain your reputation."

"It was all consensual."

"Right, well," Hogarth said, "times have changed."

"Can I still at least be involved with CLUED-IN?"

"That'll be up to Sammy. Oh, and you'll hear about it soon enough so I wanted to be the one to tell you, we're changing the name to the Center for Research on Social Transformation, Reparations, and Unfreedoms, or the Unfreedom Center."

"Why not just plant your boot in my ass while I'm walking out?" Avi groused.

He didn't need the U. He had a few ideas of his own.

"You're too old to have any more ass to boot, Avi."

166

CHAPTER 23

AFTERNOON HEADACHES AND EUGENICS

The afternoon's second presentation listed more co-authors than Bradley had ever seen crowded into the space between a title and the summary. It was like they wanted a name characteristic of every ethnic group on the planet—there was the Indian, Jawar; the Vietnamese, Nguyen; the Jew, Katz; the Japanese, Kitamura; the Scandinavian, Torvalds; the British, Smith; the Hispanic, Cortez; and ... the slide advanced before Bradley could identify the others. Maybe 25 co-authors total? Wasn't there a reason for the phrase "et al?" He was able to catch one of the affiliations—Laboratory of Molecular Systematics & Evolution, at some university in Washington state.

Geez, they needed to let fewer publish and more perish.

The speaker, a Dr. Earnest Hintz from Libertine University, might shed some light on why Dr. Washington had been especially enthusiastic about this session. It sounded like Dr. Hintz was arguing that the highest caste members of the Indian subcontinent, who generally intermarried and therefore interbred, were genetically more similar to Europeans than to Asians or Africans. That is, once he got beyond the jargon like proto-Asian, mtDNA hyper-variable region 1, restriction sites polymorphisms, haplogroups and haplotypes, phylogenetic relationships ... and that was just in the first 10 minutes.

Haplotypes, phylogenetic? What was next, Troglodytic Triptychs for Trans-Continental Breeding?

"Jesus, this is fucking eugenics!" Ashera hissed out, loud enough to be picked up by the hot mic. She caught herself. "Sorry, I didn't mean to be rude, but this IS eugenics!"

"I beg your pardon," Dr. Hintz said, looking down his nose through his glasses at her, "this is biochemical analysis of genetic structures."

"Please, let the professor finish," Bradley insisted, "one freedom we should not disrespect at a colloquium on the philosophy of freedom is freedom of speech."

Bradley looked up the printed journal paper online and quickly scanned the summary and the conclusions. Then he read the very last sentence: *Because the publication costs of this paper were defrayed by payment of page charges, the United States Code … requires us to label it an advertisement.*

What the fuck? This was as disturbing as an accusation of eugenics or the list of co-authors longer than the credits at the end of a movie. What was an advertisement doing in an academic journal or being presented at an academic colloquium? He was going to text Dr. Washington and find out. He swiped over to his messaging app, opened the text thread with Washington, but then thought: *Why should I care?*

Still, whether it mattered or not, he didn't want to be associated with genetics, eugenics, or advertisements masquerading as research. The whole thing boiled his blood. After the discussion, during which Ashera led a minor revolt, accompanied by Rolex Williams, with what appeared to be both outraged dissension and avid concurrence from Dr. Plemmons, he feigned an important call coming in on his cell.

Outside, he wished for his shades as the sun turned his field of vision into a spreading spectrum of yellow flares. He made his way past a long row of mature bougainvillea. One of the branches stuck out and he ducked. A long thorn could make a shish-ka-bob out of an unprotected eyeball. In front of him was a large planting of the omnipresent prickly pear patches, like a crowded pack of enlarged Gumby dolls, only with barbs and miniature monkey-ball-looking nodules.

He changed his mind, texted Dr. Washington asking why the hell someone was allowed to present a paper that was labeled an advertisement in the journal in which it was published?

A few moments later, the reply came back. *Ask Magellan.*

CHAPTER 24

RAJ MEETS A BOLTON

Raj Magellan's helicopter had landed on a concrete pad amidst an expanse of well-manicured lawn just outside Purvis, Mississippi, a town described by locals as equidistant from everywhere you don't want to be—90 miles from New Orleans, 90 miles from Jackson, and 90 miles from Mobile. Purvis, the alleged headquarters of the Velvet Sovereign Pact, or VSP. It wasn't a headquarters, per se, but rather the location of the Bara Plantation, home of Jabberwocky ("Jab") Bolton Leal, titular head of the secretive organization.

It had been a cool day in April, and Raj had hoped the meeting would be an opportunity for him and Jab to get to know each other. Raj had invited Jab to his last Primates Festival, and although the man himself didn't show, he did send an emissary. Based on the emissary's reconnaissance, Raj had been able to secure a deal in which he could call on Jab to dispatch a contingent of his goons when and where necessary in return for contributions to the VSP of up to $1 million annually for a period of three years. Seemed like a small price to pay for the muscle.

His trip had three objectives: 1) for the two men to finally meet in person, 2) to consummate the deal they had negotiated, and 3) for Raj to render an idea that would, hopefully, deepen their alliance.

"Welcome to my humble abode!" Jab said, with a blindingly white smile of bleached implants and a wrinkled brow suggesting he absolutely did not think a guy with a name like Roger Magellan would look like a man from the other side of the planet. "Duncan here will take your briefcase," Jab managed to say while managing—barely—to not stare.

They made small talk as they strolled along the paved pathway lined with meticulously tended shrubs, to what Raj assumed was the main house. Other buildings dotted the dozens of acres in the clearing surrounded by a dark forest of loblolly pines.

Jab had a deep southern drawl, a pudgy pizza pie of a face with faint salmon-colored splotches that made Raj want to wince, and straight sandy blond hair parted on one side and curved down and around his forehead like a protractor. Raj knew the type from the many Texans he'd dealt with over the years. Men with round faces often crowned with a cowboy hat as though they were just about to hoist their hefty bodies into the saddle and ride off to wrestle some cattle into submission, and with broad square-ish bodies, large silver belt buckles tilted towards the ground below an oversized belly, a passion for steak, and a not-so-secret desire to shoot anyone claiming to be a vegetarian or a climate advocate. Or a Democrat.

Soon they got comfortable with a couple of shots of Wild Turkey, Raj's on ice, with Abita beer chasers. With one more pour, Jab ushered him to his office, replete with a floor-to-ceiling library that contained few books but multiple taxidermied animals. They offended Raj's Brahmin background, but he wasn't one to let personal beliefs get in the way of advancing his goals.

What also caught Raj's attention was the Harvard diploma, framed with a glazed glass surface large enough to land a large drone, hanging on the wall behind Jab's desk.

"You're a Harvard man?" Raj hoped his surprise didn't show on his face.

"Oh, yes, I earned that after a six-week intensive on-site executive leadership program. It's actually a certification, not a degree. But it's certainly worth the paper it's printed on!"

Raj kept his expressions neutral. "Nice."

Jab went on. "I *am* an Oxford man, though."

Raj raised an eyebrow. "Many of my international partners over the years have been LSE graduates."

Jab gestured to a pair of overly large wingback chairs and Raj took a seat as Jab settled in, giving him a quizzical look. "LSE?"

"London School of Economics."

"London, England?" Jab shook his head. "I meant Oxford, Mississippi. Ole Miss." It figures, Raj thought. "I understand you trace your lineage to one of the original members of the Sons of Liberty?"

"Yes, yes, of course, not Samuel Adams, Paul Revere, John Hancock, not the familiar names ..."

"Who, then, may I ask?"

"Jonathan Tremaine. Mind you, he wasn't one of the big money folks, or connected to English nobility, just a humble silversmith working in Boston, but a full member of the Sons of Liberty."

"Fascinating."

"Yet he did hobnob with the big names of the time. Apprentice to Paul Revere. According to the historical record, they held their secret meetings in a dusty hayloft above a printer's shop."

"And where does the name Jabberwocky originate? It's an unusual one."

"Ha! That coming from one who should talk! My first and middle names are James and Bakke, the latter a Swedish surname which infiltrated the family lineage sometime in the mid-1800s. When I was in high school, it somehow morphed into Jabberwocky, maybe because I used to submit homework in my writing classes that was, well, let's just say, I wasn't in the gifted program."

"Ah, I see."

"I'm guessing Roger Magellan isn't your given name?"

"No, it's Rajamahedron Majundar. Many immigrants Americanize their names when they arrive here."

"Okay," Jab said, "I get it."

"My first name," Raj countered, "just by way of explanation, means royalty or king, and can be traced all the way back to Sanskrit."

"To what? Sand Grit?"

"Sanskrit. It's regarded as the first common language of the human race."

They chatted some about language, Jab conceding the bit about Sanskrit being older than English and both agreeing that although it may have been the first common world language, hopefully English would be the last. Then they got down to brass tacks.

"I've been briefed several times on your 'ask,' if you will, but I must confess, I am somewhat puzzled."

"That's why I'm here," Raj said, earnestly.

"Let me see, now, you are asking that the Bra Men Indian subcontinent heritage be included as 'white' for the purposes of membership and participation in the Sovereign Pact?"

"Exactly. Well, except that it's not Bra Men, it's *Brahmin*."

Jab turned up an eyebrow and smiled, as if to say, okay, whatever you say.

"I meant no personal offense"—Jab looked Raj up and down—"but you are not, uh, exactly, white."

"This is my point! The VSP is comprised of white males who trace their ancestors, or at least their cultural and political philosophy, to the founding fathers of this country. Out of 360 *million* Americans, you represent the elite of the elite."

"Obviously. Go on ..." Jab said, nodding sagely.

"Well, the Brahmins of India are the same. We are the top caste of all Indian society. The most educated. The most revered. Dominant across religion, education, governance, and diplomacy out of a population of 1.4 *billion* people. As the Ashkenazi Hebrews would say, we are the 'chosen ones.' The supreme sect."

"The Nazi what?"

"Ashkenazi, the white Jews who largely ended up in Europe. The other group, Sephardim, remained in the Middle East and Africa."

Jab frowned and his brows formed a deep V pointing down toward his bulbous nose. "Wait, so you're a Jew?"

"No, no!" Raj said, frustrated. "I'm saying that's what they would say, I mean, that like Ashkenazi Jews are the elites of Hebraic society, Brahmins are the supreme caste of Indian society."

"Hebraic?"

"Having to do with the Hebrews." Was this man truly this stupid, Raj wondered even as Jab's dark expression cleared.

"I understand all this, but ... you are still not white."

"What is white, anyway? It's not even really a skin color. As far as pigments go, you could just as easily say pink or rose or even salmon. Bottom line, it's a U.S. Census classification. But the VSP defines itself as an *origin* story for America, not necessarily as skin tone. Imagine what a political bloc you'd have by adding one million Americans descended from Brahmins!

"Bra Men will not replace us!"

"What?" Raj's head snapped back.

Jab chuckled. "Just kidding. It's a joke!"

What the hell, Raj thought.

Jab, still chuckling, asked, "Would most of these Bra Men become members of the VSP?"

"It's *Brahmin* and of course not. But even if we recruited 10 percent of them, the membership in the VSP would expand twenty-fold! Power and politics are all about numbers. I've done the math. The wealth American Brahmins would bring to the table far exceeds the wealth of the potential white nationalists in this country."

"It is true that our ranks include many poor rural individuals who have been fucked by the liberals, socialists, corporatists, globalists, communists, capitalists, environmentalists, and elitists. And, of course, we can't forget the Jews."

That is quite a list of 'ists'!" Raj observed, with a tight smile.

"Well, it's true. That's why white men in the country are so pissed."

"With due respect, you're being disingenuous, Jab. Many are alcoholics, opioid and meth addicts, veterans living off their pensions, farmers toiling for the global agriculture monopolies, factory workers, Walmart clerks, Amazon warehouse workers, and convenience store clerks. Many more of them are on disability or welfare and aren't even working, so they don't even qualify as blue collar. They may decide to support and vote for the same candidates, but they don't come to those decisions from the same place in the political power structure."

"That's because the system has fucked them. But let me ask, these Bra Men, do most of them look like you?"

"If you are asking, is their skin brown like mine, yes, for the most part."

"Hm, well, I'm not sure the optics work, but financially and numerically, I certainly see where you're going with this."

"I am prepared to put some of my personal fortune to work in making this a win-win."

Jab slapped a knee. "Well, I like the sound of that!"

That was encouraging. Raj leaned forward. "Just think, once we get this country fixed up and headed in the new direction, there are millions more like me in India we can recruit. The Brahmins are four percent of the Indian subcontinent population. Forty million! Can you imagine?"

"Well, I'm not sure I like the sound of *that*. Wouldn't that be dye-luting our whiteness?"

"Once again, Jab, don't think of it as color. Think of it as *supremacy*. Think of it as *power*."

Raj launched into a short soliloquy about creating an alliance among the groups of people who claim supremacy within their cultures. "Just imagine the power we'd wield working together: White Anglo-Saxon men in America and Europe, Brahmins in India, Ashkenazi Jews in Israel, the Ainu Japanese, Han Chinamen, Afrikaners in South Africa, Igbo elites in Nigeria, even wealthy light-skinned African-Americans!"

"Well, let's not get carried away," Jab cut in.

"Of course, of course. I don't want to get ahead of myself."

"Well, I'll certainly take this up with our Leadership Council, though I can't say what the final decisions will be." Jab seemed deep into a thought he could not extract himself from. "But, how would we spin this to the rank and file?"

"Scientifically, of course. The most current studies of ethnographers and geneticists show that the majority of Brahmin ancestry comes from Europe and that the bulk of their DNA actually is derived from that side of the geography, not the Asian side."

"Ah, so they could be 'construed' to be 'Caucasian' after all." Jab seemed pleased to have articulated this logic. Then he added, "As you may know, though, our rank and file aren't exactly enamored with the scientific method. Are there any religious connections we can point to? Y'all are Hindis, correct?"

"Hindus, technically."

"Any massive conversions to the Christian faith after arriving in America? Any global Christian televangelist churches gaining major footholds in the homeland? You know, like missionary-converted Christians in Africa, Jews for Jesus? Like in Uganda and how they're standing up against the sin of homosexuality. Hell, even many of the red man tribes have converted to Christianity, or at least some weird Hispano-Catholic version of it."

"I'll be sure to look into that," Raj promised.

"Fantastic," Jab said, motioning for Duncan.

Raj continued. "I cannot stress enough that I and my fellow Brahmins share a passion and insistence that men dominate in all things political, cultural, and financial. The woman's place is, well, you know where the woman's place is ..."

"That is a strong pillar of the argument, but I also like the genetic logic, I'm just not sure about our rank and file ..."

"Just look at this story from a few days ago." Raj handed Jab his phone, after tapping a few times."

Jab read out loud. "Women in a Hindi stronghold community in Idaho's panhandle attacked the home of a married man suspected in multiple sexual assaults. Later, two of the women leaders in the attack were identified, raped by a gang of enraged men, then dragged naked through the town's main street."

Leal looked up. "Whoa! VSP's got key militants off the grid in that patch of Idaho. We should introduce them!"

"We take our rightful place in the natural order of things quite seriously," Raj said, "although it is always a shame to have to resort to violence."

"This is on the scale of lynching! Community justice at work!"

Raj was relieved. He finally seemed to have impressed Jab.

"I'm only bringing this up as one of several pillars in the argument for joining forces. Genetics, man's natural hierarchy within the family, social and physiological superiority, and demographic and financial resources. And quite possibly some overlaps in the area of religion as well, which I will research and get back to you."

"Roger," Jab said as they stood up, and he walked over and put his arm around Raj's shoulder, "you make quite a case. Not air-tight, but I promise to take it up with our Leadership Council. We just need to be assured that our rank and file can get comfortable with this."

"Well, that is the least I could ask for," Raj said, smiling though disappointed. Then he had a thought.

"Jab, did you know that the elite whites of Boston, where your ancestor Jonathan Tremaine was from, used to be called the Boston Brahmins?"

Both of Jab's eyebrows shot up toward his thinning hairline. "Did not! Fascinating."

Always be closing, Raj thought, proud of himself. Always be closing.

"You should look into them."

"Will do. Absolutely. Now let's go consummate our earlier agreement," Jab said.

"Ah, yes, I almost forgot."

Magellan was expecting to be led into a room with a bar so they could toast with champagne in crystal flutes, or clink glasses swirling fine, aged Scotch. Instead, they strolled to the edge of the property where the loblollies, thick as soldiers in formation, provided a shaded canopy of green. They burrowed into the woods about fifty yards, stopped at a thick tree with a ladder going up to what appeared to be a crudely constructed tree house.

They both were huffing when they got to the top and climbed through the trap door on hinges in the floor. Jab pulled out the largest Leatherman multi-tool pocket utility contraption Raj had ever seen.

"Give me your index finger."

"What do you mean?"

"This is how we consummate our deal. Here, I'll go first."

He pulled out the knife blade from the two-dozen options, made an incision in his left index finger, and watched the blood ooze.

"We're going to share blood?"

Jab looked confused. "How else is it done?"

Raj looked at his hand, then at Jab's, and called upon his innermost sense of positivity to persuade himself that if a white supremacist was willing to mix blood with you, then he must certainly think you are white, too. Jab made a corresponding incision in Raj's left index finger and they pressed their two fingers together. Afterwards, Jab gave Raj one of two small undyed cloths and a Band-Aid. They cleaned up, dressed their cuts. Jab escorted Raj back to the mansion.

It would only be a matter of time before Jab would gain the approval of his rank and file, Raj told himself. Which would allow Raj to pivot to the next plank in his overall strategy: Lobbying the U.S. Census Bureau to define Indian Brahmins as white. Indian subcontinent citizens were fighting for a separate designation, just like the Arab-Americans had recently received. He didn't want to see his Brahmins lumped in and lost with the rest of those brown people.

CHAPTER 25

FREEDOM IS …

B radley designed the last session of the second day as informal "conversation" on the three aspects of freedom represented by the institutions on the primary panel: Freedom of expression as represented by HOMI-G, protection of American liberty as represented by the Missile Museum, and the rights of the environment, championed by Tomahawk Hill.

Once he got the session kicked off and the discussion got rolling, he texted Victor under the table.

Trust you've come to your senses re: dick enlargement?

Still thinking on it.

I'm up to 15, BTW.

Legit?

As far as my memory can ascertain.

Hey, did you know Rachel once

broke into that Primates Festival?

Bradley blinked at that. *That's outta left field. No way.*

Way.

How did you find that out?

I'm with her now!

You're in the city?

Left Florida yesterday.

Man, you are as predictable as a daily sunrise.

Wouldn't it figure? Victor runs straight to Rachel when facing women problems.

Miami-New York, baby. Dozens of nonstops a day. Better than the Wash D.C.–Tel Aviv shuttle, according to Rachel!

Duh!

I mean, I'm not at her place. She doesn't allow that. We're at a hotel called On the Avenue, 70s off Amsterdam, weird because it's not on an avenue.

Jealous. Not of Rachel and you. Of Manhattan and you.

She invited me up. After I told her about Jia.

What, do you two still see in each other?

It's complicated.

Sex?

Not since college.

He glanced again at his screen.

She wants to know if you'd consider testifying for #VeeToo in a lawsuit against Tino Lamborghini?

Gut punch! He wasn't touching that with a 10-foot pole. Last thing he wanted was to be cross-examined in a courtroom about his, or anyone else's, behavior 45 years ago. Given today's standards, Tino had probably date-raped a few women. What healthy hetero male *wasn't* in a few questionable situations back in the day? He was embarrassed to think how much he had envied Tino back in college.

He glanced up to make sure no one was paying attention to him texting under the table. Azul was speaking.

"… and so we must consider artifacts hoarded in any museum after being taken from places and civilizations around the globe as archetypes of the global power structure representing their dominant narratives. What is more, Conrad Bolton makes his money exploiting the burgeoning nationalistic tendencies of indigenous populations by playing on the sentimental value of their nations' historic currencies. He appropriates the language. He rapes the economies. And then he expropriates their artifacts!"

Geez, what a downer. Azul seemed like such a happy-go-lucky guy, Bradley thought. He'd loved HOMI-G and looking at and listening to the instruments on display. Wouldn't be much of a museum if you could only display stuff from your own backyard. Azul was almost yelling now.

"Just yesterday evening, in fact, I learn that the generous Freedom Center stipend I was to be paid for participating in this colloquium must be transferred to the museum's general funds! I don't think it is appropriate to learn something like this while you are already at the colloquium and when the museum is the brainchild of a billionaire! This is just more expropriation and exploitation!"

Gail jumped in then. "Talk about exploitation, I'm dying! Got that? I'm dying. Just putting it out there. Again. From years working in an underground bunker as a Cold War warrior. Your space to argue about pronouns? Because of people like me. I'll be dead before anyone wins that battle. Two of my Missileer compatriots are already dead. And what is the Air Force doing to help us? Not a goddamn thing. Studying the issue. Since 1988. Delaying the studies. Requesting money for more studies, even though the link was established between the materials we handled, the air we breathed deep underground in an air-tight space, and the illnesses plaguing us. Why should I give a shit what the government thinks anymore?"

Well, Bradley thought, this is going south—and getting interesting.

Gail, on a roll now, went on. "While the rest of the country was having orgies, injecting porno and gratuitous violence into mainstream movies, protesting against the Vietnam war, threatening to impeach Richard Nixon, experimenting with sex purely as carnal pleasure, communal living, and generally dropping out, tuning out, hanging out, what were we doing? Well! The sexual revolution didn't end at the missile facility's fence line. The work wasn't just monotonous. There wasn't much of it. Like, four hours out of a twelve-hour shift. That's eight hours a shift of downtime. What do you think we did? We brought liquor in. We smoked joints. We snuck friends in. We had contests to see who could fuck in the weirdest locations. Tantalizing possibilities in an isolated nine-story missile silo! They even had bunk beds and a kitchen area if we wanted to get comfortable. Emergency showers if you wanted to clean up afterwards. Even a small room we set up as a theater to watch porn, all the while waiting for the command to blow the earth to smithereens."

Talk about keeping two balls in the air at the same time, Bradley mused.

"Look," Gail said, hurriedly queuing up her slide show again. She picked up the laser pointer. "See that location right there? That's a football field away from the control and communications room." She changed slides. "You could climb up here into this missile guidance device cubby hole, get—or give—a blowjob, have your lunch, or take a nap."

Speaking of tight spaces and tall structures, Bradley wondered, had he counted that woman he almost fucked in the World Trade Tower elevator?

"And it wasn't just us grunts, either. The place wasn't crawling with security cameras like it would be today. Let's just say if you were on site, you were likely involved in the festivities."

"I'm shocked, *shocked* to hear this is what was going on in our defense facilities!" Dr. Hintz called out.

Audience member: "Surely your superiors sent out unannounced oversight crews? Spot inspections?"

"Eh, we were always aware of those 'surprise' inspections ahead of time."

Rolex Williams muttered loudly to the person next to him. "Lordy, lordy. Instead of peace through strength, they were all lathered up getting *a piece* through strength."

Gail heard him and pointed. "Ha! Like the Bible says, an idle mind is the devil's playground."

"This was routine behavior?" an audience member asked. "We all know Missileers weren't perfect human beings—no one is perfect—but you're telling us this was routine?"

"Well, it wasn't a party *every* day." She smirked. "But I wouldn't be surprised if I found a used rubber or two in some dark corner of that death chamber even today."

Dr. Plemmons stood and yelled, "TMI, TMI!"

Gail barked out a laugh. "From the one who said it was okay to say penis and vagina?"

"Those are official terms of human biology."

"These are unofficial terms of military war fighting crews." Gail went on. "No one is immune from temptation, whether of the flesh or of the pocketbook. Even Mr. Maverick himself, our illustrious former Arizona senator, may he rest in peace, retracted his threat of a Congressional investigative committee for an extra $300 million in defense authorizations."

Bradley noticed that Gail was breathing heavily, like she couldn't get enough air. Maybe it was all the attention. He looked out over the room. Everyone was laser-focused on her—except one guy in the last row looking down, busy with his phone.

"What does all this have to do with freedom anyway?" asked Dr. Zhou.

Gail looked at her like she wished she was packing her pistol. Then her expression changed, like the screen of her face went dark while her mind crashed.

"Pretty hard to think about freedom while you're waiting for orders to detonate the planet." Now her voice was subdued.

Zhou replied, "I get that, the freedom of the nation—of the entire world—resting on your shoulders."

"That's the thing, ma'am," Gail murmured, "It had a whole lot less to do with freedom and a whole lot more to do with faith."

"Faith?" Someone else asked.

"Faith that we would never receive the command. Faith that we would never have to pull the trigger. It was psychological warfare, fought through an elaborate network of highly engineered, very expensive missile launch sites. *Collective* psychological warfare. The *antithesis* of freedom. Missileers were Target Alpha of the psyops. They don't call it MAD just because it was 'Mutually Assured Destruction' against our enemies abroad. It was a war against all of us. Against humanity. Against Americans." Now Gail was almost whispering. "The nation's collective mental health was the price of freedom."

Dr. Plemmons shook her head. "My God, that's almost torture! Certainly inhumane."

"Tell me about it," Gail murmured.

The audience was still.

Gail looked up at the ceiling, then out the windows.

"Now, I will calmly wait for the Black Hawks to come take me away."

CHAPTER 26

CONSIDER THE GECKO

Bradley wanted to at least put his arm on Gail's shoulder as he passed her on the way to the podium, but what modern protocol would he be breaking?

"Okay, that was revelatory, wasn't it? What's in those energy vortexes around here, anyway?" He laughed, but the audience remained inert.

"In any case, thank you, Gail, for that blisteringly honest assessment of 'peace,' spelled as you wish, through strength." He paused, as if a moment of silence. "Ashera," he said, "come up and tell us about rights of the nonhuman inhabitants of the Hill."

Ashera did put her arm around Gail, which led to an awkward half-embrace. Why is she able to do that and not me? Bradley wondered.

"Let's give Gail another round of applause," Ashera began. "And yes, thank you for your sacrifice!"

The audience clapped heartily, a few gave her a standing ovation. The rest of the audience then stood, too, some reluctantly. The guy who had been packing his pistol earlier stood ramrod straight and saluted as if listening to "The Star-Spangled Banner" at a season opener before the president threw out the first pitch.

The guy saluting said, "Fuck that land acknowledgement shit! We should have a military service proclamation!"

"Hey!" Gail yelled, standing halfway. "I appreciate the sentiment, but don't disrespect my co-panelist's Native heritage."

The guy sat down hard like his first-grade teacher had just scolded him.

Ashera beamed at Gail. "I think all of us in this room have a better idea of the true cost of our collective freedom, however you define it. We're not even talking about the many veteran suicides for lack of mental health resources."

"Oh boy, that's a whole other can of worms," Gail said, gesturing with an outflung arm that caused Azul to duck.

Bradley added, "In my world, this is what we would call an 'externality,' the cost of an unintended consequence that is not accounted for in the economics."

Gail burst out laughing. "Figures there's a five-dollar word for it."

"Frankly, it's embarrassing blathering on about the rights of rodents and other creatures," Ashera said, "after realizing that the woman sitting beside me is dying from physiological degradation caused by exposure to nuclear weapons materials and the psychological trauma of this absurdity called MAD."

Dr. Hintz wasn't buying it: "Don't get so emotional and weepy. Every job involves occupational hazards."

Gail stood up and leaned on her arms, her hands against the dais table: "Emotional and weepy? You come talk to me after this thing is over."

Ashera: "I'm sorry, Dr. Hintz, but that is ludicrous and unreasonable. What Gail and her fellow Missileers experienced was far from 'normal occupational hazards.'" She used air quotes.

"This isn't a Pixar movie with cartoony villains and heroic good guys. But I take *your* point to make *my* point. Whether someone works at a missile site, a petrochemical complex, or on a trash truck, workers do unsavory jobs so the rest of don't have to. For a hot minute during COVID, we lauded these folks as "essential workers,' but only for as long as the rest of us were 'impeded' in our normal lives. They make us free, or free-*er*, and yet we don't care for them as if they are protecting our freedom to *not* do things we don't like and *to* do things we do—like buy shit we don't need and, uh, ruminate on the philosophy of freedom without fear of being arrested by Gestapo government goons or burned at the stake by religious thought police."

Dr. Plemmons stood and pointed at Ashera. "You go, girl!"

Ashera went on. "People ask me if I'm a vegan for health reasons. The answer is no. Is it because I'm protesting Big Ag? I am, but no. Really, it's because I love animals. I love all animals, not just the ones you can see at the zoo or own as a pet. I care deeply about biodiversity and healthy ecosystems and a sustainable planet. Maybe that sounds childish to some. But I prefer to lay the intellectual and scientific groundwork for conferring the same rights enjoyed by humans onto the other sentient beings with whom we share this planet, rather than pave over our freedoms with intellectual groundwork equivalent to white supremacy."

Ashera made the V sign with her first two fingers, pointed them at her eyes, then at Dr. Hintz.

"I'm looking at you!"

Dr. Hintz shook his head in a pitying gesture. "You can't possibly be serious. Like your cactuses and geckos are equal to humans?"

"Exactly like cactuses and geckos," Ashera shot back. "Think back over the centuries. Who didn't have rights and freedom? Who didn't have justice? Slaves brought over from Africa, child laborers, women, Jews, the Irish, you know, everyday run-of-the-mill human beings. Our dogs and cats are treated better today than most human beings have been throughout history. As Dr. Martin Luther King said, 'The arc of the moral universe is long, but it bends towards justice.' And I intend to bend it toward justice for all the 'cactuses and geckos' with whom we share this bountiful planet."

"Word!" shouted Rolex, clapping loudly from his seat in the middle of the room.

Ashera paused, lowered her voice. "It just bends so damn slowly. With human-induced climate change, we risk a sixth mass extinction event that will change the nature of what it means to be alive in the world. The cactuses and geckos you scoff at, Dr. Hintz—and every other species—will suffer alongside us humans even though they are in no way responsible for their demise. We are. You. Me. Everyone in this room is responsible."

Okay, Bradley thought, Ashera just completed the triad of depression for the day.

She continued. "Scientists have already confirmed that 80 percent of living species have already gone extinct. Climate disruption is causing humans and animals to migrate to unfamiliar habitats. Thirty years ago, no one saw armadillos as far north as northern Arkansas. Now you see dead ones along the highway in central Illinois.

Dr. Hintz muttered just loud enough for half the room to hear him. "Thirty years ago, you didn't see Guatemalans in Idaho, either."

Ashera ignored him. "The University has cut funding for studying the survivability of the saguaro cactus on Tomahawk Hill just when everyone who studies them confirms their numbers are shrinking fast. Lack of rainfall, invasive buffelgrass, rising temperatures leading to more frequent, hotter fires that spread more quickly. It's all connected."

She paused again, took a deep breath. "What are all of these living things missing? A robust legal framework to protect their rights and freedoms as living entities. Scientific studies which reveal just how much of an impact human beings are making in the new age we'd like to call the Anthropocene to support such a framework." She pounded the dais. "I want anthropocentric models of contemporaneous freedoms for *all* living things!"

Dr. Hintz now stood at the mic in the center aisle, sneering. "For God's sake, now we're dismantling the entire Darwinian explanation of life! This is beyond socialism ..."

Ashera broke in. "On the contrary, Dr. Hintz, now we are *embracing* the entire Darwinian explanation of life. We are all animals. All species subject to the same biological rules. But only one species believes itself to be so special, so privileged, as to determine the fate of *all* others."

She looked down at her hands. Cleared her throat. "Azul learned the unhappy news about his stipend from participating in this colloquium is being clawed back to the museum itself. That's unfair and exploitative. But I just learned this morning, in a text from a close colleague, that the University didn't acquire Tomahawk Hill to protect it. It acquired it to use the valuation of the land as collateral for loans to cover budget shortfalls. They are signing away one of the most valuable parcels of land in Southern Arizona because some accountant who didn't understand how to monitor their software fucked up the books. Score one for incompetent white men and drunken frat bros and score a big fat zero for the cactuses and the geckos and the Tohono O'odom and their archeological relics."

"By the way," she added, "the University will be none too happy with me for disclosing this. You know what? I don't care!"

She paused, looked out at the audience.

"You know what's really sad? Of the dozens of proposals I've submitted for research funding to study the geckos, guess who responds most positively?"

The audience looked frazzled and puzzled.

"Here's a hint." Ashera imitated an Australian accent. "Aye, mate, bundle your home and auto insurance."

An audience member in the back called out, "Progressive!"

Another audience member yelled, "That's LiMu!"

"No, that's Liberty Mutual's," a third audience member said, with a huff. "It's Geico!"

"Geico," Ashera repeated with a heavy sigh. "That's right, an insurance company wants to sponsor research about the gecko for branding purposes." Ashera paused again and put her head down on the podium, then lifted it back towards the mic. "Can you believe it? Next thing you know, the University will cut a deal with them to insure all the luxury homes they'll end up building on the Hill."

Bradley couldn't resist texting Victor.

Get this. Research about geckos surviving human development in the desert is being sponsored by Geico!

You gotta be ... even you couldn't make that one up.

How's Rachel?

She thinks you need to give up porn cold turkey. It's poisoned your mind.

Shit, you didn't ...

I used that 'just asking for a friend' line.

"Fucker, you only have one friend!"

Ashera was now sniffling. "Doesn't anyone in this room get it? We are killing off whole species. The temperature of the water off the coast of Florida right now, *right now*, no longer qualifies as an 'incremental change.' It's a step change, enough to kill off much of the marine life around the coastlines, which then kills off the larger fish and species who feed on off the marine life. Our 'freedom' is killing the planet! There will be 2.5 billion *more* people on this planet in two generations. Every one of them will want the lifestyle that you have and need the energy consumption that feeds that lifestyle. Refugees are trying to get into this country because their countries are already ravaged by climate change ... aw, hell, why am I talking?"

Ashera's sniffles turned into gushes. "The human race is fucked!" She lay her head on the podium, and put her hand over the mic. Most of the audience stayed glued to their seats, like pedestrians passing a body on the sidewalk writhing in pain.

Bradley thought he had seen everything from the podium in his career, except maybe someone get shot. Most surprising was to see someone burst into tears.

Gail struggled up from her seat at the dais, went to Ashera, and put her left arm around her shoulders. "You need to be anywhere but here."

She pulled a mic from the dais toward her. "I can't say I agree with much of what the lady just told you, but I certainly know what it is like to go home every night having it inculcated into you that the entire human race is fucked and you are responsible for unfucking it!"

From the back, Dr. Peggy Zabel lamented loudly, "We've broken the cycle of life."

CHAPTER 27

LET FREEDOM RING

Azul and Bradley were left on the dais, shellshocked. One panelist bawling, another using an academic colloquium like a Catholic confessional, the third pissed that he isn't getting his stipend. The audience, a herd of deer in the headlights of a parking lot full of trucks equipped with gun racks and all-terrain tires.

It was close to time to break for the evening. Maybe everyone would return in the morning with a clearer head. Before that, Bradley needed to wrap this shit show up. And fill half an hour.

He began hesitantly. "Uh, one thread I could pull from our conversation today is the idea of the spectrum, the gradation, between, say, black and white."

It was lame, he admitted, but it was something. He blundered on.

"After all, what is this current convention of declaring pronouns but a way to indicate where on the gender spectrum one resides? Science clearly accounts for that, but much of the public doesn't understand the science and isn't inclined to do the work to do so. So we're left with pronouns to do the trick, to act as a signal to everyone else that, here I am and this is how I identify myself. Maybe that's not so bad. And what is ethnographic DNA analysis but proof that each of us resides at our own unique place on the genetic spectrum with respect to race and ethnicity? Science accounts for that too."

He slogged on amidst the blank faces in the audience. "Let's face it. White Americans think of Barack Obama as our first Black president. But many African Americans consider him merely a white president who happens to have a father from Kenya. On a personal note, I have a friend in New York City, as lily-white a WASP as they come ..."

Dr. Hintz looked around the room, then yelled, "How come none of you complain about use of the slur WASP?"

Ignoring him, Bradley continued. "She showed me a photo of her great-great-grandfather who certainly looked African American. She pointed to her own broad nose and the way her own nostrils flared just like the man in the photo. 'How about that?' she said. 'My DNA test proves it. West Africa.' Aren't most of us products of some sort of miscegenation? Mutts of some kind? Hybrids with varying strains of genetic material—"

"Oh my God, that's so vituperative!" yelled Dr. Plemmons.

"Calm down. It just means interracial marriage," someone else said in a huff.

Rolex Williams butted in. "Laced with repulsive racist overtones, though."

"Well, at least it's not a dog whistle."

"It's a dog megaphone!" someone else shouted.

Azul pulled a table mic toward him. "Miscegenation. What a word. You must admit, it was one of the funniest lines in *O Brother, Where Art Thou?*"

Wow, Bradley thought, Azul got a kick out of *that* movie?

Azul imitated, with his accent, Homer Stokes from the movie. "I suspect some miscegenation in their heritage. How else you goin' explain it?"

Bradley turned a wide-eyed expression on Azul, who shrugged his shoulders and whispered, "It was a staple of the university film schedule."

His band is named Sambo and he loves *O Brother*.

D. Zhou spoke up. "Why do those people in Hollywood still think it's okay to malign under-resourced white people in the South?"

Dr. Hintz responded. "Because they don't have a National Association for the Advancement of Appalachians protecting them."

Dr. Plemmons turned to glare at Zhou. "Just who are you referring to when you say 'those people'?"

Bradley stammered: "Come on, comedy is supposed to lampoon and exaggerate racist situations and stereotypes of all kinds to help us learn from them."

Someone in a middle row called out, "When do you think you'll see a Hollywood movie about three Jewish settlers breaking out of prison and trying to save a Palestinian from losing his home and his olive trees?

Someone at the back responded with, "When the original Palestinian lands are completely absorbed into Israel. Then it will no longer be a threat."

Someone else called out, "*Schitt's Creek* is about a Jewish family who lost everything and rebuilt themselves in a small Midwestern town that they bought."

Dr. Zhou turned and said, "That was yet another parable about how Jews prevail even after they lose everything."

Dr. Hintz shook his head. "My point is, 'those Hollywood types' don't make movies depicting their people as bad guys. They target every other group, though. Especially Christians."

"Who do you mean, those 'types?'" Dr. Plemmons glared at Dr. Hintz.

"You know who I mean," Hintz retorted.

Rolex echoed the sentiment. "Like those Blaxploitation movies of the 1970s."

"Don't get me started on how women are treated in film," Dr. Plemmons said.

Rolex extended his arm to fist bump Plemmons who first regarded it like an alien entity, then went right ahead and clashed knuckles.

"Right on?!" Rolex said. "Nothing changes until the subgroup seizes power from the dominant class."

"Right! That's absolutely right." Another voice. "Power is never conferred. It has to be seized."

Bradley countered, "Well, you could say it has to be earned too."

"According to who? Who decides what behavior 'earns' power? Those who already have the power?"

Dr. Tseitlinsky, who had been quiet for most of the conference, spoke up. "Through revolution! Freedoms are granted by those who have the power to protect themselves."

Oh wow, Bradly thought, that's the professor who coyly mentioned he might have some things to say during the Free Will session.

Rolex Williams pumped his fist in the air. "Smash the patriarchy! Black Lives Matter!"

Dr. MacGruffin, the professor who would soon be talking on micro-freedoms, added: "Blue lives matter too!"

Bradley tried to stop that train wreck of black vs blue before it left the station. He held his hands up to quiet the crowd. "Look, we all know that genetically, identity really is a fluid thing. There's now evidence that ecosystems cooperate to enhance survival—from the tallest trees to the decaying matter in the soil. We've begun the process of protecting ecosystems through our national parks, forests, and monuments. Wouldn't the next step, the next 'gradation'"—he made air quotes around the word—"be a legal declaration of rights of some sort?"

The audience member who saluted Gail stood and put his hand over his heart. "Save our veterans first!"

Bradley looked out at the audience and exhaled demonstrably, then looked at the alert on his phone.

"Okay," he said, with renewed spirit, "I've just gotten a text from the hotel. For those wanting cocktails before dinner, they are ready for us at the bar. We'll reconvene tomorrow morning, later than usual, say 10 a.m. to give all of you time to catch up with your work back home."

In a flash, Bradley watched an Asian-looking guy in the back, who had been texting furiously most of the day, bolt from his chair and rush to the exit, leaving a backpack. Dr. Hintz saw the guy's sudden flight too.

"That could be a bomb!" Hintz dashed for the exit, too. Everyone else froze in place for a moment, then most of the audience stampeded after him. The gun-wielding Gail-saluting man with the firearm pulled it out and pointed it at the pack.

"Wait!" Bradley yelled, wishing that Gail was still in the room. She'd know what to do.

"Shooting at a possible IED might not be the—" yelled Dr. MacGuffin, as he bolted past the shooter.

The trigger clicked.

"Damn, I left the chamber empty!"

Rolex stepped up beside Bradley. "That dude's been sitting there most of the day. I talked to him at the break. He seems okay."

"Let's not take unnecessary risks, though," Bradley said, hurrying from the dais to the doors, clapping Rolex on the back on the way. He made a beeline for the front desk.

"I've been alerted!" Nascha yelled at Bradley, before he spoke.

She'd called the Yavapai head of security, Chief Clever Hawk.

"We seem to have a situation here, CH, an attendee in the conference room has left a backpack unattended."

"So?"

"Someone's gotta check it out, right? Otherwise, these Freedom folks aren't likely to go back into the room."

"I'm down at the casino, with the Chief. I doubt he will authorize me to make the drive north."

She sighed. "Figures. Okay, I'll deal with it." She'd send Rodrigo in to check it out, but then remembered he'd already left for the day. *Aw, hell, I gotta do every freaking thing myself.*

She thought for a moment, then went to the pool to get the skimmer screen, the longest implement she could think to obtain quickly, headed to the meeting room, poked at the backpack carefully, her body outside the room and around the other side of the door. If something detonated, maybe it would only take off her hand or her arm. She kept poking and prodding, until she convinced herself the pack was filled with a bunch of heavy books. With trepidation, she walked to it, located the zipper with her hands, then looked away muttering some version of last rites, and pulled the talon open. She peeked, and confirmed her suspicion.

Some minutes later, every Freedom attendee's room phone lit up red with a message that the threat had been a false alarm.

CHAPTER 28

DR. WASHINGTON CONFRONTS BRADLEY

The next morning, before Bradley could get a fork full of scrambled eggs into his mouth at breakfast, his phone vibrated. A text from Dr. Washington.

Urgent! Call me ASAP. 520-FRE-EDOM.

Bradley texted back.

Aren't you supposed to be here?

I'm dealing with a little situation. Maybe you've heard ...

Washington could wait until he finished his breakfast. He was still trying to reconstruct how the first part of yesterday's sessions went from ethnic DNA analysis to eugenics, then transmogrified from general perspectives on freedom from three well-regarded Arizona institutions into personal confessionals and venomous diatribes against those same institutions, closing with a food fight about language and nefarious connotations. Oh, and a bomb scare to boot.

He wolfed down the rest of his eggs and sausage, gulped his juice, picked up his large to-go cup of coffee, then gestured an "excuse me" with the wave of his napkin to the others at the table, and went outside past the registration area to the parking lot. Thunderstorms were threatening again. It was a few degrees cooler, but still horribly uncomfortable. He stood in the shadow of "Big Brother."

He noticed the lady from the Cave Creek ladies, who had chatted him up at the bar, approaching.

"Hello again," Bradley offered.

"Ugh, don't even look at me!" She raised her arm, pretending to shield her face beneath a wide, floppy cream-colored, Bridgewater hat.

He thought of his favorite children's picture book, *Go Dog Go!*, and the lady dog and her fancy hat.

"Aw, now, now, rough night? I do like your hat!"

"Why, thank you! I was going to have a cup of coffee delivered, but that seemed decadent ... even for me. And I had to get out of bed eventually." She laughed. "By the way, I'm sure I was not cordial enough to properly introduce myself at the bar. Catherine Keenan."

"Bradley Maniopolos." He extended his hand with a smile. She really did look like Jstacuntrygalxoxo Instababe.

"How long is your group staying here?" she asked. "I can't remember what you told me your meeting is about. Hell, I can't remember my ex-husband's name right about now."

Ex-husband, Bradley took note. "Officially, we're finished late Friday morning."

"Well, we'll be here through Sunday. Hope your conference is successful."

She turned back and smiled at him as she walked away. "Goodbye!"

If ever there was a sign that a woman was interested, that was it, he thought. It was true in *Go Dog Go*. It had been true since. And he did like her hat!

She was a cute number even without her face on. He watched her saunter into the lobby. Nice ass too. She'd look divine swinging a driver in a mini-skirt at a Top Golf party. Her boobs seemed a bit too immobile, though. He'd never fondled fake boobs.

Then he remembered Dr. Washington, dialed the number and waited for him to pick up. "Good afternoon, Kerry."

"What in the everlasting fuck is going on up there?" Washington shot back.

"Not even a proper greeting?" Bradley feigned being miffed. "I might ask the same of you. What the hell is going on down there with your down there? I mean, you know, in Tucson?"

"That's a separate matter. I'm dealing with it."

Right, Bradley thought. How the hell do you deal with a lawsuit detailing a dyke dildo debacle?

"Your colloquium up here has been in good hands, rest assured."

"Really? Then explain why I've got the Corporate Crisis Communications lady from the Bolton Foundation up my ass, the community college president *and* the University provost, the chancellor *and* the Board of Regents nipping at my heels, not to mention the fucking Brigadier General at Bagman Air Force base on line three. Hell, even the Department of the Interior's National Register of Historic places has called in—"

"Guess you didn't hear about the bomb threat we faced yesterday."

"What? And that's not even counting the #VeeToo women harassing me at every turn and this counter-protest group, slugs called the Velvet Sovereign Pact, shouting slogans like 'Jews will not replace us, Women will not displace us, Government will not deface us.'"

"#VeeToo? Velvet Sovereign Pact? Who are they?"

"One's a Femi-Nazi group. The other, best as I can figure, are white supremacists."

"Wow, you're a popular guy!"

"No shit. Those University officials *never* talk to us community college types."

"I get that."

"They're all asking what the hell is going down? at my conference in Sedona."

"What the hell are they doing down there in Tucson then? Why don't they come up and see for themselves that we're having penetrating conversations challenging preconceived notions, building bridges between traditionally entrenched interest groups and often oppositional academic disciplines."

Wow. That sounded impressive even to Bradley's jaded ears.

"I can't yet," Washington said. "The protesters are after me. The institutions are livid about what's being aired during the sessions."

"Why would white supremacists be protesting your Celebri-Dong?"

"Damned if I know."

"Wait. How do those officials know what's being discussed?"

"In case you are unfamiliar with how modern communications works, it's all over X and Threads, Instagram, Tik Tok, and whatever the hell else people use these days."

"Someone's posting about what's being talked about here?"

"Everyone's posting about what's being talked about there."

Shit. Bradley couldn't remember a conference where anyone thought the content was compelling enough to post on Twitter. And what was Threads? Wasn't Tik Tok for teenyboppers doing dance numbers for their friends?

"Why would anyone care? For that matter, why would anyone care if a former athlete had his penis replicated for sales as a dildo, or vibrator, or whatever the hell ..."

"This has Avi Kauffman's fingerprints all over it."

"Abbie Hoffman? I thought he was dead."

"Avi Kauffman. He launched a counter-offensive think tank at the University called the Collective for the Liberation of Unfreedoms and Extant Inequities, affectionately known as CLUED-IN. Or at least that's what it used to be. They changed the name, to what I don't recall. They have so little funding, they're no real threat. But Avi can be a thorn in your side when he's wearing his Fidel Castro private-label camo fatigues, figuratively that is."

"Oh, you mean against the Freedom Center. There's an Unfreedom Center?"

"Yes."

"What does Unfreedom have to do with white supremacy?"

"Nothing that I can tell. I think the VSP was dispatched to disrupt the #VeeToo group, standard counter-programming tactics."

"And VSP stands for Velvet Sovereign Pact? They sound like folks who might be interested in massaging a celebrity dong." Bradley felt his grin expand to a smile. He continued. "Who dispatched them?"

"Hell, I don't know."

He watched Catherine walk past him again, playfully saluted her, shrugged his shoulders and pointed at this phone. He mouthed the words, "Hello again!"

God, all he wanted to do right now was follow her down the landing, towards the golf course, wiggle their toes in the ultra-dwarf Bermuda grass, and find a place to nestle in a shaded crevice of those blazing rocks, make out, lift her blouse, find out just how firm a set of fake boobs might feel slathered in a mixture of olive oil and the firebrick mud from their aborted hike.

Kerry was yelling now. "Are you still there!?"

"Yeah, uh, give me the ten-second elevator pitch on CLUED-IN, just in case your buddy Avi shows up."

"It operates in a similar philosophical framework as Repa-rations, DEI, and Anti-Racist modalities, but that's not import-ant." Washington continued. "The real threat is that the Bagman Brigadier General wants to know how so much top-secret infor-mation about the Missileers program leaked out. The Board of Regents wants to know who divulged the not-yet-made-public strategic intent behind the acquisition of Tomahawk Hill. And

Bolton's corporate communications wants to know who's trashing the founder's pet philanthropic project. Someone is accusing HOMI-G of pilfering cultural artifacts?"

"Well, no offense, Kerry, but why did you insist on a presentation on eugenics? Maybe that's what set them all off."

"Jesus," Washington let out a long sigh. "Why does ethnographic DNA analysis always lead people back to eugenics?"

"Because no one wants to see whole races of people declared scientifically inferior? Or superior?"

"Look, I'm paying you to keep the discussion in that room within the boundaries of academic discourse, not personal diatribes. Big guns are coming after us and they're pissed."

"Hey, I was hired to be a facilitator, not a content referee!"

"Just keep it under control!"

Fuck you, Bradley said to the phone after he cut the call.

As he passed the registration desk, Nascha emerged from her office and came around the counter. "Good morning, Mr. Maniopolos, a guest left a note for you." She handed him a piece of folded paper.

"Geez, I hope it's not a speaker canceling. I had to fill up an extra 30 minutes yesterday. It's a tough crowd in there."

"The guest is not one of your group."

"Okay, thank you!"

He shoved it in his pocket and proceeded to his room. He had fifteen minutes before the morning session would begin. He needed some quality minutes to prep for the next session, and didn't want to be interrupted. First, he needed to update Victor.

Hey, I'm up to 18.

Eighteen what?

Women.

Oh, right.

Oh, suddenly you don't give a shit? How's Manhattan?

Would you believe, Rachel still pals around with that guy she dumped me for back in college.

The protagonist in the Penis Papers?

You had to remind me.

The lover of my lover is my enemy. Or something.

She mentioned something about 'unfinished business' with you."

Oh shit. Bradley thought. She's told him.

No idea what that's about.

How's the conference? And the state of American freedom?

It's a mess. More like quarantining the truth.

Number 18 or thereabouts.

Suddenly, it occurred to him every woman he had had sex with so far had been white. Well, except for that Hispanic chick, around number 13.

So, who was she? Number 18?

Just a girl at work. Remember that engineering company I worked for in the World Trade Center?

Just a girl at work?

There were a few of them. Some make-out sessions, second, third base stuff ...

Oh wait, he forgot about Quiana! She must be number 19 or 20.

OK, hey, gotta run. Rachel's giving me the evil eye.

Tell her hi. Keep your mouth shut about my problem.

What are you worried about, anyway? Wasn't it you who said people should talk more frequently and honestly about masturbation?

I said that?

Like, all the time.

Do as I do, not as I say.

Really, what's the problem?

You ever read Rachel's books?

No. I mean, maybe the title, back jacket. I have a vague sense of what they're about.

For fuck's sake. Ok, I'm outta here.

CHAPTER 29

THE PRIMATES FESTIVAL

Keshawn "Kerry" Washington remembered a long walk down a landscaped path lined with tall trees and fragrant flowering bushes. They smelled fine, like walking through the fragrances of the perfume aisle at a department store. Along with the other first-timers, he'd snorted a ton of coke so every sense was heightened as he sucked in a lungful of scented air. Others were tripping on psychedelics. He'd never been so amped up in his life.

When they reached a clearing with flagstone pavers, he stopped and looked up to see a tall masonry structure built smack in the middle and topped on each side with the largest TV screen Kerry had ever seen. Even in Vegas. The only light in the clearing came from the TVs. Each screen played scenes from porn movies with the sound—the *oohs* and *ahhs* and fuck me now babys—emanating from speakers like mood music. Scattered around them were sex toy dolls which, in Kerry's coked-up brain, looked surprisingly life-like. Attractive even. Desirable.

He watched one of the screens for a few minutes, along with the other men, before realizing the movie was not a continuous story line, but clips strung together, like a highlights reel. As an athlete, Kerry was plenty familiar with highlight reels and, as a man, he was plenty familiar with porn. In fact, he was an ardent fan, but some of these scenes were over-the-top orgies, some even with animals. He blinked. Did he really just see a hot dog slipping from a woman's crotch to attract that German shepherd? What the fuck? Beyond disgusting.

Yet he was hard as fucking rebar. He'd forgotten how coke could make your cock feel like a rocket ship waiting for the final countdown.

The guy next to him, the one who'd been in front of him on the path, looked up at the screens and over at the dolls, said "What the fuck," and whipped out his pecker and began to stroke. Others did the same.

Someone, he couldn't remember who, had told them that the idea was to show women who was boss and prove men were the dominant sex by masturbating to the point close to ejaculation, then pointing you rod towards the life-like female sex toys and spilling your seed onto them, or close to them, or imagine that you were spraying them with it. Or something. It was all hazy. But the guy beside him was doing it, so he did it too.

A few minutes later, he did it again.

Not sure if this was an initiation ritual or what, they stood around breathing heavily with their spent cocks hanging out, their pants dangling at their feet until someone called out, "Make way for the chiefs!"

Kerry managed to get his pants up as far as his knees when Raj, the man whose name and photo was on the invitation he'd received and whom he'd met on the first day of festivities, marched into the clearing with his entourage. Suddenly, as if a strong wind had kicked up, four dark somethings burst from the darkness of the surrounding bushes as if they had been lying in wait for the right moment of siege. Baboons! Or people in baboon costumes, maybe. They whooped and hollered and ran around and through the gathered initiates, taunting them, swiping at their limp dicks, pushing and shoving until one or two men toppled over, pants still around their ankles.

It probably only lasted a minute before the intruders fled back into the dark woods, and Raj was calmly reassuring the men that security would have them collared in minutes. Instead of worrying about the intrusion, it only added to the mystique and Kerry felt himself getting hard again.

Reflecting the next day on the fact that he'd jerked off—multiple times—in front of perfect strangers, he understood the bonding ritual for what it was. Just something guys did. No big deal.

Later, one of the guys he had gotten friendly with during the festival offered him a business proposition. He would be paid $50,000 if he allowed a prosthetic company to make a mold of his erect penis. He had been assured that the customers for such a product were largely returning veterans whose equipment didn't work like it was supposed to anymore because of injuries, PTSD, or other ailments. He figured it should be okay to help vets. The guy told him the design department preferred to make models from actual penises rather than from an idealized composite sketch. He also happened to mention that he had a very in-focus photo of Kerry spanking the monkey and spilling his seed on a pile of inflated female sex toys.

After that, the decision had been easy.

"After I signed the contract," Kerry explained when he finally got the nerve to tell his wife, "it was just a matter of having my pecker photographed from a variety of angles in its hard-on state, giving the company the rights to convert those high-res photographs into CAD drawings suitable for 3-D printing and production in a factory in Vietnam."

The money had helped him finish paying off his college loans, he explained to her, helped him make his share of a down payment on their house, buy the motorcycle of his dreams, and generally get him off the road of life-long indebtedness. His BS in Anthropology, and MS and PhD in the Philosophy of Ethics had not landed him a well-paying job, despite the claims that a Black man with such credentials would be a shoo-in for an assistant professorship, adjunct professor, or position in corporate ethics.

He ended up taking a job as an assistant coach at a small Christian college launching a football program. That got him into the system. Later, he was able to parlay that entry level position to an adjunct instructor in the college's remedial education program, euphemistically dubbed the Societal Impact Program, which provided extra tutoring in math and writing, lab assistant opportunities, coaching, and other services to low-income Native-American, Hispanic, and other under-resourced students.

When the Freedom Center conducted its search for an executive director, Dr. Washington not only had the right academic background, but had no research program of his own or other aspirations which could bias his perspective. As the money man, Raj had just needed good optics, a figurehead, someone who came across with authority and conviction. Sports heroes never hurt either.

As one of the board members put it at the time, 'We have the brains and the balls, we just need the face."

When he was done explaining, his wife had looked at him and asked, what made you think a Black man participating in a circle jerk at a *Primates* Festival would be a good idea?

Well, his ex-wife.

CHAPTER 30

CRIME AND FREEDOM

The first presenter the next morning, Dr. Waylon MacGruffin, did not win the award for longest paper title but did win for longest distance traveled. He held the Rudolf Giuliani Chair, Professor of Practice, at Blue Jay College, until Giuliani was indicted in Georgia. DEI was just getting going when it was changed to the David Dinkens Seat of Justice & Policing. Even Bradley knew Blue Jay was widely regarded as a national center of excellence in criminology.

The title of his talk: "Micro Aggressions or Micro Freedoms: Focusing the Microscope on Boom Boxes, Gay and Lesbian Public Displays of Affection, 'Petty' Public Drug Use, Street People, Windshield Cleaners, Brown Shirts, Managed Spaces, and Gentrification." The phrases in the title alone were like a walk down memory lane for Bradley.

"We're past the halfway point of our time together," Bradley said from the podium, "and unfortunately, none of us have any power over the weather. Who knew it would rain for three days straight?"

"The new climate reality," one audience member yelled.

"An anomalous weather pattern," another countered.

"Weather!" A few yelled, hoping to start a chant.

"Climate!" Several more countered.

"Okay, okay, let's not turn this into an old Bud Light commercial. Problem is, there's more rain in the forecast for tomorrow night, which makes our tour of Jerome and Tuzigoot problematic. So an alternative was suggested to me by the Song of the Sun management, an evening at their affiliated Coins of the Canyon casino. I understand a musical group with some regional notoriety is performing, too, a Nu Clear tribute band called," he shuffled through his notes, "uh, Kremlin?"

"Who?" someone yelled from the audience. "I'm from Flagstaff, never heard of them!"

Another chimed in, "Are you kidding? They had that great hit, 'No More Roads to Moscow." He started singing, "*They crossed over the Artic at dawn's early light / dozens of Titans, Siberia's fright ...*"

"Hey, good memory!" Gail called out. "That was one of our anthems at the launch sites."

"They don't turn up in Apple music," another observed, "or Spotify. Or Pandora."

"That's because they were from the Victrola era," some wiseacre cracked.

"Social media police probably banned Nu Clear," someone else said. "They're not exactly politically correct. I mean, imagine if the Jimmy Carter White House used Ted Nugent's 'I Can't Drive 55' as a theme song during the energy crisis."

"Well, Nu Clear notwithstanding, the casino has promised to give each of us $10 in chips or slot change as an inducement."

Several faces lit up. Positive murmuring in the crowd.

Someone threw cold water. "We're not allowed to accept gifts like that."

"You mean, you can accept bags of useless swag, but not casino chips?"

"Guess it depends on your institution's policy."

"Our University supports indigenous-run casinos," another chimed in.

Still another replied, "We'll be contributing to an under-resourced population." Bradley thought about Catherine and her fake boobs. What a lark it would be spending the evening at the casino with her.

"It's not really a gift. We're just going to lose it back to them, right?" He chuckled, shrugged his shoulders. "Am I right?" He said, louder.

Azul perked up. "We must think like winners!"

At least he seemed in better spirits, Bradley thought.

Ashera added, "It's important to patronize indigenous institutions, help them thrive on their own terms. I mean, without being patronizing."

Bradley said, picking up on the theme. "A past humanitarian violation canceled by an ethical good."

The audience still looked unconvinced.

"Tell you what, I'll ask Nascha, the resort manager, if they'll just consider it a $10 credit on any food or drinks we order?"

The consensus seemed to be that would be acceptable.

"Okay. Noodle on it," he said, "and we'll vote later in the day." He moved on to new business.

"Now, it's my privilege to introduce Professor Waylon MacGruffin. "He and his research team have been carrying out a massive longitudinal study of interactions in urban, suburban, and exurban public spaces. They've followed age cohorts of subjects, in different locations, surveyed their attitudes toward, and interactive behaviors in, public spaces. Plus, our distinguished guest has traveled all the way from the Bronx, or Fort Apache, as it was known back in the day."

"For God's sakes." Ashera mumbled.

"What?" Bradley whispered back. Ashera just shook her head and Bradley continued.

"I, for one, recall several run-ins in the 1970s and '80s with ghetto youth, like they'd steal our tennis balls in Riverside

Park, hassle us on the subways when we were carrying our ski equipment or golf clubs."

Dr. MacGruffin took the stage and stood at the podium, looking at Bradley. "One would have thought that a person who two days ago described himself as the darkest kid in his school, until Blacks were admitted ..."

Jesus, what made me open my mouth, Bradley wondered.

"... would have had some sympathies with the 'ghetto youth' as you described them, which I assume is code for Black or Hispanic."

"Maybe code for rough?" Bradley retorted, sensing a slight.

"A more enlightened attitude may likely have been psychologically blocked by an overwhelming white identity constructed by the prevailing forces of your white-dominated power structure."

Bradley squirmed. What? Is he implying that I'd be a less racist person if I'd been raised in the ghetto? And what was so wrong with assimilating into the dominant power structure? As if he had a choice about where he grew up or the schools he'd gone to.

As the professor got into his remarks, Bradley's mind drifted away from the offense he felt, the power dynamics of freedom, racism, and classism to number whatever. Quiana. That experience had been even weirder than being used for a quick fuck by someone who was halfway down the aisle to the altar. They were at a work retreat, and Quiana showed up at the pool in a swimsuit designed for pre-women's suffrage. Quietly, thinking he was paying her a compliment, he said her body was far more attractive than she was giving herself credit for. After a few evenings hanging out, Quiana had asked him to "help her with the problem of her virginity" at the age of 25. Even though it seemed a little weird, Bradley said he'd be "honored."

It had all been pretty awkward, but it went okay. Then things got really weird. She invited him to a party at her place, neglecting to tell Bradley her father would be there. She'd clutched Bradley's hand and presented him like some debutante introducing her betrothed.

Bradley got wigged out, tried to set her straight, she got offended, then enraged, and they'd had a confrontation. Hysterical, she accused him of using her in the worst way, when she was the one who'd asked him to take care of her "little problem."

Why was sex always accompanied by unintended consequences, guilt, embarrassment, feelings of inadequacy, sexually transmitted diseases, fear of AIDS? What was it like today? He'd been married so long, he really had no idea. He'd heard friends talk about consent this and consent that and can I touch you here and will you please touch me there? It all sounded worse than reading instructions from an appliance manual.

And why was she named for a DuPont trademark? Quiana. Jesus.

Speaking of communicating, MacGruffin spoke in code worse than anything spouted so far—spatial arrangements, opacity of barriers, olfactory circumstances, micro-normalities and abnormalities, dynamic constellations, private vs public musical spaces, subtly uniformed authority figures, nuisance elements, engagement without loitering, sanctioned vs squatter micro-performance spaces, armed defensive postures in open carry areas, etc. All this jargon was beyond pissing him off.

Loath to admit it, some of his conclusions fascinated Bradley—the observation, for example, that the more affluent you were, the more likely you were to listen to music in a Walkman in the 1980s. The less affluent blared music from a far more expensive boom box. People who smoked pot in the lines at movies in more affluent neighborhoods were far less likely to be harassed by authorities, or others in line, while those who toked in the less affluent neighborhoods were more likely to be harassed, even though pot was decriminalized back then for everyone. Yet those poorer neighborhoods were riddled with street people doing much harder drugs.

Residents of large cities in the 1990s generally felt safe when mayors hired uniformed workers to do menial jobs in entertainment and shopping areas but did not feel safe when the street people who insisted on "cleaning" your windshield for a handout at bridge and tunnel entrances wore white uniforms like they were supposed to be there servicing your auto.

In a more recent phase of the study, residents in big city exurbs with open-carry laws gradually became comfortable with seeing individuals with guns, *if they were of the same race*. MacGruffin told a chilling tale of a Black resident in Festus, Missouri, south of St. Louis, who no one bothered until he carried a gun in public. He was harassed out of town. Studies of open-carry also revealed that in the exurbs, many people brandished firearms only until they satisfied themselves that they were indeed *able to*. If everyone was like them, they didn't feel the need for displaying their firearm anymore.

Something similar was true of gay partners and public displays of affection. All these were examples of what the professor termed the "dynamic constellations of responses to localized interactions."

When MacGruffin concluded, Bradley stood. "Thank you. That was a lot of information, but salient, I trust," glancing across the audience. "Let's digest it during a five-minute stretch break without leaving the room, and reconvene for any questions or comments. Water and beverages are along the back wall."

Azul left the panelists table. Dr. MacGruffin made a beeline for someone he apparently knew in the audience. Bradley sat down with Gail and Ashera.

"How are you feeling today, Ashera?"

"Oh, I'm fine now. And I apologize. I have that affliction where you can get weepy and can't stop, even in public. It used to be called pseudobulbar affect, but now I think everyone refers to it as John Boehner syndrome."

"Please, no one needs to apologize for a little PDE."

Ashera looked at him, puzzled.

"Public Display of Emotion."

"Well, it's not very professional," Ashera countered. "Anyway, I need to rehydrate." She left hurriedly.

After an awkward pause, Gail asked, "So ... Maniopolos, I never asked before, but what made you quit leading tours at the Missile Museum?"

Bradley pondered for a second how to respond. "I thought I figured something out about those launch sites, shared it with a few of the other volunteer guides, even tried to add it to my tour narrative. Let's just say after a while, I began to feel very uncomfortable among the other guides. I got the feeling that even the people on the tour didn't want to hear about it."

"I'm all ears."

"Well, in my line of work, I spend a great deal of time analyzing systems. Complex engineered systems, as I mentioned, like energy infrastructure. My specialty became identifying the potential Achilles' heel of a system, or the fatal flaw, in a new technology and help my clients address it at small scale before it bit them in the ass at large scale. I started digging into all the available public engineering information on these launch sites, could've done a doctoral thesis on it."

"A few have."

"What I figured out is that all of the subsystems at the site were thoroughly tested. But the overall system never was. Because it couldn't be. We tested an atom bomb before we dropped it on Japan. When you build a power plant or a refinery or a paper mill, it takes months of commissioning work before the whole thing works as designed, especially if it involves new technology. It's just the reality of complex engineering."

"So, by your logic, we never launched one, so we never really knew if it would work?"

"Yup."

"Never heard anyone suggest that in all my years there. But we all did wonder whether all of this stuff would work too. Obviously. We knew how poorly designed some of the equipment was. Hell, we lived with it 24/7."

"That's called triangulation, arriving at the same conclusion from two different directions."

"You and your silver dollar words. Should have worked for the Pentagon."

"Well, I did do work for the Department of Energy."

"Figures."

"Like you said, Gail, it's not that it *would* have worked, it's that it *could* have worked. That's how I boiled down the whole principle behind deterrence."

"I often wondered if the Russians' systems would have worked," Gail mused. "Figured if ours wouldn't, theirs wouldn't either." After a long pause, Bradley asked, "So what specifically are your health issues, I mean, if you're okay talking about them?"

"You mean, what am I gonna die from?"

"Well, okay."

"A variety of ailments, non-Hodgkins lymphoma, or NHL for short, being the most serious. You've heard of cancer clusters?"

He nodded.

Well, every ICBM site is potentially a cancer cluster."

"Wow. How long has this been a thing? The cancer, I mean."

"The earliest evidence was in the late 1980s. The first "official" study was concluded in 2001. No contaminant levels above standards set by the EPA or the military, yada yada. In the early aughts, the Air Force concluded that there was not sufficient evidence to identify any ICBM site as a cluster. What was really unnerving is that the conclusion insinuates that our complaints could be attributed to 'perceived clusters,' which simply means gossip among close knit groups of people is rampant, so we're all just suffering from phantom NHL.

"Like, how many?"

"Officially? We know there are nine victims from *one site* in North Dakota."

"Shit."

"Yeah. A journalist's expose reported 30 cancer cases tied to a site in North Dakota. Anecdotal data suggests that there are well over 100 cases connected with three bases in Montana."

"I had no idea, all that time I was giving tours."

"And to think I spent my entire career worrying about the obliteration of the planet."

CHAPTER 31

SOCIAL MEDIA AND THE POLICE STATE

The day's second presentation, Social Media and the Police State, was delivered by Bradley's colloquium nemesis, Dr. Stephanie Plemmons, professor of digital forensics and anthropology at the University of California, San Diego, and assistant director of the Center for Contemporary Virtual Interactions, which she described in her bio as "residing at the nexus of collective human digital behavior and social accountability."

Bradley overheard her at breakfast saying that her department had been getting decimated from funding cuts, until they added AI to their mission statement. Now, they didn't know how they were going to spend all the grant money they'd been awarded over the last two years.

"When people hear social media and the police state in the same breath," Dr. Plemmons began, "they usually think about the police and government using people's content against them, trying to anticipate when and where crimes might be committed through surveillance, or getting some idea of a criminal's state of mind after committing a serious crime.

"Another popular conception is the digital version of the panopticon, an authority's ability to conduct surveillance over the population or segments of it. In a third popular conception, theorists see social media platform firms expanding their jurisdiction to surveillance, since they constantly analyze user data to target advertising and essentially have records in some server somewhere of every second of every engagement every individual has had on their platforms."

Bradley knew this, intuitively. It was easy to ignore that some server somewhere knows exactly how many minutes a day he spends looking at pornography online. Every email and text he ever wrote was available to a whipcrack lawyer somewhere, sometime.

Out of context, he could be labeled a misogynistic, socialist, fascist, anarchist—or a liberal, feminist, capitalist, pacifist, right wing, left wing. Hell, he could be accused of anything! We're all one emergency national security order away from a job loss, a public lynching, or a prison cell. Just depends on the definitions those in charge decide to use.

Plemmons went on. "However, in these broad situations, one's social media communications are being watched *with only tacit permission* given by the parties being surveilled through user platform user agreements. What I will present is my latest research into what I term neo-social, post-digital community policing. Within this paradigm, government regulation and policing may no longer be necessary. Communities police themselves by integrating social media, private security, weapons ownership, and public surveillance systems into every aspect of our lives."

Dr. Plemmons pulled up another slide. "We surveyed independent restaurants, analyzed reviews, social media posts, and everything searchable about these establishments, and found that 50 percent of all restaurants that went out of business in the first year had less than 3.8-star ratings on Yelp and Google. It is commonly known that 90 percent of restaurants and other independent businesses fail in the first year anyway. But we were astonished, shocked really, that the correlation to bad reviews was so high. Public opinion, in effect, is serving as a watchdog over private enterprise."

Dr. Zhou, whom Bradley privately had taken to referring to as the Tiger Lady, piped up from the floor. "At least us academics in publish-or-perish hell aren't the only ones subjected to peer-review reward or punishment."

"This isn't peer review though," Ashera said, "these are customer reviews of the businesses they've purchased goods or services from. It's a different relationship."

Rolex shook his head. "Some businesses are targeted by the bad actors and driven to failure just like one, or an entire group, can be targeted and redlined when seeking a mortgage. Banks use algorithms prejudicially for certain races. The AI you mentioned? Racist as fuck. Excuse the profanity, but every study has shown that AI been trained on racist data and imagery."

"Let's not get off track," Plemmons said dismissively, which made Rolex's face twist into a menacing frown. "What we're trying to show is the power of self-policing. A business must satisfy its customers or those customers will shut it down. While this was always true to some extent, it's the scale of the policing afforded by virtual platforms that amp up the phenomenon an order of magnitude. Whether our results will scale to larger owner/operators of restaurants and other businesses, time will tell—or an extension of our grant," she said, with a hint of a smile. "The implication, however, is less potential need for government involvement, not more."

"Now, let's widen our lens," she went on, "and consider that every participant in social media has the power to simply turn it off. We could set down our phones. Turn off our iPads or computers. We all have the power to look away rather than complain about something objectionable on the screen."

Dr. Plemmons glanced at Gail. "I believe Dr. Bartholomew mentioned this the other day."

"Appreciate the promotion," Gail said with a laugh, "but all I have is an associates degree."

"Thank you for your service, by the way," Plemmons said.

"Yeah, yeah, okay," uttered Gail under her breath, her eyes on the ground. "Enough about my service."

Plemmons continued. "We can choose to close our eyes to art we consider pornographic, distasteful, or unworthy of display. What vexes researchers about social media engagement is that the participants are all aware of this—the permanent, indelible record of their engagements, the potential for surveillance by authorities, the tracking for the purposes of commerce—and they willingly continue to not only participate but *expand* their participation year after year."

"Finally," she said, "with respect to freedom, is this question: Are social media users liberating themselves by engaging with people beyond their traditional friends, family, or geographical reach—in which case we could say that the 'voluntary servitude paradox' is actually emancipating—or are they 'voluntarily' oppressing themselves?"

Geez, everything ends in another question, Bradley thought. It's the same paralysis by analysis. Meanwhile, everything being said at this colloquium was being splashed all over social media. Then a eureka moment occurred: Maybe the assumption that there even is a right answer is its own form of tyranny?

Dr. Hintz raised a hand, then spoke before called upon. "Dr. Plemmons, were you able to determine that those restaurants weren't closed down for other reasons?"

Dr. Plemmons: "Well, correlation is not necessarily causation."

Bradley couldn't contain himself: "Damn it, if I hear one more social 'scientist' utter that statement, I'm gonna scream!" he said, pounding his fist on the table. He'd heard enough of that in his sociology classes.

The audience gasped collectively.

"What I mean is," he continued more calmly, "when are we going to quit relying on multiple regression analysis and more on direct experiments and observations?"

Dr. Plemmons looked at Bradley like she wished she had Gail's gun. "Mr. Maniopolos, how can you impugn the integrity of entire academic fields by attacking one of the most proven and robust tools of statistical analysis?"

"Okay, let's pretend I didn't say that. But look, if you don't want it entered as evidence in a court proceeding, don't enter it on your keyboard."

Gail chimed in. "Don't people just get bored with that social media crap, anyway?"

Dr. Zhou nodded toward Gail. "You Missileers didn't get bored using Pentagon facilities to conduct orgies. Why should others get bored when all this content is shoved at them 24/7?"

Bradley added, "I've heard kids in my own family say, hey, we know it's all being recorded and surveilled and could be used against us. We don't care."

Gail shook her head. "They've had it too easy. Probably never wondered whether they were being emancipated or oppressed."

"I would echo Gail's comments," Ashera said. "The only people who care or worry about all this are the people who get money to ponder whether we're all being emancipated or oppressed. Like the people in this room. I mean, I'm not knocking your research program, Dr. Plemmons, it's really a generic comment."

Dr. Peggy Zabel, who hadn't said much from the floor, found an opening. "Think about it. Who reads the academic paper about hese findings? I just looked it up, in fact, *The Journal of Surveillance, Culture, and Behavior*? I mean, who reads that? It's an online journal. Couple hundred subscribers, maybe a dozen read any one article? No offense, I do the same. Personally, I'd feel more validated if I'd made a reel from this paper and had 10,000 followers on Instagram!"

Rolex Williams agreed. "You know if *anyone* has read it?"

Plemmons protested. "I get the online surveys. It's been opened by dozens of academics worldwide!"

"Ain't hard to click and open an article," Rolex shot back. "It does take time to read it, though. Anyone respond to you about the content? Anyone who wouldn't *benefit* by responding, that is?"

Plemmons glared at him. "Just what are you implying?"

Dr. Zhou chimed in. "There are lots of people who care about this stuff, but they're not reading papers like yours, that's for sure. They're online talking about being online. You could make three times your salary in a month by hiring a hot grad student influencer in revealing clothes to make a fifteen-second reel, post it on Instagram, and suck up the ad revenue you'd get for every voyeur who clicked on it."

Bradley perked up. He didn't know Zhou had it in her to be so spicy.

"That's offensive," Dr. Plemmons yelled. "This entire audience is attacking my person!"

"We're not attacking you," Hintz shot back, "just wondering about the relevance of your work. No academic should be afraid of the truth. How many people have responded to the publication of your paper? One? Two? A grad student, your funding organization representative? Your mother?"

Gail couldn't let that one slip. "Okay, let's not bring our parents into this."

Dr. Plemmons' eyes shot virtual daggers at the audience. "I resent your implication that I am not hot enough myself to be featured in my own Instagram reels. You are belittling my experience, trashing my credentials, and objectifying me as a woman!"

"That's called getting twisted up in your panties," Bradley said, then wondered what kind of panties she wore. She did look kind of hot, in a buttoned up, school-marmish way. Did she keep a paddle in her top drawer?

Plemmons turned to glare at him. She looked even more incensed, if that were possible.

Ashera spoke up. "Influencers are paid good money to review products on-line, embellish engagement for specific accounts, and otherwise make everywhere safe for buying what someone else is selling. It's grueling work. Whether it's pornography or ETSY products. Even academic knowledge has been commodified, reduced to 20-minute TEDx talks on YouTube, fifteen-second Instagram reels, several hundred character blurbs in X, or Threads, or whatever.

"I don't care what social media platform you use, *my research is valid scholarship*," Plemmons asserted, her voice rising in pitch.

MacGuffin huffed. "Oh, please, we're all after funding and grants. Do we want to do good research? Sure, but let's be honest. We spend all those years getting a PhD and the pay is lousy and we're constantly scratching in the dirt for the next grant. It's demoralizing. None of us in the social sciences is going to get rich quick—or at all. So let's be truthful here. Even someone like you would be better off hawking your research wearing skimpy clothes and spouting soundbites on Instagram."

"They're all booty-scratchers," Bradley whispered to Azul, who gave him a small smile in return.

"*Even someone like me?*" Dr. Plemmons glared at Bradley, and pointed. "I demand Drs. Zhou, Williams, and MacGuffin be reprimanded!"

Bradley stared up at Plemmons. What was this, nursery school? *Reprimanded?* At a conference on freedom? How could this get any wackier?

MacGuffin shot back, "Go ahead. I have tenure just like you."

Azul, surprisingly, commented. "I think I need to be making more reels of my band and performances!"

Bradley heard a young woman in the third row lean over to the man next to her and whisper, "If he played without a shirt, I'd *pay* to watch his reels!"

The man next to the whispering woman smiled appreciatively up at Azul. "There's nothing sexier than a drummer!"

Dr. Zhou, in the next row back, smiled flirtatiously: "I'd watch those reels too. On repeat."

This has gone downhill in a hurry, Bradley thought, casting a glance at Azul, who appeared to be simultaneously blushing and puffing out his chest just a tiny bit. He got to his feet and stood beside Dr. Plemmons, motioning for everyone to quiet down. Then he called for a ten-minute break and encouraged other audience members with questions or comments to speak with Dr. Plemmons one on one.

After they reconvened, Bradley took the podium again. "On a lighter note," he said, "we should vote on tomorrow evening's event."

Not even close. Sixty-eight to seven in favor of the casino. As he adjourned the afternoon session, Bradley was already thinking about the odds of getting a handful of fake boob in a dark corner when Dr. Plemmons grabbed his arm.

"Jeez, two days ago, you wouldn't even shake my hand," he responded, startled.

"Aren't you going to say something to that creep?"

"MacGuffin?"

"Yes!"

"Dr. Plemmons, I honestly don't think he meant to offend you. In fact, I think he was taking pains not to."

"I have never been to an academic conference where one's stage presence on social media is impugned from the podium."

"Dr. Plemmons, I'm just the facilitator."

"I want you to know that I'll be taking this up with Dr. Washington himself. He's a personal friend of mine. This is what happens when an old white guy is put in charge. Twisted up in my panties, indeed!"

"It's just a saying."

"It's a mark of misogyny is what it is! When I tell Dr. Washington—"

At this point, Bradley didn't need tenure to not give a shit.

"Oh, believe me, I can't wait to hear what Dr. Dildo has to say."

CHAPTER 32

NASCHA TAKES CARE OF BUSINESS

On the way out of the conference room, Bradley listened to a voicemail from Dr. Washington. He ordered Bradley to muzzle that Bartholomew woman during tomorrow's sessions in whatever way he was able because the 'powers that be' were breathing down his neck. What was he supposed to do, bind and gag a retired Air Force captain? Fuck him.

Several text messages from Victor were stacked up in his Alerts pile. One asked for his latest tally. He sighed, gazed out the window and was drawn to the cliffs, flashes of bright sunlit surfaces amidst the gathering, fast-moving clouds muting their colors.

He'd had enough of Victor's juvenile antics. The more he remembered of these encounters, the less comfortable he was with them. And with himself. What kind of idiot would exert this much brain power trying to answer Victor's question?

His whole body throbbed from the stress of being "on" for two and a half days, but especially his shoulders and his calves, which he flexed and unflexed as a subconscious tic. Cocktail or nap was the question he asked himself as he passed Nascha at the desk.

"Excuse me, may I ask you a question?"

"Fire away, sir."

"Is it an ethnic slur against your people to say that the Bronx used to be called Fort Apache?"

She couldn't hide her mirthless smile. "You mean like in the movie? *Fort Apache, The Bronx* with Paul Newman?"

"Yeah."

"Well, I don't think the Bronx as a whole was ever called that in real life, but my understanding is that one police precinct had that moniker for a while."

"Hmm. Do you think it's offensive?"

"Well, I wouldn't call it, uh, a 'slur' exactly."

"But ... ?"

"For one thing, no Native Americans used the word Apache as the name of a tribe. It was just a word in the Zuni language that meant enemy."

"Ah ..."

"I mean, African Americans didn't use the n-word, did they? White people made it up to use against them."

"I see."

"But we do consider any appropriation of our experience under the oppression of the federal government to enrich Hollywood moguls, and a transference of that experience by other oppressed minorities who rightfully labeled it racist."

What? Geez, this woman should be in the colloquium with us, Bradley mused.

"So, was there ever a Fort Apache? Out here, I mean?"

"Sure, it's now a National Historic Site up near Pinetop run by, you guessed it, the Apaches."

Bradley pondered that one. Apache, a Zuni word for enemy used by white people to label a different tribe and now those people use the word as a name for themselves.

"Did you once live in the Bronx, Mr. Maniopolos?"

"No, I lived in Manhattan, though, many moons ago. Please, call me Bradley."

"You're also not supposed to say 'many moons ago.' The moon is sacred to many Native peoples."

Bradley looked startled, then bewildered. "Oh, my apologies, I didn't know."

She laughed. "Kidding! As far as I know, the moon is still unclaimed territory. Except for that patch with an American flag, though I hear there are two billionaires racing to change that."

"Whew! I've been dealing with academics who are apparently much more sensitive to language than I've been used to."

"I'm sorry ..."

"So are the Zunis like the Moonies?"

"The who?"

"Just kidding. The Moonies were a cult back in the 1980s led by some Korean guy named Sun Yung Moon."

"Oh."

"Too bad your people didn't know about him. You could have sued him for appropriating the sanctity of the moon."

Nascha was beginning to like this guy. Two more for *The Tonto Chronicles*, to boot. "Many moons ago," she muttered to herself, "that one was good. Moonies ..."

Her good humor went south when she remembered the second email exchange she had with that NAU professor about her book project. The woman had written that the title, *The Tonto Chronicles*, would be offensive to potential buyers. Really? Even though *Tonto* is also the name of an Apache reservation? Think of the irony, Nascha wrote. Think of the people walking by a display of that title in Barnes & Noble, offended, or seeing it on Goodreads, with no context, the professor wrote back.

During their subsequent phone call, Nascha countered, "You mean affluent white people who only know the name of the Lone Ranger's sidekick."

"Yes, but also women, who buy the vast majority of books."

"Even humor? These are brief, authentic accounts of micro-aggressions one Native American suffers in her daily working life." Micro-aggression, a word she learned in the Know Your Value seminar.

"Ms. Sunsee, you don't want your book classified as humor for sales. You'll want it in Book Club Contemporary Issues. Anything with Tonto in the title isn't going to sell in that category.

"How about *Dispatches From the Reservation: One Indigenous Woman's Battle Against Offensive Language?*"

"What?" Nascha wrote back. "I don't even live on a reservation. I'm not battling anyone."

"Titles are always embellished for sales," came the woman's reply. There was a long pause. "Your other problem is, Yavapai are not Apache."

"Well, that is a difference without a distinction."

"You'd be co-opting *their* experience."

"Wait. What? Technically, we don't consider ourselves Apache, but we were rounded up into the same areas. And why would buyers of *The Tonto Chronicles* care one way or the other?"

"They may not, but publishers sure as heck care about appropriation of narratives today."

This woman was getting too big for her pale-ass skin.

"How do you know all this?"

"My side hustle is literary agent."

"Oh ..."

All she cares about is her percentage, Nascha thought.

"Let me put it as bluntly as possible, Ms. Sunsee. There are a few hundred possible buyers out there who would 'get' that Tonto is a legitimate name of a Native American group. They'd be in on your inside joke. Tens of millions of possible buyers would negatively associate 'Tonto' with a television show that is now considered to have exploited the friendship between a Native American and a character turned into an American hero for millions of baby-boomer children. It would be a conflicting association that would damage the potential success of the book. Do you want your book to sell, or don't you?"

Now Nascha was plain angry. "Being an English professor and a literary agent isn't a conflict of interest?" She bristled.

"Not if you are an adjunct."

Maybe she should go back to her Have-A-Pie Bakery idea. Native stuff was too complicated in the white world. She reminisced on the traditional Yavapai berries, manzanita, juniper, mulberry, hackberry, in her fillings from her family recipes. She could sell special editions of her pies in shallow baskets made with traditional thread woven around the coiled cottonwood sticks.

Eh, then she'd end up another loser Native selling her wares out of a broken-down booth on the side of the road.

In the elevator up to his room, Bradley fished out the note Nascha had given him.

I have something for you. :-) Catherine

The Cave Creek woman! Where would he find her though? He pushed the lobby button three times quickly, and the elevator reversed, after stopping at his floor.

He waited at the front desk. The man in front of him was upset that he could not check in early. Bradley overheard him saying something about "native time," before he departed. Nascha was smiling when he approached.

"What was that all about?"

"Nothing. Hang on, I have to write something down. 'Native time.' Okay, Sorry. Now, how can I help you?"

"You wouldn't happen to know where I could find the, uh, guest who left me the note you gave me earlier?"

She pointed toward the coffee stand, adjacent to the bar.

"Thanks! I owe you one."

"The favor of your group's presence at the casino tomorrow night?"

"Oh, I should have told you earlier, the vote was overwhelmingly in favor."

Yes! Thought Nascha.

Bradley walked quickly to where Catherine was sitting. "Hey! How's it going? Good smoothie?"

"No, but Andre was kind enough to supersize a Mimosa that's just as refreshing!"

He gave her a puzzled look. "So, about your, uh, note ..."

"Yes, don't think of me as being too forward, but you seem like a fun guy. You do gummies?"

He wished he'd brought one or two from his own stash. But why did she think he looked like a fun guy? Of course, he was. Absolutely. Totally fun.

"I've been known to imbibe." He chuckled.

"Cool. Would you like one? Nascha said you mentioned it was pretty stressful in your colloquium."

"I'd say sure, and pray you weren't a narc."

"That's no longer an issue in this state."

"True, but there is the issue of Native American law, however."

"Not to worry."

She pulled out something in a Ricola wrapper from a Vera Wang handbag that could've fit a midget or two. Or were they called Little People now? Dwarves?

"This should soothe your throat, wink wink, after all that talking by the end of the day."

"Why thank you! I'd love to chat, believe me, I would, but I'm due in that meeting room down the hall in less than a minute." He pointed to it.

"Get going then!"

Bradley thanked her profusely. When his back was turned, she continued:

"Happy trails!"

He looked behind himself, tried to reciprocate with a smile deserving of the one she was giving him. A bit supersized, that smile of hers, unsupportable by such a petite body, much like the trunks of those gnarly prickly pear bushes he saw out the window that seemed no match for the heavy paddles emanating from their stems. Were they the ones with the sharp needles, or no? He couldn't remember.

CHAPTER 33

DOING THE MATH ON FREEDOM

The second half of the morning was designed as three parallel "breakout" sessions, each led by one of Bradley's core panelists. Damned if he would police them like Washington demanded.

The Freedom Center had taken a special interest in the breakout on "Quantizing Freedom." Raj had hand-picked the session leader, Dr. Fredricka Wertmuller, from California Polytechnic Institute, and sent personal notes to attendees he wanted in the room. Washington told him this session was the lynchpin for the Freedom Center's strategy to put the concept of freedom, and the Center, on the map, so to speak, by injecting rigorous quantitative analysis into the discipline.

The only thing Bradley knew about Cal Poly is that graduates of Cal Tech would rip your gonads off if you confused the two.

Wertmuller was the granddaughter of a professor at the Austrian School of Economics who, back in the 1950s, had published the "seminal" work, "An Essay on the Mathematical Theory of Freedom," introducing the concept of quantifying freedom. She'd studied at the London School of Economics, then the University of Chicago after Milton Friedman made the "Chicago School" a household phrase, at least to economists, politicians, and readers of *The Wall Street Journal*, *Commentary*, *Reason*, and similar magazines. Her abridged list of publications took up a good chunk of the real estate in the colloquium's printed program, including collaborative efforts to quantify freedom with the Heritage Foundation's State of the World Liberty Index and the International Religious Freedom Index.

Dr. Wertmuller, who could be impersonating Annie Lennox of the Eurythmics, had arrived late the evening before and had made it clear to Bradley that she would not be staying after her session. Which seemed unfair to the attendees, but okay, it wasn't his show. Bradley made sure to be at her breakout room before she got started. Of the 75 or so attendees, less than a dozen were interested in this talk.

Making small talk with Wertmuller was like having dental work. First, the professor corrected Bradley's pronunciation of her first and last name, the latter pronounced with a V, not a W. Well, fuck you, Bradley thought, how about I just call you Freddie? Each of her responses to a question consisted of multi-syllabic words and a hard, frigid stare piercing Bradley's pupils like ice picks. The woman missed her calling in the Nazi SS.

When he casually mentioned some of his own grad work analyzing complex financial models and his brief notoriety around Enron, Wertmuller kicked him the balls. "I researched your professional profile. You assimilate and regurgitate. I conduct original research."

"Yeah, well, Cal Poly ain't Cal Tech."

"Achtung, baby, I am a scholar in residence. San Luis Obispo is a pulchritudinous place from which to transfigure the economy as we know it."

Maybe she was impersonating Ivan Drago? Learning anything from her expression would be an exercise in geometry. Not a whisker of her bleach-blond cropped hair flicked when she moved.

Bradley brought the room to attention and whispered to Wertmuller that it was time for him to introduce her.

"If you insist," she replied.

Whatever. Bradley stepped to the podium set up in front of the three tables arranged into a squared off C. "Dr. Fredricka Wertmuller, ladies and gentlemen. A woman who can use the word 'pulchritudinous' in a sentence without flinching needs no further introduction." He stepped back from the podium. His quip had garnered one faint chuckle from the back of the room. Wertmuller strode forward and almost elbowed Bradley off the dais. The flex cord stand attached to the mic groaned like a bullfrog in heat as she yanked it up as high as it would go.

"Why do we revere economics, economists, and finance?" She dove right in. "And why do we worship money? What is money, anyway?" She answered before anyone could raise a hand.

"At base, money must be earned to survive, to purchase goods and services. At higher levels, money signifies growing wealth and affluence, to subvert classist systems, to neutralize ethnic prejudices, to advance our ideas and businesses." Her arms thrashed around so violently Bradley wondered if she was creating her own wind and weather system. "These are all landmarks on the road to freedom and free will. Liberty and civil rights and justice and equality and security may be provided for in documents and theoretical political frameworks, but money lubricates the realities of human desires."

Bradley settled into an empty seat. This bitch is running a four-minute mile, he thought.

"We agree that the geopolitical structure is now gilded in global finance, interlocking trade agreements, currency ratios, and defense treaties, so what should be the next great goal of nations? Money is now just a means to an end. That end is freedom! Money buys freedom. Money, as finance, is analyzed with complex differential equations and high-level math, and thus it follows that freedom is the currency of the future with which to transact human relations."

Her Austrian accent barbed her words like sharp twigs through the weaves of a basket. She was an orator, for sure. Bradley couldn't help but invoke the reels of great speeches of Churchill or Roosevelt or even Obama. Or the incendiary ones of a Hitler or Mussolini.

"The field of economics was elevated from the pantheon of 'social sciences' into the complex domain of financial engineering, so laden with higher level mathematical analysis, today you could mistake it for quantum mechanics. If we are to transform the concept of freedom into the fundamental objective of human political and cultural systems, then we must begin with first principles."

The professor pushed the buttons on the projector remote with the force of a demolitions expert plunging the detonator to take out a bridge in an essential supply line. The first slide showed an infographic illustrating analogies between important parameters in economics and freedom.

"When we dissect the fundamental parameters of economics, we can list the quantifiable ones of supply, demand, and price; the subjective ones of a transaction between two or more agents; micro vs macro activity and effect; value; and currency. To quantize freedom, we think in identical and analogous terms. Certainly, we may think about micro versions of freedom versus macro, or collective versions. We can attach a value to freedom, either at the individual level or the collective. This would be the equivalent of determining how free a single human being is, or how much 'freedom' is characteristic of an entire nation. If something has value, then we can attach a price to that value and exchange the values through the use of a currency. Instead of an economic *transaction*, we can define an economic *interaction* between two agents, individuals or progressively larger groups."

Wertmuller's thoughts were moving faster than the speed of her voice, her own version of the Doppler effect. And the sound waves were bouncing around the room, giving Bradley a headache.

"What economics has done for global society is to provide a framework for cooperation and competition through transactions which transcend familial, tribal, parochial, ethnic, and dynastic-based power structures. However, one must recognize that all societies are, and always will be, divided into elites and non-elites, even if passage between the two groups is more fluid in some political economies than others. Today, power can be equated to money and money can be equated to freedom, especially the freedom to do to someone else before they do it to you, to twist a biblical proverb."

What had Gail said earlier? There but for the grace of me goes you.

"Affluence buys freedom, in other words."

Azul said the opposite two days ago. His family's wealth made him a slave.

Wertmuller kept going. "The elites in society are those who can access and harness knowledge and resources the masses cannot. These days, the elite include those who can do, or can understand, the complex quantitative analysis inherent in engineering design, global financial engineering, aerospace technology, the mining of social media data, and artificial intelligence. By right, *they* should comprise the ruling class, not politicians who know nothing of these concepts."

"What I devote my life's work to, extrapolating from the work of my father and grandfather, is that freedom is the *next* central tenet of human political and economic experience. By quantizing the concept, we can make all human interactions, as interpolated by the elites, more fair and just. For a society without elites is a society of equals, the utopia everyone knows cannot exist in reality."

A dark-haired woman in the audience, black-framed glasses twice the diameter of her eyes, noted, "So quantizing freedom gives the elites an entirely new body of knowledge which cannot be accessed by the masses?"

Wertmuller offered more than a slight grin. She actually chuckled. "Yes! Yes! Elites in every society claim access to a specialized level of knowledge, whether they are Mayan priests, Spanish conquistadors, Jewish financiers, or Brahmin Indians. Perhaps you've heard the management edict, 'You cannot manage what you don't measure.' We have developed a mathematical framework to measure freedom, so it can be more optimally distributed and allocated. To those who will say such an abstract concept as freedom cannot be properly quantified, I say, could Adam Smith or John Maynard Keynes have ever envisioned a world in which global economic transactions are associated with differential equations, time-dependent value of money, the derivative value of one currency or commodity against another? I think not."

Damn, this actually makes sense, Bradley thought.

"I doubt anyone here has the background in differential equations or associational statistics needed to understand the math."

Bradley had taken a Diff E class in college, but damned if he remembered any of it. Associational statistics. That's Victor's field. He made a mental note to ask Victor about it.

"It is my vision," Wertmuller added, "that in 20 years, all top colleges and business schools throughout the world will have freedom engineering departments, and that all geopolitical relationships will be re-ordered based on these mathematical frameworks. Now. Any questions?"

240

CHAPTER 34

ASHERA ATTENDS TO THE LEAST AMONG US

Next door, Ashera gave her breakout attendees plenty of time to swallow a few extra gulps of coffee and tea, chat among themselves, and get seated. In her world, starting on time was an artificial constraint that just caused extra stress.

She placed a medium-sized water bottle, emblazoned with the THPS logo along with her own artistic representation of a lizard, a coyote, a saguaro, and rock art sharing the space with the mountain receding into the horizon point on the table beside the podium. She put Gordon in his travel cage front and center. Then she courteously asked for attention, and began to blow up a deflated beach ball, which brought smiles on the faces of many in her audience.

"So, I am not a fan of lectures, so I thought what we would do is, I'd just, you know, yeah, toss this ball to someone, when they have something to contribute on the rights of all living things, land entitlement, and public versus private development."

"I only have three guidelines. First, no one hold the ball more than three minutes so that everyone who wants to speak has the opportunity. Second, please think through what you wish to say, make sure it is something of interest to everyone, not an item of self-aggrandizement. Let's make this about collaboration. Third, let's not be uncomfortable with silence between comments, but rather use it to reflect on what has been said."

"Oh, and if anyone would like to meet Gordon," she said, pointing to the cage, "please feel free at any time. He's a very gregarious gecko!"

A young Asian woman Ashera hadn't noticed before—barely 5 feet tall, in stylish black 3-inch pumps below an all-business one-piece, pale-yellow dress roped at the waist, a modest pendant hanging Adam's apple length—tentatively started to rise from her chair, then sat down again.

Before Ashera finished her guidelines, a hand went up, flapping faster than the tail of a dog sniffing bacon. Oh well, Ashera thought, I tried. She threw the ball.

"Dr. Rolex Williams, Carver University. With all due respect to the gecko, why should we devote precious resources securing the rights of lizards when huge swaths of the American populace are still denied basic civil rights guaranteed in the Constitution? In every city in America, Black Americans are arrested in higher numbers, shot, and killed by those whose job it is to protect all citizens, the police. To bring it home to this region, a Black woman was recently critically injured when she tried to enter a gated community in the Tucson foothills ..."

"Yes, I understand," Ashera said. How far off topic was this, anyway? Yet she couldn't de-legitimize his point of view.

Rolex went on. "If Tucson authorities can't guarantee safe passage of a Black woman lost hiking—"

Dr. MacGruffin blurted out, "That story made national news. She *claimed* she was hiking. She was a homeless meth addict and—"

Ashera broke in. "I believe the correct term is 'unhoused?'"

"Whatever her status," Rolex went on, "her rights were violated when a policeman shot her without ever questioning her. The extent of her due process was a bullet to the chest."

MacGruffin rolled his eyes. "An African-American police officer, FYI."

"Which is an excellent example of how individuals adopt the attitudes of their oppressors in order be seen as part of the dominant group," Rolex shot back.

"Dr. Williams, thank you for your contribution." Ashera motioned for him to toss the ball back to her, which she had to do several times, once with a "please," but not before Rolex frowned.

"Now, let's pause for a minute and reflect on what Dr. Williams just said," Ashera said, in case Rolex felt slighted.

Within seconds, another hand shot up.

"Excuse me, excuse me, please," the person insisted, waving her arm for the ball to come to her.

There goes rule two, Ashera sighed. She tossed the ball.

"I am a professor at Old Tohono Community College—"

"My people," Ashera beamed.

"That actually depends on how much O'Odham blood you have, but I digress."

Well, that was saucy, Ashera thought.

The Tohono professor continued. "My research centers the basic tenets of Native American life prior to the invasion and conquest by white Europeans and examines how to apply those tenets to today's issues even as the dark shadow of the genocide of Indigenous People looms over everything and ..."

There go all the rules, Ashera thought.

" ... to redress the rights of animals, we must consider the paradox that, while in theory, any living thing with a will to live should be allowed to pursue that will to live, the truth is that animals do not possess the rationality of individual or collective governance to guarantee those rights themselves. Under natural law, every animal is subject to the hierarchy of the food chain. These contradictory situations will not be resolved anytime soon. In the meantime, we can certainly afford a renewed level of *respect* for animals, as a first step towards securing their rights, by incorporating them into our own spiritual, religious, and dietary frameworks."

She continued, barely even taking a breath. "Native Peoples hunted and killed only those animals which were absolutely essential to survival. We worshiped the animals upon which we depended. Rather than impose a complicated legal framework around animal rights, we should strive to live humbly as the dominant species capable of rationalizing how humans and animals may or may not coexist, rather than consume irresponsibly and excessively ..."

Wow, Ashera thought, this lady was her new best friend forever, even though she wished she'd shut up and even though Ashera knew that depending on people to live humbly and do the right thing was a non-starter. That's exactly why there needed to be a legal framework to begin with.

"We have worked with game theorists and computer simulation experts," the woman went on, "to show how such an approach can result in a more fair and just society for humans and animals. Our new book on this work, *Memo from Pre-1492: Advancing by Regressing,* will be available next year."

Rolex waved his hand in the air. "My book, *From Racism to Reparations: African Americans Replace Whites in the Power Structure,* is available now!"

Ashera saw Bradley quietly enter the room and stand against the wall. He gave her a questioning look with a shrug of his shoulders, raised eyebrows, and a twisted mouth, along with a thumbs up sign. She gave him a thumbs up back, followed by a shrug of the shoulders, as if to say, "I guess?"

Bradley left the room as the Asian lady in yellow rose again, and walked, as if shy, toward the front of the room. It took her a few minutes to reach the front. Ashera waved her with a smile towards Gordon's cage, nodding as if to say, go ahead, take a closer look, he won't bite.

The woman took a few steps closer.

"This whole business about defunding the police," MacGruffin observed, "I mean, you want to see people's freedoms disappear? Take the police out of the equation. I don't think there's been a stupider protest movement in my life!"

"They aren't preying on white men," Rolex countered. He looked at the Tohono lady. "At least Indigenous people get to hire your own tribal police."

"With limited jurisdiction," she noted.

The Asian woman was now by the table in front of Gordon.

"Nonhuman living things can't hire protective services. They rely on us to protect them," Ashera reminded the group.

Just as Ashera heard a low but audible metal-on-metal *click*, Gordon darted from his cage and raced up the woman's arm to her shoulder, over her head, and down her other side, where he leapt to the floor, gunning for the nearest wall. By the time Ashera could react, Gordon was up on the ceiling.

"What the hell?" Ashera cried. "Oh my God! Where's Gordon?" Her eyes darted around every square inch of the room. Finally, she spotted him in a corner at the junction between two walls and the ceiling.

The rest of the audience dashed toward Ashera and took cover behind her, as if huddling with the owner was their only means of protection. They followed curiously as Ashera hustled along the trajectory she believed Gordon had taken.

"Quick! Get some towels or something! Block the cracks at the bottom of those doors in the back!"

Someone left, and in a few minutes returned with Nascha, carrying several towels. Nascha regarded the group now huddled in a corner as if a rattlesnake was roaming the room, and wondered how to coax the gecko down from his perch.

"Something earned their freedom," she said, as she got on her knees to towel the doors.

CHAPTER 35

GAIL DRILLS THE RECRUITS

Gail banged her palm on the microphone several times in a row when the minute hand hit 10:30. "Okay, this is how we're going to roll. Our topic: the role of the military in securing citizens' freedom. I will make an opening statement, then go around the room from left to right for any comments in the order that you are seated. Once you start talking, I will use the stop-watch function on my phone. You get two minutes. If there's time at the end, you get more minutes. Make sense? Good."

A red-headed man with a neatly trimmed beard glanced up. "That seems a bit authoritarian."

Gail glared. "If no one takes charge, nothing gets done."

The man shook his head. "We're supposed to have an exchange of ideas—"

Gail huffed into the mic. "We'll exchange ideas. We're just going to do it in a way that is fair for all and no fair for anyone. Get my drift?"

"No, not really."

"Well, there are three other breakout sessions you can attend."

"We were told we had to stick with the one we selected."

"Then go have a donut or get more coffee. If you stay, you play by the rules."

Bradley looked at the text alert on his phone. Which reminded him that he still hadn't seen a text from Victor since midday yesterday. What the hell happened to him? He wanted to get his opinion on his epiphany yesterday about assumptions, right answers, and tyranny. And associational statistics.

This woman's running this session like boot camp.

Must be from an attendee. He texted back. *Well, she is retired Air Force.*

Gail opened with facts. "The whole concept of deterrence and securing borders is radically different in the post-9/11 era. Our friends and foes are fluid. Refugees are streaming into Western nations from all over the globe. We have spent trillions on a nuclear arsenal which we still claim is for defensive purposes only. Our military is actively engaged in dozens of hot conflicts around the world. We have more than 700 military bases in eighty countries. That's what the Pentagon makes public."

"The Pentagon's budget is ten times the size of the next country's defense budget. It represents 12 percent of our national budget and half of our discretionary spending. China has a larger navy than we do. Millions of illegals cross our southern border each year. Thousands of veterans commit suicide annually. World War III has already started in Ukraine. And unless anyone has been asleep for the last few decades, NATO is, in effect, America and America is damn tired of that attitude.

"We currently sell arms to 60 countries. Arms dealers get our military hardware into the hands of virtually any nation, terrorist, or despot with the money to pay for them. We've spent $1 trillion fighting the War on Drugs, remember that? That's $20 billion a year over fifty years. One hundred sixty million guns are in the hands of 33 percent of the American population. I have eight of them, by the way, including the media's favorite AR-15. One hundred thirty billion is spent by state and local police departments each year, or an average of four percent of those jurisdictions' budgets. Eighty-one billion is spent on prisons, $51 billion on the court systems. Thirty billion is spent by American citizens on home security. Security cameras and cell phone towers trace your every move in real life and virtually, online. You leave digital breadcrumbs whenever you buy something with a credit or debit card."

She took a deep breath.

"Since 9/11," she went on, coughing through her words, "the federal government has given itself broad power and authority to place U.S. citizens under surveillance. And to monitor potential money laundering, all personal banking transactions over $10,000 are subject to scrutiny by the feds. With the permission of a non-transparent FISA court, the government can demand any and all records of a person suspected of being involved in a terrorist plot or a racketeering conspiracy under the RICO statutes. With the indictments of President Trump and members of his government, the feds are about to expand that capability to anyone suspected of participating in what could be construed as an insurrection, including those protesting on January 6. The next presidential election is coming up and whoever wins will be able to tell the Justice Department how to define what an insurrection is and, therefore, who can go to prison for speaking their minds. Or not go to prison."

"Now, those are the facts. So, here is my penultimate question for all you freedom-loving academics. How free do you feel?"

Just then, Bradley walked in and stood in the back by the refreshments table.

"How 'free'"— she used air quotes—"*are* American citizens? What quality of freedom did we secure through mutual assured destruction, and everything that's come after, given everything I just said?"

She paused for effect, then repeated. "How free do you feel? Go!"

She pointed to the person sitting closest to her on the left. "You?"

"This was a bad week to stop drinking."

A person in the middle of the C-shape audience raised his hand.

"Fire away," Gail said.

"I'm Professor Rory McClelland, from the University of Colorado's Center for Political Insights, and we've done extensive surveys on Americans' attitudes toward freedom for over ten years. While there are weakly associative effects with other factors, the only two parameters which correlate significantly to Americans' sense of freedom are level of income, and, derivatively, their "whiteness. None of the other 'facts' you mention have any bearing."

Hell, Bradley thought, how many Americans even give our missile defense system any thought at all?

"Well, that is curious," Gail said, "but what do you mean by 'whiteness'?"

"Nonwhite ethnic groups tend to fall at the lower end of the income brackets. They have less income. So they report feeling less free."

A man with a cleanly shaved head and neatly trimmed gray goatee leaned forward. "So, you measured, or surveyed, income and are extrapolating a secondary effect of whiteness?"

"Yes."

"Just to be clear, your *respondents* aren't directly commenting on their whiteness, you, the researcher, are assuming it. Correct?"

"Well, I guess. Reporting ethnicity *is* part of the survey."

A young woman who looked barely out of her teens spoke up. "That makes perfect sense to me. Dr. Bartholomew, the average American is either ignorant of the facts you presented or are only superficially aware of them. In their day-to-day activities, though, the one thing that matters, in terms of feeling 'free,' is money. That is wholly consistent with a capitalist society. Because nonwhites see that white folks have all the money, they think of them as freer."

Gail nodded. "Well, I hate to *defund* my Air Force compatriots, many of whom are retired, out of work, veterans living on the street, or dead, but maybe everyone would have more money if the government didn't spend it all on deterrence, overseas military adventures, surveillance of its own citizens, supporting illegal immigrants, and constructing the police state many citizens now believe they must defend themselves against. Or, alternatively, go to war against their fellow citizens to protect themselves. I hear cries advocating for a new civil war all the time."

Shit. This was depressing. But Bradley didn't have time to sink into the doom and gloom of this session's conversation. He heard someone out in the hall yell, *Gordon's loose!* and wondered who the hell Gordon was. Didn't matter. He had to check on Azul.

CHAPTER 36

AZUL LEADS A FLOW CIRCLE

Bradley was surprised to see Azul running down the hallway. He was carrying a satchel about the size of a bag an old doctor would carry who did home visits.

"I am terribly sorry. I was delayed by a call with my boss and Mr. Conrad Bolton, the HOMI-G benefactor."

Azul was breathing hard. Bradley looked at his watch. "Not much you can do if it's the boss, right?"

"The boss, he is one thing, but the big chief, he is another."

"The big chief?"

"Usually someone at my level does not hear from such a man. But I heard plenty this morning."

"Gosh, I'm sorry to hear that Azul."

"It is very confusing. At first, I receive voice mail from my boss that I may face termination proceedings because of what I have said here. Then I receive call which made me late saying that it was a misunderstanding, and I would be up for a big promotion. I would be my boss's boss. But, we will worry about all this another time."

"Good enough. Thank you for being conscientious."

Azul rushed to the head of the room, past the 30 or so attendees chatting and texting and filling time, much like a room full of students would do, the decibel level at fever pitch. He unzipped the bag and placed his remote speaker on the table and picked up his phone.

"Please, does someone inform me the WIFI password for this room?"

"Haveapie, no caps," someone yelled.

Someone else yelled, "Isn't that a canyon you can go hiking—"

"That's Havasupai," a third corrected.

"So," Azul said. "Now I will play a YouTube recording from a live performance. What I like each of you to do is to use your stopwatch function on your phones—can everyone find that? Look for the clock icon and touch that, and you should find it."

He paused a few seconds. "All is good?"

Bradley sat down in the back.

"I shall play about fifteen minutes of a live music recording. You can find this on YouTube, but we are only going to be listening today. You, please, start your stopwatches when I start the music. Relax, take deep breaths, close your eyes if you wish, but I want for you to try to identify the time when these musicians are no longer just playing the music, but rather, when the music *flows* through them, the moment of true freedom! Please note the time on a piece of paper or on your stopwatch app. Is that good? When the musical passage is complete, we compare notes."

The audience looked eager to play along.

"This is cool, but what do you mean by flow?" someone said.

"As I explained earlier, this state of flow, or what some call being 'in the zone,' or the sweet spot, or mojo even, occurs when your mind and body are precisely balanced between what you are doing, your effort, and relaxation. Science says flow involves the release of dopamine and stimulates the part of your brain active when you are resting or daydreaming. Your performative thoughts dissipate. Your inner critic quiets. You are free, *of yourself*.

Wouldn't that be nice, Bradley thought.

CHAPTER 37

BOLTON BOLTS OUT OF THE BOARD MEETING

"Who is this punk, anyway?" Conrad Bolton demanded as he barked into one of his three cell phones to his newly hired Chief Crisis Communications Officer. He had just been picked up in a Bolton Enterprises corporate limo from the airport in Jackson, Mississippi. He was feeling a bit smug. The other family members on the board of Bolton Enterprises had almost begged him for new ideas to spur revenue growth, even though he only owned 2 percent of Bolton Enterprises and had not played an active role in the company for almost a decade.

"His name is Azul Ebola, or something," the CCC Officer said. "Apparently, he's accused you, in a public forum, of stealing antiquities on the black market."

"So? Every museum worth its salt gets accused of that regularly."

"He's an employee."

'What level?"

"Entry level, although he has been at HOMI-G for a few years."

"Why do I need to get all hot and bothered about this?"

"His family owns half of the Nigerian petroleum industry."

"So? How many currency stores have we got in Nigeria?"

"One."

"How many Bolt-Marts are there in Nigeria?"

"None. But Bolton Enterprises retails a huge percentage of automobile fuel products from Nigerian refiners."

"Oh, okay, I get it. Look, I'm headed into a meeting with the Bolton board. Talk later."

Conrad was incensed. What was an employee named Ebola doing making incendiary comments about his museum? There was a reason why all employees sign confidentiality agreements and non-compete clauses. Even if the document wouldn't stand up in court, it usually scared employees enough to keep their traps shut, especially if they couldn't afford lawyers.

At the board meeting, he quickly and very loosley hugged his brother, two sisters, a cousin, and greeted the non-family members. "Look," he said, taking his seat, "I've got to make this quick and I apologize. You wanted ideas."

"We're all ears. We've got to do something. The New York banks are all colluding against loaning any more money for fossil fuel development—Goldman, Morgan Stanley, JP Morgan, you name it."

"You've got to be kidding. Are they allowed to do that?"

"Ever since they crashed the global economy in '07, they've been playing nice with the government."

"Didn't Trump and Kushner take care of that?"

"They knocked the social cost of carbon down to near zero. With Biden, they got this policy called The Carbon & Climate Principles and fudged it up past $100/ton. That could triple our costs in some countries, especially in Europe."

"Come on, these banks fund wars, arms manufacturing, genocides in South America, Africa, the Israeli-occupied territories. You're telling me they won't fund the extraction of the resources which lubricate the entire world economy?

Suddenly, Conrad had a brainstorm, the "Bolton of genius" the family had been calling such ideas which come at the oddest times.

"Hey, remember when we used to have that number counter on every Bolt-Mart store which totaled up the time saved for customers around the world? What if we double down on the marketing ploy we've been using to sell high-carbon fuel to our loyal climate-denying customers?"

The board looked at him, puzzled.

"I'm not sure I follow," his younger brother said.

"Let's start all those counters again. Only this time, we'll total the carbon discharges estimated from the amount of gasoline each customer buys and puts in the tank."

His brother lit up. "I like it! We could even tack on an extra few cents for the customer to take home a printed receipt. We'll call it a 'brown certificate.'"

Conrad shook his head. "I've got a better idea. Let's call it a 'carbon certificate' just to confuse the libs. Customers can collect and save them, attesting to the contribution they've made to expanding the world's carbon footprint and sustaining humanity's dominion over the whole goddamn planet!"

The air in the room was suddenly energized.

"No one will be able to accuse us of greenwashing, that's for sure," his sister said with a laugh.

"We total all of the customers' contributions on the sign counters in Bolt-Mart's brand colors."

"In neon!"

"And we create a loyalty program and tout each customer's individual total which they can check on a phone app or something. Maybe we'll give out discounts at the end of each quarter—funded by those extra few cents—make it a quarter—for the receipts. A free tank of gas or a couple of lottery tickets or something. The biggest, baddest gas guzzlers will be lining up!"

His sister chimed in, "All the caged hot dogs blistered under the heat lamp you can eat! Condiments free of charge!"

His cousin slapped his knee and cackled. "I mean, this is *the* antidote to this bullshit green lifestyle. Let them eat fumes! That could be our slogan!"

Conrad laughed. "Good one. Or what about, 'Put a lib-tard in your tank today!'"

"Wait," said one non-family board member, tapping the end of his pen on the table. "Won't this shrink our customer base?"

"Nah," Conrad said. "The socialists are buying electric vehicles anyway. In the meantime, all we gotta do is keep pumping gasoline and keep an eye out for the right time to acquire the largest company installing and maintaining charging infrastructure so we can double dip if EVs ever really catch on."

"So this really is a revenue bridge to the electric vehicle future," another cousin said, "that's what we tell Wall Street."

"Should it ever come to pass."

"In the meantime, for every liberal, green-faced customer we lose, we'll gain twice the revenue from the MAGA crowd!"

"Conrad, you've done it again!"

He stood and checked his watch. "My work is done here, gentlemen. And ladies."

"Where are you off to now?"

"To Phoenix, to catch up with a wayward HOMI-G employee."

"You know, you really should come up with a better acronym," Conrad's older brother said.

"Why?"

"It sounds like a badass rap artist with an actual rap sheet."

"What do you know about rap, you're still obsessed with Lee Greenwood."

Conrad's initial reaction to the HOMI-G mess was to personally escort this Ebola punk back to the museum, put him in front of a company-wide meeting, and unceremoniously fire him, make an example out of him. A public lynching.

But after the board meeting, he'd had a change of heart. If this Ebola character really did come from oil money in Nigeria, he didn't want to piss him off. He needed to come up with a better solution, one that reflected the essential business philosophy he espoused in his book, "*Transactional Labor: How to Profess an Equitable Workplace While Running a Multi-Billion Dollar Global Conglomerate.*"

Bottom line: When in doubt, do the opposite of what you first thought you should do.

CHAPTER 38

FREE WILL—OR NOT

After he filled his plate at lunch, Bradley proceeded to the beverage table for a glass of the prickly pear lemonade. How they got a beverage so tasty from that spikey platypus plant was beyond him. He was told Ashera was still in the meeting room trying to coax Gordon back into his cage. Gail was sitting alone. Others were gathered in fours and fives at scattered tables. Several other women, including Dr. Zhou, the Asian professor who thought the hike was for pussies, were sitting at a table with Azul. Nascha scurried to and from the kitchen area. She seemed to be coaching several of the servers and filling in herself.

Hintz and MacGruffin were earnestly murmuring with several other attendees. As for Wertmuller, he'd never seen anyone leave a room with such haste. Oh, and there were the two academics who would be speaking on free will in the afternoon. He'd drop his plate there, introduce himself.

Dr. Walter Contravenir and Dr. Seth Sparksman both tried to stand, fumbling with their napkins and trying to push back uncooperative chairs. Contravenir was still not fully erect. His water glass spilled. For a moment it looked like the whole tablecloth was going to get up with him. "Please, don't get up on my account," Bradley urged.

"Dr. Maniopolos!" Sparksman said, sticking out his hand as he took his seat again.

Bradley smiled. "To be accurate, it's Mr. Maniopolos. I haven't completed a PhD. Maybe someday."

"Oh," Sparksman said, his demeanor deflating. "Still ..."

"You gentlemen have been quiet so far, but please sit, enjoy your meal, just wanted to say hi. I'll be back in a few minutes. Just need to check on the other tables. Dr. Washington told me you two have appeared on stage together before?"

"Yes. Frequently, in fact. We joke that we're the *Car Talk* of the volitionists."

"I'll take your word for it. Back soon." He made his way toward Gail, but had to pass Plemmons.

"I've put in a call to Dr. Washington about your failure to police the language in there." She pointed with her knife to the conference room.

"Whatever," Bradley said.

"Furthermore—"

Her voice trailed off as Bradley eased his way to Dr. MacGruffin's table. He sat in an empty chair and waited for a break in the conversation.

"Dr. MacGruffin, that whole bit about Walkmans and boom boxes was fascinating! Took me back to my New York City years."

"It's changed a lot," he said, blandly.

"My daughters tell me their friends are all living in Harlem. Can you imagine? I guess the Upper East Side isn't *the* place to live anymore."

"The Upper East Side was never *the* place to live, unless you were white and affluent."

Bradley paused. Everyone was so damn reactive against white people. Even other white people. You couldn't win. If people thought he was some ethnic Mediterranean type, they looked at him like he was some swarthy guy right off the boat. If they treated him like he was white, he was expected to be just as touchy as all the other white men these days.

"Well, I'll see you guys in the Free Will session," he said, as he stood up. He looked over at Azul's table, but it was clear his admirers did not want someone crashing their party. When he walked by another table, the attendees were all speaking in low voices. Bradley caught something about Dr. Dildo, decided to skip that table, too.

He'd about had enough of these arrogant pricks, their advanced degrees, their hundred-dollar words, their baleful attitudes. Looking forward to the end of the gig, he returned to the table where his plate and drink waited. Click and Clack had already left. He checked his phone while he forked food into his mouth. Dr. Mikhail Tseitinsky, whom he had met at the reception, passed him with a wink and a smile. Bradley hoped he'd sit down with him, but he continued on to the doors.

Still no texts from Victor.

As soon as Nascha got back to her office, the land line phone rang. This time it was not the Chief. There was a long pause with static on the other end of the line.

"Say it!" she heard a gruff, elderly voice say.

"No. You shay it!" This from a clearly younger man, but with some kind of thick accent.

She then thought she heard something to the effect of, 'If you don't do as I say, you won't graduate.' But it was all garbled. It could very well have been "grab a date." This must be a wrong number, Nascha reasoned, and started to hang up.

"Okay, okay," she heard, as if the microphone wasn't close to the mouth, then "MOM SHARE!" yelled directly into it.

Mom share? Nascha was puzzled. Well, they still got prank calls from time to time. She hung up the phone, and picked up *The Only Good Indians* again. A page in, she wondered, wait, did they mean *bomb scare*? She hadn't heard of anyone calling a bomb scare in years. Certainly not in Sedona. Should she be concerned? Call 911? Maybe police chief Clever Hawk? Was this tied into the earlier backpack incident?

Bradley surveyed the free will session crowd from the dais. Pretty much a full house. More interest in free will than he'd expected, especially for the last session on the third day of a conference that had, in his humble opinion, largely imploded. He introduced Dr. Sparksman and Dr. Contravenir together.

"These two consider themselves the Click and Clack of the volitionist community, so I'm going to call this session Car Talk and let the mechanics repair whatever notions about free will we all have arrived here with ..."

Dr. Sparksman: "Well, Dr. Maniopolos stole my joke, and believe me when I say not many of those are handed out in the free will department. Ha ha!"

Bradley refrained from rolling his eyes.

Sparksman dove right in, arguing that because everything humans do is based on chemical interaction and electrical circuitry, humans cannot decide anything. There is no room for free will, he said, citing evidence from neuroscience research, especially a ten-second delay between when the prefrontal cortex in your brain makes a decision and when your mind acknowledges it. He reviewed the history of this gap, from the earliest research which showed that the gap was a few microseconds to a decade ago when the gap was measured in milliseconds. The very latest experiments moved the spread from a few seconds to as much as ten seconds. He then worked backwards from that point.

"If we look at our evolutionary chart, we see that how we were raised, in what cultural and economic conditions, the genes we inherited, the ancestry we come from, the very evolution of humanity, all function together to ensure that our biological selves have 'decided' before our social selves acknowledge it.

"Thus, whatever we've done, we were going to do anyway. Whatever we're about to do has already been determined. An action has nothing to do with whether we decided to act. So, if Dr. Bartholomew were to have fired her gun at one of us in the audience in that first session, that action would be the result of everything that has come before in her life."

Gail looked at him ruefully.

"Neuroscience has confirmed what many philosophers have been saying for millennia. We have no free will."

Dr. MacGuffin raised a hand and said, "You mean to say criminals are not responsible for their crimes?"

"If they are, then everything that has happened to that 'criminal' before they violated a law is also responsible. It works the other way, too. No one deserves punishment for acts over which they had no control, nor do they deserve rewards or resources for 'good deeds' or doing what they are supposed to—work, parenting, charity ..."

Now that is a concept that could re-order humanity, Bradley thought.

Dr. Contravenir took the opposite tack. He started at the beginning of human evolution, worked towards the present, urging the audience to locate the concepts of purpose, value, and meaning in simpler living creatures, then follow how they were "elaborated on" over the course of evolution.

"All living things have some form of agency, but ..." he said.

Ashera whispered to Gail, "See? That proves my point!"

Gail elbowed Ashera back. "That proves *my* point. Humans evolved to have a higher purpose and value than lower order species. Ours were just e-la-bor-a-ted to the highest point in the food chain."

Contravenir went on. "Our future actions are informed by prior experience. I put it to you, what kind of thing are you? You are the kind of living thing that decides things!" Contravenir said, raising his arm and wagging his extended finger as he read his notes from over his glasses.

Bradley looked at Dr. Tseitinsky who seemed to be chomping at the bit.

"Free will cannot be defined simply as ions flowing through a complex system of brain circuits ..."

"Everything is a complex system," Gail whispered to Ashera, "whether it's a nuclear missile launch silo or a—"

"Or a forest ecosystem, or a gecko's physiology." Ashera completed the sentence for her.

Contravenir added, "Free will is about the *sensation* of making a choice."

Rolex Williams called out: "I feel, therefore I decided!"

"Well, your moss and mushrooms don't 'feel'," Gail countered to Ashera, in a low voice.

"They absolutely do! Scientists have made measurements of electrical ... oh, never mind. All living things feel, they just may not feel in the same ways humans do."

The woman sitting behind Ashera leaned forward and hissed, "Take it outside, you two!"

Contravenir went on. "Now I promised Dr. Washington that I would unveil a unique concept at his inaugural conference." His eyes twinkled like a kid offered a cookie.

"The hardness-softness determinism scale!" he said with a flourish, waving at an illustration of a large circular graph with an indicator dial in the middle. "We've been working on this for several years, thanks to a generous grant from the Magellan Foundation. Think of this like the speedometer on your car dashboard. It's a scale from 0 to 60. If you, like Sparksman, believe in hard determinism, your BIF, or 'Belief in Free Will, is closer to 0. If, as I do, you believe in a much softer determinism, your BIF score is closer to 60."

Jesus, how much money did they spend figuring this out, Bradley wondered. Something you can't even define, let alone measure, is being represented on a numerical scale?

Someone at the back shouted, "Where's Wertmuller? She'll love this! Quantizing freedom!"

Someone else answered, "Nah, the 'math' is too simple. Any idiot would get it."

There *is* no math. Bradley thought.

Contravenir regained control of the dialogue. "You have just validated my overarching point! Life is not a discrete state, as measured in brain pulses, or heat maps of brain activity at a specific point in time. Life is a process. You are living! You are not just alive! You are here, determining your future at every moment because you have free will! That's freedom!"

Sparksman held up a hand. "Not so fast! Having no free will is the most liberating concept ever! Imagine being relieved of the burden of living with the consequences of every action. When you understand that we are all a product of everything which came before, we have no reason to envy one another, outdo one another, kill one another."

"And ... we're back to socialism," Hintz yelled. "Nobody is perfect; therefore we're all the same. No one is responsible. That's anarchy!"

Contravenir countered, "On the contrary, when you understand that we are all a product of biological evolution, the strict hierarchy to life on this planet becomes obvious. Our free will allows us to progress and evolve within this hierarchy."

Sparksman dug in. "Aggressive behavior is not the fault of an adolescent, for example, who has a high adverse childhood experience (ACE) score, spiking testosterone, whose prefrontal cortex is not fully developed, and who is exhausted and hungry because he's homeless and hasn't had a decent meal or slept in a bed for weeks."

MacGruffin shook his head. "Biochemistry aside, what do we do for the white kid he just knifed on the subway?"

Ashera twisted in her seat and glared at MacGruffin. "You just implied the attacker was nonwhite!"

MacGruffin paused before responding. "Statistics do bear out that most violent crime, especially in NYC, is committed by a few thousand offenders, the majority of whom are nonwhite.

"He didn't say this was New York City."

Rolex chimed in, his voice hard. "Yes sir, you just automatically jumped to a racist conclusion."

Sparksman held up a hand. "Let's ask ourselves, where did the intent come from that precipitated the action? In Dr. MacGruffin's scenario, the stabbing."

MacGruffin wasn't deterred. "You're all so worried about the kid with the knife, where does the kid who's now in the emergency room go for his reparation? How does society ensure that the other kid doesn't stab someone else just because he skipped a meal? Do we reward all the kids who didn't knife somebody yesterday with a free lunch today just to keep them from committing a crime?"

Dr. Plemmons raised her voice. "All these arguments are biased because white men like yourselves have had the privilege of choosing the definitions and assumptions which drive the arguments, however rational they may seem. Nonwhite males— or females—did not have the freedom to not accept the pre-defined terms of this debate, the kind of systemic racism that we decide whether or not to buy into every single day."

"Isn't that a triple negative?" Bradley called out, not missing an opportunity to dig at his nemesis.

Gail and Ashera called out "Hear, hear!" together and then looked at each other in surprise.

Plemmons didn't stop there. "These same white men are developing algorithms that will cultivate humans based on DNA fragments associated with the most desirable traits and behaviors. And those traits all will be associated with white males."

Bradley had had it with this bitch. "Well, Dr. Plemmons, if more women would just exercise their free will to decide to be quants and coders instead of elementary school teachers and social workers, they'd have seats at the table when these algorithms are being programmed."

You couldn't hear a bowling ball drop over the commotion in the audience.

"That is positively incendiary!" Dr. Plemmons roared.

Gail wasn't going to let that stand. "He has a point. I joined the first cohort of Missileers in the Air Force. I didn't just bellyache from my tenured perch about wanting equality. I used my 'free will' and went out there and grabbed it! Plus, I needed a job."

Ashera murmured to Gail, "My dad tried everything he knew to get me into a STEM field."

Rolex stood in the middle of the room and used both hands in a placating gesture to get everyone to pipe down. "With all due respect to my esteemed colleagues, can we dial back our free-will no-free-will parlay here? I mean, you're telling us we have no free will before white America has even begun to divest itself of its racist past. We're *owned* by our histories which are, yes, owned and controlled by white men. So if we have *no* free will to *not* be oppressed, does that mean the white man has *no* free will to *not* be oppressors?"

Was that a quadruple negative? Bradley wondered.

From underneath Rolex's suede beret, his dreadlocks swayed and weaved with his words, as he rocked back and forth on his heels.

"White people aren't forced to own up to generations of genocide or stealing Indigenous lands or raping entire nations for their resources. But Black men can be arrested and incarcerated at extraordinary rates because we steal a backpack? And Black women? They can be shot in their beds while sleeping by officers of the law breaking down their doors? How about y'all let us take a deep breath of free will before you take it all away from us again?"

Bradley grabbed a microphone and nodded toward Dr. Tseitinsky. "On that note, let's take a quick ten-minute break. When we return, we'll get a new viewpoint, off the agenda, so to speak."

Bradley made a beeline to Tseitinsky. "Okay, after the break, you get twenty minutes to say your piece."

When they returned, Bradley made the introduction.

"One of our esteemed attendees, who has been patiently soaking it all in, is Dr. Mikhail Tseitinsky, a biology and neuroscience specialist from Stanford, author of the global bestseller *Pre-determined: How Lack of Free Will Makes Us Better People*. I've invited him to make some impromptu remarks."

Dr. Tseitinsky gave a courtly bow and took his place at the podium. "We are nothing more or less than the sum of that which we cannot control—our biology, our environment, our ancestry ... and not just us ... belief in free will is tenacious, but wrong, just like belief in a god is tenacious but wrong."

"Hold on, there," yelled Dr. Hintz, "this isn't a new view. Aren't you saying the same thing as Dr. Sparksman?"

"Even primates have been shown to believe in free will."

"And that bit about God," Hintz went on. "You're contradicting the beliefs of 80 percent of Americans. And remember, the freedom *of* religion in the Constitution doesn't mean freedom *from* religion. Read my monograph, *Prepositional Interpretations of Constitutional Law*."

Tseitinsky regarded the room. "I gotta love Sparksman's argument—he's on my side after all—but where any of us fall on a **BIF** meter is hardly the point. My goal isn't to slice and dice belief in free will into constituent parts because the truth is, it simply no longer has any meaning. My goal is to convince you that neuroscience is real, advancing rapidly, and leaving less and less room for any notion of free will.

"One of the conditions that will change all of us for the better is to quit trying to create 'others' and imposing our judgments, values, and preferences on them," he continued. "We don't *choose* to change, but we can *be* changed. But here's the bottom line, accepting the lack of free will *makes us all equal.* Ergo, equality is a basis for individual freedom. We can't change ourselves. But we can *all* change the circumstances in which we live, survive, and thrive. The lack of free will is a far more advanced instrument for social advancement than, say, the notion of God or any religion or morality imposed from 'above.' Or, god forbid, *quantizing* freedom."

Plemmons groaned audibly. "Then what separates us from robots and highly intelligent AI devices, once we've left the singularity in the rear-view mirror? Under your theory, we're already nothing but automatons, biological machines. Maybe we're not responsible for being short, disabled, dark, unattractive, gay, but are we really not responsible for being fat, lazy, apathetic, and disengaged?"

Hintz was incensed. "I, for one, will not stand here quietly while you disrespect the foundations of American liberty!"

Tseitinsky ignored Hintz's outburst and continued, "No, we are not responsible for being fat, lazy, or stupid because there is no such thing as a norm, or a 'right' way to be. There is only the way *you* are, *she* is, *he/she* is, *them/they* are, a way of being you have no control over. The only reason someone is discriminating against someone else is because the people who think they are superior and who have derived societal power from that belief have convinced themselves and others that it is their right to discriminate against those they deem inferior."

This was all going around in circles. Bradley still figured it was best to be an assimilationist. Become a member of the dominant class and you'll experience less prejudice. Hell, if they're the ones with all the power and if they're going to rely on algorithms to advance the human race, better to be with them than against them.

Tseitinsky held up a hand. "No one is inherently racist. The conditions in which we are raised cause racism. Small children don't even see skin color as a differentiator among their peers. So our job, as citizens of the world, is to eliminate the conditions that lead to racism and then it will, naturally, disappear. Freedom will be more abundant to all!"

Ashera shook her head. "It's too simplistic. Don't we need a belief in free will to survive? If for no other reason than to subconsciously deceive ourselves so we can function in a flawed society? Otherwise, we're nihilists. Preventing nihilism and giving people a reason for living is the role a deity has played throughout history. What do we do with no God *and* no free will?"

One guy at the back yelled out. "Kumbaya!" Followed by the whispered, "This is all absurd."

Hintz picked up the thread. "Nihilism, godlessness, and lack of free will leads us right back to socialism."

"If there is an absurdity about the human condition," Tseitinsky retorted, "it is to hate someone for something they have done or for who they are. In fact, there are deep ethical flaws in believing that free will exists!"

This could have been Washington's entry point, to wax intellectually on his philosophy and ethics, Bradley thought. Too bad for Dr. Dildo.

Contravenir apparently had had enough. "The hard determinism folks, like Sparksman and Tseitinsky—"

Sparksman was already rebutting. "Don't appropriate my position by assuming I'm a hard determinist. I consider myself a colloidal determinist..."

Colloidal? What the hell is that? Bradley was now convinced that these people were all appropriationists. They just took any old word and gave it whatever meaning they decided at the moment.

"Whatever, your argument relies too much on this neuroscientific ten-second gap between the brain and the "mind." He made exaggerated air quotes around mind.

Contravenir scoffed. "It's like imagining and constructing an entire hominid from one tooth. You can't separate a human being's mind from his brain, her thoughts from his feelings, they/them's logic from their sensations. As a whole, each of us adjusts our actions based on all new information gathered from our surroundings and experiences. We respond holistically, not as isolated body parts or neurological conceptions."

Bradley stood. "Okay, I don't think we're going to resolve a debate that's been going since the cave man decided, or not, to step out onto the steppe, but I am going to give Tseitinsky the last word."

"Wait, that's not fair," Contravenir objected, "Tseitinsky wasn't even invited! I was assured by Dr. Washington that I would get the final word. The Freedom Center's position on the matter leans strongly towards free will!"

"That's news to me," Bradley countered, "and he's not here so—"

"And I'm the only one here that presented something new," Contravenir complained.

Sparksman laughed. "Imagine, a place for the study of the philosophy of freedom having a 'position' on free will. That,

Dr. Contravenir, contravenes the entire notion of academic scholarship!"

Contravenir was thoroughly offended. "I didn't think we'd resort to making fun of our names. You're simply espousing something that you would have espoused anyway. You don't get credit for contributing to the knowledge base. Everything that came before you gets the credit. You were just ... just ... just a vessel for transporting the idea!"

Bradley groaned. He needed to get people out of the room. Right when he opened his mouth, Plemmons stood, hands on hips.

"Apparently, all we have here is a neural-scientific process to maintain a system of white male elites who maintain control over everyone else."

MacGruffin retorted. "Someone has to be in control; otherwise, the human race would destroy itself!"

"Copy that!" Gail blurted.

Not to be left out, Hintz got in his dig. "This lack of free will BS is nothing but socialism, that faux equalizer of people, wrapped in pseudo-intellectual-neuroscientific armor."

Tseitinsky leaned toward the mic. "Would you rather go through life looking down on everyone you consider less than yourself, or less fortunate, pretending they are invisible, which is frankly what most of us do every minute of every day? Or empathize and understand that they don't deserve their unfortunate fate any more than you deserve your fortunate one?

We are equal because I didn't choose to be superior, Bradley thought. Is that what he's saying?

CHAPTER 39

VICTOR GOES DARK, BRADLEY GOES AWOL

Two stiff gin and tonics into happy hour, light-headed, tilting past tipsy, Bradley decided to take a quick break before the evening's trip to the casino. Two drinks on an empty stomach. He should eat something or he might never make it out of the bar. He wanted to hear what "Mr. quant" Victor had to say about "quantizing freedom," but he wasn't responding. Maybe they could get off the topic of how many women they've had sex with, which was making him more uncomfortable with every recollection.

That CLCC babe, Catherine, was occupying the gap between his mind, his body, and his brain. He wondered what she looked like in a swimsuit. He hadn't seen Valerie in a sexy swimsuit in years.

We're not responsible for anything we do. That's what the volitionists had said. He could get behind that. At least right now.

He got into his room, made a beeline to the toilet. Why did pants have to have such short zippers these days? He couldn't get his dick in and out without snagging a pube or pinching skin. He didn't like how his balls hung precariously against the metal teeth. He stroked himself to a half hard-on but couldn't muster the energy or the interest in more.

That done, he emptied his pockets and belly-flopped onto the bed, rolled over, then lay still, savoring the quiet of the room, the heated, jagged cliffs out the window, the sun heading over the western horizon. He let their thermal energy waves synchronize with his brain waves, his mind waves, whatever. He could lie here forever, except that he only had ten minutes.

Where the hell was Victor, anyway?

He got up, checked his look in the mirror before heading to the elevator. He'd packed a more "festive" shirt, maroon and forest green paisley, to wear to the colloquium's final evening event. Did he look okay in it? Was that another red spot under his left eye, looking too much like a zit? Along with that new wrinkle on his face. He dropped the Ricola-wrapped gummy into his pocket. He looked at his vial of little blue pills. Looked again. Ah, what the hell. He tapped one into his palm and popped it.

Azul was waiting at the elevator.

"Hey, man," Bradley greeted him, a touch of his palm to his shoulder.

"Hello, Mr. Maniopolos."

"Please, Azul, Bradley is fine."

"If I may ask, Mr. Bradley, What is your ethnic background?"

"Uh, part Greek, part Lebanese, all-American. I mean, I was born in this country." He quickly changed the subject. "I hope you've found the colloquium rewarding?"

"Yes, yes, and have you have found that it met your expectations?" Azul countered.

"I guess I could say it has *exceeded* my expectations because this turned out nothing like I expected. Especially that free-for-all around free will."

They both looked at the ceiling, then the floor, then at the panel of buttons.

"Hey, Azul, isn't it a bit risky to, uh, have a band named Sambo?"

"I don't think so. When we decided to use the acronym, we looked up Sambo and found it is the name for a Martial Arts

Combat sport developed by the Russian military. We thought that was cool!"

"But doesn't it offend African American patrons?"

"Not as long as the band members are not white. It's like when it's okay that black people use the n-word among themselves."

The elevator doors opened into a bustling lobby. Azul stepped out and disappeared into the sea of bodies milling about, his Freedom Center academics and the CLCC ladies, most of whom wore foam imitation feather headdresses on their heads and Mardi Gras beads around their necks. He looked for Catherine. Nascha was directing traffic.

"The buses are a few minutes late because of the weather," Nascha yelled.

Both crowds were effervescent. The CLCC ladies—you'd think they were going to be served their chilled Chardonnay by Pocahontas at Preservation Hall on Bourbon Street. The resort hair salon must have been packed all day. Bradley hadn't seen an Audrey Hepburn beehive in decades. Another woman obviously had requested the same hairstyle Jennifer Coolidge had as Tanya McQuoid in *White Lotus*. He wanted to see those two curly-cue strands hanging down on each side of her face tickling his balls while she sucked him off.

As he was making his way to the doors, he passed Gail in a Wrangler denim skirt and camo green top, along with her MAGA cap. Her expression seemed rueful, not the look of someone about to party all night.

"Might as well go out in style," she muttered, as he passed by.

"I feel underdressed," Ashera lamented to Gail, sporting a stylish pair of sweats patterned with a menagerie of animal prints, and a Mount St. Helens College hoodie.

"Smart, though," Bradley said as he passed. "Casinos tend to be over-refrigerated. You won't freeze in that sweatshirt."

The buzz in the lobby was infectious. Bradley's mood shifted from work mode to reward mode. He had to be careful it didn't go off into what-the-fuck mode. He kept looking for Catherine.

Nascha was now behind the registration desk. He made his way over there.

"Do you ever get down to the casino?"

"I have my vices but gambling isn't one of them." She thought about Finn. That man could definitely be a vice.

"Well, we've certainly enjoyed the Song of the Sun's hospitality. Thank you for keeping the ponies running on time."

"Ponies?"

"Well, you know, instead of the trains."

She smiled.

The larger buses for the Freedom Center group arrived. Bradley and Nascha tried to get everyone pointed in the right direction.

"I'll take care of this." Nascha said. You go ahead and get a seat."

He and Dr. Plemmons couldn't help but move in lockstep with the crowd.

"Might as well try to win some dough before I go extinct," he said to her cheerily.

"You're not as clever as you think, nor qualified to facilitate a scholarly conference on freedom."

"No, but I'll retire soon, so give me credit for voluntarily taking one straight white guy out of the equation."

"Millions to go before we sleep."

"Think of me as one less spermatoid in the cervix of the patriarchy."

"I'll think of you as a recessive gene in the DNA of intelligent humor."

"Touché! I'd ask if you'd sit next to me on the bus, see if we can reboot our collegiality, but you probably think I have cooties."

"The only boot you'd get is this." She raised her leg, displaying her ankle-length black boot, suitable for a construction site, but with red eyelets, red shoestrings that could double as zip ties, and a thick two-inch heel suitable for crushing beer cans. Maybe she was into BDSM. Now that would be different!

"I'll hold you to that!" Bradley retorted.

The door opened. He hopped up the three steps, gave a breezy *hey there* to the bus driver. Bradley walked the aisle toward the very back. He felt that tingling in his body that said, the gig's almost over, and the rise in his crotch that said the blue magic is working. The tension of always being "on" coalesced in his bones, but was now dissipating from deep in the marrow out through his pores. He arched into the seat, exhaled with intention. Azul and Rolex slid into the seat in front of him. He couldn't help but overhear their conversation.

"I have only now discovered how exploited I really am by the HOMI-G."

"How so, my man?"

"I was invited to participate by the Freedom Center, then my boss snatched the opportunity away from me, then he called to say they wanted a Black person after all, and I'm not even Black, I am Nigerian ..."

"We're all brothers here."

" ... and then after I am here, they tell me the payment I was to receive would be transferred to the HOMI-G general fund. It is very triggering."

Rolex shook his head. "That's not right, man."

"I am not finishing with them yet."

Bradley laughed to himself. Here they were. An African, an African-American, and a guy mistaken for an African-American in the 1960s south, all sitting at the back of the bus.

Ashera stood in the driveway watching the crowd climb into the bus when Gail came up beside her. "You know, I hate crowds, I'm just going to drive separate," Gail said. "Wanna join?"

Ashera exhaled. "Yes. Thank you. After Covid, I'm not a fan of being packed into an enclosed space, either."

"I take it you're leaving Gordon home for the evening?"

"He's had enough excitement for the day. I still don't know why that woman let him loose! And what happened to her? It was so upsetting. I mean, he could've been stuck inside one of those meeting rooms forever!"

Once they buckled into Gail's Jeep Cherokee, a vehicle that had definitely seen better days, Gail blasted the AC and pulled up right behind the bus. Once the bus closed its doors and finally started moving, Gail followed. Nascha had told her it was better to follow since the road off the interstate was a little iffy.

Ashera shivered. "Your car's an ice box."

"Medical. My body doesn't properly cool down."

"I saw your "before" photo. You weren't always this heavy. I've had weight issues in the past, too."

Gail didn't reply. Instead, she gazed out the windshield towards the giant layered cliffs lining the road, shimmering with moisture. You couldn't go north or south without passing Big Brother. He was not nearly as bewitching wet, more blood-colored, the kind of brown blood becomes before the forensics team arrives.

Tourists strolled along the sidewalk around the resort, heading toward the fancy restaurants and shops of Sedona. These people had too much free time, too much extra money, and too much California, Gail thought. Too much metaphysical bullshit. She felt like she should warn Ashera, be more fulsome about what might be coming tonight, but she didn't know how. Whatever was in store for her, she didn't want to endure it alone.

"So just what is it about the magic of this place, Ashera?"

"Good question. There are, uh, these areas called vortices? The energy from the rocks and cliffs are said to synchronize with the natural electromagnetic waves in your body. Not sure there's anything scientific about that, but yeah, I just feel nourished. Like the earth is trying to tell me something."

Gail glanced toward Ashera and then stared back out the windshield. "Did you major in spirit-ology or something else woo-woo?"

Ashera chuckled. "I wonder if I wasn't born with it. You don't feel *anything*?"

"Nope."

"I'm planning to get up early tomorrow and go to Bell Rock and meditate."

"You tell me all about it."

Gail kept glancing at the rear view mirror and out the side windows. Were they being followed? Non-Hodgkin's lymphoma. It'd get her eventually. If the Air Force didn't.

"You know what's funny about my cancer?" She turned to Ashera.

"Nothing's funny about it."

"I'm the only patient my oncologists have seen with it that *isn't* losing weight."

Gail thought of the money she'd raised. At least she'd done her part for her fellow Missileers. She'd be leaving a legacy behind. That was something.

Ashera shifted in her seat, adjusted her seat belt. "So, what do you really think about the last few days?"

Gail snorted. "I can't believe people get paid to study this crap. The world is ablaze and we're debating something that has no definition."

"I don't disagree."

"I think that's one reason why my people love Trump."

"I don't get it. He tries to get everyone to hate everyone but himself."

Gail laughed. "That's why we love him. He's real. He doesn't take shit from anyone."

"Are you kidding me? Are we talking about the same guy?"

"Absolutely. He's a dealmaker. He looks out for himself. We all do that, but he isn't trying to hide it. He isn't bound by stupid traditions or so-called norms. He gets things done. He'd have no problem giving Taiwan back to China, even though he tries to get everyone to hate the Chinese. He'd happily give Gaza and the West Bank to the Israelis even though he's probably a rabid anti-Semite. And he'd sell out Ukraine to Putin just because he thinks Putin's a real man and Zelinsky is just an annoying Jewish comedian."

Ashera's eyes went wide. "And you admire him for those things? Because he's in it for himself, has no honor or loyalty, and foments hate?"

"Because he's taking on the goddamn government itself. He co-opted one of the two political parties and instead of having to be loyal to it, the party has to be loyal to him. He's achieved something no American leader can claim in history. He *owns* his political party. He's packed the Supreme Court. He can dismantle this global police state we're living in."

"And build a police state for the people who aren't loyal to him."

"He doesn't mean that stuff. He wants to put the fear of God into the elites, the immigrants, the people not paying their fair share."

"He doesn't seem very godly to me," Ashera said with a huff of exasperation. "Anyway, I can't believe we're debating this crap about freedom when the fucking planet is boiling over, species are dying, refugees are flooding borders across the world because where they live has already become inhospitable. Honestly, Gail,

I don't know what it takes to convince the millions of people like you that this climate and refugee shit is for real."

"It won't matter soon anyway."

"What are we even doing here? Why did I accept this invitation?

"I know exactly why I accepted this panelist invitation."

"Why?"

"To say what I said. And now I'm going to pay the price."

Bradley walked to the front of the bus and greeted a few people. He felt it was his duty as facilitator. The festive energy was accelerating. He was glad his untucked shirt covered his crotch.

When he returned to his seat in the back, he decided, what the hell? He dug into his pocket and fished out the Ricola-wrapped gummy Catherine had given him, unwrapped it, and popped it in his mouth. It would take the edge off. Cherry, too. He smiled. His favorite flavor.

Within ten minutes, he could feel the familiar sensation, his brain expanding ever so slightly against his skull, his vision getting more languid, the sharp edges of life separating, dissolving, dropping away like fuzzy fringe.

When he saw the tops of everyone's heads on the bus gently vibrating, he knew this was different. He looked out the window, thinking what he was experiencing was similar to motion sickness. The bus seemed to be going faster than it should, then slower. Passing cars floated as if on a bed of air, like pucks in a slo-mo air hockey game. The landscape was dripping onto itself, reds from the rocks sliding down the sides of cactuses, pooling on the desert floor.

Oh, God, was he tripping? He hadn't experienced anything like this since college. If he was, this was going to be a long night.

When the bus hit the dirt road and the lights of the casino were finally in view, he felt like he was in his own movie. The place was small, but it glowed, flickering against the gray landscape of dusk around it, like an alien spacecraft waiting for their arrival.

As they disembarked, one version of Bradley said normal things to normal people while another version held an entire conversation with himself. At least that's what Tripping Bradley was telling Normal Bradley.

By the time he stepped onto the casino floor, Tripping Bradley stared around the pulsating room, which seemed to wrap him in an awkward, too-intimate embrace. Clanging bells, high-pitched whistles, and blinking lights permeated his skull. He was under the glass of a pinball machine, his head was the ball, flippers shooting him this way and that, his thoughts ricocheting from one bumper to the other.

Azul came up to him and said something. Hopefully, Normal Bradley said something normal. Tripping Bradley marveled at the bright whites of the younger man's eyes, his gleaming teeth, his wide smile. Man, did he have a nice smile. He was handsome, graceful, sculpted body lithe and elegant. Bradley viscerally understood why the women in the audience wanted to see Azul pound his drums shirtless.

Did that mean he was gay? Or bi? Or whatever? Something on some spectrum someone made up somewhere? He frankly couldn't care less. The man was beautiful. Azul said something about the music playing in the distance and then walked away. Tripping Bradley could feel the music in his bones, so maybe it wasn't so distant.

Then he saw Catherine. A jaunty smile was etched on her face as she approached, and he almost broke down and hugged her. "Man, am I glad to see you!" Every word floated past his lips in sing-song treble clef.

Her smile grew even wider, cartoonishly exaggerated. "Did you take the gummy?"

Her eyes were wide, her lashes thick and curved up beneath her brows like soft, dark talons. He wondered if they were real. If she were real. The mini prickly pear cacti on her sun dress were dancing. There was something a little sinister about her, too. He leaned closer. Their thorns seemed to quiver and point straight at him. Taunting him.

"I did, "he said. "Did you?"

"Yes!"

What the hell was in it?"

"A rocking good time, that's what!"

CHAPTER 40

WASHINGTON AND THE MPS ARRIVE

Nascha thought she'd seen it all, but now her heart was clanging against her ribcage. Occasionally, the resort had reason to summon the Sedona police, the fire department, or a first responder for a medical emergency. This was a SWAT team, half a dozen heavily armed men, storming the grounds like they owned the place. She heard helicopters circling overhead.

"Ma'am, I don't wish to alarm you. We are not deliberately trespassing, but—"

"Alarmed?" Nascha interrupted. "Why would anyone be alarmed at six heavily armed and armored men invading your property?"

"'Invading' seems a bit over the top."

"This is Native American land." She pointed to the insignia on the man's arm. "You're U.S. military. I don't think 'invading' is 'over the top.'"

The leader of the group scowled. "We're Air Force MPs. Military police. Our presence here has nothing to do with you."

She held one hand with the other, hoping to keep both from visibly trembling. "Well, you didn't call ahead for a reservation, you weren't invited, so, yeah, you are trespassing on Yavapai Nation land, violating our sovereign rights."

"Ma'am," the man said, his placating and disarming voice pissing her off even more, "I'd like to reiterate that our presence has nothing to do with you or your tribe. We're looking for a Gail Bartholomew. Our intel indicates that she is a registered guest. On behalf of the United States Air Force, I'm simply asking for your cooperation in finding her."

What the hell? And she'd thought the day could not possibly get any weirder, when an hour earlier, Dr. Washington had stormed the lobby, albeit without body armor and automatic weapons. He'd been impatient, anxious, and more than a bit imperious. He'd drummed his fingers on the registration desk as if she was deliberately taking her time.

He was a big guy who'd loomed over the registration desk. "Hi. I'm the guy who signs the check for the Freedom Center colloquium."

"Ah, yes. Dr. Washington," Nascha had said. She decided not to mention the ladies' protest group looking for him earlier in the week. "What can I do for you? I trust you drove all the way from Tucson to tell me personally what a great job we've done," she said, smiling.

"Hardly. Our group was supposed to hold an event at Tuzigoot tonight. I was just there and was told that the group reservation was cancelled because of the possibility of rain. That was a mighty stiff cancellation fee, I might add, for not giving 48 hours notice."

"That's standard in the industry, FYI. But you could try to negotiate it down on the grounds of inclement weather."

"When has it ever rained like this in July in Sedona?"

"It's not unheard of. The Yavapai origin story takes place during a flood, so—"

"What are you talking about?"

"Yavapai, just think 'have a pie'."

"I don't have time for this. I have important business with several in the group that absolutely cannot wait. Traffic was awful, and there were multiple wrecks on the interstate."

Nascha sensed something not quite right was afoot. "As you're not a registered guest, I'm not sure I can help. Have you not contacted Bradley Maniopolos?"

"Are you kidding? I've been trying since yesterday. He refuses to respond."

"May I see an I.D.? This is somewhat peculiar."

"Of course," Washington said, reaching for his wallet.

Startled, Nascha turned towards the sound of voices and commotion as a group of women with signs piled into the lobby. She recognized one of them. "Hey, I remember you. Back for round two?"

"We demand an audience with Dr. Washington."

"Well, you're in luck." She gestured with her arms as if she was throwing a baby their way.

"Oh hell, they're following me!" Washington crowded back against the registration desk. "They've been harassing me back in Tucson for two days."

"Then why don't you all go to the bar and have a chat?" Nascha called out to the bartender. "Andre!"

Washington's glare at Nascha was like two arrows, so she gave him her brightest placating-an-asshole-guest smile. "Just kidding. None of you are guests at the hotel, so you're all trespassing."

"I have a reservation!" One of the women shouted.

"What's the name?

"Ivy Greenberg."

Nascha typed the name into her system. "Ah, so you do. A room with a double bed. Maximum of two guests, three with a rollaway, Where, per chance, were the rest of you planning on staying?"

The women turned away, looking at the ground or away at a wall.

"Excuse me one moment." Nascha went into her office, closed the door, and hit the Chief's number on her cell phone.

"What?" He must've had his phone in his hand.

"We've got a situation brewing here. The head honcho for that Freedom Group just arrived and—"

"Send him on down! The rest of his tribe is having a grand old time."

"I think it's more than that. Anyway, he's Black, so he doesn't do anything for my quota."

"Hm … alright, I'll cut you some slack this time. We'll apply the three-fifths rule."

"Okay, He's not alone, though. There's a gaggle of ladies following him, not sure why. Has something to do with a vibrator. Anyway, they're all white. You'll count all of them three-fifths for my monthly if I send them your way?"

"They pull a one-arm bandit, or roll the dice, they're yours."

"Deal."

Dr. Washington and his malcontents had been weird enough, but the Air Force MPs standing in front of her now looked to be a bigger problem.

"We know Bartholomew has been staying here and participating in a Freedom Center conference. The Air Force has a warrant for her custody, it's similar to a warrant for arrest. We don't want to cause undue harm to you or your property, so it's important that we gain your cooperation."

"Is that a threat?" Yet again, the federal government violating their sovereign rights.

"We don't mean it as such."

"We have our own police force, you know. I just have to make the call." She could see Deputy Police Chief ErVann Cliff Dweller and his two officers, responsible for six sites over a 2,500-square-mile area, putt-putting over in the one police car that might have enough fuel to get to the Song of the Sun.

"There's no need for them to be involved," the lead officer said.

"We don't track our guests. I'm not even authorized to confirm whether she is registered here."

"Then we'll have to stake out the facility." "Guys," he motioned to his crew, "canvass the parking lot for a 2008 Jeep Cherokee, AZ vanity plate TITAN II.

"You know her license number?"

"Of course. She still has a parking permit for the Cold War Missile Museum, located on Air Force property. Must have paid a pretty penny for that vanity plate, too."

"You gonna stake out our property in public?"

"I'm afraid so. We're not some clandestine operation. Our mission is simply to locate Bartholomew and escort her back to the base."

Nascha didn't want these heavily armed intruders hanging around scaring the guests. But she wasn't going to breach the personal rights of one of her guests either. Especially a woman.

"It is a violation of the guests' bill of rights to divulge even the guest's room number. In fact, that's a federal law. Look on the back door of any hotel guest room in America and read the certificate."

"We were hoping to find her in a public area earlier in the day, a conference room or the dining room or bar, but we were unduly delayed in Phoenix, then diverted onto Indian School Road to circumvent an accident."

Just the mention of that road made her think bad spirits were in her midst. Made her see red.

"So, you're going to stand guard on the sidewalk at the entrance? Because you do not have tribal permission to be on premises. I can't grant that. And I don't think you'll want to be scaling those wet slippery cliffs lining our private golf course. You could attempt to rappel Big Brother behind us, but I wouldn't recommend it."

"Big brother, ma'am?"

"The massive cliff on the other side of the highway."

"Ah, I see your point."

"No vehicle with license plate TITAN II in the parking lot, sir," one of the trio said when they re-entered the lobby. "But—"

"Okay, let's clear out. We'll leave a two-man team at the perimeter in case she returns."

"Wait," the guy said. "I talked to a guy out front and he said two buses full of passengers headed out for the Coins of the Canyon Casino. His daughter's a cadet at the Air Force Academy and he was happy to help."

Damn Rodrigo, Nascha thought. Always going on about his daughter.

When the troops cleared out, Nascha called the Chief again.

"There's gonna be a big pow-wow down your way. Not sure all the different groups are going to be getting along."

"Now what?"

"Air Force MPs just left here."

"You've got to be kidding me. We're fighting the U.S. military again?"

"They're looking for one of our guests. A woman from the freedom group? You're not gonna hang her out to dry, are you?"

"Are you kidding? I'm going to go find her and tell her she needs to be making tracks outta here."

"Promise me."

"You think any self-respecting Yavapai would do anything to help the Feds on our own land?"

CHAPTER 41

AT THE CASINO

Bradley and Catherine sat at a blackjack table with one other player. The dealer tossed the cards out of the shoe so fast it made Bradley rear back, as if one of the cards was going to take an eye out. Catherine laughed, leaned over and cooed. "It's so wild! Looks like a cascading waterfall of hearts, clubs, spades, and diamonds."

Professor Zhou walked by the table. Normal Bradley said, "Hi! How's that wound healing?"

"I got 50 likes on Instagram!"

He turned to Catherine. "You should have seen her after we got soaked during the hike, covered in brick red mud like she was modeling a new line of facial scrub."

Dr. Zhou scowled, then walked off. The design of the professor's blouse moved in sine waves as she receded into the crowd. He pointed it out to Catherine.

"What's a sign wave?" She asked.

"Sine wave!" He drew one in the air with his index finger.

She playfully grabbed at Bradley's sleeve, brought it close to her eyes, then away from it.

"I'm zooming in ... I'm zooming out ... zooming in, out ... in ... out."

"Just don't wipe your nose on it."

"Don't be gross," she said sternly.

Geez, she's touchy, normal Bradley thought.

All evening at the casino, they'd been casually touching and bumping into each other, giggling like grade-schoolers, asking each other if he or she had seen the same whacky image. The hallucinogen seemed to moderate what the blue pill was doing to his penis, then reinforce it.

The pattern in the carpet began to undulate. Bradley noticed the pattern was similar to one prevalent in the resort, like interlocking staples. He reached down to touch it, make sure it wasn't really moving, almost falling out of his chair and uncomfortably bending his erection. His grin was absurdly wide as he righted himself.

"This pattern must be sacred or something," he said, dreamily.

"I have a silver ring with that pattern. So cool!"

He stood, bracing himself on the edge of the table. "I need to move."

"Let's go outside. I could use a cigarette."

"You a smoker?"

She smiled and started digging in her purse. "Only when I'm partying. Or drinking coffee. Or having a drink. Only the ones that taste good."

Once outside, Catherine lit up a Virginia Slim, took a deep drag, then tilted her head back and blew a stream of smoke up into the night sky. Bradley looked up too. Noticed the sounds of the chopper overhead. Green and red warning lights on the landing gear twinkled like low-hanging stars. Casino security, he figured. Before her cigarette was finished, a third chopper lit up the sky over the casino and the canyon surrounding it, this one with a headlight beam, the kind of police chopper used to locate someone on the ground on the run.

"Come on, let's go back in."

The Chief had no problem finding Gail and Ashera, both wearing their name badges. He explained what Nascha had told him.

Yeah, okay, I know what's going down," Gail told him.

Ashera shot her a puzzled look. "Wait, what's going down?"

"Look," the Chief told them, "There's one main road in and out of this place. It's hard packed, but unpaved. There's another path wide enough for a vehicle out the back."

He pointed east.

"It's not kept up real good. You definitely want four-wheel drive. That road will take you all the way to Montezuma Castle National Monument, under the jurisdiction of the National Park Service. What you do at that point, should you make it there, I don't know. Anyway, good luck."

His cell phone buzzed. "Oh shit sticks," he blurted out. "Your pals from the Air Force are already here. My guards are detaining them at the entrance. I'll go try to hold them off for as long as possible."

He walked quickly to his golf cart. The Montezuma Mobile, his staff called it. For all the wild mythology about how the Yavapai and other Native Americans in the region took on the U.S. government, the white settlers, the pioneers in their rickety wagons, he'd never dreamed he'd have to do his part to fend off a, what? Not an attack, not an invasion, but certainly an incursion onto their sovereign land.

Several vehicles and uniformed officers were at the security huts located at the perimeter of the casino property. The Chief introduced himself to the man who appeared to be in charge.

"Well, we got ourselves a situation here."

"We sure do." The man was dressed for a SWAT raid, but had a U.S. Air Force insignia on his arm and emblazoned on his bullet-proof vest. "We seek your cooperation, not confrontation."

"Well, here's the situation. As I understand it, you are seeking to apprehend an individual who has a right to be on tribal land as our guest along with the rest of her group from the Song of the Sun Resort, our sister property. You have a warrant for her detention, according to my resort manager, but said warrant is not recognized on our land. It is within our rights to turn you away, unless you are expressly invited to take part in our facility's entertainment. I should stress that admission to the Coins of the Canyon is by invitation, not by paid admission. That is, we are not a public facility with equal access to all who can buy a ticket. We are a private facility, more like a club than a retail operation. All of which means you can wait at the boundary to the property. So, if you would, please turn your vehicles around and return to where you see the sign, facing the opposite way, that says, "Entering the Yavapai Reservation." It's just up the road a bit, and I'm happy to escort you."

Gail and Ashera walked to Gail's jeep in the large casino parking lot. Gail was out of breath almost every step of the way. It was probably the most she had walked in a few years. She was perspiring profusely. Her shirt was soaked under her pits and around her neck.

"Here." She handed her car keys and room key to Ashera. "I'm not retreating out the back way. I'm making a stand. When you get back to the resort, just throw my suitcase in the Jeep. I'm already packed. I'll figure out how to get it back to Tucson later. I don't want them confiscating my car."

"Wait, you knew this was going to happen?"

"I had a hunch. Was hoping they'd nab me in the resort, and it would have been swift and relatively painless. I didn't want to ruin your evening."

"Ruin my evening? What kind of lightweight do you take me for?"

"Hey, we barely know each other. How would I know how you would react?"

Ashera pulled out her phone. "What if I take video of you and the officers? Dark, grainy iPhone footage with the headlights of your car and maybe one or two of the MP vehicles? In the middle of the desert? At dusk? This is what the Air Force is willing to do to one of their own? I'll make it go viral."

"You're kind, but I don't want you implicated in my mess."

"The one thing I learned 'on the job' at the Hill was how to make an effective fifteen-second video suitable for propagating. It would be an honor to help a veteran Missileer after everything I've learned."

Well. That was sweet. And it sucked. No way could Gail tell her the rest of the story. "Hey, maybe you should take my cell phone, too. Send the video to everyone in my contacts list. Lots of Missileers involved in our medical advocacy activities."

Ashera had a worrying thought. "Is your gun in your car or the hotel room?"

"Neither." She patted her hip, then lifted her shirt tail. "Casino needs to up their security."

Uh-oh, Ashera thought. She got behind the wheel of Gail's Jeep and waited what seemed like eternity until Gail climbed into the passenger seat, then headed toward the casino's entrance. But they didn't see what they had expected.

"Where are the Air Force officers?" Ashera asked the guards at the security booth.

"Chief escorted them to the property line."

"Aw hell," Gail groused. "There goes our Instagram moment."

Bradley and Catherine returned in time for the Kremlin performance to begin.

"I am really looking forward to this," Catherine said. 'No More Roads to Moscow' was one of the first rock 'n' roll records I ever listened to. I stole it from my older sister's collection."

The light show monopolized Bradley's capacity to pay attention to anything. The room had screens along three walls and the ceiling showing familiar images now ingrained in popular culture—mushroom clouds over Hiroshima and Nagasaki, shock and awe CNN footage from the first War in Iraq where the night sky over Baghdad looked like a low-tech computer simulation of war rather than an invasion itself, actual footage from the Vietnam war and popular films about the war like *The Deer Hunter* and *Platoon* and *Born on the Fourth of July*. The images were sped up or slowed down to synchronize with the music. Even through his hallucinogenic haze, Bradley sensed the performance was less about music and all about the light show. The band knew fewer chords than the Ramones.

Catherine pulled Bradley down onto a couch in a lounge area in the back. He felt like he was at a masquerade where it got harder and harder to mask his hard-on.

"This just feels too good!" She yelled. She pulled out her lighter, flicked it, and held it up.

"I know! I know!" It was a little easier to hear here. It was darker too.

She pulled him closer, leaned into him, and brought her mouth towards his. Bradley was startled when he realized Azul was standing close by, just outside the door to the lounge. Luckily, he hadn't noticed them yet. He took a few steps forward, eyes focused on the stage.

"Catherine, there are people I work with here."

"So? You'll never see them again." She batted her eyelashes. "I'm really into you."

Bradley gave her a long look. In his tri-dimensional fantasy-reality-hallucination zone, he liked her too. Wanted her. Her features faded in and out while BreastBalcony3000 faded out and in. Other Instagram babes he'd gotten far too familiar with crowded his field of vision. A kaleidoscope of fragmented images started spinning like what was going on in Jimmy Stewart's head when he was looking down from the San Simeon Mission tower in *Vertigo*. Mercifully, he saw movement out of the corner of his eye. Azul was heading toward the stage.

"Wait! This guy I know, from my freedom group, he's going on stage! OMG, he's taking the place of the drummer!"

The rest of the band members did a gradual diminuendo on a standard four-power-chord riff, as the drummer relinquished his stool. Azul took up the sticks and sat down. When the lead guitar, keyboard, and rhythm guitar decrescendo-ed to a dull roar, the lead guitarist gave the cut-off sign to his fellow musicians, pointed his guitar neck towards Azul, bowed with his free arm rolling from his head to his ankles like he was announcing the arrival of an eminence, and stepped back.

"Azul Ebunoluwa, front man and lead percussionist for the Superstitious Afro-centric Mountaintop Brothers Orchestra, SAMBO!" the guitarist yelled.

Azul's solo was mind-blowing. Bradley had never seen anyone move around a drum set with such speed and precision. Was he seeing as many tom-toms and cymbals as he thought he was seeing? His vision dissociated into a smokey, hazy blur, his heart beating in syncopated time with every beat of Azul's drums, the vaporous residue of Catherine's Virginia slim mingling with his own breath and their tongues through adjoined lips, her left arm around his neck, her right hand rubbing the crotch of his pants at a tempo Bradley hadn't known since he was a young man, his pecker hard enough to cut diamond.

"It seems you're ready for me, too," She whispered—loudly—in his ear.

He struggled to his feet. "Let's go up front. I wanna watch him play."

Catherine let out a frustrated sigh. "Fine. But I'm not done with you yet."

CHAPTER 42

VICTOR AND RACHEL HEAD WEST

Victor hadn't been in New York three hours before Rachel insisted that they catch the next available flight to Phoenix, then drive to Sedona. His own big mouth triggered it. Whether he did so because he truly thought Rachel could be of help or because of his inherent envy of his friend, well, future conversations with his alter ego or a therapist he never went to would have to sort that out.

Traveling with Rachel was like traveling with his parents when he was a kid. She took care of everything. Within minutes, she'd bought their tickets online, got a hotel reservation, and before he could even say Travelocity, they were hailing a cab at 79th and Columbus.

"Once we're in Arizona, you're going to have to play the adult."

"Why? You're so good at it."

"I don't drive."

He gaped at her. "You *still* don't have a driver's license?"

"Never needed one."

"You should appear on *The Morning Show*, oldest American alive who can't drive."

"Funny."

"I can't drive ... fifty-five," Victor sang, mimicking the Sammy Hagar hit, "or any other speed."

"Lots of New Yorkers can't drive. Lots of young people don't drive. They ride-share and use mass transit. I'm in the vanguard!

Saves a few carbon molecules from going up in the air, too. And I hope you are good at navigating. Once I'm off the NYC grid, I'm lost."

"No one navigates anymore. GPS does it."

"Oh, I thought you'd use a slide rule and a sextant or something."

"Just so I am clear, we are flying cross-country to deal with my best friend's masturbation issues even as said friend rips me a new one when we show up."

"Shut up. Read my books sometime. He needs you."

"How did you get them published, by the way? I mean, it's not like you have a doctorate in sexual behavior, or even a degree in journalism. What was it you majored in, anyway?"

"Jesus, you're clueless. Don't you remember making fun of me for majoring in English, minoring in film."

"Ah, yes, what my colleagues call the welfare degrees."

"Fucketh thou! Though I will concede, it is difficult to be taken seriously without the proper credentials."

"That's what Bradley says."

"Maybe we'll commiserate about that. After the intervention."

There was no dissuading Rachel when she put her mind to something. Somewhere in the interstices of Victor's brain—the part that harbors primal fears and irrational jealousies—he wondered if there wasn't something more to it. Victor had never forgotten, decades ago, when Rachel had uttered the phrase, "unfinished business," referring to Bradley. He never had the guts to ask what she meant.

"Sounds like a classic case of CMD," Rachel said.

"What?"

"Compulsory Masturbation Disorder. More than half the men under thirty in this country suffer from CMD. They're developing a drug for it."

"Figures." He paused. "He thinks it's a side effect of taking Viagra."

"It's a consequence of having unlimited pornography available at the touch of a screen."

"I had no idea."

"You wouldn't."

"I'm not that out of touch, am I?"

"No, you just don't touch yourself enough. There's a happy medium."

"Well, it's not like I've *never* done it."

"He needs to know he's well down the rabbit hole," Rachel went on, "if he doesn't reverse course, he'll do permanent damage to his marriage, any future relationships, and to his fundamental understanding of sex in the real world. It may already be too late."

"He didn't say anything about Valerie."

"Does he ever?"

Victor thought about it. "No."

"Did he say how long he had been masturbating with such frequency?"

"I don't ask those kinds of questions."

Except how many women Bradley had sex with.

"From what I remember," she continued, "he's always willing to answer any questions about sex, bodily functions, what's playing on the tape recorder in his head. He's kind of an open book. Unlike you."

"True."

"We are at a crisis point in this country, Victor. Too often, heterosexual women can't achieve their sexual potential without men, but men are too busy submerged in online porn."

"What do you mean, crisis?"

"Porn rewires your brain! Read the brain science sometime. It's like gambling, and political power, fast food, sugary desserts, cocaine, heroin, fentanyl. They stimulate the places in your brain that seek pleasure and relief. Before you realize it, you're addicted."

"I had no idea."

"And don't get me started on masturbation. It's probably the most misunderstood act of human behavior. Some cultures worship it. Others revile it. How it ever got to be a morality play and a taboo topic of conversation, I'll never know. It's even worse if you are, like Bradley, already wired to abuse sexual gratification."

How does she know so much about Bradley?

"How do you know?"

"Trust me, I know."

Victor didn't like the sound of that.

"Nevertheless, circling back, we're flying cross-country to deal with Bradley's, uh, problems whacking off?"

"Don't minimize it." She shoved her knee into his thigh. "Have you read any of my books?"

"I've bought all of them," he said, proudly.

"Have you *read* them?"

"They're on my bookshelves." Behind another row of books and hidden from view. He didn't want any students or faculty or guest professors asking questions, or the titles appearing inadvertently in his Zoom background. He had created his own branch of science—Associational Statistics—shared across Mathematics and Engineering. Books on vaginas and penises didn't fit in.

"So, you haven't even read my books?"

"Rachel, I can barely *say* the word vagina without turning as red as that stop sign over there."

What Victor also wanted to say was that he couldn't accept the quality of scholarship and lack of validating experiments supporting Rachel's arguments and theses, at least based on what he had read in reviews of her work.

"And, the relevant question isn't whether or not I've read your books, it's what can we do for him by traveling all the way out there."

"Haven't you ever conducted an intervention?"

"A what?"

"You haven't, like, seen those reality TV shows, family members act together to save someone from alcoholism, opioid addiction, a violent spouse, obsession with higher level math?"

"No."

"Well, that's what we're doing. The element of surprise is essential, so don't text or call him."

"This is highly irregular."

"What's so important back in Miami?

"Something, I wish. Hey, have you ever read *my* books?"

"The Theoretician's Sourcebook for Advanced Associational Statistics? Volumes 1-3?"

"Wow! At least you know the titles."

"They're all the same title, and they're on the shelf with all my other 'guidebooks,' including the *Official Guide to Barely Tolerable Nerds*."

"Sounds like where they got the idea for *The Big Bang Theory*."

"So, are we going or not?" Rachel asked.

"To Phoenix?"

"Se-do-na!"

"I've got a lot of prep work for the Fall."

"Give me a break. You teach the same courses year after year. You told me yourself, your research these days is mostly acting as a nanny for grad students."

"I never said that."

"You decide when their work is ready to be published in the one journal where any of that stuff will ever see the light of day. And since you serve on the board of the association which publishes that journal, and serve as the journal's editor emeritus, they really have no other options but to follow your directives."

"You're making me out to be a tyrant."

"You control the wicket gates if someone wants a career in associational statistics."

"Some of my grad students are better at the math than I am."

"Yet, they have no choice but to be pulled into success by you. *If* you so choose. They have no real agency." She paused. "Think about it. One man controls this entire, albeit narrow, academic field. Before you, it was your mentor. That's a span of 50 years!"

"I'd rather not think about it. Anyway, I have to keep the grants coming from the Pentagon."

"It would be nice to know what the Pentagon does with all of your brain power."

"You don't want to know. Hell, I don't want to know."

"Bradley's been your best friend for more than forty years. He's been there for you during both of your divorces. He'd be there for this one, except you're here. And he's busy in Sedona."

"True."

"So we're going? You have money, 401k's. You have time. Why do you keep acting like you have to do the same things every day."

"Because I'm addicted to my work?"

"Maybe *you* need an intervention."

Long pause.

She looked him up and down. "Have you ever been to Phoenix?"

"I've attended conferences there once or twice. But I rarely ventured past my hotel or resort."

Rachel snorted. "You're as adventurous as you were in college. At least back then you did drugs. Well, I've never been to the Grand Canyon State. High time I visited."

"You have a point. He *is* a great friend. He's done far more to sustain our friendship than I have."

"Now, it's pay back time."

Other than Victor, friends were a tenuous thing for Rachel. Having parents who taught at the New Urban School for Behavioral Research, her father in Sexual Psychology and Behavioral Studies, her mother in the sociology department specializing in Worldwide Women's Suffrage and Liberation Movements, before women's studies departments became prevalent. Both happy to put their latest theories into practice raising their two daughters. She survived, barely. Her sister, her closest friend growing up, didn't. One out of two. Not bad for the social sciences. Not great for a family.

For someone who had built a profession building on her parent's work by popularizing it and, in doing so, achieving acclaim, notoriety, and respect, she had, remarkably, managed to reveal very little of herself to others. Her current work bringing what she and others called 'legal sex offenders' to justice would be her legacy. Not just of feminist importance, but for humanity, too.

Like Tino Lamborghini. Speaking of whom, she needed to line up more male character witnesses who would agree to testify against him. Victor had said Bradley wouldn't touch it with a ten-foot pole. There had to be someone, a roommate, a teammate, who could attest to his rapacious behavior. She had never forgiven Tino for what he did to her friend, Iris. Or for refusing her own advances, if she was totally honest.

At her age, Rachel was proudest of one thing: No one could define her as anything but herself: not mother, not spouse, not favorite aunt, not academic, not cultural icon, not rock star, nothing. She was her own woman. And for that, the only one who didn't resent her, despise her, envy her, admire her, try to exploit her, or try to kick her down a few pegs, was Victor. Sure, she'd had the hots for Bradley for a hot minute or two in college, but Victor was her person for life.

The plane ride would be a perfect time to come clean. Mostly.

It took two airplane-sized bottles of wine to work up her courage. And she was considering ordering a third.

"Did you ever meet my parents?"

"You never let me."

"Okay. I'm going to explain why. Soon as I get my first period, they decide they're going to teach me about sex the 'right' way, none of this beating around the bush with birds and bees hovering around. They're talking no shame, no guilt. They start with models of a penis and a vagina you'd find in any sex ed class, but then they figured that wasn't "real" enough so they demonstrate using their own genitals."

Victor choked on his beer. "Wait, what?"

"I know, believe me. But they were determined to raise their daughter without the mythologies that caused people to believe in stupid shit, like the fascists who took over their country. If you were taught about sex using birds and insects, you'd become dumb enough to believe that a dictator could be your savior. I mean, Dad even insisted I learn what an erect penis feels like."

"What the hell? Whose erect penis?"

"His erect penis. But only the one time. They did encourage me to touch myself the way they touched each other."

Victor looked around to make sure no one could overhear them. "I've never heard of such a thing!" he whispered.

"Women's lib and sexual behavior were their fields."

Victor ran a hand through his hair. Several times. His entire neck and face felt beet red. "Jesus, Rachel. Next you're going to tell me that they demonstrated intercourse for you."

"Not just intercourse, all manner of love-making styles and positions."

He was having a hard time breathing. "Oh, my God, my parents couldn't even talk about sex. My mother could not even say the word. S. E. X. Mating was the closest she ever got."

Rachel shrugged. "You're a WASP. Your kind never has to live on the edge."

"I mean, they really couldn't. Someone left a book on my bed, I guess it was my mom, *Love and the Facts of Life*, I still remember the title, when I was twelve, and that was it."

"You had no brothers, you were probably too sequestered by your teachers, and it was too early for a sex education class in high school. Probably too shy to ask a friend."

"Right. I mean, I learned more about masturbation and sex rooming with Bradley."

"Meanwhile, today my parents would be arrested by child protective services."

"Maybe back then, too."

Victor took all this in by asking the flight attendant for another beer. "I'm not sure if that explains a lot or explains nothing. About you, I mean."

Rachel shrugged like it didn't mean anything. "It was the '60s, as they say, but my experience was still, well, way out there on the fringe. And this was Manhattan, not some quaint suburban ski village in New Hampshire."

"Surprised you don't have something like PTSD about the whole thing." He checked the aisle. That second beer could not come fast enough. Maybe she did, though, Victor reasoned. That might explain her promiscuity.

"Well, the thing was, I learned too early how good all that could feel down there, especially if the vagina and clitoris were treated correctly."

"Which explains a lot of what happened at college."

Rachel nodded. She wouldn't be driving when they landed, so maybe she should order that third bottle. "My parents got divorced when I was fourteen, so I dealt with all that as well."

"I remember you telling me. And the Bowery where you grew up. What an awful place."

"It was the Ukrainian East Village, *next to* the Bowery. It only seemed like a shithole to outsiders like you. Many Jewish refugees fleeing Europe settled there."

"Well, for someone from Nashua, New Hampshire ..."

"It would figure you'd end up in a gated, whites-only community, in Coral Gables."

"It's not all white."

"Who do you know who isn't white?"

"Half the residents are Indian. Or so it seems some days."

"Well, that figures, they're the new Jews of America."

Victor wasn't going to give that one any oxygen. "So, what was it like having to, uh, touch your father's penis. God, I can hardly utter the words." He shuddered.

"I grabbed it with my right hand, started stroking it, brought my left hand to it, caressed his uncircumcised knob ..."

Victor stared at her wide-eyed then dropped his head into his hands. "Stop! God Almighty."

"Such a babe in the woods." Rachel laughed.

"Does all this have something to do with what happened to your sister?"

"You mean, why she threw herself in front of the J train?"

"Well, you said she died as a teenager."

"We'll never know. She may have been drinking. Could've fallen onto the tracks at the wrong time. It was classified as suicide at the time, though. And she had a lot of other issues besides our parents."

"God, my life was so pristine. And I feel like I'm fucked up all the time."

He chugged the second beer so fast it nearly choked him. He wished someone had choked Rachel's father. He shot her a glance while she was staring out the window at the puffy clouds below them. Jesus.

Darkness had fallen by the time they landed in Phoenix, even with its three-hour time difference. They still had a two-hour drive to Sedona according to the GPS, once they got their car checked out of the rental facility, more if the traffic didn't clear. The two travelers were at that point in the journey when conversation thins out, sentences are uttered only to serve as wake-up checks to each other.

"So," Victor said, "we're just going to check into the hotel and surprise Bradley tomorrow morning?"

"Yup. I made reservations at the same hotel he's at, the Sun Tongues Resort, or something."

"How did you know where the colloquium is?"

"How many places in Sedona have a conference on 'Neo-Anthropocentric Perspectives on Retrospective Freedoms' this week?"

"Oh, right."

"It looks like it's just off of the main road into town."

Exceedingly long pause.

"I wish we were driving during the day. The landscape out there must be stunning."

"True."

Exceedingly longer pause.

"So, we're just going to surprise him. No heads up? Is that fair? He's leading a colloquium. I sure as hell wouldn't want to be blind-sided while I was working."

"Don't worry about it."

Even longer pause.

"So, you've told me about your parents, but you never told me what happened to you in high school. You said you'd tell me sometime when we had time. We've got plenty of it now. " Although after hearing about the sick behavior of her parents, he wasn't sure he was prepared for any new revelations.

Rachel gazed out at the pitch black of the night, glimpsing walls of rock adjacent to the roadway when an oncoming set of headlights passed by.

"Slow down!"

Victor came perilously close to the back end of a semi crawling 35 miles an hour up the curving, pitched grade. "Shit! It's easy to forget that we're not the only car out here."

"You always drive too fast."

"My parents spoiled me with that Mustang for my sixteenth birthday."

Another long pause.

"I was raped."

"Oh god, no. Rachel. And you've never talked about it?"

"I've talked about it, just not to you. My parents were in the early months of their divorce. I wasn't going to mention it to the school authorities."

"You haven't dealt with this in any way, then?"

"I mentioned it to one classmate. After she told me she was raped too. We're still bonded over that.

Pause that seemed to go on and on.

Eventually Victor passed a semi, which seemed to take forever because there was no passing lane.

"So, how did—"

"That's all I'm going to say about it."

"You can't just lay a bombshell like that."

"I most certainly can. It's my bombshell."

"Okay, but you know you can trust me."

"I do trust you, Victor. But do I trust you completely? If you want to keep something a secret, don't tell anyone."

"Bradley says that, too, but with a twist ... 'unless you subconsciously want others to know.'"

"That's why he told you about his masturbation issues, which demonstrates *your* ability to keep a secret."

Victor took some time to let that one sink in. Was that true? The road continued to twist and turn around and through a mountain range, and on the other side of it, through undulating hills. Finally, they hit flat land. When they were within striking distance of the exit for Sedona, Rachel read a sign out loud. "Coins of the Canyons Casino. Boy, that's small print for a highway sign."

Long pause. Finally, Rachel broke the silence.

"Remember when Congress televised those hearings on that Supreme Court nominee, and the Dems brought in that witness, a woman who recounted how she was raped by said nominee at a party when they were in high school?"

"Vaguely. I just remember that she wasn't as clear as she could have been about what happened. Her account was pretty solidly refuted, as I recall."

"That's such a privileged white guy response! She wasn't clear because you can't be. Your brain and body have defense mechanisms which affect your memory of traumatic events. Some people might remember weird details like what the bed felt like or the texture of the ceiling, or the music playing, and hardly anything about the actual rape. That's similar to what happened to me."

"I'm not following."

"Read my fucking books, Victor! You might learn something new about the world."

The sign for the Sedona exit animated the pair, knowing they'd get some rest soon.

"Did I tell you I've got another book coming out at the end of the year?"

"Let me guess, you've done penis, you've done vagina, this one is titled, uh, anus!"

"You're too funny. This one is about Tantric Sex."

"So it is about the anus."

"And I'm using a new pen name, Nazeen Chandra."

"What?!"

"It comes from that part of the world. Tantric sex, I mean."

"Now you're going to be Indian, or Pakistani, or whatever?"

"Well, they are taking over the country. They're the new wealthy intelligentsia replacing the Jewish intellectuals of America for the next few decades. Hell, two of them are even running for President. Both of them fascist Brahmins. By the way, did you know Brahmins consider masturbation a self-control issue? Conserving semen, considered the elixir of life, supposedly promotes physical and mental health. Anyway, when did two Jews ever run for the Presidency? Well, what's his name, Lieberman, but that wasn't serious. They're the emerging ethnic power base, the new over-achievers, the *new* new money, the fists pounding at the door of the exclusive clubs."

"Isn't that, uh, cultural appropriation in the worst way, Nazeen?"

"You know how many Jews Americanized their names to get by in this country, how many non-Jews took on Jewish names to get ahead in this country, after the Jews set the standard for getting ahead? It's just part of the grand American experiment!"

"God, I hate it when you talk like this. You make lying seem so normal."

"The Victor Havilands of the world needn't worry about the nuances necessary to advance within the power hierarchy."

"I'm adopted, remember."

"Well, the adopted part gives you a sliver of cred."

"I can't help the way I was born, Rachel."

"None of us can. That's the point."

"On another subject, since we've traveled across the country to help a suffering elderly man with his masturbation problems, what, exactly, are we going to do when we, uh, 'intervene' him? What's the plan? Bind his hands? Confiscate his phone?"

"Leave that to me."

They passed through the town of Oak Creek Village. Finally, Victor got up the nerve to ask the question.

"Rachel, did you sleep with Bradley in college?"

She looked straight ahead at the streetlights illuminating their route through town but shedding no light on how to answer the question.

"I mean, while you and I were, uh, dating."

She turned toward him. "Tell me you haven't been obsessing over this for five decades. We dated for like five minutes."

"Bradley once said that you told him you considered him 'unfinished business.'"

"Put two men in a room and all they can think of is who fucked more women. Or who fucked *my* woman."

Victor's sheepish expression would have been obvious if they hadn't passed the last of the streetlights.

"Well?"

"No," she said in an exasperated sigh. "I did not sleep with him. But to be absolutely honest, I do recall trying to get him interested in having a threesome with us. I may have gone a little too far one night in trying to coax him into that."

Well, that makes sense, given the circumstances, Victor thought, the tension easing out of his body like ice melting in a warm cup of tea. She hadn't cheated on him. Bradley hadn't cheated on him. All was right with the world. Except for now knowing that Rachel had fondled her dad's erection.

Shit.

Up ahead, he saw the sign for the resort and turned on his blinker. After he pulled into the parking lot and put the car in gear, he looked over at her. "Out of curiosity, what do your books have to say about penile extensions?"

She raised one eyebrow. "You mean surgically? Or artificial attachments?"

"Surgically."

Rachel leaned her head against the passenger side window, and released an audible sigh, as if reconciling herself to the servitude of men to their cocks. "Unless your penis is shrinking the same way your height diminishes as you age. Why? Are you thinking about doing this?"

He shook his head. "God, no. Not me, heavens no, just asking for a friend."

CHAPTER 43

BRADLEY TAKES REFUGE

Bradley and Catherine stood with the crowd, rocking out to Kremlin, with Azul still on drums. On either side of the small stage were two large pull-up screens for the accompanying visuals.

On one, iconic images appeared at a very fast clip, John F. Kennedy getting shot in Dallas, Robert Kennedy in Los Angeles, MLK in Memphis, Reagan in DC, the Twin Towers coming down, the Alfred Murrah tower in Oklahoma City, Monterey Pop Festival, the naked Vietnamese girl running from the Napalm cloud, scenes from past Superbowls and World Series, the CNN correspondent reporting on "shock and awe' in Desert Storm, Abu Graib torture victims, the Million-Man March, kids running at Columbine and Marjorie Stoneman Douglas, the Women's March against Trump, Black Lives Matter, MLK's famous speech on the National Mall. It was like the greatest and worst hits of the last five decades. Even grainy mugshots of John Wayne Gacy, Son of Sam, and Charles Manson, footage of drones dropping bombs in unnamed countries. Sandwiched in between the rapid-fire repetition of images was the text image, "America: Land of the Free, Home of the Brave."

On the other screen were advertising images for every manner of product, military aircraft, hamburgers, pharmaceuticals, computers, soap, automobiles.

Some people left the room clearly unhappy, a few downright disgusted. Most stayed, however, mouths gaping.

Catherine yelled to Bradley above the din, "I don't find this very edifying. Let's go somewhere else."

"Aw, just a few more minutes. I gotta finish listening to the drummer. He's part of my meeting."

The band stopped soon after to catch their collective breath. Those remaining in the audience went wild. Bradley looked at Catherine with kaleidoscopic eyes. She had a mole that danced on her cheek. Her smile was as wide as her eyes were slits. He studied her teeth. They were perfect. Really perfect. Not a gap, not a stain, whiter than they were probably ever meant to be. He bent to kiss those teeth, and she responded by closing her eyes, ready to accept his lips and his tongue. The jolt when their tongues met was hardwired to his dick. He imagined his tongue on her tits. On her clit. Everywhere. Still, he felt like he had to keep up appearances in front of his attendees.

"What time does your bus leave?" He asked.

"Eleven, I think."

He checked his watch. "Not much time. I have an idea. Why don't we both take your bus back to the resort?"

"Spicy!" she replied, slyly.

The CLCC bus was parked behind the Freedom bus. The driver opened the door when they knocked. They were met on board with icy stares from the ladies as they ambled down the aisle, shivering from the AC.

"Let's sit in the way back," Catherine said, then whispered, "we can make out like it's the school bus!"

"No objection here!"

They got to the last row and squeezed into the seat. The familiar smell of lavatory cleaning chemical wafted around them. How romantic, he thought. In a moment of sobriety, he wondered what the dosage was of the gummy Catherine had given to him, what was even the stimulant. The moment passed. The outline of each woman walking down the aisle expanded or contracted into a new version of a human, their expressions exaggerated from neutral to morose, from slight smile to wicked grin, from worried to paranoid, weary to exhausted. His private parade of distended female forms. His hard-on would not quit.

"Those stares from some of the other ladies are wicked."

"So, full disclosure, they are probably giving me the stink-eye. I'm no longer a member in good standing of the CLCC. Apparently, their status as marital beings is more important than my status as a friend."

"I don't get it." He steadied himself by holding onto the sides of the seat in front of him.

"I'm recently divorced now. Bylaws stipulate only married women."

"That's terribly prejudicial!"

"It's all about married women exerting their freedom, and I, apparently, now have too much freedom to spare."

The bus continued to fill up with garrulous, frothy ladies. Bradley heard snippets about their casino experiences garbled into a verbal stew.

The driver walked the aisle doing a head count and scowled a little when he saw Bradley.

"I've taken him hostage," Catherine said, with a coquettish smile.

"Whatever," he replied.

At the security huts, Bradley could see the beams from the two choppers overhead, several vehicles on the ground with flashing blue and red lights, and two golf carts with yellow flashing lights attached to their roofs.

"Shit, man, what is going on?"

Then he saw a Jeep off to the left several yards behind the guard shacks. When the bus was stopped at the gate, he saw someone tall, African-American, very fit, athletic build. Then the person turned into better light.

"Oh, fuck, that's the guy who hired me! What the hell is he doing here now?"

"Which guy?"

"That guy." He tried to point through the window, while he ducked. "I hope to hell he isn't planning on getting on this bus."

"Why would he want to?"

"He's probably looking for me. Who are all those women carrying signs over there?"

He slouched into his seat but couldn't help peering out the window. The bus was motioned forward by a woman in uniform. They proceeded through the gate.

As the bus bumped down the dirt road, Catherine tried to position herself on top of him, attempting to plant a big wet kiss. This woman won't quit, he thought, as her lips descended toward his, suddenly looking more and more like the weirdly plump lips of a giant carp.

The woman occupying the seat in front of them reached up and over.

"Hey, what's going on back there? Oh, I remember you from the bar the other night."

Then she started chanting.

"Catherine and Bradley sitting in a tree, k-i-s-s-i-n-g ... first comes lust, then comes sex, then comes who the hell knows what's next!" A few of the other ladies started a chorus.

Whatever fantasy Bradley may have had earlier about having sex with Catherine was one he no longer was convinced he wanted fulfilled. Consummated. Whatever. He'd wanted a gummy buddy for an evening, not a lifelong guilt trip about cheating on Valerie again. That didn't explain why he had taken that little blue pill, though. Why were his own actions so often so bewildering? He was a conundrum. Con. Un. Drum. He thought about Azul and his drums. Wondered what he'd look like on stage with no shirt on. Or pants.

Shit.

CHAPTER 44

RACHEL AND VICTOR JOIN THE FESTIVITIES

Nascha's mood had gone from nervous to worried to panic. The CLCC ladies powwow at the 14th hole would be getting underway after midnight. Who knew what would spill over to the resort from whatever craziness was going down at the casino. This academic colloquium thing wasn't the quiet, unassuming affair she thought it would be.

Now, the bus with the CLCC group was 30 minutes late. She hadn't heard from the Chief and he didn't answer when she called. She had no idea what those military goons were up to. Whether they even made it there. What did that poor Bartholomew woman do?

At 10:30, a car pulled up under the awning out front, reminding her that two guests still had not registered. Because of a late cancellation, she was able to reserve them the last two available rooms when the request came that afternoon, although she hoped they wouldn't bitch too loudly about the condition of the room. They needed a housekeeping supervisor in the worst way.

The woman of the pair spoke first. "Hey, how you doin'?" she said, with a long exhale that ended in a sigh. Expressions from an obviously weary traveler. "Reservations for Schiff and Haviland, please."

"Good evening. How was the drive? Did you come from Flagstaff or Phoenix?" Nascha handed over the paperwork with as much enthusiasm as she could muster after thirteen hours on the job.

Victor answered, as he scribbled. "Phoenix. Is Flagstaff close?"

"About a 45-minute north. I'll need to see a driver's license. Same credit card you used to hold the reservation?"

Victor turned to Rachel. "See? You do need a driver's license west of the Hudson."

"I could use one of two passports."

"Two?"

"American and Israeli."

"Really?"

"Yeah, I got the Israeli one when Trump was elected the first time."

Victor looked at Nascha. "Just use my license for both of us, uh, Nascha? Is that correct?"

"Yes. Thanks for asking."

"Like the gnashing of teeth," Victor observed.

Nascha scowled, then smiled. At least it had been a banner week for her Chronicles.

"Sorry," he added, "we're a little punchy."

"Speak for yourself, Victor, and, uh, think before commenting on someone's name," Rachel scolded.

Nascha handed two sets of keys over the counter. "I apologize, these were the last two rooms available. It's a bit of a hike, in the old wing."

Victor inspected the keys. "Wow. Metal, what a throwback. I love it."

"We value nostalgia here," Nascha said.

"Is that, like, part of your native customs?"

"You referring to our artisan metal-working?"

"Native artists crafted these?"

"Yup, they work at ACE Hardware down the street."

Victor chuckled. "Yeah, guess I was asking for that one. I'm a little punchy too."

Rachel chimed in. "Is the resort named for a native chant or something?"

"The Yavapai are known as the people of the sun."

Rachel mulled it over. "Have a pie ..."

"Kind of like Here Comes the Sun, you know, the Beatles?" Victor offered.

Rachel followed with, "House of the Rising Sun, the Animals."

"Black Hole Sun, Soundgarden," countered Victor. "We've officially gotten giddy!"

Nascha laughed with them. "Many Yavapai sacred songs reference the sun, but none have been elevated to gold or platinum."

Rachel leaned an elbow on the registration desk. "How do you say hello in the Yavapai language?"

"Mu ham ee jah," enunciated Nascha, carefully.

"Like Muhammed Elijah or something?" Victor observed.

Nascha suppressed a giggle. Ka-ching! The gift that keeps on giving.

After Victor and Rachel headed to their rooms, they said good night on the landing, gave each other a standard Victor-Rachel hug, and decided to play the morning by ear. Immediately after shutting and locking her door, then closing the blinds, Rachel called Ivy, her #VeeTooAZ contact.

"Hey, girl, I'm in Sedona!"

"You're what? Oh wow, you're going to stand with us! You can explain why you're here later. For now, I have to tell you, the shit has hit the fan ..."

"Where are you?"

"Coins of the Canyon Casino. Military police are here, trying to nab some retired Air Force woman. Kerry Washington is demanding to see this Bradley Maniopolos character, the guy who's facilitating the Freedom Center colloquium. He's apparently not on the premises, or he's hiding out. Washington is screaming that he's the one paying the bill, demanding that someone find the guy. The casino's security goons are having a standoff with the MPs. We were waving our signs, but I had to drive back toward the highway to get a signal to call the local media to see about getting some television cameras down here. It's late."

"That explains why I couldn't get hold of you from the airport."

"We're all massed at the border between the Yavapai reservation and public property. I've got to get back there, and—wait, I see buses, or a bus, coming this way, they must have released the Freedom group. Oh, wait, it looks like a busload of women. Never mind."

Victor left his suitcase unpacked, stripped off his traveling clothes, went to relieve himself, and crawled into bed. Within minutes, his head leaped off the pillow at the banging on his door. Fire? Active shooter? He couldn't remember anything he learned from the drills in the training program the university made faculty and staff participate in. He rushed to the door, looked through the peephole to see Rachel swaying from foot to foot.

"What the hell is going on?" he demanded, as he undid the chain and bolt-lock, and pulled the door open. "Are you okay?"

"We have to drive forty minutes south of here. Now."

"You can't be serious. I quite literally just skipped the other stages and entered directly into REM sleep."

"I'll explain on the way. Now!"

"Here, just take the keys," he said, reaching towards the dresser table, then caught himself.

"Oh, right." He rolled his eyes.

"Don't start. Let's go."

"Can't it wait until the morning?" He looked down. "Oh, for God's sakes, I'm in my underwear!"

She looked. Then she laughed. "Still wearing whitey tighties?"

He shut the door in her face, pulled his pants on, then his shirt.

Rachel banged on the door again. "Victor, I wouldn't ask you to do this if it wasn't critical."

"Can you even give me a hint?"

"There's a protest taking place and I need to be there."

"Oh no, oh no, you are *not* dragging me into your femme fatale movement stuff."

"Femme fatale is a film term."

"Dangerous women, then."

"If you insist, you can just drop me off. I'll figure out how to get back with my compatriots."

"Who the fuck protests at this hour? In the middle of a desert?"

"They're at a casino. Remember? We passed the sign for it. I'll make it up to you. I swear. Or you can choose to hate me for the rest of your life. But I have to get down there."

He opened the door. "If I get arrested, you're paying my bail, lawyers, lost income, and damages for any and all harm to my reputation. If you get arrested, I'm not bailing you out."

"Whatever, let's just go!"

He grabbed the keys and his wallet. They hurried to the rental car.

"By the way, you'll have to call me Naomi when we're with my people."

"WHAT?"

By the time they'd gotten to the exit for the Coins of the Canyon, Victor had gotten the lowdown from Rachel. Didn't matter what she said. He was still confused.

"I should have read your books."

"Damn right."

"So, your group is taking down this Dr. Keshawn Washington guy, who is implicated in a, what, underperforming dildo scandal? But why are they all at a casino in the middle of Arizona?"

"It's an ongoing maximum pressure campaign. Active until he fesses up."

"Fesses up to what, exactly?"

"Victor, fighting misogyny is about going after everyone in the accomplice chain of violating women and women's rights, in this case the dildo supply company, the retail establishment that sells the goods, the branding operation, that would be where Washington comes in, instigators of the precipitating event, that would be Raj Magellan and his misogynistic, not to mention ridiculous, Primates Festival. Everyone who is even remotely connected, in other words. And it's not about winning lawsuits necessarily. It's about publicly shaming those involved, so in the future others will think twice or three times. Embarrassment as deterrence."

"You mean like a stockade in the public square? I thought we came out here to help Bradley."

"Well, that too."

They were quiet for a few miles.

"Are you sure Bradley can't be convinced to testify against Lamborghini?"

"Rachel, Bradley envied Tino. Hell, we all did. But we're here, you can ask him yourself."

CHAPTER 45

EVERYTHING COMES TO A HEAD

"**S**ince when do you approach a casino from a dirt road?" Victor said, paranoid about driving the rental sedan. The tires shimmied over dirt washboard after washboard.

"Guess we're not in Atlantic City anymore, Toto." Rachel shrugged.

"One dent in this thing, they'll charge me an arm and a leg."

As they got closer, they could see flashing red, blue, and yellow lights, and still closer, a huddle of cars parked just off one side, a Jeep on the far side of the guard house, and four helicopters hovering above, beams directed down like stage spotlights. Beyond, the casino, lit up like a fever dream from a Quentin Tarantino film.

"Jesus, what are the helicopters doing overhead?"

"Ah, I see one of our signs. Go that way!"

Rachel hopped out of the car before Victor stopped completely, quickly spotted Ivy, and hurried toward her. Victor followed well behind, looking side to side at scattered brush and darkness. What were these weird plants with the ping-pong paddles, he wondered?

Ivy and Rachel embraced. "Before you ask, your mom's doing great!"

"Oh, thank you!" Ivy gave her another hug. "That last biopsy had me so scared! Yeah, so a lot going on ... more than we ever suspected," she reported. "Best that we can figure out, there are two women in that jeep over there and they are wanted by the military police from some Air Force base around here. We think that's who's flying overhead, too."

"Wasn't our protest supposed to occur at the resort?"

"Well, you know, throw the battle plan out once the war begins. Washington went to the resort and we confronted him there. Then he came here looking for this guy, Maniopolos, who he apparently hired to run some sort of freedom colloquium. But Maniopolos, he's AWOL. The Big Chief who runs the casino took off in his security go-cart looking for him. His henchmen are holding the military guys with guns at bay because the two women in that jeep over there are on Native American property and the casino tribe has jurisdiction over the land. Oh, and for good measure, a local police vehicle just arrived, I don't know about those other two helicopters, out in the distance. Probably more military." She pointed west. "They seem to be circling each other in some sort of aerial ballet."

Victor nudged Rachel and asked. "Rachel, did she—"

She shoved an elbow into his side.

"Naomi, did she say Bradley was missing?"

"Yes."

"You mean, we flew from New York to help him, and he's not even here?" His deep sigh dropped his chin to his chest.

"Don't worry. First things first." She turned to Ivy. "So, what's the status now?"

"Well, Washington insists he's not leaving until they find Maniopolos. The military police are demanding that the two women in the Jeep be released to them. Oh, and that bus behind the security housing is full of academics trying to get permission to return to the resort. They can't leave until they find Bradley."

"Hm, I guess we have no choice, then. Victor, text Bradley and find out where he is."

Victor looked at his phone. "I have no bars. In fact, I have no service, period."

"You can get spotty service back at the highway," Ivy said.

"Victor, drive back towards the highway until you get service. He'll have to know we're here, I guess."

Victor glanced up at the helicopters converging overhead. What a shit show this trip has turned out to be, and they just arrived.

Things were at a standstill on the ground, but the noise in the sky seemed to have grown. The Big Chief paused and looked up.

"Now there are four helicopters?"

His security assistant, Clever Hawk, replied, lifting a pair of binoculars and peering up at the sky. "That's how many I count."

"Tell me we're not looking at a Chinook and a Black Hawk."

"I think we're looking at Chinook and a Black Hawk."

"Now they're violating our land *and* our air space, not to mention our naming rights? What the hell!"

Conrad Bolton's pilot looked out the window of the CH-47F. Modified for luxury civilian transport and corporate short hops, the helicopter was comfortable and fun to fly, but that didn't matter right now because he didn't like what he saw. Bad enough they had to steer clear of the Air Force birds flying directly over the target area, although he questioned whether they had the jurisdiction they claimed. He was pretty sure the Bolton board wouldn't want him to jeopardize multimillion-dollar contracts with the Pentagon by challenging their assertion.

"Mr. Bolton?" He spoke into his headset. "There's another helo in our air space. Looks like a Black Hawk."

"More Air Force? Police?"

"Don't think so. I'm gonna have to make contact, though. He's flying a little too close for comfort."

"Damn. I was hoping to get in and out without being noticed."

"I told you landing a helo on a reservation without permission isn't probably the best—"

"I know, I know. I just want to lynch that little Ebola fucker for violating his HOMI-G confidentiality agreement. And anyway, what are they going to do, shoot us out of the air?"

"Did you just say 'lynch?'"

"Metaphorically speaking, of course. The guy's accusing me of illegal trafficking in cultural artifacts! That's a crime!"

"Stealing and trafficking cultural artifacts is a crime. Accusing you of it is not."

"Defamation of character, then."

"Yes sir," the pilot said, rolling his eyes. "But like the proverbial dog chasing the car, what do you plan to do with him once you nab him?"

"After I flog his ass? Promote him and double his salary. We don't want any trouble with his family back in Nigeria. Who knew the asshole owned half the country? He never said a word. Fucker."

The Blackhawk and the Chinook faced off in the sky, like they were just about to play chicken. The clouds to the far north appeared battleship gray against the edges of the copters' lights. To the south, the beckoning lights of the Casino and the headlights of the vehicles around the security gates flickered.

Beyond them, lone property lights beamed from remote, isolated residences scattered here and there. To the west, faint headlights of an occasional 18-wheeler chugging along on the interstate.

"Please identify yourself," Raj's pilot said into the mic on the copter-to-copter communication frequency channel.

"This is license number 4B93REM. What is your business in the area?"

"This is BE070TB. We were wondering the same thing. We represent the air transport wing of Bolton Enterprises."

"We represent The Magellan Foundation. We have an interest in one of the individuals in the melee down below."

"That's curious. So do we."

Raj, sitting in the co-pilot seat, hissed, "Ask him, damnit!"

"If we may ask, how did you manage to commandeer a CH-47F? Aren't those strictly military?"

"As a supplier to half the U.S. military bases around the world, and with our global preferred vendor agreement to provide our brave and loyal service members standard discounts on all necessities from our currency stores, we received special dispensation from the Pentagon to modify a few Chinooks for corporate use.

"Damn it to hell, I wanted one of those birds," Raj whispered, "but the Pentagon brass wouldn't listen to me. Not even a $50,000 donation through my Liberty For All SuperPAC, or to my representative's re-election campaign got me the congressional approval I needed."

He looked at his pilot, defeated. "How come I always get second best?"

Raj kept muttering to himself as he tried again to get Washington on the phone. The two pilots, talking on behalf of their employers, compared notes on top speeds, altitudes, automation, safety features, communication gear, number of passengers accommodated, even the carpet and the fabric on the seats, leather for the Chinook, thick, plush velvet for the Black Hawk.

"Kerry Washington, here. What can I do for you, Mr. Magellan?"

"I've been trying to contact you!" Raj said. "Kerry, listen. I'm here. Look up and you'll see me. All I'm asking is that we meet face-to-face to figure out how we're going to rectify this mess."

"I've already apologized about the dildo disaster."

"This mess is about more than your pecker, Kerry. The reputation of the Freedom Center is at stake now. I'm not putting it all on you. I bear some responsibility. I approved the Maniopolos appointment. But we need to put our heads together and come up with a salvage plan. Above all, we need to preserve our other objective, to use Maniopolos to get to Haviland."

Like hell, Raj thought. I'm gonna have Dildo Washington's head on a caterer's platter and serve it up at the next Primates Festival.

"Raj, it's been real, but I have to sign off. Things are weird down here."

Raj turned to his personal bodyguard sitting in the back. "Keep eyes on that guy until he's in a secure area where my ground detail can nab him."

The two pilots hovered their copters patiently until their executives got bored from trying to figure out what was happening on the ground and determining whether it was safe to land with all the military, security, and law enforcement posturing going on.

"Switch the channel over for my headset," Raj told his pilot. He was at least going to figure out what a Bolton was doing out here.

"4B93REM, allow me to introduce myself: Roger Magellan, of Magellan Works Inc. and The Magellan Foundation, here. To whom do I have the pleasure of speaking?

"Uh, Theodore Berlinsky, pilot for Bolton Aviation. Let me get Mr. Bolton on the channel for you." He adjusted the comms channel and nodded to his boss.

"Conrad Bolton here, Bolton Enterprises board member, former CFO, CEO of Nostalgia Currency LLC, Chairman Emeritus of the History of Musical Instruments Gallery, HOMI-G."

Raj knew the name. He knew the names of every Fortune 500 CEO in the country.

"Mr. Bolton! It's a pleasure indeed!"

Like two circling dogs getting to know each other, the pilots began maneuvering their copters to get a better look at the other's vehicle.

"You, the Magellan of Primates Festival fame?"

"Yes, yes. That's me."

"How come the Boltons never receive an invitation?"

Hmm, Raj wondered. Maybe Jabberwocky kept his invitation secret from the rest of the family?

"To be honest, Conrad, ah, may I call you Con?"

"No. But I'm okay with Rad."

"Rad, although it's not a hard and fast rule, we encourage attendance from people in the entrepreneurial fields and venture capital-backed firms, especially for up and comers, and traditionally eschew those from large, established firms who may not be out-of-the-box thinkers. We also give priority to those who may not have earned their degrees from the most illustrious of America's universities."

"Well, I am the one out-of-the-box thinker at Bolton, I can assure you. My degree is from Mississippi State, not exactly Princeton. Plus, you invited my second cousin, once removed from the family, genealogically, I mean."

"You mean Jabberwocky? Why didn't you say so?"

"His business interests are somewhat unaligned from mine."

Raj sensed an opportunity. "Now that I have been apprised of your interest, I will see to it that you are added to the guest list for next year. I'd be delighted to have you join the festivities!"

"What is your interest in the shit show below, Raj?"

Raj sighed loudly. "I've sponsored a conference through my Center for the Study of the Philosophy of Freedom—"

"That's a tankful."

"The freedom center, for short. I've positioned it to be at the nexus of philosophy, economics, and social behavior and to scale it into the next Aspen or Davos."

The Bolton helicopter was now behind Magellan's.

"Quadruple turbo-exhausts ... nice!" Bolton's pilot yelled towards the mic.

"Shut up! Sorry, not you, Raj. What's the name of your conference?"

"A colloquium, really, Neo-Anthropocentric Models of Retrospective Freedoms."

Conrad snorted. "That's a whole tank farm."

"It's a beginning. My goal is to elevate the study of freedom to the pinnacle of academic thought by constructing a new framework for business and social behavior based on quantifying the value of freedom."

"Quite a lofty goal. Aspen better watch its back!"

"Our aspirations would be well-served with participation and sponsorship by a company as respected as Bolton Enterprises, especially its entrepreneurial wing."

"Send me some collateral."

"Happy to. Unfortunately, our debut event was marred by a rather poor hiring decision. I'm sure you understand how difficult it is to fill positions with the best people."

"Tell me about it. I'm here trying to apprehend one of them now."

Long pause.

Conrad spoke again. "What's your conference's competitive advantage?"

"Ah, glad you asked. We are going to be the first to market with a rigorous quantitative framework to support the concept—and interpretations—of freedom."

"I'm not following. Give me the el pitch."

"Let me explain. One hundred years ago, economics was a social science based on supply, demand, and price, and all the things you know from economics and MBA school, with accounting as the math. The Chicago school converted it, or at least expanded it, to financial engineering by applying complex mathematical models for valuations of transactional instruments into the future."

"I remember some of that from my MBA refresher classes."

"It kind of elevated the expertise required to analyze economics and finance from algebra to differential equations."

"So let me get this straight, the Freedom Center is going to redefine the expertise necessary to run the global economic order by going to even higher order math?"

"That's right! We're going to partial non-linear differential equations, and even associational statistics! People like you and I will never understand this stuff, but we'll hire physicists and mathematicians to do the grunt work. There's a guy out of University of Miami that I have my eye on. Dr. Victor Haviland. Pioneer in the field. The ultimate goal, however, is conceptual, quantitative language only a few will ever understand."

"Which maintains the basic social order of a dominant elite running the global financial system?"

"Exactly."

"I like it!"

"By the way, Raj," Conrad said, "I have great respect for the Black Hawk, but this Chinook is going to leave you guys in the dust. It won't even be a contest."

Below them, Raj saw the buses pulling out of the security area, moving slowly along the dirt road toward the interstate. "I like my bird just fine," Raj said with a laugh. "I'm happy to concede to your greater firepower."

Always concede to close, Raj said to himself.

The two helicopters were now side by side, facing east, away from the casino and reservation land below. With their cockpits fully lit up, the pilots were making "wanna go?" signs to each other, then a "thumbs up," and as their bosses kept talking, they shoved their respective throttles to full thrust, slamming them all back against their seats. They were burning through fuel, topping speeds of 150 miles per hour. And enjoying every damn second!

CHAPTER 46

PLEASE ... STOP ... DON'T

When they returned to the resort and disembarked from the bus, Catherine pulled at Bradley's arm.

"No, let's go this way. If we walk around the maintenance building, there's a back staircase to my room. We'll avoid anyone in the lobby."

"What if they have security cameras over there?"

She dragged him in her direction.

"They don't. I know this place like the back of my hand."

"I don't know ..."

"Calm down. It'll be fine."

Bradley was now certain this wasn't a good idea. There were no lights on this side of the property. Any minute a sensor would trigger an alarm or a security light and he'd forever be caught on grainy security camera footage. A cheater. Adulterer. Again.

"Catherine, is this ..."

"You're not going squeamish on me?"

"I mean, it's late, and I've still got a half day of this conference tomorrow."

"Everybody's blotto the last day of a conference."

They slipped into her room without flipping a switch, guided by stray light from the parking lot and wall lamps along the landing.

She launched herself at the bed, pulled him down with her. He tried to break his fall and not crush her, but she was already rolling on top of him. With a knee on either side of his hips, she sat on his crotch, smiling at the hardness she felt, pulled her one-piece sundress over her head, revealing a lacy, sheer bra corralling eager nipples, matching panties with a winking prickly pear right in the bull's eye.

"Oh God, my favorite colors," Bradley blurted out, his pecker yearning for its freedom, telling his conscience and his vows to fuck right off. Didn't prickly pear cactuses have acupuncture spines up and down their trunks and limbs?

Catherine urged, "Do you want to do the honors or shall I?"

Bradley hesitated. She answered her own question, reached behind her, undid her bra clasp, wiggled her arms like a lap dancer. Perky, gently sloping mounds of creamy white and bronze, each with a ruby red Life Saver of a center, framed by tan lines, filled his sight, a ring of sunburn, a border between two glorious surfaces. God, he loved breasts.

It was now or never. Could he swim through his lust and find enough non-hallucinatory sentences to free himself? He could still make that blue pill count with an invigorating and halcyonic session of masturbatory bliss back in his room.

"Look, Catherine, I really don't think this is a good idea."

"It's no longer an *idea*, sweetheart, it's reality."

"I'm way too high. Don't you think we should give this a little more thought?"

"Your flag staff thinks otherwise." She ground into him. Squirmed. Let out a low moan. "You want this as much as I do."

Damn right we do, his pecker said.

He never should've taken that pill. Or that gummy.

"I know, but—"

"We're in too deep for thinking. No time for 'buts.' Time to just enjoy!" She rocked on him and brought both hands up to her nipples.

He swallowed. Hard. "That was just harmless necking."

"Necking? Who still uses that word?"

"Well, making out then."

"It's called foreplay, lover boy. You know, the *play* you do before you're going to FUCK." She kept grinding her hips on him, moving forward and back along his erection, making the damned zipper of his pants dig into his dick.

She sounds a little belligerent, Bradley thought hazily, through fragmented images of Catherine, Cuddles4U, Jstacuntrygirl, and other Insta Babes, as well as numbers one through whatever he had gotten to with Victor. Past history. Wishful thinking. Mindless lust. Everything was spinning around the room—including the room—like reflections off a disco ball hanging from the empty dome of his cranium. Was he spinning inside his own head, and this was all another harmless fantasy while he held a screen and stroked his own penis?

Maybe he wasn't in Catharine's room after all. Maybe he wasn't about to cheat on Valerie.

He glanced to his right. Slivers of light crept through the gap in the curtains, reminding him that the sun, in just a few short hours, would rise, and cast its floodlights onto the red rocks. Maybe if he kept his eyes shut, morning would arrive early.

Catherine stood up long enough to separate herself from her panties. She stood over him, took his hand, made him sit upright on the side of the bed, then straddled his knees, and earnestly guided his fingers into her vagina. He recoiled, like the very first time, at eleven years old, he shoved his hand inside the top of a girl's bikini at the community pool and found her nipple, the firmness of a kernel of corn. The shock of her expression.

"Earth to Bradley, earth to Bradley."

His eyes were level with hers. "Sorry."

"You know where to put them," she said, "where it's obvious I want them."

It was obvious. She was wet and warm and sticky and he couldn't be any harder. Valerie took forever to get this wet. He kept his eyes closed. He didn't want to bear witness to what was being done to him.

After barely even a minute, a soft, highly pitched but insistent "oh!" escaped her lips, then another, and another, like she was climbing an octave from alto to soprano. She paused. Her body went limp. What the hell? Had she orgasmed that quickly? He and Valerie could be going at it for, like thirty minutes, before Valerie would finally guide and place his fingers exactly where she wanted them. Then it would take another fifteen before her climax, well after his fingers, then his hand, then his arm, went numb.

Catherine rubbed his hand into her crotch, pressed his index finger against her clitoris, and used her right hand in a failed attempt to unbuckle his belt and unzip his trousers. She paused and then used both hands to get the job done.

"Catherine, no ..."

She ignored him, opened his fly and fondled his dick. Then she returned to the pose with her left hand guiding his into her crotch, used her right hand to gently stroke him at the upper third of the shaft. Where he liked it most. Where every guy liked it most. Behind his closed lids, his eyes actually rolled into the back of his head. Nothing feels like this.

She whispered, like she was calming a child. "I know what you need. What every man needs."

"No."

"Yes."

"Please."

"Tell me to stop."

"It feels too good for me to tell you to—"

She slathered some of her own juices and a generous amount of spit onto her fingers, then gripped his shaft loosely so that her index finger would work the backside just below the rim of the tip with her thumb on the front side. She stroked as constantly as a machine. Maybe she was. At this point, why would he care.

He flipped from one woman's image to another, like a simulated moving picture on a deck of rapidly flipping cards. She seemed to know when he was almost ready, when the arrow was loaded onto the bowstring, and pulled back for firing. She accelerated the stroke, a little bit at a time, a little bit more, never allowing the index finger to waver from its position at the backside of the tip, until his moans of *no, no, noo, nooo* morphed into *ooh, ooooohh, aaaahh, oh my fucking god*, and at that point, she wrapped her lips around him to catch the eruption. When he screamed into his arm, "No! Please, God, no more!" and put his hand firmly on her head, and said, "No, stop!" for entirely different reasons, her lips retreated and she, at last, flopped back on the bed, thoroughly satiated.

As the triple point of pain, pleasure, and satiation dissipated, Bradley kept his eyelids tightly clenched.

"Aw c'mon, ollie ollie oxen free! Come find me and tell me how wonderful that had to be!"

"I have to get out of here."

"That's no way to greet a woman who just swallowed your custard."

"I did not want that to happen."

"Sure had me fooled."

"What time is it?

"Who cares?"

"I've gotta go."

"Come on. Stay a little while and snuggle. Don't be a one-and-done asshole."

"What was in that gummy anyway? Am I ever going to come down off this trip?"

"You'll be fine in the morning," she replied, her voice cold. She hopped off the bed and searched around for her underwear. She grabbed them off the floor and stepped into them.

"Alright, just get the fuck out of here then," she ground out as if her jaw was wired shut. "You're turning into a serious drag."

He sat up, rubbed his eyes, tried to rub away the high, what just happened.

Hands on her hips, frown on her face, she sneered down at him. "A waste of a good gummy."

"I was thinking the whole night we'd just be gummy buddies."

"There were a dozen off ramps. You could have taken any one of them."

"Yeah, but——"

"Just get out." She walked hurriedly to the bathroom and slammed the door behind her.

Bradley put himself back together and left. The triple pain point was the opposite now—morose, confused, violated. He wandered along the paved path. Took off his shoes and stepped into the moist grass. It felt sexier on his toes than the last hour with Catherine. The lighting on the property gave the cliffs a purplish glow. The clouds had finally moved out.

The sky was an astronomer's dream, constellations to name, black holes to wonder about, infinities to contemplate. He'd read once that only a bunch of male cosmologists could have come up with the big bang theory. Surely a pack of women cosmologists with fresh PhDs and a DEI support group at their university would dream up something very different from the universe beginning with an eruption into the void, like life itself following an ejaculation. Well, if nothing could make a guy feel bigger than a fountain of sperm, nothing could make him feel smaller than a transpicuous sky at night.

He picked up a folding deck chair from the hot tub area, and carried it far onto the fairway where no one could easily spot him. Something too imperious for his brain had just happened. It was beyond just guilt.

Was his sexual mind *that* divorced from real women, his own spouse, a hot chick with fake boobs—that he hadn't even fondled!—picking him up at a colloquium, when he was supposed to be thinking about freedom? He caught a brilliant flash and trail of light in the sky and thought, shooting star, then realized he was probably still mildly hallucinating. The joke, it seemed, was now on him. The joke was him.

Glumly, he checked his phone for messages. Holy shit. A message from Victor! Finally!

Hey, surprise, surprise, we, that is, Rachel and I, are at the Coins of the Canyon Casino, where YOU'RE SUPPOSED to be. People are looking for you. Where are you?

WTF?

I kid you not. Explanations to come. Where are you?

At the resort, Song of the Sun. But WHAT THE HELL are you two doing here?

It appears you're missing all the fun.

What fun? You mean, at the casino? God, is Kremlin still playing?

Who?

Nvm.

Oh boy, well, later, I guess. I'm heading your way. Rachel to come later, not sure.

What the hell were they doing here? He had a sneaking suspicion. Damn that Victor. He'd spilled the fucking beans.

CHAPTER 47

SHIT JUST KEEPS GOING DOWN

Gail and Ashera looked at each other in the blinding glare of the lights coming from the Air Force MP vehicles, the Yavapai police, and the casino security guardhouse.

"Guess it's decision time," Gail said, repeatedly smoothing the hair on the back of her head.

Ashera held up a finger. "Here's an idea. We can back up, drive towards the buses. You can get on the bus. That will buy some time. I'll call a civil rights lawyer to meet you there."

"At night in the desert?"

"What about those lawyers who come to you 24/7? I see their damn commercials 24/7."

"Those are injury attorneys," Gail said. "That's if you've been in an accident. *Injured.*"

"You can give yourself up, like we originally planned, with made-for-social-media filming. Just imagine: *Dying Missileer makes desperate attempt to save crew.*"

"Or I can stay on the casino property. They can't take me here."

"It's a casino, not a hotel."

"True, but it is open 24/7. I could sleep in a chair."

"Only if you're still losing money."

They sat in silence for a few moments.

"Well, hell's bells, I'm dying anyway. I can't stand the indecision."

Gail got out of the car and marched towards the MPs. Ashera stared after her, frozen.

Gail turned and motioned behind her. "Well, come on, where's my camera grip?" she said.

Ashera jumped out and rushed to get in front with her phone camera video on. Two MP goons exited their vehicle to meet them at the border. Slowly, Ashera turned with her screen to get the details of Gail's apprehension. No handcuffs, just an escort towards the vehicle. She made sure to get the faces of the two MPs as clearly as possible.

When they were next to their vehicle, one of the MPs reached for the door handle. As he pulled the door open, Gail reached into her bag. Before Gail's motion registered with Ashera, she impulsively reached into her pocket, pulled out portable 'Gordon' and tossed it at the MPs.

"Snake!" she shouted, with all the voice she could muster.

The MPs jumped and backed away like two old ladies sighting a mouse, arms flailing like pinwheels, knees bent, as if the step they planned to take toward Gail suddenly became a motion to run tail.

"Gail! Let's go!" She started towards the Jeep, but Gail did not follow. She was rooted in the ground, stunned at what had just transpired.

Portable Gordon had landed at the MPs' feet. While both men looked down, wondering which way to turn next, they realized the object had not slithered towards them. Or away from them. Nor had they heard any rattling, rustling, slithering noises. For a second longer, they stared, just to make sure.

In one smooth motion, Gail raised the barrel of her Glock to her open mouth. One MP grabbed her arm. Gail jerked her arm up and away. The gun fired. The MP caught her wrist. The gun went flying. He shoved her up against the SUV before Ashera could even gasp. The MP held Gail there, face smashed against the side of the vehicle while he frisked her and the other searched her bag.

The local police car screeched over from the north side, lights flashing, siren blaring. The casino security guards stomped the golf cart's pedal from the other direction. It accelerated slowly, like one would expect from a golf cart moving off the tee box.

Within seconds, four armed indigenous individuals were pointing weapons at the MPs holding Gail, motionless. As the MP's grip relaxed, Gail arched her body back and bent to reach for her gun on the ground. The MP holding her bag dropped it and went for the gun, too. Gail beat him to it. She grasped it and again tried to put it in her mouth.

Someone tackled her from behind.

A shot rang out.

"Fuck me!" One of the MP's fell back into the dirt as a bloom of darkened fabric appeared on his thigh.

Gail tried to turn and run, tripped over the parabolic straps of Ashera's bag, launching herself spasmodically into the barbed wire fencing separating reservation land from state land.

"For shit's sakes!" She yelled, struggling against the wire barbs that bit into her clothes and skin. With each twist and turn, she became more entangled. "I can't even off myself right."

She looked at Ashera through the twisted barbs of the 6-foot high fence to which she was now enmeshed like a woman tied to the stake. All she needed was a pile of wood at her feet.

"The gecko was not helpful!"

"Oh my God, Gail!" Miraculously, Ashera, aghast at the action, kept her phone pointed in the direction of the appalling scene, Gail, splayed against the fence like some figure laid out against a pentagram, her face twisted in anger and humiliation.

"Hold on, there!" a casino security guard bellowed, "you're on native reservation land and under our jurisdiction." He held his weapon on the two MPs, who had theirs drawn as well.

"Clever Hawk, call Emergency Indian Health Services, get an EMT out here for the wounded soldier and the airman."

"I'm Air Force, not Army," Gail corrected.

"You think I give a buffalo's ass?" he said, turning to the MPs. You're American military on sovereign native territory."

"We're not going anywhere," another MP said, "Federal authority trumps native rights."

"Not today."

Ashera continued filming.

"Well, this person is officially in our custody," said the other MP.

"Not so fast."

Clever Hawk approached Gail. Each attempt to move a limb, like being in quicksand, made her less mobile as the thick, rusted barbs pinned more of her. "Sorry, ma'am, your position is, how shall I put it, part of a serious violation here by the U.S. military. I'd help you up, but I shouldn't disturb the evidence."

He eyeballed her situation, rubbing his chin.

"Let's see, is she more than halfway on Native property? I believe she is, but I need confirmation," he said, staring at the MPs.

He radioed the Chief. "Chief, do you read me?"

"I read you, Clever Hawk, I'm a little tied up, but—"

"Uh, we have a situation here. There's a woman who appears to be mostly on native land, with U.S. Military MPs insisting on taking her into custody. Need a second pair of eyes on the percentage of her body across the fence line to ascertain proper chain of custody. Confirmation shall be conducted by a superior officer as I recall from our training guidebooks?"

"Shit. Okay. Roger. On my way. By the way, I've searched the entire premises, and there's no sign of that Manola character. So, we'll have to give up on that one."

Clever Hawk looked apologetically at Gail. "We'll wait until the Chief gets here."

Gail struggled to get air in and out of her lungs. Her attempts to get free were more and more futile, until finally she remained still among the prickling barbs and tangling wires. She'd look like a person imitating a prickly pear bush if you stumbled on her at night.

"Can I get you some water?" he asked.

"How about an oxygen tank?" she blurted out between heaves.

Ashera put her phone away and hurried toward Gail to see if there was anything she could do.

"Halt! Any closer and I'll have to consider you an accomplice," one of the MPs said. "As it is, we may have to take you in for questioning."

Ashera put her hands on her hips. "Did you really need this much firepower to take in a fellow officer who's dying of a cancer originating from her duties at the missile site and simply trying to get the Air Force to take ownership of the Missileer cancer clusters around the country?" Her voice got louder and angrier as she continued. "You, and the entire United States Air Force, should be ashamed of themselves!"

"Lady, I don't know where you're getting your information from. Captain Bartholomew is being arrested for running a fentanyl smuggling weigh station on Air Force property."

"What?"

"Step back and let us do our job!"

She looked over at Gail. "Is this true?"

Gail stared at the ground, then looked up meekly at Ashera. "I don't promote Tacho's Taco Shop for nothing."

The MP broke in. "Tacho won't be selling any more tacos. We got a tip from an insider in the cartel. He ratted out Captain Bartholomew to save his own ass."

He turned to Gail. "It's never very courteous to break up with the cartel just by leaving a note."

Gail snorted. "It's never courteous to ignore the health needs of the people who served and sacrificed, either, asshole. A little extra money to help pay for treatments and lawsuits was all I was ever after."

"Try a Go Fund Me next time." The MP snorted.

"Try a go fuck yourself this time," Gail retorted.

The county deputy walked back to his car and got on the radio. "Uh, calling for backup. At the Yavapai Casino off RR26. Standoff between U.S. Military and reservation officers, not really sure how to explain it. Protests on the other side of the road against, well, again, not sure how to describe that either. Contained for now, but chanting getting louder and louder. Anyway, shots fired. One man, one woman injured. Need the ambulance."

When Rachel got word that Keshawn Washington was on the bus with the rest of the freedom center crew, she and Ivy led the #VeeToo group, eighteen women and two guys who looked like their presence had been demanded by their girlfriends in trade for getting laid, to where the bus was still waiting to be released for return to the resort.

Back from finding cell service near the interstate, Victor trailed just far enough behind to peel off if anything bad started happening. They fanned out in the shape of an oval, surrounded the bus, and walked around it, chanting continuously, pumping their signs up and down.

"Two, four, six, eight, who do we excoriate?"

"Two, four, six, eight, who do we excoriate?"

"Kerry, Kerry, Washington, Washington!"

"Primates, primates, where are you? The only place you should be is at the zoo!"

346

"Primates, primates, where are you? The only place you should be is at the zoo!"

"Bro-thing, bro-thing, where's thy sting? You are part of a misogynist ring!"

"Celibri-Dong, Celibri-Dong, it's all wrong. Respect for women is gone, gone, gone!"

When Rachel passed where Victor was standing, he walked up to her, looking both ways to see if anyone was noticing.

"Okay, Rachel—"

"Naomi, dammit!"

"I'm outta here. This isn't my cup of tea. I could lose tenure."

"Yeah, yeah, okay, I'll get a ride and see you back at the resort."

Just then Dr. Plemmons grabbed the door handle, stepped down off the bus, and strode straight up to Naomi and Ivy.

"What on earth is going on here?"

"Hi, there," Ivy said, "Naomi here can explain it all to you."

Rachel kept pumping her sign up and down, even as she smiled and said, "Hello, I'm Naomi Wasila, Chief Advocate Officer and voice of #VeeToo—"

Dr. Plemmons' eyes went wide "Oh my God, Naomi Wasila? THE Naomi Wasila?"

"The one and only."

"The author of *Dismantling the Patriarchy: Penis by Penis*."

"Well, that was quite a while ago, but yes."

Rachel paused, then said "Excuse me a sec."

"Two, four, six, eight, who do we excoriate?" Rachel yelled with the rest of the group.

She looked at the lady's nametag. "Would you like to join us, uh, Ms. Plemmons?"

"It's Dr. Plemmons, but absolutely! I'm going to tell everyone else on that bus, too. But first, can I get a selfie?"

"Of course! I'm flattered."

Victor shook his head. "For God's sakes," he whispered, audibly, before discharging a diaphragm full of disgust into the desert air. "I. Am. Outta. Here. Rach ... Naomi, I'm heading back to the resort."

She gave him a happy wave. "Right, I'll meet up with you later."

Rachel and Dr. Plemmons embraced like they were old pals. Plemmons reached way out in front with her phone so that the #VeeToo protesters and their signs were in the background. Then she went back to the door of the bus and started banging on it.

"Jesus, Joseph, and Mary, okay, okay," the bus driver muttered as the woman he'd just let off the bus pounded the doors to get back on.

"You'll never guess who is leading that rally out there! Plemmons yelled, hopping back up the steps toward the driver. "Naomi Wasila!"

"Seriously?" Dr. Zhou and several of the other women stood up. "Let's show our support!"

"What are they protesting?" someone asked.

"For fuck's sake, they're protesting me!" Dr. Washington yelled. "Anyone leaving this bus and joining that mob will never get a dime of freedom center grant money. Ever!"

"Until you're fired!" Plemmons fired back.

"What the hell did I do wrong, but allow my, uh ...."

"Your Bro-Thang!"

Kerry stood up in his seat and tried to look intimidating, even as he was hunched over under the overhead storage compartment. "There's nothing illegal about that."

"That's the point," Plemmons said. "Misogyny isn't illegal, but the violence and aggression against women that it leads to is, and it's rarely prosecuted because the misogynists are in charge! C'mon! This bus isn't going anywhere for a while anyway.

We might as well show we're capable of something besides publishing or perishing."

Several others followed, including Dr. Zhou, who threw her arm in the air and yanked it down like she was pulling the emergency horn on an 18-wheeler. "Let's rumble!" She climbed over her seat mates into the aisle, and stormed to the front. The driver opened the door, before they even got there.

"Have at it," he said with a loud sigh, then rested his head on the steering wheel.

Professor Hintz stood up. "Dr. Washington, will you please go out there and see what they want? Perhaps you can come to terms and we can get the hell out of here."

MacGruffin chimed in, too. "Yeah, nothing good is gonna happen until you confront those maddening sirens."

Kerry walked the aisle like he was walking the plank and, shoulders hunched, disembarked.

"Okay, okay, what do you want from me?" he yelled to the group, arms wide as if offering himself as a sacrifice.

Rachel approached him as the others kept yelling. "Two, four, six, eight, who do we excoriate?" With Ivy at her side, she turned her back to the protestors and huddled with Washington.

"At the end of the day, you are just one small fish," Rachel said, pointing her finger at him. "We're really after Raj Magellan, an end to his movement and his festival. You help us get to Raj, we'll cease our harassment campaign against you."

"That shouldn't be too hard," Keshawn said, and looked up into the night sky. "He's been flying overhead for half the night."

"If you go back on your word, we'll be right back out in full force—at your office, at your home, in your neighborhood. Now you know what we're capable of."

"You're capable of publicly lynching men before they've even been accused of a crime, that's what you femi-Nazis are capable of."

Rachel beamed. "And we're pretty damn good at it!"

In the spirit of 'keep your friends close but your enemies closer,' Rachel and Washington walked off out of earshot of the rest of the crowd for a tete-a-tete. To Washington's surprise, Rachel divulged that she was one of the women who had broken the gender barrier at the Primates Festival Washington he had attended, where all his troubles had started.

"You were the one in that baboon outfit?!" Washington exclaimed.

To Rachel's surprise, Washington divulged that his benefactor, Raj Magellan, was keenly interested in getting close to Dr. Victor Haviland and explained why. Rachel wanted Magellan held accountable for his misogyny. Magellan wanted Haviland to further his aspirations to make freedom the ultimate currency of human interaction and transaction. So they had the basis for a deal.

"He'll be directing his conference from a prison cell eventually," Rachel promised, "but I'll get him an audience with Haviland if he keeps you employed. You'll serve as #VeeToo's mole on the inside."

Victor left Rachel to her protest, drove even more carefully on the dirt road toward the interstate, but then kept it at 80 mph until the exit for Sedona. He glanced at the text that just came in on his phone, couldn't make out the time stamp.

Sitting on the golf course under the huge willow tree. Can't miss it.

He texted back, clumsily. His car phone charger was missing. He must have taken it into the room when they checked in.

10 min awaay Bout to lose battery

Minutes later, he turned into the Songs of the Sun parking lot, pulled into a space, and got out of the car. He leaned against it for a moment. He looked up at the night sky. As a kid, he'd wanted to be an astronomer, a cosmologist. Where did that ambition go? Instead, I'm creating complex statistical models for the Pentagon. Where's the wonder in that?

What he really wanted for his legacy was an equation or a constant or some formula in the annals of statistics. Like the Bernoulli equation, Euler's Identity, the Fourier transform, Weibull distribution. It didn't necessarily have to penetrate the public's consciousness, just invoke the reverence of his future peers. Maybe they'd name a branch of Associational Statistics, Haviland's Framework. He'd be up there with Bayes' Theorem. He'd be remembered. Respected.

The Big Chief climbed out of his golf cart and addressed the MPs. "Well, hasn't this been a gross misunderstanding. Why didn't you tell me this woman was being sought for fentanyl smuggling? I'd have been more than willing to cooperate. Fentanyl has devastated our people."

"I'm afraid we'll have to impound that Jeep Grand Cherokee," an MP told Ashera.

"It's Gail's," Ashera said, "I was just a passenger for the short ride from the resort to the casino."

"And we'll need your contact information to question you later. Tossing that lizard wasn't your brightest move. Makes you an accomplice."

Ashera sighed, shell-shocked and dejected. She gave the details while the MP scribbled in a pocket notebook.

"We'll also be looking to confiscate your video."

"I know my rights. You need a warrant from a legitimate police authority. I'll just walk over there to the bus, and pretend the last few hours never happened," she muttered to no one in particular. By the time she got there, the protesters had broken up and the Big Chief had released the bus for exit.

Ashera slumped into a seat next to Azul. "What a night, huh?"

"Yes, I am still coming down from the euphoria of playing with Kremlin. What a wild ride that was! The band members surprised me!"

"That, by the way, was AMAZING!"

"Thank you! I have always had this dream of pairing music with images, ever since I watched Mr. Francis Ford Coppola's *Koyaanisqatsi*. Kremlin was on board with the idea. I thought about a performance like this at the museum, but knew that wouldn't happen. After I learned that HOMI-G was taking my stipend, I called my Kremlin friends and they were willing to change their set list and concept."

"Oh my God, I love that film, that juxtaposition of nature with humanity's destruction of it. I watched it for a film class at college."

"It was very popular anti-imperialist film in Nigeria. Do you know what Koyaanisqatsi means?"

"No, I don't recall."

"It means 'land out of balance.' I believe it is from the Apache language. Or maybe Hopi."

"Well, if Earth was out of balance when that film was shot, you'd have to say it is irreversibly disconfigured today."

They both contemplated that idea.

"I have heard that our fellow panelist member, Gail, has met with an unfortunate circumstance."

"If being arrested for using Air Force property as a staging ground for fentanyl smuggling is a 'circumstance,' you are correct."

Dr. Plemmons, in the seat in front of Ashera, popped her head over the head rest.

"That's Naomi Wasila out there! I got a selfie with her." She reached around the seat with her phone in her hand and showed it to Ashera, like a fan girl sharing her latest Taylor Swift concert pic.

Ashera sat straight up. "OMG! Her books were, like, Bibles at university."

Ashera strained to look out the window. Then she rose from her seat. "I never do this celebrity kind of thing, but I'm making an exception. C'mon, Azul, she's got to be one of the coolest women on the planet."

"I am happy to go with you."

"The bus is leaving, Miss," the driver said. "Take a seat."

"But I have to get off! Just for a moment. Pleeeease?"

The driver groaned and opened the door.

Rachel and Ivy, along with the other protesters, stowed their signs in the trunks of the cars they arrived in and all piled in like schoolgirls after a soccer game, dusty, clearly exhausted, brimming with pride about their success. Just when Rachel was about to step into the back seat, Ashera bounded up to her, Azul in tow.

"I'm sorry, I don't *ever* do this, and I know we've all had a long evening, but I am a great admirer of your work. I mean, you kept me sane in college. Can I, can I, just, uh, give you a hug?"

Rachel and Ashera embraced.

"Oh, I'm Ashera, by the way. This is my colloquium co-facilitator, Azul."

"It's really wonderful to meet the both of you!"

"I don't know where you are going next, but I would love the chance to have coffee or a drink with you sometime."

"It's a little late for a drink, but I'd take a rain check! Here's a card with my information on it." She reached into her bag.

"Hey, we're caravanning anyway," the car driver said. "I'm Ivy and I'm driving Rach—Naomi—back to the Song of the Sun resort anyway. Why don't you ride along?"

"OMG! That would be super-cool!" Ashera turned to Azul who shrugged and then waved goodbye to the bus driver. She'd never been so excited in her life!

Once they got close to the interstate and cell service resumed, Rachel saw a text alert on her phone.

Bradley in good hands. Ready to split with us in morning. Intervention going well.

CHAPTER 48

MEANWHILE, BACK AT THE RESORT

Nascha, on her latest attempt at a nap in the office, had legs propped up on the desk next to *The Only Good Indians*, as Victor approached.

"Excuse me," he said, timidly. She did not stir.

"Excuse me!" he exclaimed again. She jolted forward, the book slipping to the floor. She left the book there, and stumbled to the registration desk.

"Ah, yes, what's up? I mean, how can I help you?"

"I'm really sorry to bother you, but where is the, uh, big willow tree?"

"Oh right, you checked in not too long ago, didn't you?" she said, squinting, rubbing her eyes. "Go out this way, until you pass a rack of bicycles, then take a left. The walkway will curl around and up some stairs, then connect to a long pathway. You can't miss it."

"Thank you, and apologies again."

Nascha's faculties were slowly returning.

"Sir, sir!"

Victor turned around. "Yes?"

"You just returned from the casino, right?"

He walked back to the desk. "I did, as a matter of fact. Your directions were spot-on."

"Did you happen to notice if anything, uh, weird was going on there?"

"If you call a gaggle of women protesting, security lights flashing everywhere, a bus full of people detained at the security shack, and four helicopters circling overhead weird, then I guess so."

"Okay, that confirms an earlier report."

Victor didn't want to say more in case it might incriminate Rachel later. He noticed the book.

"Hey, is that a good book?" He pointed.

"What book? Oh, that one, *The Only Good Indians*?"

"Yes, A Native American reading a book about 'good Indians.' That seems to be, well, something."

"How so?"

"Well, I don't know, wouldn't you find it ironic if you saw me reading a book titled *The Only Good White People*?"

Nascha considered Victor. "You probably don't know the significance of the slogan to Native American history. The quote means the only good Indian is a dead Indian."

Victor looked like he was stumped for an answer on a test. Then his eyes widened. "Oh, I get it now. The author is Native American too, then?"

"Yes."

"His name doesn't sound native. Aren't we not supposed to use the word 'Indian'?"

"*You're* not supposed to use it."

"Me?"

"White people."

"Oh. Well," he said, backing away. "I guess I should go find that willow."

Avi Hoffman and one of his grad students, driving Avi's meticulously restored 1973 Volkswagen bug, pulled up to the resort's registration area.

"Okay," he wheezed, "you wait here. I'll handle this. Since you totally fucked up the bomb scares, I gotta do everything around here."

He teetered on his cane, slowly navigating the curb and the step. His back arced a 20 degree angle to the vertical. His unkempt hair, coarse and colored like the coat of a gray wolf, grew from the sides and the back, some of it tied back in a ponytail, all of it uncontained by his French beret. He wore a light navy-blue hoodie. Each leg of his baggy khakis could fit two of his spindly legs. The spread of his nostrils was wider than the length of his lips. His forehead, cheeks, and chin bore uneven crevices and depressions where one could imagine rivulets of sweat running down. No one Avi ever ran into wanted to imagine that.

"Excuse me," he said loudly, rapping his cane against the counter. "I'd like a room."

Startled, Nascha, who had nodded off again, almost fell to the floor trying to right herself in her chair.

"What the fuck!" she screeched, to no one in particular. She looked over to see a disheveled man tapping impatiently at the counter.

"Sorry for the adult language. Can I help you?"

"I'd like a room with two beds."

"We're booked up for the night."

"There's nothing available?"

"We are booked solid for the next three days."

"Can you make a call for us to one of the other area hotels? My cell phone is dead."

"I'm not sure you'll have any luck finding a room in town at this hour. Maybe Oak Creek Village has rooms available. Rim Rock probably a better bet. But that's a ways."

"Not even a smoking room?"

"Booked."

"Surely there's something you can do."

This was one customer she didn't mind losing. "Look, your inability to plan does not constitute an emergency on my part."

"Okay, okay, I'll have to think this through. Would you mind if I and my traveling companion just sit in the car in your lot while we figure something out?"

"I guess no problem," Nascha responded. "No sleeping in the parking lot, though."

"Do you happen to have a spare car phone charger?"

Nascha gave him a look.

"I need the kind that plugs into a cigarette lighter."

Nascha exaggerated her look.

"Okay, okay." Avi returned to his car. "Okay, drive over there," he instructed his student. He pointed to a corner of the parking lot away from the streetlights.

"Yes sir, Professor."

Nascha scanned through her security camera screens. Why were they going over there? How could he even get in that car? Could he exit the vehicle without a chiropractor? Or a winch? Eh, he was too old to make a fuss over at this hour.

Her phone rang. The Big Chief.

"What a night, Nascha! But good news. You just eked out your quota for the month."

"Great! I'll sleep better," she replied, yawning into the phone.

"We had to detain those Freedom Riders for a while on account of a little situation with one of their members. We even lost one of the group, thought he was roaming on casino property, that, uh, Mani-pedi character? Had a lady in tow. We looked all over for them. Unless he's in a broom closet."

"Oh, he returned earlier with the CLCC ladies." She had spotted him sneaking in on the security camera.

The Big Chief paused. "Nascha, we could have avoided a lot of grief down here if you had let me know that."

"I had no idea it was a thing that needed to be known."

"In any case, you can expect the Freedom Riders bus to show up soon."

"Roger that."

"Good night, then. We'll debrief in the morning. Got a feeling most of this will be kept on the QT."

"Got it. Night."

Moments later, the bus chugged by Big Brother and pulled into the lot, made its way slowly to the awning leading to the lobby. Even the bus looked like it would tell you it had a long night if it could speak.

In the Volkswagen bug, Avi nodded with renewed vigor when he saw the bus pull off the road into the resort. "Ah, okay, plan B," he said. "Don't turn on the headlights. Start the ignition, and follow in behind that bus. When it stops, you stop a few meters behind it. Got it?"

"Yes sir, Professor."

"I'm going to show you how it used to be done!"

"We're not going to get hurt, are we?"

"You have to make sacrifices to achieve social progress."

"I just want to finish my PhD!"

"You're not getting that degree without my approval. You don't get my approval until you experience what participating in a social movement is all about."

"I don't recall that from the graduate sociology program mission statement."

"Let me quote it for you, then. 'Each PhD candidate, after completing the coursework, works closely with his or her advisor(s) and under their supervision to complete the dissertation' and defend it in front of a panel comprised of several department professors and/or independent experts. The advisor is solely responsible for ensuring that the candidate's dissertation defense is prepared and for scheduling the defense session.'

"In other words, I own you."

Nascha watched on the security screen as the VW bug crawled slowly from the parking lot corner with no lights.

"Well, that is peculiar," she thought. She went quickly to a small closet.

The bus stopped by the curb. Nascha flipped through the security screens. She couldn't see the car anymore behind the bus. The bus door opened and one passenger, a lady, got off.

Avi reached into the glove compartment and pulled out a pistol.

His graduate student put his arms over his head and cried out. "Oh save me, Confucius, we're going to die!"

Fighting against the slight incline the car was parked on, Avi pushed the car door to where the hinge would lock it open. He couldn't get himself out of the car without placing his gun on the roof of the car, bracing his hand against the side, and pulling himself out. His cane fell, but thankfully at an angle that it would not roll away. He sneaked behind the bus, waited, then continued on stealthily, hunched over with his back against the side of the bus so that no one could see him from the windows.

When he reached the door, he made his move.

"All right, no more passengers are getting off," he said from the pavement to the two weary academics gathered at the steps, ready to disembark and get some sleep. He brandished his gun.

"I am taking this bus hostage in the name of Unfreedom Ideology until I have Dr. Washington in my custody!"

"My god, he's got a gun!" the man on the steps yelled, stepping back, nearly sitting on the woman behind him.

"O Lord, when is this ordeal going to end?" Someone yelled from the back.

"Where're the good guys with the guns when you need them?" Another lamented.

A third called out, "Where's Gail?"

Rolex patted Washington on the shoulder as he passed him in the aisle, trying to get off. "Niggah, you are one popular dude tonight!"

The driver looked down on Avi. "We've already been held hostage for two hours."

"Really? Why? Never mind! I demand to see Kerry Washington!

The driver groaned. "They don't pay me enough for this."

Washington got up from his seat and made his way to the front. He stepped around the two people on the steps and stood face-to-face with the old man. "Ardent Avi! Krazy Kauffman! This is no way to have an ideological debate."

"Debate, my ass, we're not having a debate. CSPF has all the resources at your disposal. That white supremacist, Magellan, is behind all this. Our center gets nothing. Our department is being dismantled. We have no choice but to make our voice heard in other ways! We demand Unfreedom!"

"How could Magellan be a white supremacist? He's darker than me. He's a fucking Indian, for fuck's sake."

Avi ignored him. "We demand Unfreedom!"

"Who's we, Avi?"

Meanwhile, Nascha quietly made her way from the lobby and sidled in the space between the wall and the bushes lining the walkway. With the speed of a mountain lion leaping at its prey, she jumped and planted herself within 20 feet of Kauffman, a bow with gut string pulled taught, an arrow ready to be discharged at her cheek and shoulder.

"One wrong move, and your liver will be dangling in front of your chest, quivering off the tip of this arrow!" she yelled.

Avi immediately dropped his weapon and put up his hands.

When the grad student saw Nascha and her bow, he jumped back into the VW, plunged in the clutch, and threw the stick shift out of neutral, stomped on the gas pedal, and was doing 40 before he got to the street. He minnow-tailed out towards Sedona, not even looking to see if traffic was coming either direction.

"There goes your ride, Avi," Kerry said.

"Now, you move over here." Nascha motioned to the side of the bus, and then inserted herself between Avi and the open door.

"Pick this gun up, will you?" she asked the person on the first step.

"I'm a strict pacifist. I don't touch guns."

Kerry sighed. "I'll get it. He wanted me, after all."

"Everyone off the bus now, it's all going to be fine, it's all okay now. The threat has been eliminated," Nascha called out. "Please accept our deepest apologies."

Washington walked over to hand Avi back his gun. "Avi, really?"

Avi's shoulders slumped even more than they already were. "I just wanted a taste of that '60s energy. I miss those days. Columbia, Wisconsin, Berkeley, you know, Kauffman's last stand kind of thing."

"And look at you. You don't even have a car now."

"Oh, he'll come back with it. He's a non-resident Chinese PhD candidate on a student visa and I'm his advisor. He can't take a shit in this country without me vouching for him."

"Ah, yes, the dissertation advisor as master, grad student as slave. I remember those days."

"My dignity, though. That's gone forever."

"Well, it looks like he's got the upper hand now," Kerry said. "Give the poor guy a call, and tell him to come back and get you. The coast is clear."

"My phone's dead."

"God, you are pathetic. Here, use mine. Call him."

Avi looked even more dejected that he had to use his adversary's phone.

"Aw, hell, I don't know his number by heart."

"Let's walk to my car. You can charge your phone and call him."

"What an embarrassment."

"At least you're not going to jail. No one's going to press any charges. I'll just find a repository for your gun."

"There's not even any bullets in it."

"As for you and your contretemps with the Freedom Center, look, I don't make the rules. Nowadays, the billionaires are running the show. You need one for a benefactor. Otherwise, you can't compete."

"Did you really model your cock for a dildo company?"

It was Washington's turn to look a little sheepish. "Afraid that's so."

"Damn, that's cool. Al Goldstein would have been so proud."

"Who?"

"Way before your time. He published smut, but he was a liberating force in his time, friend of mine, well, maybe not friend, but we ran in similar circles back in my NYC days."

"Avi, you are a legend out of time. Hey, here's your ride pulling in now. Cool car, by the way, is that yours? You should apply for one of those AZ historic vanity plates."

Well, that was a thrill, Nascha thought. It had been a long time since she'd pulled out that bow. She saw the VW return on the security camera, and the Asian guy getting out of the car. Something clicked in her head. She went to a closet, retrieved the backpack that had been left in the meeting room the day before, and walked it out to the car.

"I think this belongs to you," she said.

"How do you know?"

"All the books inside have Chinese characters?"

In all the excitement, though, Nascha realized she hadn't done her final checkout of the 14th hole for the CLCC "Darkness to Dawn" all-nighter powwow. It really would be nice if there was more help around here. She hurried back in.

Andre had prepared the punch, laid out the glassware, and barely even scowled when she asked him to set up the stools and the tom toms. They'd set out a powerful wireless speaker on a table, so they could play whatever music their hearts desired from their own devices. Why they needed any punch was beyond Nascha. They'd be soaring on their gummies, passing an imitation peace pipe bong back and forth. She didn't understand the ritual, but whatever. They paid good money for the privilege. They even bought the last of the Sedona red rock face paint she sold in the resort's store. It was sourced in Vietnam, but she doubted any of them would ever read the fine print.

CHAPTER 49

VICTOR AND BRADLEY REUNITE

Victor looked for the big willow tree. No one was around to ask. He looked behind him at the big window and door to the bar/restaurant area. Closed up. He walked a football field or two down to the grass, then noticed to his left a faint outline of someone sitting in a chair. He got closer.

"Bradley?" he asked, meekly. It was pitch dark.

"Victor!" He got up, shook his friend's hand, giving him a half-armed hug. "What in the everlasting fuck are you and Rachel *doing* here?"

"Thanks for asking how I'm doing. Despite the exceedingly long trip out here, we're fine."

"No, really. What the hell is going on? I mean, my birthday is in a few weeks, but I doubt you flew out to help me blow out 67 candles."

"Is there another chair? Never mind, I'll sit on the grass."

"It's wet. I'll go get you a chair." He walked to the hot tub area and brought back a chair. "Level with me, buddy. What the hell's going on?"

"Well, I'm a bit confused by it all myself. I left Rachel down at the Casino protesting with the #VeeToo group."

"What? The bunch that's after Dr. Washington? Rachel is one of them?"

"Apparently. You're to call her Naomi when she's with her peeps."

"The other alias she used to publish books?"

"I guess, though I've not read them."

"We've established that."

"Yeah, well, now it's been established with her too."

"Well, that explains why she's here. But not you."

"Did you know she doesn't have a driver's license? Doesn't drive at all."

"She's Manhattan, through and through."

"Not having a car is different from not being able to drive. What did she do when she was in LA those years?"

"Good question."

Long pause.

"So?"

"So what?"

"What the fuck are you two doing here?"

"Aw hell, we're supposed to be conducting an 'intervention.'"

"On who? On what? What intervention?"

"Well, uh, on you."

"What do I need to be intervened about? Aren't interventions for addicts or victims of violence and abuse?"

"I guess."

"Oh wait, you didn't."

"Didn't what?"

"You told her. Jesus fucking Christ, you told her!"

"Told her what?"

"About my problem. Your big fucking mouth. You told her. If I wasn't so fucking glum, I'd slug you."

"What are you depressed about?"

"I'll explain that another time."

Long pause.

"Is there anywhere close we can get a drink?"

Bradley ignored him, "Now, she knows about my problem and she's going to fix me."

"Fix you with what?"

"Victor, if you've ever read any of her books ..."

"I haven't."

"You're not kidding! You're not even curious enough to skim through them?"

"I don't read much outside of my research and coursework."

"For God's sakes, could you not have kept your big fucking mouth shut?"

"Well, I haven't read her books, but we do talk. I know she's a sexual dysfunction expert."

"In the area of guys whacking off?"

"Well, she's supposed to be, although her research methods have been called into serious question."

"Another reason not to let her intervene."

"She came under fire for not having the credentials to conduct such research or come to such conclusions, but she dismisses it as right-wing cultural politics."

"I can relate to that. But I'm here finishing up a colloquium on Neo-Anthropocentric Models of Retrospective Freedoms without those credentials. And now you two are going to work on my whacking-off problem."

"Not me, I'm not going there with a ten-foot pole."

"Or a six-inch cock."

"Shut up!"

Long pause.

Victor asked, "How did you get this gig anyway? Or maybe the better question is, why did you take the gig? You don't need the money, do you?"

The question he'd been asking himself since the reception the first morning in Sedona. Maybe it was time to answer it honestly.

"I don't know, I guess I was hoping to be recognized for my academic quality publications and books. I've published on concepts researched as deeply as any doctoral thesis, and just as original, but academics don't take me seriously because I don't have the goddamned degree. I figured this Freedom Institute was hiring me because they respected some of that work. All of you fucking PhDs don't want to be associated with anyone who doesn't have one. Having one doesn't make you better at analyzing stuff, it just means you met the requirements of a doctoral program. Hell, I could have gotten a University of Phoenix PhD or some equivalent. I've read a ton of dissertations, some from illustrious institutions, and most have little real-world value."

Victor remained silent.

"You PhDs hang out with three kinds of people: your students, other PhDs, and anyone who might provide funding for your programs."

"You don't have to get vicious about it, Bradley." He thought for a moment. "But you're not wrong."

Bradley reverted into gloom. No one mentioned his work over three days. A pounding headache was firing up. He'd had sex against his will with a woman he met two days ago. Well, he didn't fuck her. Small consolation. But still, it was sex. Rachel and Victor were here for an intervention. The gummy's effects were rapidly descending to zero. It was well past midnight.

He was crashing. Fuck. He tilted his head back, looked up at the night sky, and wondered what it was all about.

CHAPTER 50

THE PARTY AT THE 14TH HOLE

Victor leaned out of his chair.

"What's that?"

"What's what?" Bradley sat up.

They both gazed in awe as a procession of women dressed in white gowns, wide hats adorned with feathers and bows and colorful wraps, some with western-style vests, leather frills hanging off the pockets, belts gathering their dresses at the waist, and fancy cowboy boots or ankle-high soft leather booties, a few with moccasins, made their way across the expanse of green fairway sloping away from where they were sitting. They each held a candle in one hand, a palm from the other to protect the flame.

Bradley wondered, was this the sirens scene in *O Brother, Where Art Thou?*

"Where do you suppose they're going?" Victor asked.

"Okay, good, you see them too. Just a reality check."

"Should we be going where they're going?" Victor said, with that cherubic smile that always suggested he was embarrassed by whatever thought triggered what came out of his mouth.

"They're wealthy married women who come here twice a year for a week away from their spouses. They were at the casino earlier. I met one of them at the bar."

After a few minutes, they heard music, a Native American flute soaring over background instruments from where the women were headed.

"Maybe there's alcohol down there."

Bradley wanted to see if Catherine was in the group. They got close enough to see that the women had formed a wide arc of sorts. They were quiet, solemn even. Some were tapping lightly on small tom toms fitted into their laps. Others moved languorously into and through the soft music, some on their own, some in pairs. One had streamers attached to her sleeves which billowed out as she moved. Another made wide circular motions with her arms as if to gather fruit or soil from the ground.

Bradley said, "They must all be on uppers. They were at the casino for hours before this." He scanned the group for Catherine, but didn't find her. She should be with them.

Both were startled by a voice. "You boys got a reason to be here?"

Bradley and Victor looked behind them to see Nascha.

"Oh, we were just sitting over there and saw them walking over," Bradley said. "Wondered what it was all about."

"Well, let's give them some space, shall we? It's their Darkness Becomes Dawn powwow. Ladies only."

The exhausted academics finally disembarked from the bus and walked toward their guest rooms like ghouls from *Night of the Living Dead*. Behind him, Bradley overheard snippets of conversation.

"Can you believe it? We're discussing the concept of freedom and are detained at a Native American casino by military police, then almost taken hostage by a rival freedom center? You cannot make this shit up."

"Who was that guy with the gun?"

"No idea."

"What happened to our fearless facilitator?"

"I think he went off with that chick he was feeling up on the couch."

"What about Washington?"

"He left with the old guy with the gun."

"What a night!"

In the distance, the sounds of calming music, the steady beat of drums caught their attention. As they headed toward their rooms, a few of the tiki torches were visible. Strings of holiday bulbs made the grounds festive. A few of the women academics seemed pulled toward the party, trance-like, not against their will, but in obeisance to something deeper within. The clouds and the fog had fully cleared. The colored lights seemed like a bridge, a conveyance through the cliffs to the canopy of constellations beyond and above.

"Did we just see that?" Victor asked.

"What?"

"More ladies gravitating toward the party."

Oh, them, yeah, one of them is Dr. Plemmons. She spoke at the colloquium. They all hate my guts right now."

"Why?"

"I ditched them at the casino to hang out with one of the CLCC ladies, that group partying over there. She slipped me a gummy. Jesus, was I tripping. God knows what I said to those people." Bradley looked over at his friend, then dropped his head into his hands.

"Hey," Victor said, gently pushing Bradley's chin up with his hand. "Look at me."

Bradley looked up, but not like he wanted to be acknowledged by the world.

"You still got it!"

"Got what?"

"Your mojo, man. So ... was she number 37, or 28, or whatever?"

"Aw, fuck you, Victor, it wasn't like that."

Victor arched a brow.

"Well, it was kind of like that, but not," Bradley admitted.

"How come you aren't down there with her?"

"It didn't end well. It didn't start that well, to be honest."

"You mean, you just did gummies with some babe, had sex, and now you're moping around like you used to do when you got your grades."

"Was I really that bad?"

"You were inconsolable every time you got a C on a midterm or a final. We had to put up with your sour ass attitude all weekend."

"Yeah, Well, I didn't have the PRIVILEGE of being a fucking GENIUS in math."

"Maybe not, but you did have the foresight to know what you wanted to do after college and you did it. Who else did that?"

"Aren't you doing what you wanted?"

"I had no idea what I wanted to do. I just followed the path carved out for me by these professors and advisors and mentors who—"

"All knew you were a genius at math."

"All I knew, I was told from an early age how good I was at math and I was shepherded around to advanced classes and mentor teachers like a pet on a leash."

Bradley thought about the free will session. "Didn't you always want to be a professor in some ivory tower?"

"Hell no! I wanted to be an astronomer, calculating spacecraft trajectories, the movement of celestial bodies, solving the three-body problem. A latter day Tom Swift. And I wanted your success with women. Bradley's harem, remember?"

"You guys totally misunderstood all that. I didn't have some 'harem.' I had a girlfriend who had roommates and lots of friends. They just happened to do everything together. You happened to go out with the one girl, Rachel, who kept her girlfriends and her guy friends very separate."

"She was kind of a loner. Speaking of, she still wants to convince you to testify against Lamborghini."

"She was a controller, not a loner. By being at the center of different groups but minimizing how much the groups interacted or overlapped. And the answer is no on Tino."

"I've never thought of it that way."

"I didn't study sociology late in life for nothing."

"Which reminds me," Victor said, "why didn't you major in that in college? You always loved it. You always got A's in your humanities courses.

"Yeah, they sure brought up my grade point average. I only studied engineering so I'd be assured of getting a job. Anyway, why are we still talking about all this? It was almost 50 fucking years ago."

They took in a long moment of silence with the bracing, brittle desert air, that minerally aroma, wisps of creosote.

"She finally told me what that 'unfinished business' was between the two of you."

The circulation in Bradley's veins stopped. Oh shit, here we go.

"Would you believe it? She was just trying to maneuver us into a threesome."

Bradley exhaled like the weight of history had just been lifted. "For sex?"

"What other kind of threesome is there?"

"A frank discussion of *Our Bodies, Ourselves*? Hell, I don't know."

"Ha ha."

"Too bad she didn't push for a foursome with Iris. She was pretty hot."

"That's what I told her. Imagine, our own three-body problem!"

They both contemplated the constellations, the ends of the bowed branches of the willow nearby, the pond with its fountain in the center, Big Brother which in a few hours would be as irradiated as the lights around the 14th hole.

"So, how was it? All these years later. Your gummy lady tonight."

"Terrible. I don't want to talk about it."

Azul and Ashera walked by. Bradley thought it a little strange Gail wasn't with them. He overheard Azul mutter excitedly. Something about staging the multimedia show.

"Hey, you two!" Bradley stood and called out. "Victor, meet two of my facilitators for the colloquium. Victor's a good friend from my college days."

Victor stood and Azul shook his hand and mumbled, "That's cool."

"That was some performance, Azul!" Bradley exclaimed.

"I was honored to be called by my peers. Very humbled by their gesture." He turned to walked on toward Ashera, who had kept walking.

"Ashera, wait." Bradley called out. "Where's Gail?"

Ashera stopped abruptly and turned around, fury in her face. "Oh, right, you haven't heard because you abandoned us at the casino. She's in the custody of the Air Force, hopefully receiving medical treatment for lacerations she incurred from being trapped in barbed wire fencing."

"What?"

"Yeah, it was quite a scene. She tried to put a bullet through her head. Too bad you missed it. Want a hint?" She pulled out her phone and opened her photographs.

Bradley walked toward her.

"How's that for an ending to her conference participation?" She asked.

"Holy shit!" Bradley gasped. "You mean, because of that stuff she divulged in the conference?"

"You'll figure it all out. Nice to meet you, Victor. Your friend's an asshole."

"Well, that wasn't very nice," Victor muttered.

The two watched the pair continue on to the party in the distance. They could overhear Azul and Ashera's conversation until it trailed off.

"Twelve hours ago, I received a voice mail from my boss saying that I could be terminated," Azul was saying. "Then just before my breakout, I received a text that I would be promoted with a big pay raise. Now I am reading a bulletin from HOMI-G stating that our benefactor, Conrad Bolton, has died suddenly and tragically in a helicopter accident ..."

"OMG, you don't think—" was the last thing Bradley heard from Ashera, then could no longer hear them.

"Who is Gail?" Victor asked, settling back in their chairs.

"The third primary facilitator for my colloquium."

"She tried to commit suicide??"

"This is the first I'm hearing about it. I was frolicking with the gummy girl. Fuck, now I feel twice as bad."

"Good thing you're about to retire, right?"

"For once in my stupid life, I decide to have some fun at work instead of being 'oh so responsible' and it's all coming back to haunt me."

"You're haunting yourself, Bradley. You're a prisoner of your own conscientiousness. No one is going to care about any of this tomorrow. That Gail chick, whatever she's getting thrown into the slammer for, had nothing to do with you. That Catherine chick, she came on to you, right?"

"And all you seem to care about is how many women I slept with in my life!"

"That was just supposed to be a bit of fun, Bradley. I didn't think it would end up making you crazy."

"And all I do all day is whack off to these babes on social media. Sometimes I think it's fine and sometimes I feel like I'm cheating on Valerie. And now ..."

"Well, Rachel will take care of all that for you. I mean, I guess."

The Darkness Before Dawn party was getting more boisterous. At least one reveler was taking her drumming seriously. The constant, steady beat had been replaced by someone who obviously knew their way around a set of bongos. The air filled with beats reverberating between the canyon walls.

"They must have recognized Azul from the casino, given him some bongos to play."

"He's quite a cat on those skins," Victor said.

"Since when do you talk like a jazz aficionado from the '30s?" Bradley countered.

"Every so often I try not to sound like a dorky math professor from the 2020s."

"You sound like a poser who just looked it up on the interwebs."

"They're having a much better time than we are. Because you're moping and morose."

Rachel and a bevy of #VeeToo protesters finally arrived, after dropping off Ashera and returning some folks to Sedona. They walked with haste into the lobby.

"Yo!" she called out, in her oversized New York accent.

Nascha once again lost her legs, crossed and anchored on the desk, as they sprawled towards the floor. This time she managed to catch *The Only Good Indians* from sliding off her chest.

"Wha-what? For God's sakes, I've got to get a couch in here. What can I do for you?"

"What's going on back there?" Rachel pointed toward the golf course.

"Oh, lord, thanks for reminding me. I've got to get them a few more jugs of spiked punch! Yeah, it's a private party for some of the guests."

"Oh, far out!"

"Women only, though a few plus ones are allowed on a discretionary basis." She thought about calling Finn and inviting him. They could do a Darkness Becomes Dawn adjacent party. But it was late and she was bone tired.

"Even better!"

Rachel walked back to the parking lot.

She told the group, "Hey, I know you young ladies were going to drive back to Phoenix tonight, but it's late. There are festivities going on, and you've surely earned your right to party! You can crash on my floor after and drive back whenever you wake up. I don't want to be a mother hen, but I do have seniority."

After a few minutes, Victor spied Rachel and the group approaching them.

"Oh, wow, here comes Rachel! And her #VeeToo followers, I guess, who all look way too young for me. Oh, remember, call her Naomi."

"What? Naomi?" Then Bradley remembered.

"Okay, I get it."

When Rachel saw Bradley, she dashed off ahead of her group to meet him.

"Bradley! How long has it been?"

"Rach ... Naomi, God, at least a decade or two!"

"Let me step back and get a good look!"

"I think I had at least some hair the last time we saw each other."

"I think I had a few strands that weren't colored to hide the gray! Anyway, these wonderful ladies have had a hectic day, a long week, in fact. Do you know what's going on down there?"

"At this point, I don't think they'd mind if a few more women showed up."

"You sound a little down, Bradley."

"Ah, we can talk about all that later."

"We certainly will."

"I think I know what's in store for me."

"That's because you've read my books, right, Bradley?" Rachel said, with a stern glance at Victor.

"All of them."

"We'll deal with all that later."

"Yes, we'll be dealing with all that," Bradley said raising his voice, "because a certain somebody has a big fucking mouth." He gave the evil eye to Victor and let it linger.

"Hey, can't we go? To the party?" Victor asked.

"Women only, according to the proprietor," said Rachel.

Victor looked at Bradley. "That guy Azul's down there."

"Well, no old, privileged white men, then."

"Speak for yourself, Victor. I'm brown, when it's convenient." Bradley finally smiled.

"I'll put in a good word for you two," promised Rachel.

"That's not gonna happen. They all hate me down there."

Rachel thought a moment. "I'll make a deal with you. Testify against Lamborghini and I'll get you an invite as my plus one."

Bradley looked at Rachel, then at Victor, then back at Rachel. "You know what? I'll think about it."

"As for you, Victor," Rachel said, "I've got a prestigious job opportunity for you, but we'll talk about that later, too."

"I don't need a job."

"Do you want to retire on a professor's pension and retirement fund, or buy a yacht and sail the Inter-coastal the rest of your life?"

"Well…"

As Rachel was walking away, Victor yelled, "Hey, uh, Naomi, how come it's okay to have a ladies-only bacchanalia, but Raj Magellan can't have an exclusive guys-only Primates Festival?

Rachel turned around and flipped him the bird.

"I guess we're really not invited," Victor lamented.

"Guess so."

"We're going to take off first thing in the morning, right?"

"Right."

"Good, I'm going to bed," Victor said. "See you in the a.m."

"It's already the a.m."

"You're not going to do anything stupid, are you?"

"You mean, like spending $30,000 for a pecker extension? No, nothing that stupid."

"I'm just weighing my options," Victor conceded. "I'll see what Rachel thinks."

"Go get some sleep. Oh, and Victor, it's good to see you. Seriously."

After a few minutes, Bradley decided bed was probably a good idea, too. He ventured to the top of the hill one more time to see if Catherine was at the party. And there she was, with the rest of them, smiling no less, undulating to Azul soloing on a set of bongos, the ladies dancing together, arms appearing to be swimming breaststroke through water, or reaching up to the stars for enlightenment, ribbons and frills tangled up into the wisps of air which one couldn't see but the dancers could surely feel, a kaleidoscope of colors, a warm cacophony of chants and murmurs.

In a few hours, the sun would be making its appearance yet again, the cliffs would brighten up and heat up, and at the optimum angle of the sun's magical beams, the red rocks would make their appearance, and the dew and whatever precious moisture the unprecedented rainfall left, would evaporate and everything would—

Bradley felt his shirt collar constrict his throat, his entire body yanked from the back, an angry hand grab his left shoulder, spinning him around and tumbling him to the ground. His right hand caught the weight of his body. He righted himself, but he knew whatever had just happened to his wrist was going to be painful in a few hours. Before he could turn around fully, his attacker shoved him again. This time Bradley fell fully to the ground. He rolled once and winced when the weight of his body crossed over his hurt wrist.

"I should just fuck you up!" Dr. Washington grunted through clenched teeth and pursed lips, obviously not wanting to make too much of a scene.

"Dr. Washington!" The lines of his facial hair grooming seemed even more precise than when he saw him at the interview a few months ago. It was almost like his head was 3-D printed.

"You haven't returned my texts or voice mails for two days. You ruined my colloquium, and our shot at launching the CSPF into the same orbit of the Aspen Institute and Davos! That woman you're palling around with and her pre-pubescent followers just destroyed my career. Not to mention the liability fallout to the CSPF from an invited facilitator's attempted suicide and arrest by the Air Force."

"It certainly didn't unfold the way we expected it to, now did it?" Bradley tried to get to his feet.

"Fuck you, you smug, smart ass!" Washington yelled. He grabbed at the front of Bradley's shirt, popping a button, and cocked his right fist to within an inch of Bradley's cheek.

Bradley cowered. "Look, the last time I was in a fistfight was

1975, in the football team's frat house. I was not on the winning side."

The words rode on his deep heaves like a bad surfer drowning in a wave. "Shut up! Just tell me. Why?"

"Why what?"

"Why ... all this?"

"Look, this wasn't some premeditated plot against you, your career, or the Freedom Center," Bradley said. I just, I don't know, all this talk about freedom, went to everyone's head. How did I know some mole was posting all our stuff on social media? I really enjoyed Dr. Wertmuller's talk on how to quantify freedom. I thought I'd manufacture some freedom of my own. You know? Blow off one gig. See how it would feel. These facilitators, and even some of the attendees, the conference seemed to free them too.

"Wasn't anyone monitoring social media in real time?"

"Maybe that someone should have been you as I was busy, you know, facilitating. Look, Kerry, no one tweets or twits or tic-tac-toes at the conferences I've managed. All I did was allow your invited speakers and facilitators the freedom to let themselves go a little, liberate their tongues."

"This was supposed to be a conference on concepts, not everyone's personal grievances."

"Talking about freedom can be a powerful thing."

"That's how the Center sees it," Kerry said with a long-suffering sigh.

Bradley got to his feet. "That stuff about your 'bro thang,' and the Celibri-Dong, well, I hate to break it to you, but that's on you."

"Now I'm on the hook to get the #VeeToo chicks to Magellan."

"Your billionaire sugar-daddy."

"I am up the creek."

"What's his game, anyway?—Magellan."

"He's an ardent believer in personal liberty and the natural order of things."

"Natural order? So, he'd be proud of what went down at the colloquium, right?"

"Doubtful."

"And his Primates Festival?"

"Ugh, don't remind me."

Washington walked off, dejected. Bradley yelled after him.

"Hey, Kerry, why did you guys hire me for this gig anyway?"

Kerry paused and turned around. "Because you *don't* have a PhD. Magellan admires daring and courage. And he liked one of your papers from your sociology grad work."

"Which one?"

"I can't recall the title. The one where you survey homogenous ethnic group trust networks dominating national economies in many parts of the world. He loved it."

Ah yes, thought Bradley, the one for which I was accused by my classmates of advancing anti-Semitic biases.

"Oh, and I almost forgot," Washington continued, "he's keenly interested in that friend of yours, professor by the name of Victor Haviland."

The sun had now peeked above Big Brother over the eastern horizon, and the cliffs on the other side of the road to the Song of the Sun were about to light up. The revelers were straggling back to their rooms, the daylight signaling that the end had, indeed, finally arrived and whatever one's state of freedom was, daybreak surely signified at least a new beginning.

At least there was that.

Ashera and Azul, arms slung around each other and holding each other upright, passed Bradley who looked morose and dejected, his party shirt ripped at the front buttons, grass stains on his khakis, left arm cradling his right.

"Hey, asshole," Ashera said, nonchalantly, "looks like you got what you deserved."

"Maybe we can get a cab into town and have breakfast," Ashera said to Azul. "I'm starving."

Bradley clutched his right fist with his left hand. He could barely move it. Only an X-ray would tell if it was sprained or broken. Hell, now he'd have to masturbate with his left hand. Then again, if this truly was going to be an intervention, maybe he'd have to quit cold turkey. A right hand in a caste would help. To add the insult to the injury, they'd wanted Victor all along.

Nascha bounded out of the lobby, carrying a large bucket, and grabbed a recycling bin on wheels almost as tall as her, located a few yards from the door. She stopped suddenly to take a phone call from the Big Chief.

"Thought you should know, one of those helicopters ran into a butte on the way back to Phoenix and exploded. Thank God the wet earth kept a wildfire at bay until the fire department showed. Mercifully, it didn't happen on our land."

"That's awful! But Chief, I've really—"

"That's not all. The other whirlybird did an emergency landing on the casino parking lot. They'd run out of fuel. This guy, he's standing next to me, Ram Gamella?

Nascha heard a faint voice, "Did I pronounce that right, Ram?"

"Anyway, Ramen here wants to know, is there a guest named Haviland up your way?"

"Chief, you know we're not allowed to disclose to outside parties whether guests are registered or not—"

"He's about to drop a sizable, and I do mean sizable, number of Ulysses S Grants on our craps tables, Nascha."

Nascha thought for a moment. "Short answer, yes."

She rolled the bin down the hill toward the 14th hole and past Bradley.

"Hey, Nascha, when does your restaurant open?" Bradley yelled, with the last of his metabolic energy and joy about his mental state.

"Seven a.m., but don't bother me, I've got to clean up down there. We've got a golf tournament for a bunch of local sales folks this weekend.

"Wasn't that powwow last night an appropriation of your culture?"

Nascha stopped for a moment. "Well, my people have been caretakers of this land for ourselves and others for centuries. We do the same thing today, only now we charge for the privilege."

THE END

READER DISCUSSION QUESTIONS

The following Q&A, between the author and the author's alter ego, is intended to prompt inquiry and discussion among book club enthusiasts.

Q. First, why do you label the novel brutalist satire?

A. I thought about calling it savage satire, but the alliteration bothered me.

Q. You are echoing brutalist architecture though, right?

A. Yes, I thought an art form associated with socialism would be ironic for a satire about capitalistic versions of freedom. And the fact that the decline of the architectural form was largely due to it becoming associated with urban rot (in this case, academic rot) and totalitarianism (read, unfreedom or *imposed* freedom).

Q. Did Catherine "date-rape" Bradley at the end?

A. I'm not sure you can conclude that because they really weren't on a date. The ambiguity is certainly deliberate. You might say that's just semantics, but I say everything is just semantics. Or is it?

Q. Why did you locate the party at the end on the golf course's 14ᵗʰ hole?

On a billiards table, the fourteen ball is green and striped and green is my favorite color. Also, I grew up near a golf course and the 14ᵗʰ hole was a fairly easy par 3 after the brutally long par 5 thirteenth hole. I'm not saying that the previous chapters were brutal, but then again the whole thing is labeled brutalist, so maybe they were. You have the freedom to determine that for yourself.

Q. What was your process for creating your main characters?

A. Much contemporary art, notably sculpture and collage, makes use of and recycles everyday "found" objects. You could say I just picked up fragments of the personalities and behaviors that have surround me over the course of my life, recombined them, then threw them in the crucible of fire and recast them.

Q. Ultimately, Gail is the tragic hero in this story?

A. If you must pick a character, I suppose so. They all seem tragic to me. Which is good for a comedy. Haha. I'm a big believer in the idea that if we don't laugh at life, we'd spend every minute curled in a corner crying. Especially in times like these.

Q. Still, why Gail?

A. I've always made fun of the quaint notion heard too often in writers' workshops and seminars: "The characters write themselves!" However, I have to say, Gail really did write herself in *Wrequiem*, and in the end saved me a lot of work fleshing out other characters as they responded to her.

Q. That didn't answer my question: Why Gail?

A. You're the one who identified her as the tragic hero, why do you believe that?

Q. That still doesn't … oh, never mind. Moving on…

Q. How did you select the three institutions which anchor the Colloquium?

A. I challenged myself to pick three of my favorite destinations in Arizona and do my best to depict them in a way that would make me not like them.

Q. I suppose you don't have to look too hard to find satiric material in Sedona?

A. Indeed. The locals don't call it Crystals and Pistols for nothing.

Q. It's clear Bradley's character is autobiographical if you do a forensics-level web search on your name.

A. Superficially, perhaps, but I never achieved any notoriety in professionally. Plus, I was never able to masturbate more than three times a day.

Q. Seriously, though, there are character details which mirror your own life pretty exactly.

A. Small doses, perhaps. In the end, it's taking fragments of reality and extrapolating or exaggerating them for fictional purposes or comic effect. Like how one learns in data analysis to measure a few points, graph them, and find a curve that "fits the data."

Q. What's that supposed to mean?

A. In geometry, an asymptote is a boundary line that a curve approaches but never quite arrives at. The word comes from the Greek and means "not falling together." Or maybe it's more of a Schrödinger thing: Bradley is me and also not me.

Q. Why freedom?

A. When I heard about a university opening a center on the philosophy of freedom, I thought, how can you conduct "objective" research around something that, just in the attempt to define it biases anywhere you'd care to go with it. So, it kind of became the poster child in my mind for much that is wrong with academia today. All research comes back to two things: assumptions and definitions. Both can be ambiguous. (Add inherent and often unacknowledged bias to the mix and, voila, you have…what?) Importantly, you must have the credentials or money or political power as a "player" to even be allowed to conduct the kind of research that would be taken seriously in such a setting. This precept applies regardless of the kind of research you do, humanities, STEM, quantitative, qualitative. Ultimately, freedom has everything to do with power, and is, therefore, dependent upon it. Without power, you can't set the agenda and you can't define the terms, and you certainly can't control the narrative. So, no power, no freedom. And where does that put us?

Q. You really hit ethnicity hard, but Indian subcontinent folks really take a knock-out blow.

Correction. Brahmins perhaps take a knock-out blow, just like any group that espouses some form of inherent superiority over others. The concept of a superior class or race, like Sedona as a place teeming with magical vortexes, just begs for satire. In most comedy, it seems, one undeserving group of people takes the majority of the punches. Recently, two Indian-Americans were popular and legitmate candidates in their party's nominating process for president of the United States so it seemed like an opportunity I'd be stupid to pass up. In a brutalist satire like Wrequiem, it's a testament to Indian-American success to be pilloried.

Q. How did your ideas for this novel evolve?

Like many people, I suppose, when I moved to Arizona, I was captivated by the Native Americans and that fact that they are visible and active members of the community, unlike everywhere else I've lived in America. In Tucson, their stories, their myths, their art, their culture, their reservations, their continued oppression by the rest of America surrounds us. In the beginning all I knew was that I wanted the story to be "centered" on Native Americans, but not in a way that would be considered "about them." I started a notebook for ideas. It got all serious and too deep, Then I decided I wanted to write humor. Somewhere along the way, I had mapped out some plots that incorporated the three institutions I mentioned above. It got more complicated. Too complicated. The epiphany that allowed me to move forward was to bring representatives of the three institutions to one place. Other than that, over my career, I really have had enough of academics and other professionals and their jargon, illegible papers no one reads, exploitation of their graduate students and employees, suspect research methods, abused analytical tools, biased funding partners, commodification of education, etc., especially in non-STEM fields. I could go on and on. American universities impair all the things they ostensibly strive to support—equal access, equal opportunity, educational excellence, intellectual inquiry, the meritocracy.

Q. Which authors and what novels inspired you while writing Wrequium?

A. The three funniest novels I've ever read are *Catch-22* (Joseph Heller), *A Confederacy of Dunces* (Jonathan Kennedy Toole), and *The Sellout* (Paul Beatty). But I also have my favorite movie comedies, which should be obvious when you read *Wrequiem*. My goal was to write a novel as intellectually rewarding as those three but with a straightforward comedic structure like *Animal House*, *Dazed and Confused*, or *The Forty-Year-Old Virgin*, or even one of my favorite early reader books: *Go Dog Go!*

Q. Let's return to Bradley—and Victor. Why does Victor make Bradley count all his sexual conquests?

A. Lots of reasons, obviously. What could be less intellectual during a high-brow academic colloquium than an obsession with whacking off and two white guys reminiscing about how many women they've slept with? The contrast was too rich to pass up. Second, I imagine any man with a sliver of a conscious and a history of even mild promiscuity has searched his databank of sexual experiences for any behavior that might have been too Trumpian, Weinsteinian, or Cavanaughan (is that a word?).

Q. Who is your favorite character?

A. That's easy. Nascha Sunsee! Robert Sapolski's work, *Determined*, uses the illustration of "turtles all the way down" to support his thesis that there is no such thing as free will. That is, if you catalogue everything in a person's life, his brain/mind chemistry in the preceding moments, environment, heredity, ancestry, etc., that influenced the action the person just took, you have to conclude he/she did not make a choice to do the thing. If you apply this concept to oppression and prejudice in America, it's "turtles all the way down" until you get to the Native Americans. Here's this woman, Nascha, just trying to get by, do her job with a lack of resources (like many of us), and pursue a dream or two, while the rest of American society has the "freedom" to prattle on and on about freedom and unfreedom, essentially ignoring the most important aspect of the whole concept, i.e, that it is constructed by those with power, given to some, and denied to others.

Q. The penis plays an outsized role in *Wrequiem*.

A. It sure does. Doesn't it everywhere?

EXTRA READINGS

The following list includes, in no particular order, books and articles that have stayed with me, inspired me, and challenged me while writing *Wrequiem*.

- P.D. Eastman, *Go, Dog. Go!*, Random House Inc, New York, NY, 1961.
- Esther Forbes, *Johnny Tremain*, Dell Publishing, New York, NY, 1943.
- Chimamanda Ngozi Adichie, *Americanah*, Alfred A. Knopf, 2013.
- Stephen Graham Jones, *The Only Good Indians*, Saga Press/ Simon & Schuster, New York, NY, 2020.
- Andre Gabor, "The Concept of Statistical Freedom and Its Application to Social Mobility, *Population Studies*," Vol 9, No. 1, July 1955.
- Denis Gabor and Andre Gabor, "An Essay on the Mathematical Theory of Freedom," *Journal of the Royal Statistical Society*, Vol. 117, No. 1, 1954.
- James Gwartney and Robert Lawson, "The Concept and Measurement of Economic Freedom, *European Journal of Political Economy*, Vol 19, 2003.
- Peter Graeff, "Measuring Individual Freedom: Actions and Rights as Indicators of Individual Freedom," in *Towards a Worldwide Index of Human Freedom*, Fraser Institute, 2012.
- Robert M Sapolsky, *Determined: A Science of Life Without Free Will*, Penguin Press, New York, NY, 2023.
- Robert Sapolsky, Behave: The Biology of Humans at Our Best and Worst, Penguin Press, New York, NY, 2017.

- Kevin J Mitchell, *Free Agents: How Evolution Gave Us Free Will*, Princeton University Press, 2023.
- Nikhil Krishnan, "Make Me: Is Free Will an Illusion? You Decide," *The New Yorker*, November 13, 2023.
- Naomi Wolf, *Vagina*, Ecco Books/Harper Collins, New York, NY 2012.
- Andrea Long Chu, 'My New Vagina Won't Make Me Happy,' *The New York Times*, November 24, 2018.
- Ava Kofman, "Measure for Measure: On the Frontiers of Penile Enhancement, Competition for Patients Grows Cutthroat," *The New Yorker*, July 3, 2023.
- David Friedman, A Mind of Its Own: A Cultural History of the Penis, Free Press, November, 2001.
- Ewa Stefanska, "The Relationship Between Atypical Sexual Fantasies, Behavior, and Pornography Consumption," National Library of Medicine, April 2022.
- Gabriele Kuby, The Global Sexual Revolution: Destruction of Freedom in the Name of Freedom, Angelica Press, December 2015.
- Jeffrey Escoffier, "The Sexual Revolution, 1960-1980," www.glbtq.com, 2015, Glbtq Inc.
- "Liberalism and Our Sexual Rights and Freedoms," www.aeromagazine.com, January, 2023.
- J Michael Bailey, "Academic Freedom and Sexual Hysteria: Three Controversies," November, 2020, FIRE Faculty Conference, Northwestern University.
- Eric Schlosser, *Command and Control: Nuclear Weapons, the Damascus Accident, and the Illusion of Safety*, Penguin Books, New York, NY. 2013.
- Richard Nisbett, *Mindware: Tools for Smart Thinking*, Farrar, Straus, and Giroux, New York, NY 2015.
- Chuck Penson, *The Titan Handbook: A Civilian's Guide to the Most Power ICBM America Ever Built*, 2008.

- David K Stumpf, *Titan II: A History of a Cold War Missile Program*, University of Arkansas Press, 2000.
- Maria Streshinsky, "The Apocalyptic Optimism of Christopher Nolan," *Wired*, June 2023.
- Titan II Veterans Health Survey and Deaths as of June 13, 2023, https://sites.google.com/site/titan2vetshealthandwellness/health-surveys/titan-ii-missile-veterans-health-survey-responses.
- Tom Mueller, "The Home Front" (Book Review), *The New York Times*, August 20, 2023.
- Gayle Harrison Hartmann and Peter C Boyle, Editors, *New Perspectives on the Rock Art and Prehistoric Settlement Organization of Tumamoc Hill*, Tucson, AZ, Arizona State Museum, 2013.
- Michael Stancampiano, "Tribal Membership" (Letters to the Editor), *The New Yorker.*
- Sterling HolyWhiteMountain, "False Star" (short story), *The New Yorker*, March 20, 2023.
- Margaret Talbot, "Hot and Bothered: How Candida Royalle Set Out to Remake the Porn Industry," *The New Yorker*, March 25, 2024.
- Moira Donegan, "The Catalyst: Betty Friedan and the Movement That Outgrew Her," *The New Yorker*, September 18, 2023.
- Fonteini Stamatelopoulou, "Being in the Zone: A Systematic Review on the Relationship of Psychological Correlates and the Occurrence of Flow Experiences in Sports' Performance," Psychology, Vol.9, No. 8, August 2018.
- Christina Sharpe, *Ordinary Notes*, Farrar, Straus, and Giroux, New York, NY.
- Peter Baker, "Foreign Policy Veteran Says Real Threat Is 'Us,'" *The New York Times*, July 2, 2023.
- Daniel Bergner, "Let the Body Do the Talking," *The New York Times Magazine*, May 21, 2023.

- *Universal Declaration for the Rights of Mother Earth*, Global Alliance for the Rights of Nature, April 2012.
- William Sturtevant, General Editor, *Handbook of North American Indians*, Volumes 9 & 10, Smithsonian Institute, Washington DC, 1983.
- Yarren Hominh, *The Problem of Unfreedom*, Doctoral Thesis, Columbia University, 2021.
- Lisa Magarrell, International Center for Transitional Justice, *Reparations in Theory and Practice*, September 2007.
- H Matthew Kramer, "Sources of Unfreedom," Oxford Scholarship On-line.
- Ann M Eisenberg, "The Geography of Unfreedom," *Michigan Law Review*, April 2023.
- Pablo de Grief, "Repairing the Past: Confronting the Legacies of Slavery, Genocide, and Caste," Seventh Annual Gilder Lehrman Center International Conference at Yale University, October 2005.
- Raj Chetty et al, "Diversifying Society's Leaders: Determinants and Causal Effects of Admission to Highly Selective Colleges," Opportunity Insights, Harvard University, July 2023.
- Marianne Keppens and Jakob de Roover, "The Brahmins, the Aryan, and the Powers of the Priestly Class: Puzzles in the Study of Indian Religions," *Religions Journal*, 2020.
- Michael Bamshad, "Genetic Evidence on the Origins of Indian Caste Population," *Genome Research*, June 2001.
- Sumitra Badrinathan, "Social Realities of Indian America: Results from the 2020 Indian American Attitudes Survey," Carnegie Endowment for International Peace, June 2021.
- Sahiba, "Unsettling Complicities: An Autoethographic Mapping," Kalfou: Journal of Comparative and Relational Ethnic Studies, Vol. 9, No. 2, 2022.
- Aadita Chaudhury, "Why White Supremacists and Hindu

Nationalists Are So Alike," Al Jazeera, December, 2018.
- Robert Edward Gordon, "The Philosophy of Freedom and the History of Art," *Philosophies*, 2020.

ACKNOWLEDGEMENTS

Here, I am supposed to recognize those who are and will be important in scaffolding my fiction publishing career to the heights of success. There just aren't any. To be honest, I didn't follow any of the guidance I've ever received about how to write a novel. I just tried to write guided by the spirits of the three authors I admire most for their satire: Joseph Heller, *Catch-22*; Jonathan Kennedy Toole, *A Confederacy of Dunces*, and Paul Beatty, *The Sellout*.

As a lifelong writer (engineering and business writing and short stories) publishing his second novel at the dawn of his eighth decade on this planet, I can't feel anything but gratitude for everyone I have encountered over my life for every single moment they've contributed to the deep pool of inspiration my brain draws from, and my fingers type to, at any given moment. Those who directly mattered to *Wrequiem*—family members and friends, probably want to remain anonymous—except for Kristina Blank Makansi, my editor, muse, critic, publisher, spouse, and intellectual sparring partner, as we enter our fifth decade of partnership and love.

I would be remiss not to acknowledge the members of my writers group in St. Louis, informally and affectionately known as Big Jim's Slaves of Fiction, who helped this engineering magazine journalist hone his skills in fiction. While they numbered in the dozens over a period of eight or nine years, I hope all of them, and all the writers I have encountered throughout my life, have, as I have, ultimately found joy, salvation, redemption, social and psychological renewal, and/or perhaps even success expressing themselves on the printed page.

ABOUT THE AUTHOR

Since launching a family newspaper in the 6th grade (it lasted two issues), Jason Makansi has considered himself a writer all his adult life. He wrote bad poetry in the 1980s and 1990s, a few published in vanity collections; short stories for fifteen years, a dozen of which were published in reputable (though now largely defunct) literary journals. His first novel, *The Moment Before*, came out in 2018 to a small but quite enthusiastic readership of about a hundred.

Other publishing credits include several professional books, including the industry-acclaimed *Lights Out: The Electricity Crisis, the Global Economy, and What It Means To You* (John Wiley & Sons, 2007) and the 2016 IPPY Gold and and Foreward Reviews Indie Silver winner, *Painting By Numbers: How to Sharpen Your BS Detector and Smoke Out the "Experts,"* a layman's guide for strengthening numerical literacy.

Makansi earned his BS in Chemical Engineering from Columbia University in New York in 1974, worked towards a higher degree in Sociology at the University of Missouri in the late 2000s, and attended the Sewanee Writers Conference in 2009. Other than the epigraph in the beginning, his favorite quote, from a long-ago Saturday morning cartoon, is "A pie in the face is worth two in the mouth."

Find out more about Jason's work,
including his music, visit:
kristinamakansi.com/jason-makansi
Threads & Instagram: @jasonmakansi
Substack: https://jmakansi.substack.com/